# Shark
# Point

ALSO BY ERNEST HAMILTON

THE IMPOSTOR
FREE AT LAST
GO FOR THE GOLD
ASLEEP AT THE WHEEL
THE FORGIVEN
AN INVISIBLE HAND
THE ART OF LIVING

# Shark Point

A Novel

**ERNEST
HAMILTON**

All of the characters and events in this book are fictitious, and any resemblance to actual persons, living or dead, is purely coincidental.

ISBN-13: 978-1482741216
ISBN -10: 1482741210

Cover Design by Nancy Bell

Printed in the United States of America

April 2013

First Edition

# Special Thanks

To my wife, Nancy, who offered
gentle critiques, listened patiently to
all expositions, and helped edit and re-
edit the final manuscript.

To my daughter Karen Yvonne for
asking the question 'what if' to a short
story I wrote.

To my granddaughter Nancy Bell
Hamilton for her rendering of the
knife.

## CHAPTER 1

**B**uddy Harrison jerked awake at the sound of a snapping tree limb. His hand encircled the shotgun lying by his side. The sound, like the white-hot crack of a whip searing the air, still echoed inside his head as he aimed the gun towards the darkness. His heart pounded. He strained to focus his eyes on the edge of the woods just twenty feet away, searching for the slightest movement – expecting men to emerge any second. With his right thumb he eased both hammers back. The sound of the ratcheting hammers, which he knew was just an inaudible click, resonated in his ears and was carried, or so he thought, in all directions by the soft breeze.

He waited. The snapping sound, this time much weaker and farther away, caused an eerie tingle in his spine. Hair stood straight up on the back of his neck and shoulders. He lay without moving, his finger light on the double triggers, ready for anything.

Five feet away Robert Harrison, with bare feet protruding from the edge of the blanket, lay sound asleep. Could the sounds have anything to do with him? Somebody trying to get even? The Brown boys? *Won't wake him till I'm sure what's out there.*

The moon in the south was quartered, the dark morning sky awash in stars – about an hour before first light. A small breeze drifted off the Gulf of Mexico and rustled the leaves as it passed across the spit of beach where they camped, carrying with it the confusing smell of salt air and seaweed. The night fire, positioned between them, was smoldering and just barely visible. Wisps of thin smoke trailing upwards, were dispersed and carried away by the breeze. The bluish tint at the edge of the sky barely outlined the solid front of the woods.

The birds were quiet, but he knew they were there, they were listening, too. His eyes became more accustomed to the dark as

1

the beach and surrounding woods lightened in the wash of the faint moon glow. There was neither movement nor sound. Then he saw the eyes, low down to the ground, glowing in the light of the moon. His stomach muscles tightened and his finger pressed the trigger – but wait – the eyes were familiar – a coon. He felt a sudden relief but uneasiness lingered – the sound that woke him was not that of a coon.

Another five minutes dragged by while he waited, leg muscles cramped and aching. He heard no more sounds, except his own breathing, the beat of his heart and the waves lapping against the bottoms of the two skiffs tethered at the water's edge. He eased the hammers back and relaxed his grip on the gun. The palms of his hands felt sticky with sweat. *Probably nothing to get so het up about – a panther more'n likely.* Several had been seen in the past few months all along the coast as far north as Lostman's River, and all the way south to Cape Sable.

His eyes lingered for a moment on the stars. There to the northwest was the Big Dipper, about forty-five degrees above the horizon – four fists held at arm's length.

Flo came to mind. Three months ago they had been together on the beach at Rat Key. She had been so happy when he taught her the trick with the balled fists to estimate a stars position above the horizon. He chuckled when he thought of her small fists – for her, it took five fists. The children had played themselves out and had fallen asleep next to the fire. He and Flo had lain there looking at the stars, relaxing and enjoying each other. She always tried to remember the names of the different star patterns. The Big Dipper was her favorite and she always seemed amazed as the bowl turned upside down during the year. She got in the habit of tracing its course from the east in August, with its bowl at the top, to the northwest in February, with its bowl at the bottom, like now. The five years since they married had gone by in a heartbeat. Lost in his thoughts, he reached for her, only to feel the gritty sand.

The black face of the woods gave up no sign to his probing eyes. His bladder was sending urgent signals; he'd have to make

2

a move soon. He threw off the blanket, pulled on his rubber boots, and with gun in hand and ready, ambled down to the water's edge. The coon beat a hasty retreat – a missed opportunity to get the stores next to the smoldering fire. Buddy relieved himself into the Gulf.

Cautiously, he walked east along the creek shore, gun at ready, eyes and ears tuned for the slightest sound or movement. A quick sideways glance at the skiffs pulled high on the beach assured him of nothing amiss there. After another hundred feet or more, mangroves growing well out into the water blocked his forward movement. He stopped and listened. Far up in the creek a fish jumped. A moment later the wail of a mama panther far off to the east rose to a high pitch then trailed off. All was quiet.

Buddy retraced his steps to the mouth of the creek. A tree limb snapped somewhere near the edge of the woods and brush rattled. He spun around and dropped to his knees in the sand, gun leveled at the sound, cocked and ready to fire. Hair on his back felt like it was standing straight up again. He waited, not a muscle moving, straining his eyes to pierce the darkness of the woods. Nothing stirred. When his pounding heart calmed, he walked the few feet to the mouth of the creek and the wide expanse of the Gulf, stared for a few minutes back to the east trying to form a picture of the sounds, then walked north along the shore.

The beach, half covered with seaweed and littered with rotted tree stumps and limbs, fronted the Gulf and stretched for about a half mile north from where he was standing. In that direction, with the exception of a few scattered live buttonwood trees and mangroves near the edge of the water, the beachfront was wide open for a good forty feet before touching the dense woods to the east. It would be near impossible for anyone to get into the woods without being seen or heard. Maybe the sound of the breaking limb was just the end of the bad dream he'd been having lately. A panther had been in all those dreams, too. Yet, the sound was so real – too real to be a dream. *Somebody's up to no good. I better get on home. Can't take the chance. Flo needs me.*

Determined to head for home without further delay, Buddy walked, without making a sound, back to the camp. He picked up a stick and poked it into the smoldering embers. Sparks scattered into the air, quickly lost their heat and disappeared. A small flame came to life and spread fast to the small pieces of unburned wood. He placed new wood on the flames and the morning fire was soon ready for the coffeepot. Robert stirred.

Buddy splashed water from the jug into the washbasin and some into the coffeepot. He put a measured amount of coffee grounds into the pot and found a place for it at the edge of the fire. He washed and dried his face and soon the smell of boiling coffee filled the air. He filled his tin cup to the brim, rolled a cigarette and lit it with a glowing ember from the fire.

Robert tossed off his blanket, pulled on his boots and strolled leisurely down to the water, relieved himself and stared for some moments out over the Gulf. Buddy, squatting by the fire and sipping his steaming coffee, studied him as he went through the morning ritual. Robert was a lean hard man, well-liked by most but a pure hellion when stirred up. At six feet tall, Robert liked to say he was 180 pounds of 'floatin' hell'.

Buddy squinted his eyes and watched as Robert made his way up to the fire. Robert took a cup from the cardboard box near the fire and poured it full of coffee, being careful not to stir up the grounds in the bottom of the pot. Daylight strained through the tree tops, and with the help of the meager moonlight, the skiffs, piled high with animal hides, were now visible on the beach. The pale blue sky behind and just above the dark outline of the trees gained a deeper color as it climbed. The air, fresh and cool, had just enough breeze to ward off what few mosquitoes still lingered.

Robert spoke as he splashed fresh water into the basin and washed his face. "Damn, I slept like a baby. It's gonna be a great day for the traps. This is gonna be the best haul we ever made. By the way, happy birthday. What is this, number twenty-eight now?"

4

Buddy, brow furrowed in deep thought, grunted in Robert's direction, but said nothing. He sat near the fire and stared blankly out across the open sea. 1932 was turning out to be one hell of a year. Price of mullet down to one cent a pound, hardly no market for much of anything and the cost of everything way too high. *It's just getting too damn hard to make ends meet.* He finally spoke. "My birthday ain't till day after tomorrow."

"Well, no mind. You're gettin' old as the hills anyhow." Robert squatted near the fire to get its warmth. He filled a cigarette paper with tobacco from the little sack, rolled it between his fingers, licked the edge with his tongue and lit it with a burning stick.

"Robert, I been thinkin'. We got us a pretty good haul of hides these past four days, maybe we oughta high tail it outta here and head for home. I'm mighty itchy to see my young'uns, and tomorrow bein' Saturday, Flo'll likely be wantin' to go downtown."

"We done all right that's for damn sure, but you know we planned to go on down to Oyster Bay today. We always had plenty luck down there, and besides, we got to clean out our traps anyhow. Jake ain't to come for us till tomorrow."

"I know you're right, Robert, and I know it's a damn long way to pole all the way to Wood Key if we don't wait for Jake, but I'm just ready to head on out. Got a strange feelin' in my gut." He put his cup down beside him, took the makings from his shirt pocket, fashioned and lit another cigarette.

"Somethin' eatin' at you, Buddy?" Robert paused, and when Buddy didn't respond, continued. "I tell you what. I reckon it's about five-thirty now. Let's go as far as Little Shark, work the few traps there and get an early start back this afternoon. We'll probably meet Jake soon after we pass here on our way back."

Buddy stared at the water's edge and ignored Robert's words. He felt like hell. His coveralls, smeared with dried blood, were dirty and reeked of rotten animal. He wanted to wash all over and snuggle up to his woman again. His mind refused to merge the snapping limb into a dream – he wondered again if there was somehow a connection to Robert. "You had any run-ins with Rufus lately?" He rubbed the four-day stubble on his chin and looked straight into Robert's eyes to read any meaning hidden there.

"Don't recollect I've seen Rufus or any the rest of that Brown bunch in some time. You got somethin' on your mind? Rufus got anything to do with that feelin' in your gut?" Never taking his eyes off Buddy, Robert took a long careful sip from the coffee cup, rolled another cigarette, lit it and took a deep drag.

Buddy kept his eyes locked on Robert's. He started to mention the morning noises then decided against it – maybe it really was just a dream. "No, not really, just wonderin'. Know you got into a ruckus with him awhile back, somethin' to do about his old lady I heard tell." Buddy grinned to ease the building tension.

Robert frowned. "Oh hell, Rufus is a damn cry bag. You know that. He ain't man enough to take care of his woman, and she gives me the eye ever time we meet. I have to help her out now and again, you know." He laughed out loud, slapped his knee and yelped when hot coffee spilled along the inside of his upper leg. "That whole damn bunch are worthless as tits on a boar hog." He stood up and turned to face the Gulf.

Buddy poked at the fire with a stick and watched as the end caught fire. Robert was smooth as silk with the ladies and easy going as a politician running for office when trying to smooth someone's feathers, but he was meaner than a wildcat when crossed or riled. Buddy got a kick out of watching him get steamed up. He started to push a little further then stopped short. No need to go on with this line any more. "I reckon you're right there. Ain't much to 'em."

Buddy took a long sip of coffee and cursed under his breath when he burnt his lips on the hot tin cup. He put the cup down near the fire, picked up his shotgun and stood, towering to his full six feet two inches. His shadow, cast eerily by the flames almost to the edge of the woods, competed with the shadows of the trees, which now stretched, long to the west. The sun, soon to be above the trees, would not be denied its daily ritual much longer. If they were going south, they'd better get a move on. He spoke to Robert's back. "You make us some johnny cake for breakfast. I'll be back in a few minutes." He didn't wait for Robert to respond.

Buddy walked past his bedding and into the woods where he'd heard the sounds and was soon out of sight of the camp area. A few of the sun's rays filtered through the treetops and provided meager light. He didn't expect to find anyone, but kept his gun and himself at the ready just in case.

The brush was thick with familiar pines, cocoplum, palmetto, buttonwood, seagrape and several varieties of low growing ferns. Mosquitoes covered his long-sleeved shirt and crashed into his face and neck, but the salve he'd rubbed on earlier kept them from doing any damage. The Curlews, still perched high in the trees, would make a mighty good breakfast and satisfy his hunger for a decent meal. No time now, though. He was ready to get this hunting trip over and get on home. Some old broken tree limbs caught his attention, but he couldn't tell whether they broke from weight on them or just old age. He walked through the brush to the southern shore where the mangroves grew into the water, then walked back along the beach, past the skiffs, and finally saw Robert bent over the fire with a frying pan.

The vast Gulf, now almost mirror smooth, stretched as far as the eye could see. The breeze had lightened and the sun's rays were already warming the air. He turned and strode into camp to the welcome smell of fresh fried bread.

"Everything come out all right?" Robert grinned as he passed the frying pan.

Buddy took a piece of johnny cake out of the pan and poured a fresh cup of coffee. He sat cross-legged on the ground by the fire and took out the makings. "Yeah, everything's just hunky dory. We goin' south or north?"

Robert bent down and worked the frying pan into the edge of the embers, taking care they were all around the pan to keep it warm. He straightened up. "Buddy, I been doin' some tall thinkin', and I reckon that just maybe you're right. Maybe we oughta head on back right now. I'm kind a ready for a little night life anyhow." He paused, then slipped in. "But I bet we could clean up down around Little Shark."

Far to the south Buddy could just barely make out the long, dark shape of Shark River Island hugging the horizon and jutting way out into the Gulf of Mexico. He didn't want to argue. He just wanted to get away from here and head for home. "Yeah, you're probably right. Let's get the job done." He sipped the hot coffee and flicked the ash off his cigarette.

"You gotta lighten up some, boy." Robert produced that well-known devilish grin that let you know he'd been serious long enough. "You're just too damn tight. When we get back home, you and me are goin' into town. I'll show you for sure what makes up a good time – what life's all about. I'll fix you up good and proper. You done forgot what a good time is." He sat cross-legged at the western edge of the fire facing Buddy.

"You gotta remember, Robert, I got a wife and two young'uns to tend to. My hell-raisin' days are over. I done my share of that in the old days."

Robert's face took on a somber look. "I sorely miss them good old days, Buddy. You were a rounder then and liked a rumble in the cane fields and in the honky-tonks just like the rest of us. Nobody I know of could take you then. I don't reckon they could now neither." He looked long at Buddy as if trying to figure him out. "Women, when they put the chain on you, drain all the steam from your body. I know you got to look after your woman and kids, but it'd do you good to let your hair down ever now and then and forget about all that book larnin' and quit foolin' around with all them contraptions so much."

"A body just can't get enough book larnin' as you call it, and I'm sure enough missin' out on a bunch of it stuck way down here in these swamps. I aim to get out of these woods one day and see that my boys get a shot at the learnin' that books can give 'em. We missed out on a lot, Robert, you and me, not gettin' to go to school like other folks done. And them contraptions you talk about is what's gonna get me out of these woods sooner than you might think. Don't you go lettin' on to Papa about what I said though. He's sure countin' on me stayin' around here the rest of my life." Buddy reached to the frying pan and took another piece of bread.

Robert took a bite of the bread and washed it down with hot coffee. "Don't worry none about me tellin' that old man nothin'. The talks out, though, that he's figurin' on you takin' over for him when he gets too old."

"He's got the other boys to take over for him. He don't need me." This talk was getting old and Buddy yearned to get moving.

"Who's gonna do it? None of them boys got what it takes. That younger bunch ain't got the stomach for this hard life. They see how the folks in town live and want to be part of it. Face it, Buddy, without you Uncle Jim'd be a broken old man in a few years."

"I don't believe that for one minute, Robert. Papa's still a mighty strong man, and I reckon he'll be that way for a lot a years to come. Hell, he's only forty-nine or so. I've whipped a many in my short life, but I'd think long and hard before I had a go at that old man. They don't call him King James for nothin'."

Robert fashioned a cigarette. "Old Jim Harrison's like a chunk of iron all right, but I reckon you could take him if it ever come to that. You remember that time we—"

"Enough, Robert, let's get the hell out of here." Buddy stood up and tossed the remains of his coffee into the fire, which hissed back at him and sent a thick wisp of smoke into the air in retaliation. "We have had some good times though, ay? Even Papa don't know about some of 'em, huh? I don't reckon he'd laugh too much if he did. Maybe I get my serious side from him, you reckon?"

Robert stood, "That old man's hard as a rock, that's for damn sure. You better get the hell out of his way when his back is up. You remember how mad he gets about them stories goin' around about old man Harrison. Why I don't see—"

"God's sake, Robert, let's don't get into that one now. Granpa ain't much darker than you or me. His ma was a full-blood Choctaw and his pa a dark-skinned Portagee. Come on now, let's see to them traps down south and get on home. I'm achin' for my woman and boys." He put the cup by the dying fire and headed for his bedroll.

Robert picked up the coffeepot, both cups and the frying pan and headed to the water's edge. "I can understand that itch. You got a good woman in Flo. You all plannin' any new young'uns any time soon?"

Buddy continued walking but turned his head towards Robert. "She don't think I know, but I figure there's another'n in the basket right now."

Robert stopped in his tracks and turned towards Buddy. "You don't mean it? When you reckon?"

"I do mean it. Maybe August, September. Now let's see to them traps." He tossed the words over his shoulder as he continued on to his skiff.

Robert put the pan, cups and coffeepot in the water, grabbed a handful of beach sand and scoured them good. After all the sand was rinsed out he stowed all the supplies and bedding in the cardboard boxes and took them to his boat. Buddy covered the smoldering embers with sand. Neither man spoke.

The sun was just breaking over the treetops and shadows had shortened considerably when they pulled away from shore in their skiffs, loaded with animal hides and stores, and began poling south for the one hour trip to Shark River Island.

After about fifteen minutes, they slowed to a more manageable pace and caught their breath. Buddy broke the silence. "You never give up, do you?"

"One of these days I'll take you. Bet on it." Robert leaned on his pole and fought to catch his breath. "You think we ought to stash our hides before we work the traps?"

Buddy breathed heavy, too. "I'd rather go straight to the traps and get done with it, but I reckon we'd be smart to hide 'em."

"We put into Little Shark?"

"Let's go just this side, up in No-Name Creek. Not many knows that one, but as you know, we've lost skins there before. We'll catch that smart bastard one of these days. Never seen no sign of him except on weekdays, though."

Buddy scanned the entire coast all the way up to Shark Point, looking for a sign of anyone. He turned into a small creek which had not been visible a few minutes ago. Robert followed and, after about five minutes, they beached their boats in between mangrove legs growing on the beach and out into the water. The cool breezy air and the gunk on his skin warded off the mosquitoes. They each grabbed an armload of hides and made their way through the tangle of mangroves until they came to a high sandy spot. Pines and buttonwood towered skyward, their young hugging the ground. They located the stash, a simple hole in the ground with a top fashioned out of limbs and old tree trunks scattered around to look natural, and soon had all their hides and excess gear safely stored. They were both sweating when they returned to the boats.

CHAPTER **2**

It was about seven thirty when they beached the boats at Shark River Island and made their way inland, with guns and croaker sacks, to work the traps marked with the Harrison brand. It was taboo to touch another man's traps – definitely a killing offense.

The first trap had only a leg in it. Robert was the first to speak. "That bastard done chewed his leg plumb off. The will to live is some kinda strong when you'd take your own leg off. This is where your trap would come in handy. When you gonna get it made?" Robert forced the jaws of the trap open, removed the leg and tossed it into the brush, then reset the trap and moved on.

"I got the patent on it and made one, but ain't tested it yet. Know it'll work, though." Buddy moved towards the next trap, just out of sight of the first.

Robert caught up. "You reckon you'll ever make any money off it?"

Buddy removed the animal from the trap and placed it in his croaker sack. "Been offered $1,700 by a company in Canada. Didn't take it, though. Might still. The big money will come from the distributor I made."

"What's that? You never told me nothin' about that." Robert reset the next trap and they made their way deeper into the woods.

Buddy brushed aside a tangle of vines and stopped at the edge of a small clearing. This island was much like their camp at Shark Point, high sandy ground, thick and lush, with the same kind of trees, including some pine. Curlews were plentiful, too. They'd roost just before sundown. No creatures stirring this time of day. "You know how cars backfire all the time?" Robert nodded. "Well, that happens because all the spark plugs ain't timed just right to each other. The answer to the problem is to

12

have 'em all firin' at just the right time. That's done with a distributor, but far as I know, nobody's come up with the right way yet – except me."

Robert perked up. "Christ almighty. How'd you come up with an idea like that?"

"Same as the other ideas, I reckon. My mind just works like that. I see problems and my mind finds the answers." He removed a large granddaddy raccoon from the trap and re-set it.

"You made one yet? When you reckon it'll be ready for everybody to use?" Robert started moving again and Buddy followed.

"Got it at the lawyers in Ft. Myers right now. They're supposed to be filing for the patent this week."

"You shore gonna remember us pore folk when you get rich, ain't you?" Robert flashed his famous grin. "I can see you and me now, strollin' real fancy-like downtown with all the other big shots. Me with a beautiful babe on each arm and you dressed in your fine Sunday go-to-meetin' clothes. Fine houses and cars and clothes and food and all the rest that goes with it. Toilets and runnin' water inside the house – electric lights. Whoee, sounds good, don't it?"

"We ain't there yet, Bobby boy, but all my family'll be taken care of real good – even you." They both laughed heartedly.

Soon their croaker sacks were filled to the brim and they headed back to the boats. At the beach they both brushed the mosquitoes off their clothes and set to the task of skinning. The breeze was refreshing after the confinement and closeness of the woods.

Buddy took the skinning knife from the bow of his skiff, ran the blade across the whet-rock a few times to be sure it had a good sharp edge and picked up the first carcass. Robert gathered some wood, started a small fire, and got the coffee going.

Buddy deftly slit the animal from just under its jaw all the way to its tail hole, cut the neck clean through, grabbed the head, and with one swift and continuous motion, pulled it and the skin right off the animal's body, and tossed the carcass into the water.

13

He scraped the remaining meat from the hide, spread the insides with salt, laid it aside for the sun to do its magic and reached for the next carcass.

Buddy, engrossed in the skinning task, jumped when Robert yelled, "God damm it, I cain't find my knife. I always put it in the same place and now it's gone. What could I have done with it?"

Buddy picked up another animal and looked sideways at Robert. "You remember puttin' it in the skiff after we skinned that last batch?"

Robert seemed beside himself. "Sure do. This ain't makin' no sense at all." He rummaged through the cardboard boxes as he removed them from the skiff.

You didn't often see Robert this upset and bewildered. Buddy felt a tinge of pity for him. "Did you use it for anything else while we were at Shark Point?"

"Don't remember. Reckon I could've. Just know it ain't here and that grieves me sure 'nough. That knife was give to me by Uncle Walter who said he got it from one of them Injins what used to come up around his place. That knife can hold an edge better'n any I've ever seen in my life."

Buddy continued with the skinning. "I've got an extra blade under the bow. Put an edge on it and help me with this skinnin' and treatin' so we can get on outta here. I'm mighty anxious to get on home now." He gestured with his knife towards the skiff.

Robert found the knife and honed it on the whet-rock. "Buddy, we're just gonna have to stop by the camp at Shark Point for a minute or two so I can look for my knife. It's gotta be there somewheres. Cain't be no place else. Cain't go home without that knife." Robert seemed incapable of movement, bewildered.

Buddy gazed at Robert with a touch of pity and growing impatience. *Damn, damn, it's always something with that boy. He'll be the death of me yet.* The plan was to by-pass Shark Point on the way back and meet Jake halfway to Wood Key. Aloud he said, "Yeah, I reckon we can stop for just a minute or two." The smell from

14

the coffee pot filled his nostrils. He filled a cup. It was now going on ten o'clock. "You wanna get a bite to eat before we go?"

"I'm powerful worried about my knife now, Buddy. I'd rather get it, then have some vittles later if that's okay with you."

"Okay by me. Let's get this skinnin' done." Buddy knew how important that knife was to Robert. He remembered the old Indian who used to come up around the place at Lostman's. Uncle Walter and him would go trapping way up in the woods and sometimes be gone for days. The old man had fainted dead away one time and fell headfirst into the water. Would've drowned if Uncle Walter hadn't pulled him out in time.

The old man was dying when Uncle Walter last saw him again deep in the swamps. In his trembling hand was the knife. The hilt was carved to resemble a snake coiled around the middle of the knife, with protruding eyes at the end. The old Indian said the knife had been handed down from his great grandfather, and that whoever owned it, and led an honorable life, would have a long and fruitful life. His eyes said he wanted his best friend to have it and he handed it to Uncle Walter as soon as he saw him. Tears welled in the old man's eyes. He didn't say a word, just smiled, closed his eyes and died. Uncle Walter had thought so much of Robert that he had given him the knife with the extracted pledge that Robert would lead an honorable life like the old Indian.

Buddy and Robert worked fast and soon were on their way. They made good time to the stash and reloaded the hides. Their boats were over-loaded now. It would be slow going on this leg, but Buddy figured they would have time to stop for the knife and still be well on their way before nightfall.

Just a little after high noon Shark Point lay dead ahead. Buddy was in good spirits and absorbed with the thoughts of home. With this catch there would be enough money left over to get that new stove he'd promised Flo. They would go into Ft. Myers this weekend. Maybe even take in a moving-picture show.

15

# CHAPTER 3

As soon as they hit the beach, Robert jumped out and ran up to the camp. Buddy remembered the morning noises and a feeling of anxiety engulfed him. He shot a quick glance towards the edge of the woods. Robert's skiff began to drift away from shore. Buddy secured his, turned around and grabbed the bow-rope of Robert's.

His back was to the camp when he heard the shotgun blast. The sound stayed in his ears for a long time. He stood dumbfounded for a long moment – his hand unmoving on the rope – the reason for the blast would not register.

He spun around in time to see Robert propelled backwards from the blast that tore his chest out of its mooring. Robert hit the ground and grains of sand sprayed into the air and seemed suspended there. Robert lay still – dead when he hit the sand. In the same moment, Buddy saw Rufus Brown at the edge of the clearing with smoke wisping out of one of the barrels of the shotgun still pointed at the spot where Robert had been a moment before. To his right and just emerging from the woods was Guy, the younger brother of Rufus. The shotgun Guy carried was leveled and pointing straight at Buddy.

The rope slipped out of his hand and sank into the water as he reached for his shotgun in the bow of the skiff. He kept his eyes on both of the Browns as his hand circled the stock of the gun. He'd used this gun many a time, but never against another man. His calmness amazed him. The morning sound again flashed in his mind. He wondered how he'd missed the sign. It must've been these boys. The cocking hammers had scared them off. *These boys are aiming for another killing right now.* He thought of Flo and the boys – the tyke yet to be born. He thought of the patents and riches and the learning to be had. Twenty-eight was too young to die.

The gun hadn't cleared the side of the boat when he heard the words loud and clear in the breezeless afternoon, "Don't do it, Buddy, we got no truck with you. It was Robert we were after. We don't aim you no harm." It was Rufus who spoke as he moved from the edge of the woods toward Buddy, reloading the empty barrel. Rufus was a man about his own age and size – six two or so and probably 200 pounds – all lean. In a way they were a lot alike. Same dark complexion and hair, rugged good looks and easy manner, but Rufus had an oddity about him that had caused him a lot of ridicule. He bobbed to the side when he walked – one leg shorter than the other – that way all his life.

Buddy's mind raced – seeing everything and processing it. The gun was just now clearing the boat. Maybe it was true. Rufus had it in for Robert and had publicly vowed to do him in sooner or later. Was it about his wife or the traps? He didn't believe the accusations about the traps. Robert could be a bad boy, but a thief or liar he was not. Did they really mean to let him go? How could they? If he could get his gun up and cocked, he might just have a chance. Neither one of these boys had a reputation for bravery or for being any too smart. Maybe he could bluff them. His thumb brought back the double hammers as he continued to raise the gun. The simultaneous clicks resounded in the still air. Only seconds had elapsed. He still had said nothing – his eyes locked on Rufus.

Rufus now turned his gun toward Buddy.

Guy pleaded, "Don't try it, Buddy, we'll cut you down like we done Robert. Drop that shotgun and get on outta here. Do it, boy, for God's sake." Buddy looked at Guy and hesitated. What a puny little bastard – blond and nasty looking – probably too scared to fire a gun at a man. If he had to, he'd take Rufus out first, then Guy.

Rufus moved closer to him now and said. "Go on, Buddy. Turn around and get. If you tell what happened here, we're comin' after you. We'll do you just like we done Robert. Now get your hand off that gun and get. We didn't come here after you. We could've gotten you this mornin' if we was a wantin'."

17

Maybe they really were dumb enough to let him go. It sure made sense that they could have killed him this morning if that was their mind. These boys were both dead shots. He knew he could get one, but his chance of getting both was slim to none. His only chance was to run. He lowered his gun and laid it on the front seat of the skiff. "You boys gonna let me take my skiff and high tail it on outta here, ain't you?" Robert's skiff started drifting away from shore trailing the sunken rope after it.

"Naw, that ain't our plan, Buddy. We're gonna take your hides and your skiffs as fair trade for the traps and hides stole by Robert. You just get on up the beach there and keep movin'. Somebody'll be along for you soon enough, I reckon." Rufus menaced with the shotgun and shot a glance at the drifting skiff.

*Just go for the skiff, Rufus, you dumb son-of-a-bitch. I'll blow you to kingdom come.* He tried to stall. "Come on, Rufus. That ain't fair damn it. I ain't done you all no wrong. You got no cause to treat . . . ."

Rufus looked him dead in the eye and cut him off. "I figure Robert stole four, five times that amount from me and my family these past few years. I told him I'd get even. That boy got me powerful riled up."

"But you didn't have to kill him. Why take my skins? We been all week gettin' this bunch. Goddam it, Rufus, it ain't fair."

"I'm tired talkin', Buddy. You better get on now while the gettin's good." Rufus raised the shotgun level with Buddy's belt.

Buddy controlled his anger knowing that time had run out. Rufus wouldn't look at the drifting skiff. He felt like a trapped animal and knew the only sensible way out was to fight. Sweat flowed from his forehead into his eyes. Fear and anger merged. He regretted now that he'd put his gun down. He would rather go out fighting than running. He glanced downward to the gun. It was still cocked. It would take a long time to get that gun up, aimed and fired.

Rufus was now just fifteen feet away, his gun pointed right at Buddy's belly. "Don't even think on it, Buddy. I can fire this thing before your hand touches the stock. I'm givin' you one last

18

chance to high-tail it outta here. You best get, boy, if you wanna keep on livin'."

Buddy looked into Rufus' dark eyes and saw the hatred and determination there. He calculated his chances of getting the gun up and fired before they could. Guy stood just twenty feet away with his gun leveled at Buddy's midsection. The sun was almost directly overhead and the wind had completely died away – the heat stifling. "Okay, okay, I'm goin'." He looked at Robert's skiff – Rufus didn't. Maybe playing to their selfishness would soften them some. "Rufus, I'm damn sorry Robert did you all dirt. I never had no problem with you boys. You know that. I hate like hell to leave my skiff and hides this way, but I'm much obliged to you for lettin' me go. Flo'll be waitin'. She'll be beholden to you, too."

Guy spoke, "We know that, Buddy. You always been fair with us and our family. We always got along good with you and your daddy. Like Rufus said, we got no truck with you."

Rufus prodded again with the gun which was now just ten feet away and moving closer all the time. "You get goin' now, Buddy. You hightail it, you hear? I'm gettin' damn tired of your talkin'."

"I'm goin'." He glanced again at the gun, gauged the two boys advancing on him and concluded a gunfight was not in the cards. Only one chance and that was to run for it. He turned around and walked along the beach to the north. These boys he'd backed down before, and there was just a small chance that he could've bluffed them again. He wondered if he really could've taken them, then and there, even though they had the drop on him. He kept a weary eye on Rufus.

When he felt he was out of range of the shotguns, he took off in a fast run. If he could get around that clump of trees just ahead at the water's edge, then into the main woods, he could elude them for days in the swamps. They were swamp men, too, and like him, had grown up in these woods, but he was smarter, stronger, and braver than they were. Those dumb bastards would pay for their stupidness one day soon. They would be mighty sorry for not killing him on the spot like they did Robert.

The sound of the shotgun blast reached him just as the buck-shot tore into his skin and propelled him face first into the sand. The thunder of the shot reverberated off the trees at the edge of the woods and echoed along the shoreline. Then there was silence – an eerie empty silence.

It was then he realized what had happened. "You lyin' no good son-of-a-bitch, Rufus," he shouted at the top of his lungs as he tried to raise himself from the sand. His energy spent, he found it hard to breathe. The now blistering sun beat down unmercifully on his back – the breeze suddenly gone. Sweat drenched his face, and grains of sand clung to his eyes and lips. He tried to spit the sand out of his mouth but no moisture came to his aid. Sand clung to his tongue, and his back pained something awful. He would just take a minute to catch his breath then get on into the woods – and safety. He rested the side of his face in the sand and measured his breathing – the breath from his nose cut a groove in the sand.

He thought of Flo and the boys – the young one yet to come. His life on the water wasn't so bad, after all. As a matter of fact, his life had been pretty good. After the inventions were sold and he was rich, he would have a big house in town, but . . . at least one camp in the swamps, too. He really did love some parts of this life. He was free as the birds in the trees. Where else could he have this much freedom and independence.

He longed to hold his sons. He remembered them on the beach at Wood Key the day he left for this trip. Junior, only four, wanting to come with him, said he could hunt as good as any grown up. Francis, just three, crying, holding on to his legs, not wanting to let him go. He thought of the new one to be born – surely another boy.

Flo, he longed to hold her. He could still see her standing at the shoreline with the water lapping at her bare feet that morning so long, long ago. *I've got to get up from here. Flo needs me.*

*She can't make it by herself – with the kids.* He struggled to raise himself from the ground. "Flo, I'm comin'."

"Goddam it, Rufus, what'd you go and do that for – you gave your word . . . ." Guy rushed towards Rufus.

"Shut your damn mouth, Guy. I know what I'm doin'." He ran towards Buddy, reloading on the way.

Buddy, unable to move, heard all the sounds. The sounds of water lapping at the shoreline; the sounds of birds, quiet now, watching from their vantage point high in the trees; the sound of his breathing and of his heart beating furiously within his chest; the sounds of the two men arguing and running towards him; the sounds of men shouting out on the water to his left, beyond the mangroves. He heard one shot. He didn't hear the others.

CHAPTER 4

J im Harrison pushed the Donella to her limits as he made the
right turn from Northwest Cape heading for Key West. She
was a good boat and had stood him in good stead many a
time in the past. She wouldn't fail him now. The sun had
been up about an hour. The clock in the console read 7:30.
Farther south was a raging storm that could be the dreaded
hurricane predicted to hit the upper keys. His plan had been to
skirt the storm to the west and be well out of its path before
now. It had apparently shifted, but if his reckoning was correct,
and he was seldom wrong in matters such as this, he was still
well to the west of the main force. He hoped it was not the full
hurricane. Damn these radios anyhow – more static than
anything else. He had little confidence in weather reporting, but
right now any news would be welcome.

A sudden shift in the direction of the wind and the cold bite
of it penetrated the tear in his oiler just over his chest. A cold
shiver ran the full length of his body. Big drops of rain splattered
against the windshield one at a time and slithered away to the
side. Nor'easters spelled real trouble and he felt a sudden pang of
fear. They would be in serious trouble if he didn't make Big
Spanish Key in time to ward off the full blast of the treacherous
northeast gale. Just a little more time and they'd be out of it.

On deck with him was his nine year old son Jimmy, who was
going back to school in Key West. Jim wished now he hadn't
brought him along on this trip. He wished, too, he hadn't
brought his daughter-in-law and her two small children – she
swollen with child. Jim had vowed that his youngest son would
get an education come hell or high water. Up to now he'd kept
that vow. Maybe the high water would do him in this time.
School would start on September fifth, just six days from now.

As he looked at Jimmy now, hanging onto the railing while trying so hard to show that he was a man and capable of weathering a storm with the best of them, a pang of sorrow caused Jim to shudder as the image of his eldest son flashed before his eyes. Buddy, his first-born, the heir to his throne, the one who, above all, would lead his family out of these swamps to a better life, the one who teachers ran out of things to teach, the one that everything seemed to come to so easily, was no more – shot down in cold blood by murderous scoundrels. At least that's what most folks said.

Jim wasn't so sure about that – nothing added up. No bodies or any other evidence of foul play had ever been found. Yet, on the other hand, Buddy was not the kind of man who would run off and leave his wife and kids to cope alone. But if he wasn't dead, where was he? Six months was a long time to be traipsing around with no word. Jim shook his head to rid it of negative thoughts. He had to skirt this storm and put into Key West so that child could be born to take his daddy's place and make some kind of a mark in the world. *What's the purpose of life anyhow?*

He yelled now, "Jimmy, go below and see to Flo. Tell her we'll put into Big Spanish about ten o'clock. It should be calm there for a while. We can have a bite to eat and put into Key West by one – two." A quick glance assured him that all was secure on deck and ready for the worst.

Jimmy scampered below deck as Jim strained to see ahead through the ever-increasing intensity of the rain that now came down in heavy sheets. He would've been soaked to the skin, but for his slicker. The pelting rain shifted direction every minute or so. The gray of the sky, so solid and rain-soaked, hung just above the boat – a little lower and it would engulf him.

The storm had come up suddenly and unexpectedly, but he felt certain he was at its edge and would be clear in short order. A look at the big compass on the dash reassured him he still headed west. The darkened sky hampered his forward view and he had to rely almost entirely on the compass. He'd been taught as a little boy to trust his compass in weather like this. The swells grew and the ride worsened. He looked to the emergency equipment lying near at hand just in case.

None of this was new to him, and would be of little concern if it weren't for the others aboard. Braving the seas and facing down disasters was his life, and he'd been at it since he could lift an oar. This trip to Key West he'd made a thousand times if he'd made it once. He worried some, but didn't want to let on to the others – important they remain calm. "God all Mighty, what am I to do?" He muttered into the wind, inaudible to all, even to himself as the wind scattered the words far ahead.

They were nearing Big Spanish Key when the seas increased without warning, and he put all the strength of his massive arms against the pull of the steering wheel. With the rope lying on the dashboard he secured himself to the control station. The waves, at least six footers, now pounded the boat obliquely from the stern and posed a real threat of swamping if he lost his grip and control of the wheel for but a moment. He had to keep the boat running with the waves. "How in the hell did that storm get this far west?" He asked out loud. Waves broke across the stern and he had a moment of respite, then the strong pull of the wheel tried to wrench from his grip. His muscles ached from the struggle.

Little Jimmy tried to emerge from the cabin door and Jim yelled for him to stay put. The rope cut into his back as he fought against the pressure of the waves and wind. The big boat heaved and groaned as the waves pounded it incessantly. Would they never reach the safety of the key? He could not see it through the heavy rain. The compass gyrated like a yoyo moving from side to side. He hoped he was still on course. They probably would not survive if they didn't reach the key soon.

Flo Harrison yelled for the children to come to her as Jimmy entered the cabin. He looked at her and started to speak then turned around and stuck his head out of the cabin. The rain poured through the door. She heard Jim yell something, and

Jimmy came back into the cabin and forced the door shut. The boat shuddered.

"Papa said we'll be out of the storm in a little while," Jimmy yelled and held onto the rail as the boat movement tried to wrench him loose.

Flo reached for Junior and Francis just as a wave hit the boat and tossed her to them. She braced herself against the opposite bunk and gathered the boys to her. Francis started to cry. A searing pain, like a red-hot scalding iron, flashed across her lower stomach. She screamed, released Junior and clutched at her stomach. "Oh God, no, please don't let this baby be born now." Both boys looked stunned and started bawling. The wave subsided and she huddled the boys to her and moved back to her bunk. The pain eased.

She looked at Jimmy. He was white as a sheet and looked a little scared, but still had a tight grip on the rail and tried mighty hard to put on a strong front to show that he was a man. He would take care of the woman and children – that was his daddy's charge.

"Are you all right, Jimmy? Come on over to the bunk before the next wave hits." He looked at her with eyes wide and bolted for the bunk which she had just let go of. "Hold on tight," she said. "There'll be more comin'." The words were barely out of her mouth when another wave hit from the same side as before. They were ready for this one and weren't so badly shaken.

Junior looked up at Flo and asked, "Why'd you scream, Mama? You scared, Mama?"

Francis burrowed his face into her bosom, hungry for the comfort to be found there. Flo caressed his head and stifled her building emotions. She pulled Junior close and forced a brave smile. "It's okay now, son. You stay close to Mama."

It had now been more than five years that she'd lived in the Everglades with Buddy, and she was fairly used to a hard life, but, for the most part, she'd been sheltered from this kind of weather.

The only other time was back in '28, a few months before Francis was born. She and Buddy had gone into the swamps to seek shelter from another hurricane. It was not uncommon to do that. Folks felt safer in the swamps than in their houses. Once in the swamps, with all their belongings, they would simply tie their boats to mangroves and ride out the storm. This time she and Buddy had not left soon enough and got caught in the middle of the hurricane. They were lucky then.

The trouble was greater now, she could sense it. The intensity of the weather increased. Would she be lucky again? She stifled an audible cry. She couldn't cry now, not in front of the children – must remain calm.

Junior jumped from her arms and ran to Jimmy on the other side of the boat. At that very moment another wave smashed into the side of the boat, lifted it high on its side and threw Junior back into her arms. She banged her head against the bulkhead. Both children started to cry. She gathered the boys to her breast and tried to comfort them. A quick examination revealed no damage this time. Pain shot from the back of her head and she reached for it – panic tried to wrest control. It felt like part of the skull had been torn away. She touched it and found only a big knot and a finger-long shallow gash. Blood ran into her ear, but panic retreated. She reached for a towel from the end of the bunk and pressed it against her head. Jimmy held onto the bunk railing with a stunned look on his face. The children quit crying except for an occasional whimper. "You okay?" She asked Jimmy.

The color had returned to his face but he held on for dear life. "Yes, ma'am, I'm all right."

Another wave hit. Then another and another in rapid succession. The children whimpered and wanted to get up and walk around. She kept them to her. Her arms felt tired and weak, and she knew she would not be capable of much more. There had to be a way to lash the boys to the bunks to keep them from being tossed around the cabin and getting lasting damage. She looked around and saw nothing close that would serve the

26

purpose. She held them to her even though her arms ached. *Where are you, Buddy? I need you now more than ever. How could you just go away and leave me in this wilderness all by myself as some say you did? I just know you wouldn't do that. If you're out there somewhere and can hear me, come to me. I'm not strong enough to get through this by myself. Please come to me.* A breakdown was near, she knew it. She had to hold on, if only for another minute. She squeezed the children to her and sobbed within.

Finally she noted a change in the pounding waves. They seemed to be just as big as before and had the same wallop, but were more rhythmic now – they rolled rather than smashed. She relaxed her grip on the boys and gave a sigh of relief. Except for the throbbing in her head, she felt rather good again. She ordered the boys to stay on the bunk and hold on tight.

Holding on to bunk railings, she made her way to the cabinet, got a bottle of aspirins and took two, using only her saliva to wash them down. She'd been banged up pretty bad and her tensed position for the past hour or so had strained her muscles to the breaking point. The gash in her head had stopped bleeding and the pain eased some. The children edged off the bunk and back onto the floor looking for lost toys. The weather seemed to be letting up.

She relaxed a little and surveyed her surroundings as if for the first time. The cabin had been built to accommodate fishermen for not more than two weeks at a time. Families could adapt for a short time in normal weather, but it was always a trial because of the extreme cramped quarters. It was just eight feet in length and wide by about a little less. There were three bunks on each side of the narrow aisle, one hung above the other. Near the door to the outer deck was a very small galley with a gas camp-cook with two burners. Cooking utensils were stored in a cabinet overhead. At the very bow of the boat a small toilet was cramped even for one person, and in heavy seas like now, near impossible to use.

Jimmy opened the cabin door and the rain poured in. Just as he went out a huge wave smashed over the stern and seawater

27

gushed through the door, and just as suddenly the bow went sky high and the water went out again. Flo lost her grip on the bunk post and was flung against the rear wall of the cabin. Terrified, she grabbed for the door and pulled it shut. Junior smashed against the same wall and started screaming at the top of his lungs. She grabbed for him and looked for Francis. He was lodged under the edge of the bottom bunk and safe for the moment, but howling like a coyote. She and Junior were pressed against the wall. The bow went down into a trough and they were both flung toward the forward cabin. Both boys continued screaming, Francis still lodged under the bunk. She held on tight to Junior and grabbed the leg of a bunk and held on for dear life – this could very well be the end.

# CHAPTER 5

When the cabin door opened Jim heard a scream and looked in horror and disbelief as his child slammed against the console. At the same time the massive stern wave hit him in the back with force like a sledge hammer and pinned him against the steering wheel. He reached for Jimmy just as the bow shot skyward. Jimmy slid along the deck to the stern and only the end of the boat stopped his movement. In a moment he would be washed overboard.

Jim gasped. He struggled to keep the boat from being swamped while he fought to undo the ropes that bound him to the wheel. If he let go of the wheel they would swamp. If he didn't get to Jimmy quick, the boy would be taken by the sea. Another wave came from behind and poured into the boat. They veered off course and were in danger of capsizing. He looked for Jimmy and didn't see him. A dread came on him like nothing he'd ever experienced before. His son was lost. He fought to get the ropes off. The bow rose again as he tore free from the wheel. He had to hang on with both hands or risk losing his footing. Out of the corner of his eye, he saw Jimmy pressed against the bulkhead. Jim was so happy his chest constricted and a sob escaped his throat.

He tied the wheel tight to the right window to keep the boat turned into the waves ahead, and ran to Jimmy. He gathered him in his arms and dashed back to the wheel just as the rope snapped and the bow turned to the southeast. They were parallel to an oncoming wave and would surely swamp. With Jimmy lodged between his legs, Jim tugged at the wheel with every ounce of strength to turn the boat west and away from disaster. His arms were so tired he could hardly feel them.

Jim dropped a section of the rope to Jimmy and told him to lash himself to his legs, then he lashed himself to the steering wheel again. Jimmy shivered against his legs. The waves came without let up. The stern waves poured over the bulkhead and lifted the bow, then raised the stern and pushed the bow into the trough in front, and then the water flowed over the bow like they were diving. The rain presented a solid impenetrable front – the bow lost to view. The compass pointed to the southwest, but how far off course he'd drifted posed a problem to be solved later. It wouldn't make any difference at all if he didn't get out of this storm, and real soon. A taste of a disaster he had never known was strong in his mouth. He spit the terrible taste out onto the top of the console. If he weren't lashed to the steering wheel, he'd surely drop. He couldn't remember ever being so tired. Jimmy screamed. Jim realized that his legs were squeezing the boy. He forced his legs to relax and kept the engine running with just enough speed to let him control the direction of the boat.

Through a momentary break in the rain and overcast, a flash of white caught Jim's eye and was immediately gone. He strained to see. Was he seeing things? There it was again, almost dead ahead about a hundred yards. *My God, it's a boat with only the cabin and gunnel showing.* He felt lucky to have seen it at all, but how was he going to avoid complete disaster? If he moved too far off course, he'd be caught between waves and meet the same fate. If he kept his present course he would ram the wreck and still suffer the same fate. He lost sight of it and eased his course slightly to the east, being ready to turn back if he was threatened by a wave. Jimmy fidgeted between his legs. Jim ached all over.

Jim strained to pick up sight of the boat again. There it was off to starboard and still about thirty yards away, just barely visible in the rain. Furious waves beat against it. He edged farther to the east to be sure of good clearance. His vision dimmed and he struggled to keep the boat in view. The waves tried to tear the wheel from his grip. The rain let up and he saw the boat just off the port side. As the boat drifted to the rear, he saw what appeared to be a person hanging onto the far side. He wiped the mist from his eyes and stared hard to be sure they weren't playing tricks on him.

A wave smashed against the side and almost capsized him. He was in a quandary. If what he had seen was really a person, he must make an attempt to save him, but how was he to do it without risking the lives of all on board.

He turned back to the west and plowed through the forward wave. The boat had disappeared to the northeast. Just as he went through the forward wave, he cut hard to the right and ran along the trough for just a moment then hard right again and headed north against what was once stern waves. Now the stern waves were smashing into and over the bow. Once in the trough, he could see ahead. The boat was just barely visible above the water. A white, empty life vest, tied to the side, bobbed in and out of the water as waves washed over it in rapid succession. No person was in sight.

He came up on the right of the upturned boat as close as he dared. Just as he came alongside, the bow lifted violently atop a wave and just as quickly plunged deep into the trough. He turned to the right again and managed to avoid capsizing and came along side again. This time he was running with the waves and would have a better chance to throw a lifeline if necessary. His legs ached from being in one place for so long and bound to Jimmy. He longed to move them. Salt from sea spray built up on his upper lip. He licked it with his tongue and spit it out.

The boat came up on the right. Jim readied the line. With wet, numb, fingers he rubbed his eyes, straining to see any people – there were none. A sense of relief surged through him. Maybe others had rescued them, or, more likely, they were traveling with other boats. Jim felt sure that was the case. He wished he had been as smart.

The wave hit him broadside and lifted the side of the boat out of the water. The propeller whirred faster without any resistance. He jerked back on the throttle. If he lost the prop now the fight was all over. Water poured in from the left side and washed over Jimmy. They were all goners now for sure. How was Flo and the kids doing down below? He fought the wheel with hands and arms that moved without concious

31

thought. When his legs gave out he would surely crush Jimmy. The boat settled back in the water and completed the turn. They were safe again for the moment. He felt like collapse was near – it would be so easy to just give in. Only his instincts kept him going. He had to go on. The people he had on board were his main concern now.

Jim turned back to the southwest and braced himself for more of the storm. The going was slow, but the weather had abated somewhat – smaller waves and less rain. He edged his way into calmer water.

On the verge of complete exhaustion, Jim maneuvered the Donella to the lee side of Big Spanish Key. Jimmy, still soaking wet, but now sitting huddled against the cabin door, at the signal from Jim, stood and dropped the anchor from the bow and secured the rope to the stanchion. They were in about six feet of water he reported to his dad. When the boat tugged at the anchor, Jim cut the engine and stretched the tarp from the edge of the cabin to the rear poles to provide shelter from the light drizzle. Clouds thinned out and allowed some blue to get through from the sky, and on this side of the key at least, the wind had died to a heavy breeze. The boat rocked gently. Jim knew the storm still raged farther to the northeast, but they were out of it for now. He leaned against the console and took in a deep breath. He brushed the hair out of his eyes and looked around for his cap. It was gone – lost to the winds.

The cabin door opened and Junior and Francis bounded out onto the deck followed closely by Flo. She looked haggard to Jim – worn out from the tossing around he knew she'd been subjected to below deck for the past four hours. She tried to smooth out the wrinkles in the long, plain, white cotton dress she wore, and seemed happy as she stretched her arms wide and took a deep breath of fresh air. Her dark blue eyes seemed to delight in the whole openness.

She saw Jimmy, went to him, gave him a big hug and held on for a while. "Thank God you're all right, boy. When that wave hit I just knew you were a goner for sure." She tousled his hair.

He looked up at her proudly and then at his dad. Then to Jim, she said, "You okay, Papa? Did we get right in the middle of it?"

Jim struggled to light his pipe in the wind. He bent down close to the floor. Smoke climbed and quickly dissipated. He'd always liked Flo, even from the start. The thought of Buddy leapt into his mind. He frowned as he straightened to his full six feet and quickly put the thought out of his head. "No, thank the Lord. We were just on the edge, but much farther into it than I reckoned. We're okay now, though." He took Jimmy by the arm and aimed him toward the cabin door. "Boy, you get below and get some dry clothes on." Jimmy scampered away.

Jim busied himself coiling the ropes at his feet and reflected on the unseen, but still raging storm just over the horizon. Out of the corner of his eye he watched Flo put her hair in place and tie a bandanna around it. He'd seen her looking much better than she seemed today. She would probably never know just how close she'd been to death.

"Papa, you want me to fix us somethin' to eat?"

"That'd be just dandy, Flo, but a cup of steamin' hot coffee first would take the chill off these old bones. There's lots of food in the cupboard. You fix whatever you want. I'm game for anything after the coffee. We'll just be here an hour or more, then we'll head on in to Key West. Should be pretty smooth sailin' the rest of the way. You all right?" He noticed the dried blood on the edge of her left ear.

"Yes, I'm fine." She rubbed both hands over her swollen stomach. "This baby's been kickin' the livin' daylights out of me, though. I reckon he's gettin' ready for the world. Where are we anyhow?"

"We're just north and west of Marathon. This little key has good high ground underneath all the mangroves. Good beach on the western end. Spent time here in the past. Used to pull up here to rest after a long day fishin' the Gulf in this area. Note some blood on your ear. You cut?"

Flo touched her ear and scraped off the blood with a fingernail. "Small gash on the back of my head. It's okay now, though. No need to worry none."

Jim surveyed the woman who had been his daughter-in-law these past five years. He'd always admired her courage and stamina. Just a wisp of a woman, little more than five and a half feet and normally about a hundred and ten pounds soaking wet he reckoned, but now swollen with child – her face a little puffy looking – overbite more prominent than usual. Her dark hair, always worn short, framed her plain, but handsome face. He couldn't remember ever hearing her complain about anything and, God knows, there's enough for anyone to complain about in this hard country. He worried about her, though. Unless she found another man pretty soon, she would probably have to go live with her mama. The country was just too unforgiving for a woman alone, especially with three small children. There weren't many eligible men in these parts either, and the chance of snagging one was pretty slim.

The thought of another man in his son's place sent tremors racing through his chest. Buddy and Flo seemed made for each other and there could be no good substitutions. Up until February their marriage had been about as good as anybody could expect, and probably better than most. Buddy was not much of a drinking man and Flo seemed very contented with him. When Buddy was not fishing, hunting or trapping, or helping him with one thing or another, he was tinkering with his darn fool inventions – some already with patents. This from a man with almost no schooling at all. Jim's heart ached whenever he thought of his son and the promise God had set aside for him. But now as he gazed at Flo he thought he detected a faint glow emanating from her simple white linen frock. Was it from the child to be born?

Flo went back into the cabin and soon emerged with two cups of steaming hot coffee. The wind carried the steam away as soon as it materialized at the edge of the cup. "Papa, here's some coffee. It's very hot. It should warm you up some. When do you think we'll put in to Key West?"

"We'll stay here a couple of hours till the wind dies down some. Should make Key West before nightfall, about seven, I reckon. Flo, if you're gonna stay up here any time, you ought to wear an oiler to keep you dry and warm. This cold wet weather could make you sick." He was concerned about the child as well as the mother.

"I'm all right, Papa. I'll have some vittles for us in a few minutes. I hope the boys runnin' in and out won't aggravate you too much. Mama was expectin' me this afternoon. I hope she won't worry."

"She won't have to wait long." Jim responded, and experienced a moment of anxiety. The wind was picking up. Could he have miscalculated the direction of the storm? The wind should be moving to the southwest soon. He turned to the radio as Flo made her way below deck.

The radio yielded only a crackling noise. He faced the wind as if to dare it to take him on. By God, he was King James, master tracker of animal and man, hunter, fisher, guide for the rich, and Special Deputy Sheriff for Monroe County. He'd lived in these parts since he was born in 1883 and had braved many a real storm. This little puny wind wouldn't come close to testing his grit. They were safe for the time being. The wind would slack off in due time. The coffee warmed his innards and he thought of his life in the Everglades, and it wasn't all that bad of a life either – something akin to paradise, maybe.

As far back as he could remember, he loved his life. Some people were always looking for something better, but not him. He'd found his place in life. Life had, for the most part, been wonderful even after the death of his wife three years ago. All his children were generally in good shape with healthy families of their own. Buddy was the oldest and had more promise than any of the others – but no need to dwell on that now. Children were good things to have in this wilderness, but most times they were

35

a great problem or aggravation. All told, though, a pretty good life.

He was startled out of his thoughts by the sound of children running on deck and young Jimmy yelling that dinner was on the table. At the same time, Flo called for him to come into the cabin to eat.

The meal was simple, but good and satisfying. More coffee warmed him. Jim returned topside and surveyed the abating weather. They could move within the hour. Flo and the children came back on deck. He looked at them with some pity, but mostly with hope. He wondered just what she would do with the rest of her life. She was only twenty-three. He thought again of Buddy. The promise that had been his had been taken from him so early in life by a God who Jim simply could not understand. Why give a person talent and promise and then rob him of it before there was enough time to use it for its intended purpose – whatever that was. In a sudden inspiration he envisioned God's wisdom – Buddy's potential for greatness would be inherited by this yet-to-be-born child.

Looking directly and solemnly at Flo he said, "Flo, your child will be a boy, and he will perform great works. He will not have the chance to look upon his daddy and is therefore destined for greatness. It's God's will." He was astonished at what he heard coming from his mouth. Flo's look was one of amazement. He had never spoken to any of the kids that way.

Flo moved closer to where Jim was working idly with a pile of rope and smoking his pipe. "I've heard tell that a child who's never seen his daddy has the power to heal. Is that what you mean, Papa?"

"It's more than that, Flo. Buddy had natural talent. I feel this child will inherit that as well as the power to heal." He felt a little uneasy talking this way with her. He was not used to talking at any length with a woman anyhow, but they were both lonely and way out in this desolate sea. It was good to talk to someone.

Flo lit a cigarette and tossed the spent match overboard. "Papa, what do you think really happened to Buddy and Robert down there at Shark Point? You think they were killed by somebody that had it in for them?" The kids were playing at the stern with Jimmy.

Jim re-lit his pipe, drew in a deep breath and exhaled the smoke into the air. The thought of that day he first arrived at the scene came to mind. Even after six months he still found it hard to focus on the scene at Shark Point without a pang of sorrow and a quiver to his lip. He hesitated until he was in full control of his emotions before he answered her. "I went straight there from Key West the minute I heard the news. Except for the ashes of the campfire, I didn't find no sign. Found some footprints and trash lying around, but that's just normal from so many trappers and fishermen usin' that point for a camp. When I came back the next week with a posse from Key West, we searched the area better and found some blood splattered around in two different places. As you know their skiffs were never found. If somebody killed them they sure cleaned up real good. Flo, it's mighty hard for me to believe that Buddy would just go off without tellin' somebody somethin'."

Flo interrupted, "I've heard some rumors that Buddy's been seen around. You checked up on them, haven't you?"

"Yeah, I've heard probably the same ones you heard. I've checked all of them out and it seems that's all they were, just rumors. Didn't want to dwell on any of them till I had some good news for you. Don't want you to get up any false hopes. I'll keep followin' up on all I hear of, you can be sure of that." Jim's mind simply would not allow him to believe that Buddy was not alive. "Flo, if Buddy's out there somewhere, I'll find him. Make book on it."

Flo stood. Jim saw the tears in her eyes. He turned his face into the wind and busied himself with preparations to depart. The kids were still busy with their games at the stern. Jimmy came to his side as if awaiting sailing orders. Flo went below.

They turned into the wind as they made their run for Key West. The Gulf was still choppy, but the wind had abated and was a lot less than gale force. The wind had shifted to the southwest, which was a good sign. They would make it in two hours with only a little discomfort. The blue sky revealed more of itself, the heavy overcast now way up high. The wind was strong in his face, but with no rain and only an occasional splash of salt spray. He loved it, the wind, the spray, the challenge. He loved the sea, the hunt, and the chase, whether it be man or animal. He closed the windscreen and wiped his face with the towel he kept there just for such purposes.

The talk with Flo brought Buddy back to mind. All the questions and known facts now poured back into his mind. Did Buddy run off on his own for some unknown reason? Jim had a deep itch to believe that Buddy had run off, but it just didn't fit. Buddy was a devoted father to his boys and a loving husband to his wife — or so it seemed. Of course, you never can tell what goes on behind closed doors. Jim refused to believe that Buddy would just run off and leave them to fend for themselves in this hard country. The idea that Buddy's life had really ended wouldn't sink in either. There had to be some rational explanation. Surely he would get in touch with his family any day now. But that idea, too, was dimming fast. Jim didn't now know what to think.

Bad blood existed between the Harrisons and other families in the area for sure. None of it, though, should lead to murder, but Jim couldn't rule it out. He had been a law officer too many years to rule anything out. There had been rumors since that it was the Brown boys who had ambushed them, but with no hard evidence and no one willing to testify against them, not much could be done about it. He remembered the time the Browns had tried to do him and his family in over a long simmering feud under the guise of trying to patch things up. But time had mostly eased the tensions. Had they let their guards down too soon?

There weren't too many people in the area that had any hard feeling toward Buddy. He was fair and easygoing with just about everyone. Now, that Robert Harrison was a different story altogether. That boy was a rogue, a lady's man and quick temper all wrapped into one. It was always wise to keep a wary eye on

Robert when he was in the neighborhood. There were likely many men who had it in for him. In this country not many deaths were ever resolved. It was difficult, in most instances, to determine foul play even when circumstances and evidence pointed to such a conclusion. Of course, he would rather believe that they had run off somewhere even though it grieved him no end to think that Buddy would just abandon his family that way.

# CHAPTER 6

Flo was on deck standing next to Jim when she saw the familiar railroad trestle over the northern end of Garrison Bight. It was a welcome sight, the safety of the harbor just beyond. She reckoned another hour and a half before nightfall. In ten minutes they would be docked and on dry land again. *Never want another trip like that one as long as I live. Next time I'll go by train.* They passed beneath the trestle and made their way into the calm of the Bight. Inside, the water was calm with barely a ripple. The wind had practically died out.

She looked at the blue sky with only one small cloud, way out over the airport on the southeast side of the island. She heard a plane roar, then saw it rising in the sky heading east. Most of the fishing boats that used the Bight were in for the day and tied at the docks along Ocean View Drive. Most of the fishermen had gone home. A few still lingered – taking care of the remaining details of the day. Several tourists lingered, too – chatting with the boat captains – making plans for tomorrow or beyond.

Jim turned the Donella to the east and headed for the docks at that end of the Bight. The railroad crossed Ocean View Drive just east of the docks and just beyond old run-down and unpainted buildings.

Flo saw her mother standing by the black Buick sedan – bought new in 1924 when times were much better on the lime farm. She looked taller than normal for some reason. Maybe it was the effect of the light blue, lacy dress, belted tight at the waist, which hung to her ankles. Hopefully, she wouldn't be mad because they were late – knew she would, though. That woman would raise Cain for days about making her wait for hours in the hot August sun. She was a very impatient and strong-willed woman, accustomed to getting what she wanted when she

40

wanted it. If she was on this dock to pick up her daughter, no matter all the complaining, you could bet she would be looking after her daughter and the expected child. Flo had a good warm feeling inside just knowing her mama was there. Would she ever grow up and be secure without her mama around? Her child could now be born without worry. Mama would take charge and see that the right people were on hand to deliver the baby properly.

Jim backed the Donella in, and Jimmy looped bow ropes first over one pole then the other, then ran to the stern and jumped onto the dock with the tether ropes. Flo thought he was such an expert boatman to be so young. You learn early in this country. Jimmy made the ropes fast, got back into the boat and busied himself with the chores he knew by heart. Junior and Francis both scrambled up on the stern trying to get off the boat. Jim nodded at Mildred and pushed the boys up onto the dock. They ran to see the other boats and the fish spiked to a big board. Flo accepted Jim's arm and climbed up. She took the luggage he passed up to her and hugged Mildred.

Mildred spoke with a question to no one in particular, but Flo knew it was directed at Jim. "I can't imagine why you all would even think of makin' this trip in that kind of weather. You all could've been killed. I've been worried to death about you." She looked at Flo and gathered the children to her when they ran up to her pulling at her skirt.

Jim glanced at Mildred, then away when she fixed him in her stare. Flo let out a sigh of relief when he didn't respond right away. He looked like he wanted to take up the fight, but busied himself instead with securing the boat. It seemed like he didn't relish the idea of crossing swords with this tough woman today. Mildred kept staring at him as if to lay all the blame at his feet.

"Nothin' to worry yourself about, Mildred, everything went just about as planned," Jim finally responded, Flo thought, with just a taste of testiness. Here it comes, she thought, but Jim turned away and kept about his business.

Flo stepped in front of Mildred to block her view of Jim, hoping to change the subject. Both of them meant a lot to her, but she knew that neither cared two cents for the other. The safety and security of a good house and a clean bed was all that occupied her mind now. She could sleep for a week.

Mildred ignored Jim and spoke to Flo. "I just hope to God nothing has happened to that young'un. You wouldn't listen to me and come by train like I told you to. Just because you've got young'uns don't mean you're all grown up. You got to listen to your ma when she talks to you. You still got a lot of learnin' ahead of you."

Flo felt weary and wanted to get away from there before a fight started. She couldn't understand why her mama had to pick a fight with everybody she met. Sometimes she wanted to tell her so, but always knew better. She could still taste the blood from a good slap in the face for putting in her two cents. "Aw, come on, Mama. We're here and the baby's fine. He's been kickin' my sides out. I bet he's healthy as an ox. I'm tired. Can we go now?"

Jim spoke over his shoulder. "How's old man Joe doin', Mildred? Ain't seen him in a coon's age. He plannin' to do any more fishin'?"

"Joe Patavia is the same as he's ever been. Mean and cantankerous as ever. Just like old man Jim Harrison," Mildred flung back.

"You tell old Joe we miss him on the long nights in the bay," Jim said to Mildred. To Jimmy he said, "Jimmy, come on. Let's go. We can finish up here tomorrow. I'm tired out." He climbed out of the boat onto the dock. To Flo he looked a tired and beaten old man. Not nearly as old as Joe Patavia, but certainly tired-looking today. Age gets on you if you worry and fret too much.

Mildred said something as Jim turned away from them to speak to a dock attendant. He acted like he didn't hear.

Jim turned back toward them and spoke directly to Flo. "Flo, I'll be in town for the next two weeks. If you need me, get word to me at the house. I'll see to the place at Wood Key till you

42

decide to come back. Let me know what you expect to do after the baby's born."

Flo nodded. "Thanks for everything, Papa. I'll be in touch with you soon as I have any news. I imagine I'll be goin' back when the baby's about five or six weeks old. Papa, don't pay no attention to Mama. She don't mean nothin' by what she says."

"Don't worry none, Flo. I don't pay that woman no mind."

Mildred was walking away toward the car with the two boys in tow. Jim returned to the dock man and his tasks. Jimmy followed the father he adored. Flo said goodbye to Jimmy and turned and headed towards the car.

Mildred retrieved the crank from the trunk and handed it to Flo when she came up to the car. She reached in under the steering wheel and turned on the ignition switch and set the spark. Flo moved to the front of the car, stuck the crank into the slot just below the radiator and gave it a couple of good turns. The engine sputtered to life and began to purr like a kitten. Junior and Francis climbed onto the back seat and Mildred slid in under the steering wheel. Flo deposited her things in the back seat next to the boys, stepped up on the running board and climbed onto the passenger seat.

Mildred backed around and came within a foot of the water's edge, then moved slowly along the west side of the tracks just as a passenger train came chugging towards them, belching smoke and red ashes from underneath the engine. The train wasn't more than three feet from them. The conductor, hanging half out of the engine compartment, seemingly within touching distance, pulled a cord by his side and the blast of its whistle shattered the calm and serenity of the Bight. Francis screamed and clapped his hands to his ears. Mildred turned right on Ocean View and headed west.

The highway merged into Rocky Road and, as they passed Bayview Park, Mildred broke the silence of the past five minutes. "I don't care what they say, I just don't like that rude Jim Harrison. His kind are all the same. Think they know it all, but don't know a damn thing. I told you not to marry into that

43

family. They're good for nothin' and never will amount to nothin'. Now here you are with another young'un and no man to look after you. You shouldn't even think about goin' back into that God-forsaken country. Them people don't give a tinkers' damn about you. If you don't find a man soon, you'll be out on your ear. I tell you—"

Flo cut her off. "Mama, please. Papa Jim and all his family have treated me as part of the family for all these years Buddy and I've been married, and especially since he went off last February."

"Don't interrupt me, girl. I've heard the gossip . . . . But, no matter, you're better off shuck of 'em. They're nothin' but white trash anyhow. Maybe not even white. It's been said around that old man Richard was actually a slave. So you stay right here with me and we'll find you a good man soon enough."

Exasperation overwelmed Flo. She loved her mother and would never do or say anything to hurt her, but sometimes she felt a strong urge to just choke her to keep her from hating so much. The choking part was just as quickly put out of her mind. She knew she could never do anything so drastic. But oooooh! She had heard this argument a hundred times if she'd heard it once. She said as calmly as she possibly could, "Mama, we've been over all this time and time again. I don't believe a word they say, and how the heck could they know anyhow? Sure, the Harrisons are dark skinned, but most of that comes from bein' in the sun all day long." Mildred tried to interrupt, but Flo pushed on without let up. She didn't look at Mildred, and pretended that she didn't hear. "It's also been said that old man Harrison is mostly Indian. His mama was a full blood Choctow. His nose is narrow and his hair is straight as a board – with just a teensy little wave to it. He looks more like a dark white man to me." She stole a look at Mildred.

Mildred was plainly flustered and probably would've slapped Flo if she hadn't been driving the car. "Well, just look at your Buddy Jr. He certainly gets his dark complexion from somewhere. He sure don't get it from me or from the Portagee's on your daddy's side."

Flo hadn't received a slap yet and became braver in this conversation. *Maybe Mama realizes that I've grown up.* She blurted out. "What about Mary's boy, Rodney? He's more dark complected than Junior, but he sure has plain white features just like Junior, and there's no Harrison blood in him. And how about little Francis here, why his skin is the fairest in the family and his hair is almost white. Junior calls him cotton top."

Mildred thought on Flo's last statement, but said nothing. Inside she fumed. She looked straight ahead and tried with all her might to control her temper. It would do no good to get into a fight with Flo over the damned Harrisons. Flo would always protect them, at least until they turned on her, and she knew they would one day.

Mildred continued on Rocky Road past the elementary school at White Street and turned right on William. She noticed the Catholic Church on the southwest corner and felt a pang of guilt for having missed so many masses during the past year. She knew she was too ornery to be a good devout Catholic, but did like to go and have confession every now and then to cleanse her soul. Be important to go while Flo was in town so the church would help them with the midwife, milk, and other needs which were sure to crop up. God knows she didn't have the where-with-all to pay for everything herself.

Joe was sitting on the porch swing when Mildred parked the car next to the low cement wall in front of the house just across from the graveyard. They'd been renting there for the past two years, ever since letting the farm on Key Largo go back to the owner. She halfway expected Joe to get a farming job on Captiva. He had corresponded with the owner several times.

Joe came down to the car to greet Flo. "Ain't you a sight for sore eyes now," he said. "Bigger than the County Courthouse, looks to me." He gave her a big hug and, before she could even respond, grabbed her belongings from the back seat and went

45

back to the house with them. The porch boards squeaked under his weight. He opened the screen door and sat the things on the floor of the living room.

Mildred wasn't particularly happy to bring her daughter to this place, but it was all she had, and was what they had all been used to most of their lives anyhow. Poorhouse Lane certainly lived up to its name. Everybody on the street was poor as church mice. Most of Key West was poor in these trying times. There had even been talk of turning in the city charter. Poorhouse Lane was more of an alley than a street, but since it began on William Street and ended on Solaris Hill it was not really an alley either. Only the house right near the bend going out to Solaris Hill was painted. The other five on that strip of the street hadn't seen a coat of paint in many a year, and probably wouldn't see one in many more. She was sick and tired of living so close to others. There wasn't more than five feet between the houses and everybody got a whiff of everybody else's out-house. A twenty-five foot lot was just not big enough for a comfortable house. Maybe Joe would take that job on Captiva and they could leave this dying town.

Junior and Francis scampered out of the car and took off after their Papa Joe. Mildred came around the car and she and Flo followed all of them into the house. Twilight was settling in. It would be dark within the hour. Joe had turned the electric lights on and the living room just off the porch was snug. A cool breeze came in through the open windows and from the scupper on the roof. Mildred showed Flo into the back bedroom just off the long hall next to the kitchen at the back of the house. She then went into the kitchen and began to rattle pots and pans. In a little while she had a dinner together and went to get Flo. She found her stretched across the bed fully clothed and sound asleep.

After the children were asleep Mildred went out on the porch and chatted with Joe until he tired and went inside. She sat alone for some time, enjoying the taste of snuff and staring off into space. Her mind pulled persistent thoughts in from times past.

46

All her life she'd wanted to be something better than she was, both money-wise and in the social world, but somehow she couldn't seem to break out of the mold her culture had set for her. Marriage and children, that's all there was. Each one of her nine children all seemed to be on the road to the poor house. All married to fishermen or poor white trash with not much more promise than a bare living. They all seemed to have just accepted their lot – not a spark left in the bunch.

At one time, she had high hopes that one of them would do better than their start in life, but she knew it was darned near impossible to move or marry out of one's class. The old way of selecting a daughter's husband had lots of merit. Flo, at one time, had an ambition to get a higher education with an extreme interest in archeology, but here of late, she seemed to be heading in the same direction as the others.

Now this damned depression was about to kill them all. There was no work anywhere. Fish were plentiful, but no one had the money to buy them. The men could just barely get enough money to keep their nets and boats in repair. There were no jobs anywhere either. From the men's talk, she'd heard there were as many as twelve million people looking for work. She didn't understand it at all – just knew that times were damned hard and a decent living was hard to come by. Of course, the men could somehow always find a way to get a bottle of whisky somewhere, even though it was illegal. She reckoned Roosevelt would be elected in November, and there was powerful talk about lots of government jobs which would put the men back to work, get the economy back on track and make things right for everybody. *Hopefully some of that will filter down to our boys. We'll make it, we always have.* She spat well-chewed snuff spittle into the coffee can near her feet.

Mildred thought she had finally broken the mold when she convinced Joe to move to Key Largo. They had begun the small key lime farm, which had grown over the years. This was the start she'd been looking for to get her away from the poorhouse door.

Then came the 1926 hurricane which wiped out their crop, and that was followed by the collapse of the land boom which erased the value from the farm. The storm, together with the economic downturn destroyed their farm and, with it, all their life savings. They were crushed. Their subsequent return to fishing had resulted in Flo marrying into that awful Harrison family. Maybe she was too harsh on the Harrisons – she doubted it, though.

Tomorrow she would pay a visit to the church to get some help for the new child. She'd given enough in the plate every Sunday most of her life and it was high time they paid some of it back when she needed it.

She didn't know what they were going to do to survive. As usual, Flo had no inkling of their situation. Mildred didn't want to move back into the swamps, but she didn't see any other way. Fishing and farming was all Joe knew and he now seemed content to do no more than that. The old spark from long ago was gone and so were her chances to make something of her life. Time had about run its course. Joe's job working on the guide boat didn't pay enough to keep them and wasn't all that steady either. He was a strong man for seventy-two, but she wondered if even he could last under the rigors of farm work.

She would go over to the Columbia Laundry tomorrow to be sure they would take Flo on as they promised. Laundry work was hard as hell, and she felt some shame putting Flo to work in her ninth month, but what else could she do? She didn't have enough money to feed all these mouths. Life could get damned hard. Things had never been this bad before. Roosevelt would make things better. She spat out all the snuff into the coffee can, stood and went in to bed.

# CHAPTER 7

At the top of Solaris Hill Flo nodded to the old Cuban man sweeping the front porch of the two-story grocery store. The building, like everything in Key West, was old and in great need of repair. On the way home tonight she would stop at the store and pick up a loaf of Cuban bread and a plug of Brown Mule tobacco for Papa Joe as she did every evening. Mama had to have her Cuban bread for supper. Flo liked it a lot, too, especially the crust and more particularly the hard bead on top running the length of the loaf. The store made the bread fresh in the morning and in the afternoon.

Manuel looked up as she approached, but kept right on with his sweeping. "Buenos dias, Flodeenda".

Manuel pronounced Florinda like her father did. "Good morning, Mr. Aguilar." Flo smiled and continued past the porch and the other grocery store on the north corner, still shut tight, and just as old and in need of repair as Mr. Aguilar's store. She paused to catch her breath before continuing on to the laundry at the bottom of the hill to the west. She had worked at the laundry every day except Sundays ever since she arrived in Key West, near to three weeks now. The stifling hot plant and the grueling work almost did her in at times, but the seventeen cents an hour helped keep the wolves from the door, or so her mama said. Her advanced stage made it hard to climb the steep hill and she knew she would have to quit the job any day now.

She turned and looked back down the hill. The sky, a bright blue, close to the horizon, lit up the spiked iron fence surrounding the graveyard. The tombs and graves looked like ghosts in the dancing shadows. A chill crawled up her spine. The sky overhead was dark blue, sprinkled with a thousand stars. There to the southeast was Orion, lying on his side with his dagger pointing to the ground.

The thought of Buddy tugged at her heart and she choked up momentarily. He had taught her so much about the heavens. There in the north and high up, Cassiopeia formed a big lopsided 'M', and she knew just below it was the North Star and below that, hidden by the horizon, the Big Dipper. That dipper was the best of all for her. She always thought of Buddy when she saw it. The unmoving air hung heavy with moisture. She wiped away a tear with her sleeve. With heavy heart she turned and went on toward the laundry.

Just before reaching Simonton Street, she cut across the marl-covered parking lot and saw Mathilde, standing by the dilapidated and rusty Model-T, waiting for her, as she did every morning. Only six other cars occupied the lot. Mathilde was dressed as always in blue coveralls with the red and white bandanna wrapped around her hair, blondish strands hanging loose across her right eye. She would be a knockout if she could lose some of the weight she carried. Underneath the puffy face was, or had been at one time, a very beautiful woman. That weight, plus her two teenage children, prevented her from snagging some eligible man. A fat thirty-five year old woman working the steam press in a laundry wasn't much of a catch.

Flo had been assigned to Mathilde and had taken a liking to her from the first day on the job. Mathilde, though, had been reluctant and apprehensive with having to put up with a woman about to give birth. But after that first week, when Flo showed that she could work with the best of them, Mathilde became her protector and tried to assign her to the better jobs. Flo had started off lugging bags of dirty laundry, then graduated to loading the machines and now she was ready to handle the dry cleaning machines all by herself. The baby had been a constant kicker and she knew it would not be denied its birthright much longer.

"Mornin', Teal. Sorry I'm a little late. That hill is gettin' steeper and steeper by the day – have to stop and rest part way."

50

Mathilde joined her and they walked toward the big white frame building fronting on Simonton Street. "No matter. You look like you're about to bust. Any day now, huh? You okay?"

Just as they stepped inside the door the whistle blew and the medley of voices coming from the large open space was soon drowned out by the steady hum of machines. There must have been a hundred machines with women of all ages attending to about half of them – not enough business to work them all. Mr. Martinez looked their way with just a hint of contempt as they went on down to the floor. As long as she was with Mathilde, old meany Martinez wouldn't jump on her for being a few seconds late or for her bulging belly under her plain sack dress.

"Yeah, I'm doin' just fine. Lookin' forward to workin' the dry cleaners all by myself. Maybe another week for the kid, I reckon." They walked to the opposite side of the room from Matilde's usual work station.

On the floor next to the first of five large machines sat several cardboard boxes filled with clothing to be dry-cleaned. The first two, big round vats built on legs that kept them about a foot off the floor, were large washers, both connected to an electric motor by wide flat belts hooked together through a series of pulleys. The belts were frayed and she worried they might break, fly off and hurt somebody, especially her. Both machines could be operated at the same time or separately by throwing a switch on the motor. She would run them both this morning.

"All right, Flo, we'll go through one complete process. Go to it, but before you start anything, tell me exactly what you're going to do before you do it." Mathilde stood to the right side of the first washer. Heat inside the building had grown since they entered, the noise deafening.

With her foot, Flo moved one of the boxes up to the first washer, threw open the curved door, opened the perforated smaller inner door and piled the vat full of all sorts of men's suit clothing. She filled the other washer that was just behind with women's clothing and shut the doors on both machines. With a nod, Mathilde gave the okay to proceed. Placing her hand on the gate valve, she said out loud for Matilde's benefit. "I'll turn this valve and let in the naphtha fluid from the outside tank on the roof, and with the switch located on the motor, start both machines." She opened the valve and flipped the start switch. The big machines came to life with a rumble and motion which would have ripped them from the floor had they not been bolted to steel plates. The noise drowned out the human and machine noise from the rest of the room.

After twenty minutes, she stopped the washers, removed the dripping and foul-smelling clothing and placed them into the third machine in the line to spin the fluid out. This machine was a round, tub-like affair also bolted to the floor that loaded from the top. Here the clothing would spin at high speed until all the fluid had been removed from the clothing and pumped into a cleaning tower sitting up against the wall. There the naphtha would be cleansed and returned to the tank on the roof.

After another twenty minutes, and with the approval of Mathilde, she removed the clothes and placed them into two large dryers where the clothes were steam-heated and tumbled until all the naphtha fluid was completely removed. After the clothes dried she removed them from the dryers, placed them in a canvas cart and had them sent to the pressers. The material still smelled of the liquid.

Mathilde watched the whole process and turned to leave. "Okay, kiddo. You're the master here now. Don't overdo it. How're you feeling?"

"I feel great. Should be able to get all these done today." She motioned to the boxes filled with clothes. Mathilde looked doubtful, but only grunted and walked off.

The 3:30 whistle blew to announce the afternoon break just as Flo moved the last load from the washers to the spinner. Her side ached and she was exhausted and drenched in sweat, but she was almost finished. She would just get the spinner loaded and started, then take her break. She felt a surge of pride in having accomplished her goal. She remembered the look of doubt on Mathilde's face this morning when she announced to the world that she would get all the clothes in the boxes finished and to the pressers before quitting time. Martinez was at the window, his usual perch. The machine noises in the room gave way to friendly chatter amongst the women as they made their way to the outside for cooler air and smokes.

The searing pain hit like a scalding iron. The wet clothes scattered across the floor as she collapsed in a heap. She heard an ear-piercing scream and tried to locate it before she realized it was coming from deep in her throat. Curled up on the floor in a tight knot she tried to squeeze out the pain – it just got worse – she knew there was an end and hoped it would come soon. She should have recognized the signs earlier and stopped, but it was important to prove that she was as tough as any of them. Blood ran hot against the inside of her leg – her time was here. She cursed herself for not resting more. Mathilde would have been so proud of her if she could have finished the job before the day ended. The sound of running feet and Mathilde's yell was the last she heard.

# CHAPTER 8

It was dark when Flo awoke. Confused, she tried to see in the dimness. The boys were asleep on the cot across the room – she was home. The events of the afternoon returned. She remembered the extreme pain and shuddered. Her throat felt dry as a bone. She got out of bed and stood warily in the doorway. The voices of Mildred and Papa Joe, talking out on the porch, drifted in on the soft breeze. She eased her way into the kitchen and filled a glass with water from the tap. The screen door squeaked, and she turned to see Mildred approaching.

"So you made it through yet another day. You okay? Hungry?"

Flo sat in a chair at the kitchen table. "I'm starvin' to death. How'd I get home?"

Mildred busied herself with pots and pans. "Mathilde brought you. Said you screamed like a stuck tiger and fainted. You don't remember any of it?" She removed some covered bowls and plates from the icebox and placed them next to the stove.

Flo took one of the cigarettes from the pack, tapped it on the table and lit it. "Only remember droppin' the clothes and watchin' 'em slide across the floor and knowin' I'd failed. Next thing, I'm here."

Mildred placed the warmed-up food on the table and set out a clean plate with knife and fork. "Mrs. Thompson came by and looked in on you. She expects the young'un in the next few days. You go ahead and eat. Want to tell Joe somethin' before he goes off to bed. You come on out on the porch when you're done." She turned and left the room. Flo sat alone with her thoughts and meal.

She was drying the dishes and putting them away when she heard the voices on the porch get louder. *Better putter around some more before going out there.*

The screen door opened and she recognized the familiar footsteps of Papa Joe. He stuck his head in the kitchen. "Flo, I'm goin' on to bed. You okay now?"

She turned at his voice. "Yeah, Papa Joe. I'm all right now. Don't know what came over me at the laundry. The heat, I guess."

"You best take it easy gal, till after that young'un gets here. Can't over do it, you know." He turned to go. "Good night, Flo. Get a good night's sleep. I'll see you in the mornin'." He spit tobacco juice in the coffee can he carried and walked away.

"Good night, Papa Joe. I'll be careful." *Wonder how long he's been sleeping in the back room? Guess it's easier to sleep apart when you get old.*

She washed the rest of the dishes and put them away, then strolled out to the porch and sat in the empty rocker next to Mildred. The night was dark, with just a hint of a breeze. She lit another cigarette. Mildred stared straight past the bright red bougainvillea that covered the far end of the porch out to the alley. She didn't look to be in a very good mood.

Flo broke the ice. "You got some ironin' to be done? I'll be able to help you with it tomorrow – don't think I better go back to the laundry till after the baby's born." The rocker groaned a little when she started rocking.

Mildred spat snuff spittle into a can she had by her chair. "You gave me quite a scare, girl. I thought for a minute both you and the young'un were goners. Couldn't get no doctor, but Joe went and got Mrs. Thompson. You better try to take it easy for a spell." She put the can back on the porch and folded her hands in her lap.

"Can't just sit around and do nothin'. Go stark ravin' mad if I do. Got near four days' pay comin', better see to it tomorrow. You all gonna move back up to Sanibel?"

"That's what we were just arguin' about. He's been offered the job of runnin' a farm on Captiva – sharecroppin' like white trash. I like it right here. 'Course can't make no money in Key West. He fishes some with Jakie Key, but that hardly puts beans on the table. If it wasn't for my washin' and ironin' they'd have to send us all to the poorhouse. It wasn't always like this. At one time, we were really on our way but . . . ." She paused and took a deep breath. "Oh well."

Flo threw the cigarette butt into the spittle can. A hiss sounded and smoke rose from the can. She looked intently at Mildred. "Is he gonna take it?"

"Reckon he'll have to. But he's just too damn old though to be responsible for a farm that size. Probably kill him. Of course he knows a hell of a lot about farmin' and I reckon the owner knows he knows, otherwise he wouldn't be makin' the offer. We came damn close to out-runnin' poverty back in the twenties and would've, too, if it hadn't been for the crash of '26 and, right on top of that, again in '29. Times were good before then. There's a lot of luck to life – lot of hard work, too, though."

Flo leaned back in the rocker and sighed. She gazed out into the clear night at the emptiness of Poorhouse Lane. "I remember the lime farm on Key Largo, and I remember the happiness I knew at pickin' time when we'd go into Miami or come down here. You'd always take us shoppin' for new clothes and shoes. They were the happiest days of my life. Papa Joe would load up the truck and we'd follow in the Buick. I remember the new leathery smell of the seats. Still smell it to this day." She lit another cigarette and mused out loud. "Why do we have to grow up anyhow?"

"Right after me and your daddy parted ways we all loaded up and headed for the farm. Joe had already been workin' it for six months by the time we got there. Times were good back then with the excitement that growin' your own business brings. Best years of my life, too. Joe and me been together near on thirteen years now. Been a good marriage. Don't regret it none."

"Mama, why did you and Daddy break up anyhow?"

"I don't care nothin' in this world about dredgin' up them old memories. They're gone now and best stay that way."

"But I need to know somethin' about Daddy. You always put me off when I ask about him. I was just ten then, but now I'm grown-up and think I can understand what goes on between a man and a woman. Never get to see him. How'm I ever gonna learn anything about you all?"

"Your daddy was a swashbucklin' Portagee from Oporto, Portugal. Nephew of a Gaspar pirate. Came to this country when he was twenty-two, lookin' for his uncle." Mildred paused. "The year must've been about 1877 or thereabouts. I met him much later on Captiva, and he swept me right off my feet. I was a very impressionable little girl and he was a dashing pirate – at least in my eyes. I was down there visitin' a cousin and never went back to Mississippi. We were married on May the thirteenth, 1885 on Captiva."

"I never heard nothin' about him bein' a nephew of a pirate."

"Story has it that Francisco's uncle, John Gomez, was a cabin boy for Gaspar. After the Navy busted up the pirates, John ran down into the Everglades where he died sometime around 1900. Some people claim he lived to a hundred and twenty-two. That's how your daddy happened to be in that God-forsaken country in the first place." Mildred's voice trailed off.

Flo leaned forward in her chair to catch every word. "You said his name was Gomez. Ours is Alvarez. Why the difference?"

"When Francisco came to this country he took his mother's name. His father's name was Gomez, the same as John's."

"How come you to divorce Daddy?"

Mildred stood up. "Enough of this. I've got a hard day tomorrow and I'm tired out."

Flo stood, too. She thought she had better drop the subject. She'd gotten more than she could have hoped for. "If you all go to Captiva, when will you go?"

The screen door squeaked when Mildred opened it. "Joe will probably leave right away to get us a place and get started on the farm. I'll follow after I get all my business taken care of. You better get some rest, too." She went inside.

Flo stood at the edge of the porch looking out into the night. *I'm her business.* Light flashed in the pitch-black sky followed soon after by rolling thunder. The wind had picked up, the smell of rain heavy in the air. Her mama was sometimes hard as a rock on the outside, but usually good as gold on the inside. She went in.

Mildred awoke with a start. What had awakened her? A noise? She listened. Nothing. The air was heavy and warm. Her nightclothes clung to her damp body. A fly buzzed her face. She nodded off. There it was again. This time she recognized the sound. It was Flo. It was time. She lay still and looked at the clock – 5am. At 5:11am the muffled cry came again. Mildred rose, slipped on her gown and went to where Flo lay tossing and moaning. After a long moment she stole out the door without a sound and made her way through the graveyard to Ashe Street and the home of Winifred Thompson, the mid-wife. When they returned to the house, the labor pains were just five minutes apart. The child would be born soon. Mildred wondered to herself, as she heated water for the mid-wife's chores and for a cup of coffee for herself, if there was anything to the old wives tale about a child who had never seen his daddy. What if this really was an historic event?

Francis came into the kitchen and sat at the table. Mildred gave him a glass of milk and a cold biscuit from the night before. She heard Mrs. Thompson talking to Junior, and in a minute he, too, came into the kitchen. The door to the bedroom shut. "Granma, why is Mama cryin' and who's that woman in there with her?"

Mildred sat a glass of milk and biscuit before him. "That's Mrs. Thompson, the doctor, come to help your mama bring your new baby brother."

Flo screamed. Junior jumped up and ran to the bedroom door and tried to open it. Mildred caught him and brought him back into the kitchen. Francis started to cry and Junior shouted, "She's a mean ole doctor. She's hurtin' my Mama. I want to go in there and help my Mama." He struggled to get away.

"Bring your breakfast and let's go out on the porch. Your mama will be all right. She wants you both to be big boys while she tries to bring the baby into the world." She took them by the arm and led them to the porch. In a little while, Joe had them amused and they forgot their mother for a while.

At exactly 10:13 Saturday morning on September 24 she heard a baby's cry and knew the time was at hand. Warren Eugene Harrison was now a part of this world. Junior and Francis hadn't heard. In five minutes the door opened and Mrs. Thompson stepped out of the room. Junior ran up to her. "Did you bring the baby in that bag?" She paid him no attention, and he went into the bedroom where Flo was lying on the bed holding the fresh baby. Junior looked at the baby, then at Flo. "Mama, where's your belly?"

She smiled big and pulled him to her. "The doctor took it out in the black bag." He seemed to understand.

Mildred, watching from the doorway, got the okay from Flo, and went into the kitchen and busied herself preparing a late breakfast for them all. She thought about the new child. Regardless what old wives had to say about the special powers of children who haven't seen their daddies, she knew this was no time for new mouths to feed. This was a very serious and difficult time. There were no jobs to be had and even a little money was hard to come by. This baby could only bring harder times to a person already eaten up with hard times. There was a time when more children were a boon – but not in this year. Damn Buddy Harrison anyhow.

# CHAPTER 9

Standing just inside the door of the one room shack which had been his home for the past three months, Curly peered through the dingy screen and watched old man Andre working in the garden. Earlier in the morning, he'd worked right alongside the old Indian and felt a little ashamed not being out there now. Weeding the rows of vegetables was a never-ending job. Weed, fertilize, weed, reap, weed, plant, weed and so on – day in and day out. Was it all worth it? At suppertime, yes. He could do more if he could get some strength. Seemed he was just too sick all the time to be of much help to anyone. When the dizziness hit him this morning, it had been all he could do to keep from fainting dead away. The heat had been too much to handle. It had been that way ever since he came to live with the old man. The headaches, too, were continuous.

The first two weeks here he had stayed to his bed, just hauling himself up long enough to eat a little bit and go to the toilet out behind the shack. He grimaced at the thought of the struggle to get there and the awful heat and smell when there. He'd vowed then, even in his weakened state, that someday he would change that stench and he had. A good application of lime had done the job. It was a mystery why the Indians never learned the trick. A mystery, too, how he'd learned it.

He couldn't remember hardly anything about the past and didn't have enough energy to worry much about it. He didn't even know who he was or where he came from. To this day, there was not a good clear picture of how and when he left the hospital. They said he had laid in a coma there for three months. Said the gunshot to the head had caused it and the reason for his lack of memory now. Andre pumped him all the time about it, but there were no answers to be had. Every now and then little tidbits of the past crept into his mind and sent him to

60

wondering. There was the recurring dream about a woman standing at a shoreline with water lapping at her feet. Two small boys ran around her playing. He always strained to see her face, but never quite could.

Toby, his savior, had left soon after bringing him here from the hospital, and he hadn't had a chance to ask him any questions. If he could only get rid of the headaches and dizziness and get some strength he would set off to find his past. He would help Andre more, too. That old man, near sixty, was so frail, a good wind would blow him away. Curly knew he would get better if he could eat and work more. He couldn't do much work because of the sickness. The lack of eating was because the food was just plain awful. He had to find his past, though – the woman and children in his dreams just might be real – may be needing him something powerful.

Curly half-turned to go back to his bunk when he heard the car approach. Still leaning against the door jamb, he watched with detached interest as it pulled up and stopped in front of the old man. The dry road dust kicked up by the car caught up and swirled around and over it. He'd seen a car like that before – 1927 Model-T Ford, two-door roadster with a rumble seat. *Where had he seen it?* He tugged at his brain for a picture. No images came to mind.

The door opened and a big man stepped out and walked toward the old man. About six feet and 180 pounds or so – broad shoulders. A deliberate walk that showed off his toughness. A hard man, used to trouble. Curly noticed the gun on the man's right hip and saw the silver badge on his left breast. The man's face lay hidden under the shadow of the brown felt hat he wore cocked low over his right eye. *Police? What are they doing here?* Curly moved farther back into the room. Too quick – the dizziness again. He could still see out, but knew he couldn't be seen from the outside.

Andre leaned on the hoe and turned to face the big man. He took the kerchief out of his back pocket and wiped his brow and the inside of the straw hat he'd been wearing. With the hat back on his head and the kerchief in hand, he waited for the lawman to approach.

"Are you Andre Gonsalves?" The man didn't wait for Andre to answer and his voice sounded loud and bossy. "I hear you've got a man named Buddy livin' here with you." He looked like he was accustomed to getting his way.

"Buddy?" The old man yelled in a shrill tinny voice. "I don't know a Buddy."

"Buddy!" The name leapt into Curly's brain and everything seemed clear for an instant, as if his head had lifted out of a fog, then, just as quickly, nothing – the name remained, though. "That's my name," he said under his breath – astonished at the revelation. "By God, I did have another life somewhere. The Indians call me Curly, but my name is Buddy." He took control of himself and looked again at the big man with the star on his chest. He still could not make out the face. *If I'm the Buddy this man's lookin' for, what's he want with me?* This Buddy must have done something mighty wrong for the law to come into Indian country looking for him. He felt the back of his head where the shotgun blast had tore into it. *Did I kill somebody?* He eased farther back into the shadows of the room, grabbed his shirt off the back of the one chair in the room and donned it as he pulled on his rubber boots. Andre was saying something to the sheriff, but Buddy couldn't make out what it was. The screen door was too dirty to see through from his position in the room. He picked up his cigarette makings and eased out the back door, trying with all his might not to make a sound. The door squeaked – he froze.

His heart raced a mile a minute, but otherwise he remained calm. The calmness in the face of danger seemed to be a knack of his. It had happened a few other times since he came here. Both of his hands were steady. He rounded the back of the shack, ran headfirst into a tree growing near the building and fell to his knees. The dizziness returned. Everything seemed to be spinning out of control and he thought he would puke. He held onto the tree and leaned against it until the dizziness left. With the aid of a low hanging limb, he pulled himself up, moved around to the opposite side of the shack and peered around the edge towards where Andre had been. Neither man could be seen. Fifteen feet from the shack was the old man's wood-frame house. Only a few flakes of old white paint still clung feebly to the sides.

He did a slow, low run across the space between the buildings and made his way quietly around to the side of the building away from the two men. He crept to the corner, crawled on his belly under the front porch to the garden side and looked into Andre's eyes just thirty feet away. The slight breeze carried their voices clearly to him. The coolness under the porch refreshed him. The old man seemed to look right at him but showed no sign of recognition. Only a few moments had elapsed since the lawman first arrived.

"I'm from the Monroe County Sheriff's Department. I heard there was a white man livin' in this village. The villagers said a stranger was stayin' with you." The man stood head and shoulders over the stooped old man, but spoke calm and in a regulated tone. Buddy hadn't realized before how frail and skinny the old man was until now, standing next to the powerful looking sheriff.

"There's no white man staying here, Sheriff." The old man said defiantly, standing his ground. None of the Indians in this part of the world ever cooperated with the law or white men voluntarily. Stories of betrayal were kept alive amongst the many South Florida camps – not wise to trust any white man. Harboring or simply catering to them could be punishable at the hands of the Elders. Buddy was tolerated more than accepted. His contact with the Indians around the lake was skimpy at best. Even old Andre didn't give him too much attention. He did eat what little there was with the old man most of the time and had been to Okeechobee City a few times for supplies, but for the most part, he had not been accepted by any of them.

The lawman remained calm and stared directly at the old man. "Look mister, the man down at the village said you had a feller stayin' here with you, and I'm wantin' to find out if he's the man I'm lookin' for. You got somebody livin' with you?"

"No white man round here, Sheriff." The old man wiped his forehead again and spat tobacco juice on the ground in front of the sheriff.

The sheriff looked exasperated. He removed his hat, wiped his brow and looked up at the sky. The September sun was almost straight up and baking everything underneath it. "I didn't come here to cause you no trouble, mister, but I need to locate this Buddy, and I need to do it right quick like. If you got somebody livin' here with you, you got to tell me now. If I have to drag you down to the jailhouse to get you to tell me, I'll damn shore do it."

The old man turned his eyes toward Buddy then back to the lawman. "I told you, there's no white man here. Breed been living with me for two, three months. Been staying in that shack back there. He's not here now, though. What's he wanted for?"

The sheriff ignored the question and sprinted toward the shack. The old man watched him go and looked directly under the porch. Buddy wasn't sure the old man saw him, but he backed out from underneath the porch and stood against the wall on the far side of the house. Keeping the house between him and the garden, he did a walking run into the woods. From the shelter of the woods he could see the front door of the shack. The sheriff was not in sight. Buddy waited. He felt dizzy again and leaned against a tree. After about ten minutes, the man came around from the back of the shack, looked around, went towards the front door and headed towards the old man. Buddy went back to the side of the house and crawled under the porch again. He panted heavily but relished the coolness.

The sheriff stopped by Andre, removed his hat and mopped his brow. "Where's the breed now? When you expect him back?" He wiped the inside band of the hat with the kerchief and looked hard and threatening at the old man.

Andre stopped digging and leaned on the hoe, seemingly unconcerned about this man and what he wanted. He mopped his brow and spit tobacco juice on the ground. "He wanders off every now and then. Sometimes goes down by the lake and just sits. Sometimes visits with the neighbors some. No telling where he goes most of the time." He looked directly at Buddy under the porch. "Don't do his share of the work around here I can tell you that much. Doesn't eat much either. Should be back before nightfall, I reckon."

The sheriff stared at Andre and asked impatiently and in a sort of low growl. "Where'd he come from? How'd he come to be stayin' here with you? What's he look like?"

Andre limped to the edge of the garden on the far side of the house and stood in the shade of a large oak tree with Spanish moss almost touching the ground. He seemed to favor his right leg more than usual. Maybe he was trying to get the sheriff to offer him some pity. The sheriff followed.

Andre said, "He's a tall man. About six three or so. Kinda puny and pale now, but I reckon he was a big man at one time from the looks of his hands and feet. Natural dark skin, but you can tell he's a breed by the green in his eyes and curly hair. My nephew and another man brought him here about three months ago and asked me to look after him for a little while. The poor man was more dead than alive and almost as white as a ghost – still don't seem fit. I didn't want to 'cause I'm not set up to look after anybody, specially a man can't look after himself. Toby forced me. I owe him, so I agreed to keep the breed for a couple weeks. It's now been three months. I don't—"

The sheriff cut him off. "How'd he come to be with your nephew? What'd you say his name was?"

"Toby. I don't know how they came to know each other. I asked him the same thing, but all he told me was the man had been in the hospital for two, three months."

"Where's this Toby now?"

"Don't know that either. He vowed he'd be back in a couple of weeks, now it's—"

"Who's the man your nephew was with that day?"

"Only know him as Marty. He hangs around with Toby a lot."

"What's Toby's last name and where'd he use to live?"

Andre hesitated, fussed with his hat and kerchief and didn't answer, like he hadn't heard the question. Buddy realized he didn't know Toby's last name either. He waited anxiously for Andre to respond, as if the answer would somehow help him find his past.

"What's Toby's last name?" The sheriff growled.

Andre looked straight at the sheriff as if pleading to not have to tell that. "Last name, Cypress." He turned away.

"You sure?"

Andre turned back and with shoulders squared in a fighting stance, faced the sheriff straight on. "God damn it, Sheriff, I ought to know my own nephew. Why don't you leave me be now. You wanting to get my family in some kind of trouble?"

"Where'd he come from?"

"Boy wanders all over. Had family down south. Down around Ochopee somewheres."

"Where's he at now?"

"Wish I knew."

The sheriff started for his car and flung over his shoulder. "All right for now. I'm gonna look around some more. I'll be back. I hope for your sake you've been square with me."

Andre spat on the ground where the sheriff had just been and looked at Buddy as if pleading for understanding.

Buddy, sweating now, scampered out from under the porch, crawled alongside the building, stood up and braced himself against the wall. His hands trembled. Sweat dripped from his forehead and beaded up on his nose. Bent over, and keeping close to the ground, he sprinted to the woods again. This time he didn't stop at the edge. The dizziness started again. He tore through the thick tangle of palmettos and pines, but took great pains to remain quiet. If the sheriff heard him, all was lost. There was not enough strength left in him to outrun anyone. His legs were heavy as lead and ached through and through – he could barely lift them. He stumbled over a fallen tree and plunged head first into a pile of dead branches, pine cones, and leaves. A sharp branch gouged the side of his neck, and it felt like a hot branding iron had been placed there. He rubbed the area with his hand and felt the stickiness of blood and the mushiness of a deep gash. For a short moment a paralyzing fear took hold of him – he shook it off. His hand, smeared with blood, he wiped on his pant leg. He pressed his kerchief against the wound and held it there until the blood stopped oozing out.

He tried to lift himself, but his arms didn't have the strength. They wouldn't budge him. A picture formed in his mind. His face was in the sand and his back on fire. There was the woman and children again, wading in the water. With all the strength he could muster, he lifted his body with his elbows and drew his legs underneath and forward. He pushed his body backwards and sat on his haunches. Once standing, he teetered, but quickly moved to a tree and held on to it until the dizziness passed. He moved from tree to tree with slow, but steady progress. The palmetto fans, saw-toothed and sharp, cut his hands and arms as he plowed through them when the path petered out. A sense of dread overcame him – he was spent. He dropped to his knees and sat back on his haunches to rest a minute. He picked a handful of palmetto berries from a nearby bush – supposed to make you get better. The taste was like spoiled cheese and tobacco juice combined. He chewed several, hoping for some miracle to come forth. The taste was the same as before. When he tried to swallow the juice he gagged. He tried again and forced a little into his stomach. Finally, he just gave up and threw the rest away. He'd recuperate by himself. He started to move and fell to his knees again, tried to rise up and sprawled flat out on his body. There was no more movement left in him. His arms had no feeling – not a part of his body. The sheriff would just have to take him. What little breath he could muster was evil-tasting and scratched his throat. Somebody was crashing through the brush. This is it. He closed his eyes, resigned himself to his fate, and fainted.

# CHAPTER 10

When Buddy finally opened his eyes everything was a blur and unfamiliar, the smell of coffee strong in his nose. He rubbed his eyes. They were sore to the touch. Sunlight came softly through the trees and drew dancing patterns on the ground in front of him. Mid-morning he reckoned. The old Indian sat with his back against a tree. Buddy looked at him in disbelief. *What's he doing here? How did he find me?* A woman he didn't recognize was stirring something in a big black pot suspended over the fire. A coffeepot with steam filtering out of the spout sat just to the edge of the fire. The smell of cooking meat and vegetables filled the air. The smell brought back memories and momentarily he was on a beach somewhere. The ocean breeze, cool on his face – salt and seaweed smells deep in his nostrils. There was a woman and two little boys playing in the water – running, splashing, yelling happily. The picture disappeared. He tried to sit up and couldn't. The woman at the fire turned towards him, but said nothing, her expression a blank. He had seen the woman somewhere, but couldn't place her. He rubbed his eyes again. The old man came over to him.

"So, you finally wake up, eh?" Buddy tried again to sit up. Andre supported him and spoke to the woman. "Consuella, give a little coffee and a bowl of soup for my friend. That will return some strength, I think."

Buddy felt dizzy and awfully weak. "How'd you find me? When? What day is it? What time?"

Andre helped him get comfortable against the tree. "Whoa. Take it easy. Take some coffee and soup. I will explain everything." Andre took the cup from the woman and held it to Buddy's lips. He sipped the hot coffee and cherished the warmth as it made its way to the bottom of his stomach. The woman came with the soup and held the cup to his lips. The soup had chunks of turtle, boiled swamp cabbage and other unrecognized vegetables. The taste satisfied him and he took the cup from her and drank it all. He indicated with his eyes a desire for more. She was soon back with another cup, which he drank in a few quick gulps, chewing the meat for its life-giving energy. He leaned against the tree and sipped the coffee.

Andre fashioned a cigarette, lit it and handed it to Buddy. He sucked smoke into his lungs and held it there for a long moment before exhaling. Half the cigarette was gone before he spoke again. "All right, what happened? Did that sheriff come after me?"

"I came looking for you right after the sheriff left and found you sprawled out with your face in the dirt sound asleep. I went and got Consuela to help me, and we pulled you to this clearing. I came and spent the night with you here. Consuela brought the coffee and soup this morning. Are you feeling stronger?"

"Yeah, I'm feelin' much better now. Thanks a hell of a lot, Andre. You're a true friend. I owe you a lot. One day I'll pay you back. Thank you, too, Consuela. The soup hit the spot." Consuela looked into his eyes – her face expressionless. She just nodded. He took another drag on the cigarette.

Andre looked first at the woman then at him. "Consuela is a good woman. She is my sister. She cannot speak. Been like that since she was a little one. Our mother went into the swamps alone to give birth to Consuela. When her father found her she was passed out on the ground and Consuela lay between her legs, still attached with the cord."

Buddy looked at Consuela with a new sense of admiration, for her and these good people who had looked after him for so long. They didn't seem to have much, but gave of it without hesitation. He seemed to remember someone who couldn't speak. Who was it? He searched his mind. Nothing. "Is she Toby's mother?"

"Yes, but let's talk of that another time. We need to get you a place to stay until you can get back on your feet. You can't go back to the shack. That sheriff won't give up that easy. He'll be back."

"Did he come back after I ran?"

"Yes. He came back and went through the shack again. Went through my house, too. Went to the lake and asked others about you and Toby. Said he'd be back. Said he'd find Toby. I think he knows Toby may be in Savannah. Somebody told him."

"In Savannah? You know he's in Savannah?"

"Don't know for sure. When Toby brought you here he said he'd be back in a couple weeks to get you. I got a letter from him about two weeks ago saying he'd found work in Savannah and that he'd send for you soon. That's the last I heard from him. Are you able to walk? We can talk more later."

"Where we goin'?"

"Consuela has a friend who lives farther to the south near Fish Eating Creek. She will take you in for a little while until the sheriff cools off. Then you can come back to me until you get your strength back."

Buddy stood up, bracing himself on the tree. The dizziness returned, but was as quickly gone.

Andre put his arm around Buddy's waist and guided him away from the camp. "Consuela will see to the fire and things. Nice lady there where you're going." He coughed and glanced knowingly at Consuela.

They walked back through the woods to Andre's house. At the edge of the woods, Andre put his hand on Buddy's arm, and they stopped and surveyed the property. Nothing stirred except the animals and flies. The animals and their droppings smelled to high heaven and the dreaded flies were into and on everything, especially the wound on Buddy's neck. He'd have to get it dressed soon or that would be one more thing to hold him back.

Buddy collected what little he had and piled it on the buckboard Andre had waiting. Andre seemed overly nervous. He could be in real trouble with the Tribal Council down in Dania if he was caught harboring a criminal. The Elders at the local camp wouldn't look too kindly on him either. Buddy knew he was causing a lot of trouble for these good people. He had to regain his strength and get on to finding his lost life. He knew that meant finding Toby first. The doctor had told him his memory would come back little by little as his senses recognized things – like when he heard the name Buddy. If he could just get back to familiar surroundings, the memory would come back. He had to find Toby. With him dwelt his memory.

The rutted, single-lane, sandy road had high grass growing between the ruts. On the left was a barbed wire fence with high bushes and weeds growing in it. Four crows sat on the top wire looking east towards the trees and paid scant attention as the riders passed, leather and wood creaking and groaning. Grassy plains with cabbage palm hammocks scattered here and there ran into another forest of pines and palms far off to the west. A few head of cattle lolled about far out in the savanna. The morning was quiet – nothing seemed to move except the horse and wagon and the fly that went from one of the horse's ears to the other. Andre drove without talking and Buddy sat, consumed with his own personal thoughts.

After about two hours they crossed a swampy plain and came to a separate village off to the right, surrounded by huge oak trees with moss hanging low from the branches. It was mid-afternoon, and few people were about. The blazing fury of the sun roasted everything under the cloudless sky. Ten hand-hewn platforms, raised up off the ground and supported by posts, with roofs thatched with palmetto fans reaching almost to the ground, made up the village. The platforms appeared to be about ten feet long and almost as wide. The chickees, as Andre called them, situated in a large semi-circle around several large chickees with no sides and no wooden floors, fronted on the narrow creek that ran along the side of the road. The large chickees, Andre said, were shared for cooking and other communal affairs. Stretching for what looked forever, far out behind the village, were fields of corn on the south and sugarcane to the north, with a wide expanse of other crops in between. Andre said they grew cabbage, carrots, beans and tomatoes all year round.

Buddy noted the wisps of smoke curling towards the ceiling of the middle chickee. The smell of slow-cooking meat, mixed with the unmistakable stench of unseen cattle and hogs, hung heavy in the still warm air. A big black pot with steam drifting upward hung on a spit over a smoldering fire. A mangy looking dog lumbered out from under a chickee, had a look at them, then went back under. Two chickens moved about near the fire pecking at some unseen morsel on the ground. He pointed to the pot. "Turtle soup?"

Andre looked in the direction of the village. "More likely sofkee with deer meat. They keep a pot of that on the fire all the time."

"How come you don't live in a village like that, Andre?"

"Consuela lives there." With a skinny, crooked finger he pointed at a chickee. "Fourth one back on the south side. Long as I can remember, I always lived where I am now, or near by."

"You say she's your sister. How come she lives here and not in a place like you?" Buddy continued to study the village just across the creek. "Where's everybody at, you reckon?"

Andre pulled the buckboard into the shade under a large oak between the road and the creek, and tied the reins off. He removed his hat, mopped his brow with his bandanna and dried the sweatband. "Consuela married a man named Charlie Cypress back in '96 and moved in with his family back then. He was a no-good scoundrel. Never cared for him none. He provided for her and the kids okay, but stayed drunk all the time. He took Toby with him into the swamps to hunt and got him in to alcohol and ornriness early on. Never spent too much time with the other kids. Killed in La Belle in a fight with whites in '09 over traps or something. Consuela could've come to live with me then, but chose to stay on with the others." He spit out the wad of tobacco and bit off a fresh chew.

The thought of having been killed over traps sent a chill running down Buddy's spine, and he had a flash of men with shotguns trained on him. They were accusing him of stealing their traps. The image was gone quicker than it came and he struggled for a moment to regain it. No luck.

Andre droned on. "Consuela makes her living now making and selling dolls and trinkets to white folks in the towns around here on festival days. Of course I help her some with meat and vegetables. She and Elizabeth, the woman we're going to see, team up and sell a lot of stuff."

Buddy interrupted. "But you all grew up together, I reckon. How come you to be livin' in a house rather than in a chickee with the others"?

"Comin' to that. Patience, young feller. My father and mother worked for a Spaniard by name of Antonio Gonsalves on a big ranch that stretched far west from the edge of the big water. The forty acres I live on is all that's left of it. Before the old man died he cut out the forty acres and gave it to my father. The whites tried to take it from him, but he had the good papers for it and they finally gave up and let him keep it. It had some old buildings on it, but they've long since rotted away. My father built the buildings you see there now, probably when I was about ten years old. Consuela lived there, too, until she married that no-good Charlie Cypress."

"How about this woman, Elizabeth. She live in a chickee?"

"No. She also grew up around whites and took some of their ways. She lives in a house like mine. She owns about twenty-five acres. Her mother bought it off the man she worked for. Mother and father were rodeo hands for a big white rancher. Her father was gored to death by a bull when Elizabeth was just a young woman. She's lived right there all her life."

"She married with kids?"

"She had two but both died – one during birthing and the other in a train wreck, in 1912 if I remember right. Henry Russell, her husband, died then, too."

"What happened?" Buddy chewed on the end of a piece of straw.

"The story goes that Henry and the little girl were in Okeechobee City, known as Tanti then, when she ran onto the railroad track and fell down. Henry saw the train coming and ran to save her. The train smashed into them and drug them three hundred yards before it could stop. Their bodies were torn to pieces. Elizabeth never got over it. Don't bring it up when you're talking to her. Look, we better get going if we're to get there before dark." Andre picked up the reins.

Buddy put his hands on Andre's to delay movement. The coolness under the tree felt good and he was reluctant to get back out into the sun. "Are there more Indians living in villages like this one?"

"I hear there are about thirty camps like this one from here on down near . . . ."

"Indians own the land like you and Elizabeth?"

"Indians own the land because they were here when the whites came. They figure the land's their's, but the whites don't see it that way. If you don't have that little piece of paper that says you own it, you don't, according to them."

"So the Indians are just squatters?" Buddy spat out the chewed straw and picked up another.

"That's what the whites say. There's talk the government is planning to buy up a lot of land and settle all the Indians on it. They're scared that more and more white settlers will come into the area and buy the Indians' land right out from under them, and then kick them off. Been some people already bought land for the Indians, but the Indians won't move onto it. Same old distrust. Some of the Indians want it, though, and they believe the government owes it to them. That's why we have to be so careful with you. If the Tribal Council knows you're hiding out here, and if they think it would hurt their chances of getting reservations for all the Indians who want to live on them, they'd have our scalps. Don't know what will happen to our land anyhow if they buy all this up around here for a reservation." He picked up the reins and whacked the horse. The wagon lurched forward.

74

The sun hung high in the west when they came to a little house on the edge of a swampy area near a large lake and just off the main road. Dust swirled up behind them and the horse was lathered with sweat and foam. Andre pulled the buckboard through the creek bottom and into the front yard loaded with the remnants of old cars, wagons and everything imaginable. *This woman must be a collector of junk.*

Buddy absorbed the picture of the property in one quick glance. The three buildings visible were all weather-beaten and in bad need of paint and repair. *Likely hadn't been a man around here in a long time.* Off to the far left of the main house straight ahead was a tall barn with the doors swung wide open. In between, and farther to the rear, was a small, long building with a flat roof. Junk everywhere. Must be a garden somewhere, but he couldn't see one. All Indians had gardens. The still air hung heavy with a mixture of smells – oil, cattle and chicken dung. A proud rooster strutted his stuff over near the barn.

Buddy saw the portly woman in tight denims and long-sleeved colored shirt come onto the porch from inside the house. She stood with legs spread and hands on hips – gray black hair down to the middle of her back. About fifty, he reckoned. Proud as the chicken walking by the barn. She wore a broad-brimmed white cowboy hat and boots with pointed toes. A scene flashed before his eyes and was as soon gone. *A big man with high cheekbones and a set mouth, dressed in dungarees and denim shirt with a brown floppy felt hat, standing on the porch of an unpainted wooden house.* Nothing more came. Buddy, now tired through and through, thought, what am I in for now?

# CHAPTER 11

Elizabeth heard the wagon as it drew up in front of the house before she stepped out on the porch. A large, black Great Dane followed her through the door and stood by her side, eyeing the strangers coming onto its territory. Its big head reached above her hips. The growl came from low down in its throat. She leaned against the post near the wooden steps leading down to the yard and peered from under her broad-brimmed white felt hat at the men in the wagon. Even though she hadn't seen Andre in several years, she recognized him right off. He had once aroused a strong passion in her when they were both younger and it might have worked out differently had he not upped and married pretty little Moon Maiden, the daughter of a Tribal Council member. She knew then the marriage would not last and it hadn't. Things never worked for them after that.

The man sitting next to him she'd heard about, but never seen. He sat proud with his shoulders squared, but he was thin and pale with a scraggly beard and uncombed curly black hair about half-way down to his shoulders. *Guess that's why they call him Curly.* She'd heard he was a breed. Could be taken for an Indian under the right circumstances. At one time she figured he was a strong man, but now he had the look of someone very sick. *What have I got myself into?* Promising Consuela to take the man on as a hired hand for a while might turn out to be the biggest mistake she had ever made. No doubt, though, someone was needed for the many chores around the place. From the first appearance of this man, she harbored grave doubts that he would be anything but trouble. She walked down the steps and out into the yard as the two men stepped down from the wagon.

"Andre, you old son of a gun. Haven't seen you in a month of Sundays. Where's Consuela?" Her voice was whispery –

gravelly, and rasping. She gave Andre a big hug like he was a long-lost friend, then turned to Buddy. In a quick glance she measured his gaunt frame. About six two and a hundred and sixty-five, she figured. "And you must be Curly. I've heard some about you. We'll get on just fine, I reckon." She reached for his hand.

"Mighty pleased to meet you, ma'am." His voice was deep, but weak. He extended his hand and she shook it, the grasp firm. She liked that in a man. She looked deep into his dark green eyes. His probed just as deeply into hers. *He'll do.*

Andre butted in. "Lizzy, you're sure a sight for these sore old eyes. Haven't laid eyes on you for many a moon. You haven't aged one little bit. Still pretty as a picture and slim as a rail. Why I'll bet—"

Elizabeth interrupted and pulled him towards the porch. "Come on up to the porch out of the sun." She knew if she let him he would run on and on forever. That man always could talk a blue streak. She motioned for Buddy to follow.

Andre was not to be stopped. "I see you're still collecting junk, just like always. Last time I was here it was just out back – now it's all over the place. People not buying? Where do you get all this stuff? How do you handle—?"

"Andre, how you do run on. Never heard a man talk so much. Suppose that's the reason I ran you off before. Hold your tongue for a while. Your mouth runs like a bell clapper. You don't give Curly a chance to say boo. I'll get us some tea." She left them standing there and went through the screen door.

She emerged with the tea and spoke directly to Buddy. "Curly, you can stay yonder in the bunkhouse." She pointed to the south side of the house at the low frame building just west of the two-story barn. "There's four bunks in there. Take your pick. You'll have the whole place to yourself. In better times, I had four men living there, but those times are long gone now. You can go on over there now and take your things. When you hear that bell ring come running." She pointed to the small bell hanging from the porch rafter. "It'll either be an emergency or supper time. I'll come and see you in a little while and we can chat some. I'll say goodbye to Andre now."

Buddy went to the buckboard, got his things and walked towards the bunkhouse without a backward glance.

When Buddy was out of ear shot, she said. "Now, you old coot, give me the lowdown on this poor man." She moved to a wooden rocker and eased her heavy frame into it. It groaned under her weight. "Where'd he come from?"

"Not much to tell. Toby brought him up here about three months ago. The man was half-dead and, to hear him tell it, he doesn't even remember his name. Toby said when he came upon him he had been buck-shot in the back and head – just barely alive. Laid him up in a hospital in Miami. Out of his head for three months. Hasn't regained his strength since he's been with me. I probably don't cook too good, huh?"

"And you probably work him too hard out in that hot sun all day long. Where did they find him? Does he remember anything about his past life? Why did the sheriff come looking for him around here?"

"He didn't say. May have something to do with him being shot. Toby didn't say where he'd found him, and I wasn't too interested at the time. I didn't want any part of him – not set up for it. That sheriff came onto me mighty hard, and you know me, I can get my back up right quick when somebody comes at me that way."

"Did you tell the sheriff what you told me?"

"I told him that Toby had brought him here. He asked about Toby. He learned from somebody that Toby's in Savannah. Toby was supposed to be back here by now to take Curly away with him, but I haven't seen hide nor hair of him in near three months."

"Has Curly tried to leave?"

"Naw. He wanders around the area some, and he's been in to Okeechobee City a few times with me. He seems too weak for most anything. Claims he's dizzy all the time. Don't eat much either. Like I say, maybe he doesn't like my cooking any too good."

"Well, let's see what I can do with him. I've heard tell the Tribal Council don't want him around here – especially since that sheriff came snooping around." She stood up, walked to the edge of the porch and looked toward the bunkhouse. *Wonder if this Curly is just a no good wastrel. Didn't seem that way, though. May really be sick.* We'll see. "You better run along now, Andre. Let me have a chat with Curly and see where we go from here."

Andre walked to the buckboard. "I'll check in on him every now and then. Check in on you, too. Thanks for the tea. And thanks one hell of a lot for taking Curly in. Don't know what I'd have done if you weren't around."

"I don't know why I'm doing it really. I owe Consuela a lot for helping me during the hard days when I was down. Maybe I even have a soft spot in my heart or something."

"I doubt that." Andre turned the horses and headed out before she could respond. The shadows stretched long to the east – a few more hours until sundown. She went in, fixed a good meal and rang the bell.

"That was a mighty fine meal, Miss Elizabeth. Ain't eaten that good long as I can remember." Buddy looked sheepishly at her and pushed his plate away. She stood at the sink cleaning up and showed no expression one way or the other at the remark. He'd eaten like a starved man and she had remained silent all the while. She poured a cup of coffee and took it to him.

"Thanks again. Mind if I smoke?" Buddy pushed his chair back and removed the makings from his top shirt pocket.

"No. You go right ahead. Think I'll have one, too." She poured a cup of coffee for herself and sat at the table across from him. "By the way, you can drop the Miss. Just call me Liz."

"Yes, Ma'am." He fashioned a cigarette, lit it and passed the makings to her.

"And drop the ma'am, too. What do you know about yourself, Curly?" She lit the cigarette she'd just made and leaned back in the chair, exhaling smoke in a gush.

Buddy leaned back and crossed one leg over the other. He looked into her dark brown eyes as if searching for her hidden character. "Not much. I've lost my whole life it seems. Only know since I woke up in the hospital. Don't even remember that too good. Remember the headaches – mighty bad in the beginnin'. Still have 'em, but not nearly as bad. Dizzy a whole lot, too. I'm mighty beholden to Andre, and you, too, ma'am, for takin' me in. Hope to be on my feet real soon. I'll never forget you all. I'll be forever in your debt. I'll do what I can to repay some of it soon as I can get on my feet."

"But what happened to you? How did you happen to end up in the hospital? How did Toby happen to find you? What were you doing at the time and where were you?" She put the cigarette out in the ashtray and moved to the stove for the coffeepot. "Has Toby told you anything?"

"Toby brought me to Andre about three months ago, straight from the hospital. He didn't stay around very long. I was still groggy as hell and didn't know what was goin' on. Andre told me later that Toby promised to come and get me and take me back to where he found me. The doctor said I should get my memory back piece by piece as I saw and heard familiar things. He said if I was lucky, one thing might trigger the whole memory and it would all come back in a gush. I sure hope that's the case." She filled his cup with fresh coffee. He lit another cigarette and passed the makings to her. "Thanks."

She fashioned and lit another cigarette. "Did the doctor say what caused you to lose your memory?"

"He said I had buckshot in my back and skull. The shot didn't go through and touch my brain. He said the shock of the blast to the head caused the coma for three months and the memory loss. Said he thought the memory loss was likely short lived."

"Have you been able to get much of your memory back since you left the hospital?"

80

"No. But when the sheriff came up and asked for Buddy, I remembered that my name's Buddy. I had a flash of other people, but couldn't place 'em. Know I can read. Know a little about farmin' and know how to fish. I can fix machinery. Been too damn weak to do much of anything, though. If I can just get next to more things maybe more memory would come back."

Elizabeth was growing tired of the conversation and tired from all the activity of the day. Besides she had to get an early start in the morning. From the looks of him, he wasn't going to be much help anytime soon. She looked steady at him and probed, hoping to get some insight on his willingness to work or if he was just another good-for-nothing. "What kind of work did you do at Andre's?"

"Did most everything when I was able. Worked in the garden, repaired the buildings, helped with the horses and hogs and fed the chickens. Did some fishin' at the lake, too. 'Course, I reckon I was just too sick to handle my share. Feel right sorry about that. Couldn't shake the dizziness. Andre, bless his heart, seemed to understand and treated me right tolerable. I can more than carry my own if I can get some strength back. You won't be sorry you took a chance on me, ma'am."

Elizabeth's expression was reserved, but she said, "Well, there's lots to do around here. We'll try to fatten you up some before we get into the hard stuff. Curly, I want to make something clear to you right from the start. I consider myself to be a fair person, but you'll find I speak my mind. I don't mince words. Some folks say I'm too hard on my hired hands. I expect a day's work for a day's pay. I'm not a giving person. Don't believe in it. Times are hard. Not much money to be had. I've taken you on here because of Consuela. I won't put up with a good-for-nothing for long. Not that I think you're one, but I need someone to help me with chores that are piling up. You look like you were once a strong man. About thirty or so today, I'd say. I'll expect you to earn your keep until you're ready to move on. You'll sleep and clean yourself in the bunkhouse and take your meals here. Breakfast at six, dinner at noon and supper at seven. The toilet's out back of this house. Pay is room and board. Any questions?" She stood.

Buddy rose, picked up the cigarette makings and stuffed them in his shirt pocket. "What you want me to do tomorrow, Liz?"

"You say you know machinery. We'll keep you in the barn, out of the sun, for a few days and see if your health gets any better. There's a lot of work to be done there. I'll expect you on the porch at six. How do you want to be called?"

"Curly's all right. Been called that now for three months that I know of. When I came in I saw a guitar near the door. I think I can play it. Can I try?"

"Take it with you. There's a pick stuck in the strings. What makes you think you can play?" She followed him to the door.

"Don't know. The thought just came to me when I saw it." Buddy picked up the guitar, opened the door and stepped out into the night. "Goodnight, ma'am, and thanks for the meal and for takin' a chance with me." It was pitch black. He held onto a porch post until his eyes adjusted, then cautiously made his way to his quarters.

# CHAPTER 12

Buddy watched her coming, trailed by old Wilbur. Wherever Liz was, you could bet that old dog was not far behind. She was still a mighty good-looking woman. Always dressed in pants, long sleeved shirt, boots and that ever-present wide-brimmed white hat. *Wonder why she never wears a dress.* He had cleared a path through the junk between the barn, his quarters and the main house. Here lately she had taken the habit of dropping by late in the afternoon to talk about chores for the next day or just to see how he was faring. He suspected she was beginning to soften towards him. She still kept her brusque attitude and manner, but she seemed unable to hide her tenderness, although she tried hard. Maybe she had decided to adopt him as she had Toby. A woman's instinct to have someone under her wing more than likely.

He kept on with the milking, playing like he didn't see her coming. It was nearing six and would soon be suppertime. She probably had it on the stove now. He felt hungrier today for some reason – could almost taste her biscuits. These were different somehow from the ones he remembered, but mighty good just the same. Her discipline had been the right medicine. His weight was now up to 190 and his energy seemed boundless.

He hoped she made money on his labor because he figured he was eating her out of house and home. The first two weeks had been easy enough, but now he worked a full ten hours every day except Sunday. That day he kept open for fly-fishing at the creek that opened out on the big lake. Her husband, when he was alive, had been a regular fisherman and kept a whole slew of fishing rods and gear. Some of the stuff brought back no memories, but he had soon learned how to use them effectively. She liked the fish he brought home and always fixed up a good meal with them. She had, on occasion, come to watch him handle the rod, but had not tried it herself even though she had expressed an interest – said her husband had tried to interest her, too. She had no interest then and didn't now. A waste of time she said.

Liz came through the ceiling-high doors. "Curly, you're getting to be pretty good with that guitar. I listen to you of a night. Voice not too harsh on the ears either. You sure you didn't play in a band somewhere?" She went into the nearby stall, talked soothingly to Honey and started to rub her down. He couldn't understand why she kept that old mare around anyhow. That old horse was far past any usefulness to the place. Another piece of her insides she couldn't hide.

That bit about playing in a band had become her favorite joke. Since he picked up the guitar and found that he really did know how to play some, she had been teasing him about it. He knew he didn't have the voice to sing in a band, but with a little guidance, he probably was good enough with the guitar to at least play second. He could even pick out a few tunes he must have known before. "Yeah, maybe I can get a job in the city that pays more'n you do." He laughed, moved the full pail of milk, put another pail under the cow and resumed milking.

"Don't go getting any fancy ideas now. We've got a lot of work to do, starting next week. The Tribal Council has given me one month to move all my scrap back away from the road. They don't want to see it when they drive by. We'll need to clear about five acres and dam it up so no run-off will get into the creek. Then we have to move all the scrap back there."

He stopped milking and looked at her. "How you plannin' to do all that in one month? You got some other workers and heavy equipment lined up?"

"You let me worry about that." She closed Honey's stall and turned to face him.

"Yes ma'am." He started milking again. "What's the Tribal Council got to do with you? You're not part of none of the camps."

"I know it's hard to understand, but they still have a lot to say about what I do so long as I want to be a part of the Seminole

84

Nation. There's powerful talk about bringing all this land around here into a sort of reservation for all Seminoles that want to live on it. My land happens to be right smack in the middle of it. There's even some question if I'll be able to keep my ownership."

Buddy stopped milking and looked quizzically at her. "I sure don't understand how somebody can come along and just take your property away from you because they want to give it to somebody else. Don't seem right to me."

"The Council says I can get paid for it and still live on it the rest of my life if I clean it up. Otherwise the government will buy it from me and the Council will make me move. I can try to fight them, but it'll probably be easier to just clean up the place. Anyhow, we'll get it worked out." She came around behind the cow and placed her hands on its rump. "Look, Curly, tomorrow's Saturday and there's the annual fair in Okeechobee City. I always go to it and set up a booth to sell my dolls. People come from all over. Lots of excitement. I'd like you to come with me. We'll be gone most of the day. You can help with the booth. Andre and Consuela will meet us there. Maybe there'll be something there to spark your memory. Will you come?"

"You're the boss. Just do what I'm told." He lifted the two pails of milk and set them outside the barn. Liz picked up the pails and headed towards the house. She called over her shoulder. "Supper in one hour."

Buddy waited until she had gone inside then strolled into the yard on the far side of the barn. He had found something else about his past since he began working for Liz – his love for mechanical things and how and why they work. In amongst all the old wrecked cars, wagons and broken down equipment of every description, he had been restoring a 1918 La Salle. It was now close to being finished. Up to now he had been able to keep it a secret from her. Since he came she rarely ever ventured into that part of the scrap yard. She had become increasingly dependent on him to get the customers what they wanted and collect the money. Now she's saying everything will have to be moved. He would have to squeeze more hours into the project and find a way to delay moving this area of the yard until last. Just how he was going to get that done, he wasn't sure. Where would he find the time?

The feeling that he may have left people behind who were dependent on him grew stronger by the day and he wanted to be leaving soon to find Toby and his past. Just how was he to tell Liz that his time here was getting short? Travel with no money would be next to impossible, but at least he now had most of his strength back. He removed the distributor assembly and went back to his quarters. He had to find a way to keep the engine from backfiring. An idea had been rumbling around in his head – he'd work on it tonight after supper.

# CHAPTER 13

Liz wakened early this Saturday morning. She had breakfast ready for serving and the boxes packed with her dolls when Buddy stepped up on the porch before sun-up. Wilbur barked and ran to the door. "Hush up, Wilbur, it's only Curly." The dog lumbered back to the kitchen in the rear of the front room and plopped down under the table. "We'll only have time for a quick bite. Need to get there early and get set up. Should be able to get my normal stall if I'm there early enough. You hungry as usual?"

"I could eat a cow and sit up on the fence and ring the bell for the calf." He removed the white cowboy hat which she had bought him for this occasion and eased his long frame into the wooden chair. He gave her his usual broad and boyish grin.

"Curly, you do come up with some of the darndest sayings. Where'd they come from?" She brought the plate filled with eggs, grits and fried bread and put the pot of coffee in the middle of the table. "I saw your lamp on late last night. Reading?"

"Yeah, I was readin' the book by Charles Dickens you gave me, Oliver Twist."

She studied him as she banked the wood in the stove so that it would soon go out untended. He paid little attention to her as he hurriedly ate his food. She had bought his clothes just for this occasion and he looked the part she wanted for him. The denim pants and white shirt with colored beads over the pockets went very well with his long muscular frame. He wore boots although he said he preferred dress shoes for town, something he apparently was used to from his other life. She wondered if he would ever find it. She had been hard on him in the beginning because she thought she had another loser on her hands, but he was different. He worked hard, was bright and seemed hungry to learn everything. He read every book she'd given him – kept them as a treasury in a bookshelf he put together out of scraps he'd found around the yard. His hair he now wore long like most Indian men – one pig-tail with a leather thong tied just below the skull – curls now stretched into long waves. She cared a lot for him – the son she never had. Even Toby hadn't gotten this imbedded into her heart. She wished he could stay with her or near her forever, but she knew he longed to find his other life.

She downed the last of her coffee, put the cup in the basin and pumped water into it. She walked to the table. "You about finished? We need to get a move on. Need to put the boxes in the truck."

"All done." He stood up, drank the last of his coffee, put his hat on and moved to the boxes stacked up by the door. "I'll see to it now."

The sun had just peeked through the trees on the far side of the lake when Liz turned the Model-T truck onto Highway 78 and headed north. It would take a good forty-five minutes to reach Okeechobee. Neither spoke for about twenty minutes, each consumed with their own thoughts. Finally, she said. "Curly, when do you suppose you'll be pulling out from here?"

The question stunned him for a minute. Her blunt ways still caught him by surprise more often than not. He didn't want to abuse her trust and yet he knew he had to make his move soon. The dream with the woman and children came more often of late. "Tell you the truth, I was plannin' to talk to you about that real soon. Got a big itch to find my lost life. Likely some folks back there needin' me powerful bad. Been gone a long time now, but don't want to leave you in a bind either. You said we had to move all that stuff to the back of the property right away. You ain't wantin' me to go before that are you?"

"No, I don't want you to go at all, Curly, but I may have no choice but to let you go. Tribal Council keeps on me all the time about you. That sheriff has been back several times trying to get information about you, but nobody will even talk to him anymore, they just say they don't know anything. It's become a big problem for the Council. They're worried about their connection with the outside law and government and whatever outcome that might have for all Indians. They've allowed me to keep you on to help with the move, but unless something changes, that may be all the time we have." Her eyes betrayed the hurt hiding there.

Buddy looked into her eyes then straight ahead, not really seeing anything. *This thing is working out better than I figured.* Help her move, then head for Georgia to find Toby and do it without causing any hard feelings. He wanted more than anything to leave on good terms with her and the others that had helped him so much. "Now don't you go and fret none. Should be on my way now, but it'll keep till we get the move done. Got a little surprise for you anyhow."

"A surprise? What kind of surprise?"

He kept his eyes straight ahead. "Surprise ain't a surprise once you tell it. You'll know soon enough. You got to stay away till I'm ready. Deal?"

"Deal." She turned onto Highway 441 and went straight through town and directly to the fair grounds on the northwest side of the city. Except for the fair participants heading for the fairgrounds, the city streets were deserted.

Buddy noticed grass growing between cracks in the road and the un-repaired holes, washed out by the heavy rains. "This city looks like it may be on its last legs. You sure folks'll come and buy things?"

"They'll come. They won't have much money to spend, but I guarantee they'll come. They'll forget the hard times for a few hours. They'll laugh and even spend a few of their hard earned pennies." Her eyes moistened. She dabbed at them with her kerchief.

Liz seemed wistful and truly sorry for the poor folk. Even though she tried to hide it, he'd seen this soft side of her on more occasions than one. "You've spoke of hard times before. Why're these times harder than others?"

"You've lived in better times Curly, but I reckon you've forgotten them. All you know are the past few months. The whole world has been turned upside down. No jobs for hardly anybody. Nobody's got any hope of anything better. I guess the only hope the country has is this man Roosevelt. He says he'll do something for the every-day man. He'll find them jobs. You've read the newspapers some. Next month we'll find out something when the voters have their say." She turned onto the fairgrounds and spoke to the man at the gate who gave instructions and waved her through.

"Yeah, I've looked at some of your old newspapers and did read some about Roosevelt and people bein' out of work, but I've been so busy tryin' to get well and workin' that I just didn't give other folks that much thought. Little selfish of me, I reckon." He felt a little of what she must feel that caused her to cry.

In a short time, the stall assigned to Liz was ready for business. The smell escaped first as Buddy tipped the thermos bottle and poured a cup of coffee for both of them. Liz continued to putter around with things. He took his cup and relaxed in a chair at the front of the stall. He built and lit a cigarette as he surveyed the various stalls and people along the walkway which ran the length of the fairgrounds. The clang of pots; the bang of a hammer; the curse from somebody that something hadn't gone just right for; the mixed smells of coffee brewing, sausages and other things cooking; animals sweating behind tents, was the Okeechobee Annual Fair getting underway. Another Indian couple across the pathway were setting up to sell woodcarvings from tree stumps. He had just finished his cigarette when he saw Andre, Consuela and Laura Mae coming towards him.

There was no question that these folks were Indians. Andre dressed as usual in Levi pants held up with a wide, brown leather belt with a large, bull-head, brass buckle, boots, long-sleeved, multicolored shirt and a ten gallon white hat. His gray hair, tied in one pigtail, hung out from under the hat and down to the middle of his back. He was proud as a peacock even though he favored his right leg more than usual, and a good strong wind would likely blow him away. His dark leathery face and big protruding nose didn't help his appearance any. Consuela wore a flowing multi-colored dress that went to her toes. The brown frilled moccasins showed as she stepped confidently beside Andre, her shoulders draped with a shawl and her head bare. Her coal-black hair was braided in two pigtails tied with bright colored strips of cloth. A big wide grin showed on her face as Liz came out of the stall. Laura Mae lagged behind, sticking her head in and out of other stalls and taking her own sweet time.

Andre spoke as he put out his bony hand to take Buddy's. "Curly, how you been, boy? Haven't seen you in a coon's age. Let me look at you. Damned if you haven't put on some weight. You're not the same boy I left off at Liz's place a month ago. I knew you'd grow out to be a big man with the right vittles. How come you here? I didn't know . . . ."

Buddy turned away to ward off the strong whiskey breath. That man could talk a blue streak and drink you out of house and home. He acknowledged Consuela with a tip of his hat. Consuela greeted Liz and they went inside the stall. Laura Mae was nowhere in sight. "Liz wanted me to have a little time off, I think. Pull up a chair and take the weight off your bones. You been all right?"

"I've been just fine. I need somebody to help me, though. Miss you over there even though you didn't do a hell of a lot." He grinned from ear to ear. "Better go in and say hello to Liz. Be right back." He went into the stall.

Buddy rolled and lit another cigarette. Laura Mae came out of a stall and started walking toward him. He felt a stir in his lower gut. It was the same feeling he felt another time when she came to visit Liz and had brushed against him accidentally. She was a good looking woman and well built, too. He had not been with a woman since his accident and couldn't remember having ever been with one. There had been dreams about a young woman and some kids, and he and Andre had talked about it some, but that's all there was. Laura Mae's dress was much like the others, a cross between traditional garb and cowboy. The long-sleeved white shirt, tucked neatly into Levis, was held up with a plaited, brown leather belt with a large buckle. Two black pigtails showed from beneath the black cowboy hat and extended past her shoulder blades. She seemed to glide over the ground as she moved towards him. She noticed him for the first time and the smile spread across her face. He smiled back and waved to her. Must be about his same age.

Laura Mae had been taking his measure since she first spied him after they left Consuela's stall and had not let on that she had even seen him. She remembered the stirrings in her stomach from the last time she'd brushed up against him at Liz's some weeks ago. He seemed like a good man, quiet, strong and loyal – a man she could go for. Liz said he was a wonderful person. He would make some lucky woman a fine husband. She wondered if he was a married man and maybe even had some children. She had purposely stayed away just because of that possibility. Now the stirrings were back again – would she be able to control them – did she owe any responsibility to another woman? From a distance she caught a blue glint from his otherwise dark green eyes. She wondered what kind of people he was made from.

Laura Mae was kind of hopping and bouncing along when she came up very close to him and held out her hand. He stood and moved towards her. Her fresh scent lingered. Liz and Consuela didn't have the same smell. This girl stirred something long forgotten in him and he felt a strong desire to take hold of her and crush her to him. She took hold of his hand and said, "Curly, it's so good to see you again. Have you been here long?"

He took her outstretched hand in his big hand and placed his other over it. Her dark brown eyes seemed to be laughing along with the rest of her – her whole body and manner filled with excitement. She bubbled over with glee and happiness. "Been here about an hour, I reckon. What're you so all fired up about?"

"So happy to see you, Curly," she teased. She playfully punched him in the stomach then backed away just as quick. "Just love the fair, don't you? It's better than the rodeo. So many more things to marvel at and wish for. Don't you just love it?" She backed towards the stall. "Consuela and Liz inside?" Before he could answer, she saw them and stepped inside. Her smell lingered. He was in a stew.

He sat down in the chair again, made and lit another cigarette. Girl stirred him up something powerful. Was the woman in his dreams his wife in the other life? He should put Laura Mae out of his mind until he could sort out that past.

Andre came out of the stall. "Curly, can you help me move Consuela's stuff out of the stall down the way? She's been given the one over here next to Liz's." He motioned to the stall over his left shoulder.

"Sure. Where's her stuff?" Buddy stood up and ground the cigarette into the hard-packed dirt.

Andre started walking in the direction they had come a few minutes before. "Come on, this way. Wanted to talk some to you anyhow. Heard from Toby a few days ago. Said he planned to come down this way early next year."

"Been plannin' to go lookin' for him. You got his address?"

"Yes. I'll get it for you. No use you traipsing off all the way up there if he's coming down here."

"Got a problem. Council wants me to be gone right quick. They've given me about thirty days. Just about enough time to help Liz move all her junk to the back of her property. They planned to boot me out right now unless she agreed to move the junk away from the highway. Got a mighty powerful itch to find my past, too, Andre."

Andre pulled the flat bottle from his back pocket and took a swig. He turned the bottle upside down and nothing came out. "I need to go into town for another bottle. Will you go in with me, Curly?" He threw the bottle in a trash bin near the edge of the walkway.

"Sure. Why not? Let me check with Liz first, make sure she won't be needin' me for a while."

They reached Consuela's stall and entered. Andre said, "Yes, I knew it wouldn't be long before they found you. That sheriff's been back a number of times asking questions from everybody he could find. Threatening the Council with State action if they don't help out. What's this about moving all her junk? Ten years ago you wouldn't know the place. When Henry Russell was alive most of the scrap was towards the back of the property. He saw to it that the property was as neat as a pin most of the time. She's kind of just let it go. More interested in her dolls than anything else, I guess. Does just enough to keep the Council off her back. Guess they're tired of it now. They see you as the chance to get her to do something." He started placing smaller boxes of trinkets into bigger boxes.

"Who's Henry Russell? Never heard no talk about him. Where you want this stuff?"

"I'll pack the stuff up, you load it on the truck. Henry was Liz's husband. He died about twenty years ago. Married thirty years or more, I reckon. You remember, I told you about him that day I first took you out to her place. He and his little girl were killed by the train . . . ."

Buddy stacked boxes on the truck. "Oh yeah, I remember now."

Andre continued. "Had an eye for her myself before he came on the scene. Didn't work out."

Buddy stopped loading. "What's that? You and Liz had somethin' goin'? When was this? What happened?"

Andre kept working. "Wasn't nothing. Long time ago."

Buddy didn't press the issue.

Andre drove the loaded truck around to the back of the newly assigned stall, unpacked it and told Consuela it was ready for her touch. Buddy told Liz he was going into town with Andre and the women went into Consuela's new stall. Buddy and Andre went back to the truck.

# CHAPTER 14

The pool hall on the southwest side of town was a long white building with a rusted tin roof positioned parallel to and just off the highway. Andre pulled onto the gravel parking lot in front of the building and parked alongside a dilapidated Model T truck with a huge black dog in the back. The dog looked at the two men and issued a low growl as they passed by. Only two other vehicles in the lot.

Buddy opened the front door to the building and held it for Andre. Smoky heat gushed from the opening. Sunlight from outside splashed into the room and cut a deep swath through the almost impenetrable darkness. The light made the swirling smoke and dust the only objects visible. Smoke concentrated at the low ceiling.

Andre stopped just inside and Buddy allowed the door to close before moving farther into the room. A vision from the past brought the room into focus and, as if from habit, he took in all there was to see with one slow sweep of his eyes. The swarthy bartender to the left turned to face the intruders, placed his two hands on the bar and waited.

At a table to the right and against the far wall sat five men. They all stopped whatever they'd been doing and stared at the two men entering the room. Four pool tables farther back in the room were unoccupied.

Buddy's gaze held the men in focus for a long moment. A tingle of excitement raced along the full length of his spine. He'd never been in this particular bar, but he knew it just the same from some other time – birthplace of trouble. These men were the type to make it happen. There was one old man with a full long beard, dressed in denim overalls, three others about Buddy's age and one pimply-faced young boy about fifteen. They looked like people he'd known all his life, a dirty surly lot, always against strangers. An image of two such men with guns facing him flashed across his eyes and was instantly gone. The clock on the wall behind the bar told him it was 11:45. Buddy followed Andre to the bar. He moved with ease, but felt uneasy in the now quiet room.

Finally the bartender broke the silence. "What'll it be, gents?"

Andre bellied up to the bar, hooked his right heel in the brass foot railing and acted like he owned the place. "Give me and my partner a beer if you've got some and I'll need a pint of whiskey to go."

Buddy stood sideways to the bar with his back to the pool tables where he could see the front door and the table with the men without letting on that he was eyeing them. He figured Andre would be of little help to him if anything started. He spoke directly to Andre, "Maybe we should just get the whiskey and get on back to the fair?"

"Let's just have one beer then be on our way." The bartender had already brought the two beers from somewhere under the bar. The men still had not spoken. They just watched what was going on at the bar.

The bartender set the bottles of beer in front of them. "That'll be thirty cents for the beer and eighty-five cents for the liquor." He turned and reached under the counter for the bottle of whiskey. Andre fingered coins in his pocket.

"Charley, you ain't sellin no whiskey to Injins, are ya? Don't ya know that's aginst the law?"

At the first sound from the man's mouth Buddy fixed him with his gaze. It was one of the younger men – a dirty man with sharp features and a three-day-old scrabble on his face. His hair, worn long, was uncombed and dirty looking. The man's teeth were black with tobacco stains, except for the two missing front ones. Buddy knew this kind of man from somewhere. As the man spoke, smoke trailed from his mouth and inched upward. Buddy was now accustomed to the darkened room.

Andre, with his beer in hand, turned to look at the men and leaned his back against the bar, one heel still hooked in the foot rail. "There's no such law, mister. You know that. Same law for Indians as for whites. No liquor for anybody. What've you got against Indians anyhow?"

"It's the law if I say it is, Injin. In this county we don't allow no Injins to drink hard liquor. They cain't handle it. Never could." Raucous laughter erupted from the table – the old and young the loudest. The young one's mouth showed missing teeth. The bartender remained silent.

Buddy tensed, glanced at the door and back to the men. If they came, he'd go over the bar. There would likely be something back there he could fight them with – maybe a shotgun. He'd have to take the bartender out right off.

The old man interrupted the laughter. "What you doin', Ronnie? You tryin' to pick a fight with that old Injin? He's so skinny you could blow him over with a puff." They roared with glee again.

"Just don't like Injins, young or old – got a bad smell to 'em. The big one'd probably blow over, too. Never seen a Injin worth his salt." The man started up from his chair.

Buddy grabbed Andre's arm. "Come on, Andre, let's get out of here. Give the man your money and let's go."

Andre stood up straight with both feet wide apart as if to invite the world to take him, one hand still in his pants pocket. "You don't like Indians, mister, come get yourself a piece of one. There was the day I could whip any two white men with one hand tied behind me."

As the man at the table rose to his full six-foot frame, Buddy squeezed Andre's arm harder and turned him toward the bar. "Give the man your money now." His voice now strong and stern. This could get serious quick. Andre complied. From his pocket he produced the right amount of coins and laid them on the table. He picked up his bottle of whiskey and looked hard at Buddy. Buddy could see the shame in his eyes. This little frail man really did want to take on all those men.

Buddy, with his hand still on Andre's arm, turned to face the four men coming toward them. "Hang on, fellers. We don't want no trouble here. My friend has had about one too many. We're goin' right now." He pulled Andre through the door. The men's laughter rang in his ears. He, too, was ashamed of backing away from a sure fight. An image of him running from another fight flashed in his mind and quickly faded. The men came to the door and jeered, but didn't come outside.

Andre drove most of the way back to the fairgrounds in silence. Buddy tried without success to recall the image of a few moments ago. Was he a coward?

Andre seemed mad as hell. Finally he spoke. "Goddamn it, Curly, you shamed me. I thought you would have more grit than that. Goddamn it, man, I'm near sixty and I would never run from a fight, no matter what. All the folks at the camps figured you had a lot of spunk to stand up for what you've been through. Now you turn tail and run at the least bit of trouble. Don't know if I want to know you anymore."

"I ain't yeller, Andre. I didn't take us out of there 'cause I'm yeller. Figure it's always better to walk away from a fight if you can. Don't mean you're a coward if you do. Besides if you got to fight it's better to do it at your place of choosin' – with lots of room to move around in." Buddy looked sadly at Andre who looked straight ahead, apparently not convinced that he wasn't a coward. Maybe he should've taken the men on. He never could understand men who always felt a need to show others how brave they were.

Andre didn't say another word and, when they arrived at the fairgrounds, walked off without even a nod in Buddy's direction. Buddy, saddened at the loss of a friend over such a little matter, went to the stalls where the women were, checked in with them, then took his chair in front. He felt bad for the way Andre was taking his reaction to the men at the bar. Although he felt a little shame himself, he never did, all through the moment, feel any fear at all. He made and lit a cigarette and tried to relax and put the events of the past hour behind him.

Laura Mae brought him a lunch of two ham sandwiches and a bottle of Coca-Cola. She had a sandwich, too, and pulled a chair alongside his. "Where's Andre, Curly?"

Buddy took the food gratefully. "Thanks. He felt a need to take a walk and maybe have a little snort. He'll be back in a little while, I reckon." He dug into the lunch.

"The medicine show starts in thirty minutes. You want to go with me to see it? I haven't seen one since last year."

Buddy spoke with a mouth full. "Don't know I've ever been to a medicine show. What is it?"

"It's where they bring out new medical cures. Patent medicines as well as snake oil medicines that cure whatever ails you. I don't ever buy anything, just go for the show. They usually have comedians and all kinds of skits. It's free to get in. Usually lots of fun."

Buddy seemed to have some remembrance of such a show. He tried to recall a picture but was unable. "Sure I'll go with you. Ought to be fun and relaxin'. How's sales going for Liz and Consuela?"

"It's been pretty slow so far. Lots of people, but not many buyers. There'll be more this afternoon, I suppose."

# CHAPTER 15

Three white men, with eyes and lips circled in white paint on black faces and dressed in brown suits with tie and a bowler type of hat, came on stage. Two danced and one played the banjo. The music was rousing and Buddy's foot began tapping in tune to it unconsciously. He remembered the music and the banjo and right then realized that he, too, could play the banjo. An image flashed in his mind. *A large fire at night with grownups sitting round. Lots of kids running all over the place, a large body of water nearby. He was playing the banjo and singing that same song. There was another man playing the guitar in time with him. The people were clapping their hands in tune with the music and some were dancing around the fire.* The image vanished.

Laura Mae placed her hand on his leg just above the knee. The touch felt electric. The heat from her hand warmed his leg and he looked at her, searching for meaning. Her dark eyes were penetrating and inviting. The music stopped and broke the spell – she removed her hand. The minstrels' left the stage and were replaced by another tall man, also in a business suit. A very pretty girl wheeled a cart on stage filled with dark-colored bottles with white labels. She just as quickly darted off the stage leaving the man alone. He began talking about the medicines he was trying to hawk.

A young woman with two small boys came into the aisle. The youngest boy came first and sat next to Buddy on the wooden bench, then the oldest boy, then the woman. The young boy, with white skin and many freckles, had blond hair cropped close to the ears, but long in the front so that it hung into his eyes. He was about four or five, wore white linen pants and a short-sleeved brown cloth shirt. The pants had patches on the knees and rear. The older boy, with dark hair and dark complexion, about a year older, was dressed like the younger, but with his hair combed back slick. The handsome woman, with dark hair pulled back in a bun and covered with a wide-brimmed white hat tied with pretty ribbons, acknowledged him when she entered the aisle. She quickly became taken up with the spiel the man on stage was delivering. Something about this family peaked his interest. He wondered about their daddy.

The man on stage was giving an electrifying spiel about the powers of a certain liquid contained within a peculiar shaped dark green bottle that could cure everything from colds to moles to tired blood. At the end, and because he said the supply was limited, a lot of folks rushed forward to purchase the bottles before they ran out.

After all the bottles were sold, two men in denim overalls and straw hats came on stage, one with a fiddle and one with a guitar. Buddy instantly recognized the fiddle. He owned one somewhere and he could play it. The image of the gathering around the fire came back for an instant and he was playing the fiddle. The tune roused his spirit – he recognized it – Sally Goodin.

The little boy next to him spoke. "Mister, why do you pat your foot like that?"

Buddy had heard that voice and question before. In his mind he saw a little cotton-topped boy with freckles groping onto his legs and looking up at him. The boy was crying. Who was he? Was it his child? Didn't favor him. Maybe a nephew or something. An older, darker skinned boy held onto a shallow boat near the water's edge. The boy looked familiar. *Maybe I do have a family back there. They must think I'm dead or run off.* A deep sadness engulfed him and he fought off the urge to get up and leave right then and there.

Buddy looked at the boy sitting beside him. He tousled the boy's hair. It felt fine and clean – washed just for this event, he reckoned. "You try it. Just pat your foot with the music." He removed his kerchief from his back pocket and dabbed his eyes. He glanced at Laura Mae. She had seen him wipe his eyes.

"Anything the matter, Curly?"

"No, not really. The little boy's question sparked a memory that's all." Buddy turned back to the boy. The boy was looking at his feet and trying to tap them in time with the music.

He looked up at Buddy. "Look, mister, I can do it, too."

*Buddy stood on the beach with the water lapping at his bare feet. Two little boys in patched britches and shirts held onto his legs and a woman in a simple white cotton dress down to her ankles stood farther up on the beach. Tears ran down her cheek and she tried to smile through trembling lips. She fingered the apron over the dress. He moved the boys off his legs and went to her.*

The image faded and then disappeared. "Yes, son, now you can feel the music just like me." He rubbed his eyes with the tips of his fingers.

Buddy and Laura Mae left the medicine show and started walking back to the stalls. They stopped and watched a man throw a baseball at a clown in a cage. The clown ridiculed the man and tried to get his goat. The man took the ribbing in good stride and threw the ball straight and true. The clown plunged into the water and quickly climbed back up to his perch and continued ribbing the man who just laughed and walked on.

Two young boys strolled by licking at ice cream cones. "I'd like an ice cream cone, Laura Mae. Would you like one? I guess I haven't had an ice cream cone since I can remember." He took her arm and steered her towards the ice cream wagon off to the right.

"Do you have money to spend on such things, Curly?" She knew Liz didn't pay him much, if anything at all.

Buddy dug deep in his pockets and brought out three nickels, two dimes and several pennies. "I've been savin' what little money I earn helpin' Liz. She don't pay much, but every now and then she slips me a few coins for cigarette makin's and such. I'm able to put a little away for the rainy day that's sure to come. What'll you have?" They stepped up to the counter. She gave him a questioning look.

Buddy was engrossed with his cone and felt good being with Laura Mae. She could tempt him under the right circumstances, he was sure of that. They turned a corner and he immediately knew something was wrong. A crowd had gathered in front of Liz's stall but he couldn't make out what was happening. He threw the unfinished ice cream into a waste drum and started to run. He saw the man then, one of the young ones from the saloon. The man faced Andre who tried to stand tall, but clearly was no match for the man. Then he saw the other three. Only the old one was missing. Buddy reached the group and pushed his way through the growing crowd just as the man pushed Andre. Andre tried to stand tall but tumbled backwards and fell in a heap in the dusty street. Consuela rushed the man with a stick and he backhanded her as if she were a mere fly. She went sprawling with a cry of agony and pain.

Buddy caught the man by the shoulder and swung him around. The other three moved in on him, the young pimply-faced boy leading the pack. Buddy saw the shock on the man's face as he hit him with a powerful right hand square on the nose. The nose gave away and blood splattered. The man's face reddened with blood as he flew backward and landed on his back near Andre. The dry dust swirled up around him. Buddy spun around just as the boy took a swing at him. He sidestepped the blow and grabbed the boy by the back of the neck and propelled him face first into the dirt. He punched the next one to get near him and downed him with one punch. The other one started to back up and Buddy caught him and knocked him down to his knees. The man tried to regain his footing and Buddy hit him again full in the face, pulled him forward and shoved his face in the dirt. Buddy's blood ran hot and his chest throbbed. He looked around for others. All four men were on the ground. The boy tried to get up and Buddy hit him full in the face and knocked him out cold. The man who had pushed Andre tried to get up. Buddy stood over him and waited. The man tried to bully his way up. Buddy grabbed him behind the head and hit him again. This time only mush remained in place of the nose. His fist, covered with the men's blood, hurt and felt like it might be broken. On the outside he looked like a wild man, but was extremely calm inside. He walked to the other two and stood over them. They didn't try to get up. They crawled through the crowd and disappeared.

Buddy cooled off some and took the time to look at the crowd that had gathered. They circled him and the men on the ground. Andre, with a shocked look on his face, pulled himself up and looked at the man's face next to him. Buddy now took stock and realized the police would soon be here. He stepped into Liz's stall and pulled her to him. She gaped at him wide eyed. Laura Mae was nowhere to be seen. Consuela backed into the stall and he noted her red face, but she appeared to be okay. Everything had happened so fast. Now he was cool and thinking fast. "Liz, I've got to get away from here before the police come. I don't know why they're after me, but I can't let them get me yet. Get Andre. I'll meet him at Consuela's truck. He can take me back to your place and come back for Consuela and help you pack. You okay to drive by yourself?"

Liz grabbed him by the arm and ushered him to the back of the stall. "Go now, I'll be all right. I'll send Andre to you." She pushed him out the back. He sprinted for the truck and climbed inside. Soon Andre jumped into the truck and backed out slow and easy. Police sirens sounded everywhere. Buddy's heart beat a mile a minute. Neither man spoke until they had turned onto highway 78 heading south.

"Curly, I got to eat crow. I was ashamed of you this morning. Now I'm proud as hell to know you and to be your friend; that is if you'll still let me. That was one hell of a fight – never in all my born days seen anything like it. Where'd you learn to fight like that?" He looked at Buddy then back to the road, then back to Buddy.

"Just keep your eyes on the road, old man. We don't want to get picked up by the police. I ain't never stopped thinkin' of you as my friend. You're a damn good friend and you've always done right by me. Figure I owe you a whole lot. I can understand how you might've thought poorly of me. Never been one to pick a fight and never been one to run from one neither, that is, not that I know of. Just seem to know to pick the right time and place if I have to be in one – second nature I reckon."

Andre looked long and hard at him. Buddy looked at Andre. Then they both laughed long. Andre said. "By God, I've never seen anything like it. Whooee. They'll be talking about that fight for a long time to come I bet." He patted the steering wheel with both hands. "I'll never forget that calm look on your face and the cigarette dangling out the corner of your mouth. You seemed to be in hog heaven. Damn, damn. What a sight." He took out the pint, took a big swig and passed the bottle to Buddy. At first Buddy waved it off then changed his mind and took a big drink. The whiskey burned its way into his stomach and left him feeling warm and fuzzy all over. He put the cap back on the bottle and leaned his back into the seat. Neither man spoke for quite a while.

Finally Buddy broke the silence. "Old man, I'm gonna need your help one more time." He placed his hand on Andre's shoulder.

"Anything Curly, you just name it, boy. If I can do it, I will. What can I do for you?"

"Next week we begin movin' the junk back from the front of the property. Got to get it done in a month. I've rebuilt an old LaSalle and I want to give it to Liz as a present, but I want it to be a surprise. She's sure to see it when we start movin' all the stuff. Maybe you—"

"You done what? You rebuilt a car? How in the hell? Where is it? I—"

"Hold on, hold on, old man. I'll show it to you when we get there. You've got to help me hide it until I'm ready to give it to her."

"Her birthday's next Saturday. Give it to her then. You can keep her out of that part of the yard until then. We'll all come out and give her a big birthday."

"Damn good idea, old man. You can help me keep it from her till then." Buddy smiled and patted Andre on the shoulders. "Damn good idea. Didn't know about her birthday. Let's see, that would be," he counted the days on his fingers, "the 5th of November." Maybe Laura Mae would come, too. He would like to see her again before he took off. He was a little afraid to get too close to her though – can't tell what nature would have him do. *Wouldn't be proper to go sparkin' another woman if I was married and had young'uns of my own.*

"Just one more question, old man, what was this thing between you and Liz?"

Andre looked long and hard at Buddy. Looked about ready to brush off the question. "Me and Liz were about to be married when I got another girl with child. I was forced to marry the girl and it broke Liz's heart. Sorriest thing I ever did in my life."

# CHAPTER 16

By Monday afternoon the back acres were cleared and the dike built to prevent runoff into the creek that led to the lake.

Buddy had the workmen start with the big items and had them place the old autos in such a way that provided a shield around his prized LaSalle. The plan was working perfectly so far, and, by Friday, this part of the job should be finished. It would likely take the slow rumbling crane at least five days to move all the large material, then another few days to finish with the small stuff. He looked again at the sky, then went to his room and got his windbreaker to shield the coolness of the morning.

He spent the necessary time with the workers so that scrap was laid out as planned. The time not spent dealing with the workers and on normal chores, he spent on the LaSalle. He had made good progress. It would be ready for Saturday.

His luck had held. Both Tuesday and Thursday Liz had been gone most of each day. Today, she left right after breakfast and said she would be gone most of the day. This was the last chance to get that distribution system fixed to stop the backfiring. After giving the crane operator instructions for the day he went to his room and carefully removed the distributor he'd fashioned out of scrap-metal parts and wires from other junked cars on the place. After checking the wiring again he clamped the metal ends to the wires and shoved them into the holes on the distributor.

He experienced again the strange feeling that he had made one of these devices before. His memory kept trying to gain a foothold, but slipped up each time. One of these days, and soon he hoped, it would come flooding back with all the lost knowledge. These feelings had happened many times with different experiences. There would be a flash of memory which would last only a brief moment. Each time he thought this was the event that would trigger the flood of memory the doctor had spoken about, then nothing but the present. The past would not come back. His thoughts turned again to finding Toby. That seemed to be his only hope of finding himself. It had now been over eight months since he had been hurt and lost his memory. Whoever may be waiting for him was sure to give up soon. He had to make his move.

Satisfaction came after two hours of working on the distributor, and now was the time for the test. He wrapped the wires around the device and headed for the door. The loud barking of the dog stopped him in his tracks. *God, what now?* Through the screen door he saw Liz pulling up to the porch in her old rattletrap. She was supposed to be gone all day. What was she doing back here at this hour – not even noon yet. This thing had to be tested today if he was going to have it ready for her birthday tomorrow. Not much chance of testing it with her here. He fumed and watched as she got out of the car, looked his way then went into the house. Standing back from the screen so she would be unable to see him, he bided his time impatiently. He was about to go back out to the yard for a talk with the crane operator when Liz came out the door and headed in his direction. "Good God." She stopped, looked long in his direction then turned back and strolled to the car. In another minute she turned onto the road leading to the village center. Once out of sight, he walked to the yard and back to the LaSalle.

When he stuck his head out the door Saturday morning, the sun was nowhere to be seen, but evidence of it lay in the hazy blue light that dimmed what few stars were out. The light brightened and concentrated behind the dark clouds bunched close to the horizon. The sun would lift its head above the cabbage palms in about an hour. A slight breeze coming off the lake a half-mile away cooled the air and gave it just enough chill to cause him to shiver. The tops of the palms and pines barely moved in the breeze.

The old rooster stood on his roost in the chicken coop and let out his ear-piercing wake-up call. He repeated it four times before he climbed down and began his morning strutting. There would be more if no response was soon received. Buddy knew the hens and chicks would soon be coming out of the house – the daily routine. He'd watched it unfold most every morning.

Buddy removed a Chesterfield from the pack, tapped it on the back of his hand and put it in his mouth. He favored his makings, but Liz had bought the pack that day at the fair and he figured it would be best if he used them up before he left. The flame flared from the match when he rubbed it against the doorjamb. He cupped the match in the palms of his hands to ward off the effect of the breeze. Darkness engulfed the main house. Liz would sleep for another hour.

He looked around the grounds. Most of the old wrecked cars and other big stuff had been moved to the back of the property. The week had been a frantic one. Andre had kept his promise and had somehow managed to keep Liz busy and away from the place so he could finish with the LaSalle. It purred like a kitten and shone like a new dime after the paint job he'd given it. He'd been unable to find black paint so he'd painted it with the only paint available, sky blue. Probably the only blue car in creation. He laughed to himself at the irony of it. He had started out to just get the thing to quit backfiring, and ended up with a new car that would stand out from all others by its color. During the process he had found out something else about himself – he was good with machinery and he was now sure that he'd faced the problem of backfiring before. The flash of memory when he made his drawing had him dealing with men in suits and ties. They were discussing something about patents, but the memory disappeared before he could tell where he was or how he was involved. Slowly, but surely, he was finding himself, though. He hoped it would come in time. He had to get back to where Toby found him – his memory lay there.

Buddy flipped the dead cigarette away, stepped back into the room and grabbed his windbreaker. He walked to the back of the property where a good amount of the scrap was now located. His planned organization was taking shape. Another week or so with the crane and he would be ready to head for Savannah. He could just make out the LaSalle in the dim light. The starlight glittered in broken strands from its finish. The brush strokes didn't show at a distance in this light. He had taken extra pains to remove as much of the strokes as possible. Would've been better if he had a spray gun handy, but, as someone said, "you have to play with the cards you're dealt." *Now where did that come from?*

Liz would love the car, he felt sure of that. The entire population knew her as a tough old gal who stood on her own two feet. This car would give her more of that independent feeling. She would stand out from the others. He felt good, and the hour for presentation was near at hand.

He heard the rumble of a wagon just before noon. Andre, dressed in his finest white shirt and hat and sitting proud as a peacock on his old buckboard, turned onto the property. Consuela, dressed in her traditional multi-colored dress, sat next to him. As always, her coal-black hair hung in pigtails down to the middle of her back. Like Andre, she wore a brightly colored bandanna around her neck, but wore no hat. She sat proud, too – back straight as a ramrod. He felt a moment of disappointment when he didn't see Laura Mae with them. *Sure would like to see her again.* A woman is no doubt a necessity – surely must've had one in the other life. He longed to regain that past. *Hopefully I'm not a criminal or murderer or something worse.* Ever since that sheriff came around looking for a Buddy some months back, that idea remained as a distinct possibility.

Buddy caught Andre's attention, and motioned for him to come to the backyard. Andre nodded and continued on toward the main house. Buddy turned the corner of the bunkhouse and headed straight for the LaSalle. The chill of the morning air was fast disappearing. He removed the canvas topping and the other scrap placed on and around the car for security. He was inspecting it from a distance when Andre strolled up.

Andre pulled a small bottle from his jacket pocket, took a big swig and passed the bottle to Buddy. Buddy hesitated. Much too early for whiskey. Then he said, "Oh, what the hell," reached for the bottle and took a nice pull. He winced and blew breath through his teeth with a gush like a steam engine leaving the station, trying to push out the toughness of the liquor. "Aaaugh." Andre laughed.

Andre walked around the LaSalle several times. He hadn't seen it since that first day when they came from the fairgrounds a week ago. Then he had his doubts that Curly could make anything of it. He had said then that it was like trying to make gold from a sow's ear. But now, here was a new car right down to the running boards. He took another swipe at the whiskey. "Curly, where'd you get the new rubber for the running boards? This car looks brand new except for its color. Never seen a blue car before. Of course never seen any new car before either." He laughed in his familiar high-pitched squeal.

"You like that paint job, uh? Listen to her run." He climbed under the steering wheel. The engine purred like a kitten. He relished the sound. No backfiring.

Andre climbed into the passenger side and leaned back in the seat. A loose spring nudged his back. "What you gonna do about the seats?"

Buddy looked at the upholstery, which was a sight for sore eyes. "Nothin' I can do before I give her the car today. Maybe I can fix it up some before I leave."

Andre looked soberly at him. "When are you expecting to leave, Curly? I suppose it's getting about that time, huh?"

Buddy turned the engine off and looked at Andre. "Been meanin' to talk to you about that. Yeah, I got to get goin' right soon. Would like to leave early Thursday mornin' on the first day of December. If I have a family somewhere, I'd sure like to get back to 'em by Christmas. Be a good Christmas if they're still waitin'. Need you to drive me to the other side of Okeechobee City. Figure I'll hitchhike right up 441 all the way. Can you do that? We can use Liz's Model T."

"I'd be much obliged, Curly. You're like my son, boy." His lip quivered and he turned away and sucked in a deep breath. "Know you've got to go, but I've grown too fond of you, and just hate to see you go. Kind of feel like I won't ever see you again." He stepped down out of the car.

A tear welled up in Buddy's eye. He had grown mighty fond of the old man, too. "Now don't you go gettin' mushy on me, old man. You're damn tootin' I'll be back around here. Imagine I'll be comin' back through here with Toby and Marty in a couple of weeks after I leave. Come on. Get back in here and let's deliver this thing to Liz before we lose the daylight." He started the engine again. Andre climbed in and passed the bottle to Buddy.

Liz, dressed normally, in denims, boots and white hat, and a crisply-pressed white shirt with an open collar, mingled with guests on the front porch. She sported a bright blue speckled bandanna looped and tied around her neck with the knot hanging rakishly over her left shoulder. She was in animated conversation with one of her guests when she spotted the big blue car turn into her driveway. *Who in the world?* She continued the conversation, but strained to see the driver of the car. She could make out two men in the front seat. She had never seen a blue car before. She wondered if it was someone from the Tribal Council coming to check on her progress with the junk relocation. *Why would they be coming on Saturday?* They had been out several times during the week and had seemed satisfied with the progress. They had even followed Curly around one day, checking environmental concerns and so forth. The car drew nearer and she recognized Andre in the passenger seat. "What the hell", she murmured under her breath. She broke off the talk and walked to the edge of the porch as the car stopped just short of the porch in the final arc of the curved gravel driveway. Although she could not clearly see the driver, he bore a great resemblance to Curly.

She left the guests gawking at the car and its occupants as she stepped off the porch and approached the car. "Andre, you old coot, what the hell are you doing?" She broke off in mid-sentence when she bent down with her hands on the car door and got a full look at Buddy. "What in the world's going on here? What tom-foolishness are you scoundrels up to now?" Amazed, she watched Buddy as he opened the door on his side and got out. She stood erect and looked him full in the face over the top of the car. He wore a broad grin like he had a cat up his sleeve. "Curly, will you please explain what you all are doing in this car? Where'd you get it and why do you have it here?" She fixed him with her demanding gaze and his grin widened even more.

Buddy quit grinning long enough to say, "Little Squirrel," he rarely used that name when talking to her, "this car belongs to you. It's yours." He tried to continue, but she interrupted.

"Wh . . , wh . . , how's it mine? I've never seen the likes of anything like this before." She couldn't understand what was happening. She turned toward the guests and fixed her eyes intently on Consuela as if asking for solid answers to this greatest of all puzzles. Consuela just grinned. Liz turned back to Buddy as he continued.

"This is your car. It's a 1918 LaSalle. Been here all the time. I'm surprised you've never seen it before. Of course you had so much junk around the place, maybe it's not so surprisin' after all." His grin spread as he came around the car and stood before her. The guests had come down off the porch to try and get a better fix on this slowly unfolding drama. They formed a sort of semi-circle around the players, eager to catch every word.

"What kind of a game are you playing, Curly? Surely I would've seen this car if it had been on the place, no matter how much junk was around." She looked to the group for approval that she had not been so lackadaisical that she could've missed seeing such a thing.

Before Buddy could speak, Andre broke in, as he pushed open his door and forced Liz to back away. "Of course it didn't look like it does now. Curly had to dress it up some. Add a part here and there, little dab of paint there and here, lots of elbow grease and one hell of a lot of smarts and know-how. Beats me where he got it all, but he did it and there sits the finest automobile in the entire state, and it's all yours. Where's the food?" He started through the crowd towards the porch. He took a big pull on his whiskey bottle before he got too close to the food.

"Happy birthday, Liz." Buddy moved to Liz and took her in his arms. She wrapped her arms around him and looked over his shoulder at the big car.

"I still don't get it." She untangled from him, and while holding onto his shoulders, looked him sternly in the face. "I don't understand how you were able to do this. Not only how you could keep it from me, but most of all, where you got the learning to take an old wrecked car and make a thing of such beauty. You must've found a part of your past. What were you, a mechanic?" Some of the others had wandered back to the porch while the most inquisitive milled around the car.

"I found that I'm good with machinery and the like. Once I got started, I found that I knew some things without havin' to figure too much. Know there's a lot more I could do if I had the time." He placed his hand on her elbow and steered her towards the porch.

Her eyes watered and she looked away from him. The thought of him leaving had been with her constantly this last week. Ever since the fight at the fairgrounds, she knew the day was not far off. "Yes, I know. You've got to be on your way pretty soon." Her quivering voice betrayed her emotions. "I'm going to miss you mighty bad, Curly." She broke away from his grasp and went into the house.

Buddy moseyed over to the big long table at the far end of the porch and busied himself with the food spread out there. The food was as varied as the guests, since each one had brought their specialty. He fixed a plate heaping over with swamp

114

cabbage, venison, boiled turtle, roasted beef, potatoes and all the trimmings.

During the next three weeks he worked like a Trojan. He had moved all the remaining junk, using the flatbed trailer pulled with Liz's Model-T. He must've made a hundred trips if he'd made one. Even all the scraps had been picked up and placed in small piles, ready to be moved to their place in the backyard. The front yard was now ready for the grass that had been trying to break through for the past several years. He had even built, with scraps of lumber lying around the place, a high fence between the barn and the bunkhouse with a gate just as high. With the gate closed, the backyard, with all its salvage parts, was completely blocked from view. With the rear entrance, which also was gated, she could keep dumpers from coming through the front yard. He still had a few days before his planned departure. Perhaps he could get the fence painted to match the buildings he had painted during the last three months.

It was Sunday and he walked the main road back from the lake and his weekly fishing. The day had been a good one. He had a string of wide-mouth bass that would be good eating tonight. Liz would be glad to fix them up. Only a tuft or two of white clouds remained in the sky and the air was cool even with the sun, bright as a new dime, yielding its warmth to the body. He wore his long-sleeved shirt rolled up above the elbows and opened to the waist. The cool air circulated around his body under the shirt. The homemade rope belt held up his pants as usual. He passed the entrance to the back property and walked on up the road until he stood directly across from the front entrance to Liz's property. His accomplishments, especially during the last month, pleased him. He remembered the day he first arrived here. Liz had been willing to take him in as a favor to Consuela, but she had given him the impression that she was reluctant and almost certain that he was just another laggard that she would have to feed and board. He had vowed to himself that day that if she would take him in, he would make her proud that

115

she had. Looking at the place now and thinking on her attitude towards him, he felt certain he had succeeded in his vow.

The three buildings were all painted white. Most of the rotted boards had been replaced and the roofs mended and tinned in where necessary. The buildings proved to be dry as a bone in any kind of rain. The rows of plants in the garden, now clear of weeds, and the dark green leaves on the vegetables indicated the benefit of fertilizer applied. Sprigs of grass grew in the frontyard and the hibiscus plants Liz had planted along the road and at the edge of the house had taken root and would soon be high and full enough to shield the grounds from passersby. He knew the council was pleased although they had not said anything to him or, to his knowledge, to Liz. He suspected they would be around soon enough.

He had worked these months primarily for room and board. He had saved the few dollars she had given him on occasion for the eventual trip which was now almost at hand. He could sure use more money. The money in his jar, counted just this morning for the umpteenth time, came to just nine dollars and thirty-two cents. That likely would not get him very far. He had thought about asking Liz for some money even if it was a borrowing, but each time he got up the nerve, he backed down. She had been good enough to him by letting him stay on the place and providing him with some mighty tasty meals. He would get by somehow.

# CHAPTER 17

Bill Parkins's letter arrived one day before Flo planned to leave Key West to return to her house on Wood Key.

*November 10, 1932*

*Dear Flo*

*I will drop you a line or two to let you know that I am loving you as much as ever and hope you are well and all of your kids. I reckon the new one is born by now. I hope it is a boy. Tell Junior I said happy birthday and happy birthday to you on November 2nd. Sorry I missed it. I'll make it up to you when you marry me and we are always together. I would have wrote before now but I did not have no paper. How is your mama? Are you getting plenty of work to do? When are you going back to Wood Key? I guess I will go on down to your Brothers from here. I am not such a good writer but I guess you can read it. I am thinking of you all of the time and hope you are the same of me. Well I guess I will close for this time. With love for you only.*

*William D Parkins*

*I don't know when I will get it but write soon.*

> *Almarada Fla.*
> *Care Buice Hines Monroe County*

Even though she had told him over and over again that there could be no relationship between them so long as there was even the slightest chance that Buddy could return, Bill had literally buried her with letters and personal attention these last several months. This one was no different, expressing his undying love for her and promising to take care of her and her children. With no children of his own he looked to having a ready-made family. He had already spoken to Jim Harrison who had a rather high regard for him. She would talk with Jim about it when she returned to Wood Key. Although she needed someone to look after her, and Bill could no doubt fill the bill, she must wait for Buddy – she must not lose hope – she had to be strong – she would be strong. Her eyes watered as she re-read the letter and stuffed it into the bag with the others.

The shuttle launch from Chockoluskee pulled into the net spreads at Wood Key a little before noon. Flo looked along the shore to see if anyone was there to welcome her home. She desperately needed someone to talk to, but now realized it was a bad decision to arrive on Saturday. But surely, everyone had not gone into town. Nary a soul in sight, though. After the launch pilot helped her debark her things and the supplies she had purchased at Chockoluskee, she headed towards her house a hundred yards up the beach. Junior and Francis ran along the shoreline looking to see who was at home to play with them. She carried little Warren, now eight weeks old, wrapped in a light blanket over her breast.

Wood Key had been her home for the last three years and she had loved every minute of it, except the last nine months or so. The Harrisons' had homesteaded the Key off and on for fifty years or more, ever since Grandpa Richard Harrison settled in the area back in 1872.

As she walked towards the house a pang hit her heart and she paused by the water's edge. *Just there, beyond the net spreads, Buddy loaded his boat for the fateful trip from which he would never return.* The cherished vision vanished as soon as it appeared, but she knew it would be forever imbedded in her memory. How could she even think of marrying someone else? No one could ever truly and completely take his place. Her heart ached for him. Mosquitoes swarmed over her face and arms. She would have to get used to them all over again. *How quickly we forget. Thank God, it's not summer time.*

Once in the house, she settled Warren on a pallet in the bedroom and lit the carbide in the coffee can lids to kill those mosquitoes that managed to enter with her. She put wood in the stove, and after several tries, got a fire started in the kindling. When the flames grew enough she placed larger pieces on the fire. Thoughts of Buddy filled her mind again and she walked to the bookcase near the door to the bedroom and removed a well-worn book. Idly flipping the pages, she walked the few steps to the kitchen table and sat down. She held the book in her lap and caressed it lovingly as her mind wandered to things past.

She had not told him that she had missed her period and that another child was likely. The timing had never been exactly right before he left for his last hunting trip with Robert. The night before his trip, he had sat in his chair under the seagrape tree behind the house playing his guitar and singing. He always seemed to be at peace in that spot with his guitar and fiddle. He had a natural ability to play any instrument and he learned quickly – everyone said so. From the kitchen window, she had watched him admiringly and just loved everything about him – his walk, his easy-going manner in any situation, the way he tilted his head ever so slightly when waiting for an answer to a question he had asked. He was tall and solid as a rock with broad shoulders – not an ounce of fat anywhere. He had never, to her knowledge, used his size or abilities to put anyone down. She knew some who, because they were large, were brutish bullies, always picking fights with those much smaller. That kind always gave Buddy a wide berth or prettied up to him to become his friend. Although he was a quiet man, it was known far and wide that he had never backed away from a fight and had never lost one that had been brought to him. He never tried to dissuade those who would have a go at him, but he never encouraged anyone to try him either.

They had talked about their life and what the future held for them. He had received an offer on the trap he made and was trying to get patents on some other things as well. When these things started paying off he had said, they were leaving the swamps for good so his children would have a better chance for some real schooling. He was special. Now, that dream was no more. She silently cried. The image of that day, so long ago, clouded her consciousness and she gave into it.

There was no hint of impending danger as Buddy readied for a rather normal hunting trip down to Shark River that morning. He had made the same trip hundreds of times. He made several trips from the house to the boat with his traps, camping gear and provisions for a week. The pale blue sky outlined the tops of the tall mangroves to the east and hundreds of stars provided just enough light to make out the skiff tugging at the anchor rope at the shore line.

It was still an hour or more before sun up when he came back to the house for his guns – a rifle and shotgun. On our walk down to the shore with him, Junior, wide awake, ran out ahead while Francis, still half asleep, stayed close by. The kids always enjoyed the excitement of watching their father make preparations for a trip. Junior waded into the water, climbed into the boat and yelled, "Daddy, Daddy, can I go with you this time?" Junior always asked to go, but the answer was always the same.

Buddy propped his guns in the bow of the skiff. "When you're seven you're ready for trappin' and not before, but it won't be long now. You'll both be grown before long."

There at the end of the net-spread Robert poled his skiff, heading to place it just next to Buddy's. Papa would be pulling the launch around any minute now to tow them down to Shark River. Papa had timed his trip to Key West so he could lighten the boys' load a little. Robert called out, "Hey, Buddy, you ready? I saw Uncle Jim untying the Donnella a minute ago. You know him, he won't wait for nobody when he's ready to go."

"I'll be ready for him. He's never had to wait on me and never will." With the guns safely stored under the bow, Buddy turned to the children who were now at his feet holding onto his legs with both arms. He picked them both up in strong arms and hugged them hard. "Which one of you is seven?" Junior piped right up, "I am, I am . . . almost."

As he walked toward me, he put them down and tousled their heads. "It won't be long now." He put his arms around me, squeezed tenderly, and walked with me back to the boat. "Flo, when I get back we'll go into town and get you that stove you've been wantin'. We'll get you boys somethin', too, maybe even take in a movin' picture show. I been meanin' to tell you that I got an offer on the trap the other day which oughta mean that we'll be rollin' in money pretty soon now. We can afford to let loose of some of our savin's then. When I get the patents on the others we should be pretty rich. Of course, we don't want to count our chickens before they hatch, now do we? You look after the boys, I'll see you Saturday." He rubbed the boy's heads, turned and strode towards the skiff.

A tear formed and spilled over her eyelid. I said, "Buddy, I love . . . ." Robert yelled that Papa was coming around. I wanted to tell him that I loved him. He answered Robert, turned and waved to me and got into his boat. Papa, in the Donnela, pulled into view and Buddy shoved off to meet him. I didn't leave the shore until he rounded the point and raised his arm in a final wave of recognition – and then he faded from view. The morning was chilly and the sun barely filtering through the mangroves when I headed back to the house.

Flo replaced the book, went over to the stove and began preparing lunch for the boys and coffee for herself. She heard the familiar squeak of the front step, then heard Lucy's voice and turned at the sound.

"Flo, I see you're back. Can I come in?" The screen door opened noisily and Lucy, big as a house with child, walked into the living room. Flo moved from the stove to the kitchen table and stood wiping her hands on the dish cloth. At least somebody cared enough to stop by.

Lucy Harrison had married Flo's brother, King, in 1925. Richard and Albert had come in rapid succession and she expected the new child in December. She wore a simple white cotton dress with ruffled-ended sleeves down to her elbows. Her hair, worn in the usual manner, and pulled tight against her head, hung in a ponytail down to the middle of her back. Flo had always wondered how Lucy could stand the hair pulled so tight against her head. Flo preferred her own style, cut short just above the ear lobe and hung loose all around her head. She couldn't deny, though, that Lucy's slightly dark skin and usually slim build made her a natural beauty. Of course the slimness had gone with this child she was now carrying.

For one who didn't usually care about anything but himself, King worshiped the ground Lucy walked on. King was a wiry little banty rooster who relished a fight with anyone bigger than him. He loved a challenge and, like most people, looked for a way to make a quick and easy buck in these hard times. Someone said that he was now running liquor from Cuba and making a handsome profit. He had tried unsuccessfully to get Buddy involved. They had, earlier on, stolen whisky from a yacht whose owners were the guide clients of Papa. Buddy and King had slipped onto the yacht while Papa had taken the owners on a short fishing trip. They took almost all the liquor and transported it deeper into the swamps where it was later retrieved and sold at a handsome profit. Buddy had been quite agitated by the whole thing and would never engage in it again. The episode had only whetted King's appetite. Papa was hopping mad when he found out, but no formal charges were ever made because the liquor was illegal, even for the yacht owners. Everyone seemed to believe that King was somehow involved, but no one linked Buddy. Flo knew he was, though.

Lucy sat in the chair at the kitchen table and her rear-end lapped over the edges. "I saw the shuttle launch drop you off. I had begun to wonder if you were ever gonna come back. How you doin' and how's the little one? I hear it's another boy."

"I'm doin' all right, I reckon. Yeah, it's a boy, cute as a bug's ear. He's in the bedroom. How you been? I reckon that child's about ready, huh? I thought about not comin' back, not knowin' how I'd make a livin' for me and my young'uns. But I had to come back for my things anyhow. I've got to decide what to do." She stood behind the chair with her hands resting on the wooden back and looked intently at Lucy.

Lucy slapped the palm of her hand down hard on the table. Flo, momentarily startled, removed her hands from the chair and stood back. "What do you mean you thought about not comin' back? What's the matter with you, gal?" Lucy pushed her chair back and stood. Their eyes locked. "You just gotta get that nonsense right out of your head. This is still your home, even if Buddy ain't here." She moved toward Flo.

The coffeepot started to whistle as the steam fought to escape. Flo backed toward the stove. "I was just now thinkin' about Buddy when you came in. No matter what I do, I still can't get him off my mind for long. That day back in February is still so fresh." Using the dishrag she moved the pot to a cool spot on the stove just as it began to howl. The wailing stopped when she removed the lid. "Just made some fresh coffee. Want some?"

Lucy walked to the stove and put her hand on Flo's shoulder. "It's gonna take a lotta time, gal. I don't know what I'd do if King was to go off like that. Probably kill the son of a bit . . . ." She didn't finish the sentence.

Flo poured coffee for both of them and they returned to the table. "I just can't seem to accept it that those two men could have been killed down there. Both of 'em could fight their way out of any fix. No one could come up on 'em without them hearin' it. They know these swamps like the back of their hand. Just how could it have happened, Lucy? Who would want to do it? Do you cotton to the idea that they ran off somewheres?" Flo wiped her hands over and over on the dishrag.

Lucy sipped her coffee too quick and spit out the scalding hot coffee. "Aieee. Damn, that's hot." She wiped her mouth on the sleeve of her dress. "No, Flo, I don't believe for one minute they ran off. There've been some rumors floatin' around that the Brown brothers did 'em in."

"The Brown brothers? Rufus and Jacob?"

"No. Rufus and Guy. The story has it that when Buddy and Robert put into Shark Point and set up camp, the Browns were watchin' their every move. They kept their distance and shadowed the boys as they made their rounds. When they came back into camp, the Browns were waitin' for 'em. Surprised 'em and shot 'em both, then towed the bodies and skiffs out into the Gulf."

Flo's eyes moistened and ran over with the thought that Buddy's body had been dumped at sea. She stood and turned towards the stove. Her voice quivered. "So you think they're dead?" With the hem of the apron she dabbed at her eyes.

"Oh, God, Flo, I don't know what to think. Buddy wouldn't just run off and leave you and the young'uns here all by yourself. There's just no reason he'd do such a thing. He has to be dead." She stood and walked to the stove with her cup.

Flo, calmer now, poured them both more coffee and leaned against the sink. She lit a cigarette and sipped her coffee. "Papa don't want to hear nothin' like that. He wants to believe they're both still alive – that they ran off for one reason or another."

Lucy blew on her coffee and took a careful sip – she sucked it up, making a kind of slurping sound. "Papa may want to believe that, but he's too much of a lawman to pass over the signs." She walked back to the table and sat down.

Flo followed. "But what about all the rumors that Buddy has been seen here and there?" She sat wearily down in the chair.

"I've heard all the rumors, too, and Papa's checked 'em all out and found nothin' to none of 'em. King and the other men all believe the story I told you. I don't know what else to say, Flo."

Flo, overwhelmed with the finality of Lucy's opinion, started to cry, got up, went over to the washbasin and sloshed water on her face. She was fussing around with things on the sideboard when the porch produced its familiar groan and the screen door squeaked. Jim entered the room, followed by young Jimmy. Lucy got up to leave and Flo waved her down.

"How're you and the young'un, Flo?" Jim asked as he entered the broad living room. He nodded to Lucy and said hello.

Flo retreated into the bedroom and emerged with the baby wrapped in a bluish white coverlet. Jim looked intently at the baby for a long time and moved the cover off of Warren's face to see it more clearly. Certainly he was remembering his prophetic statement back in August. Well, it was a boy anyway, and time would tell if he would follow in his daddy's footsteps. She knew Papa wasn't really here to talk about the baby, though. He wanted to know when she planned to return to work at the farm.

Jim turned away from the baby and, as if reading her mind, said, "Flo, I sure do hate to rush things for you, but we're short-handed as all get out at the farm and need you bad. You plannin' to come back to work for a while?"

Flo didn't try to answer until she had taken Warren back into the bedroom. When she came out of the room, she said, "Yes, Papa, I do. Just tryin' to sort things out here and figure how it'd work with the new baby and all. But I should be ready for full time again startin' Tuesday if that's all right with you."

"Rather have you Monday, but I understand, and your schedule will be okay. We'll make do till you get there."

Lucy's statement that claimed Buddy was dead flooded Flo's mind. Should she . . . ? She needed to speak to Jim about Bill Parkins, but didn't want to while Lucy was still here. She'd best wait for a better time, but that might never come. Papa was always off somewhere with all the demands on his time. Lucy seemed to realize her plight and rose to leave.

Flo said, "Lucy, are you leavin' already?"

125

"Yes, Flo, I've got a hundred things to do and not enough time to do 'em in. Papa, you comin' to supper tonight?"

"Can't do it tonight, Lucy, your aunt's plannin' to, though. Got to run up to Everglades and won't make it back till late. Maybe not till tomorrow. I'll see you later. Guess I better be goin', too." They both turned towards the door.

Flo walked them to the door and put her hand on Jim's sleeve. "Papa, can I have a word with you before you leave?"

Jim turned. "Sure Flo, what's on your mind?" The screen door squeaked as Lucy and Jimmy went through and out onto the porch.

"Papa, I wanted to talk with you about Bill Parkins. I know it's right soon, but Bill's been comin' on and I just don't know what to do about it." She watched his face, looking for a sign, but detecting none. His face was impassive and his body reflected no discernable movement. *He's like the wooden Indian. What's he thinking?* "He asked me to marry him, and he wants to do it right soon. I've told him time and again that I must wait for Buddy. No one can ever take Buddy's place, I know that, but like you said, there's not many men around here willing to take on a wife and three small children," she blurted the words out in rapid succession. There, she'd gotten it all out. She fidgeted. His brow creased and he shifted his feet, as if agitated. She waited in fear for his judgment.

"Do you love this man, Flo?"

"I love Buddy with all my heart and soul, Papa. I don't believe I could ever love anybody again like I love him. I haven't known Bill all that long, and haven't spent any time alone with him, but I've heard and believe that he's a good, decent and hard workin' man. I think he could make a good husband and a good father for my kids if I have to make that move. God knows I don't want to but . . . what're my choices?"

Jim was looking intently at Flo as if trying to delve to the bottom of her being and sift out her true feelings. Unable to withstand his steady stare, she walked to the screen door and looked out, as if looking for the children.

126

"Flo, you know that Buddy's body has never been found. Even though the law might assume that he was murdered, he has not been legally declared dead." His voice broke. She sensed that his heart hung heavy with this conversation. He never did like to talk of Buddy's death.

He continued, "I believe the law requires you to wait seven years before a missin' person can be declared dead legally. We'll have to look into this matter to see just what you'll have to do to marry Bill. But I agree that you gotta look out for yourself and your boys, and Bill is a pretty good man. You could do a lot worse, Flo. Life is damn hard now for anyone, especially in this country and especially for a single woman with kids. You've got my blessings to do what you gotta do, but first let me look into this legal thing."

Flo almost swooned with relief. She had not been sure of the position he would take and she was still not sure if she should even be considering such an idea. She found it hard to imagine being married to someone else. She blurted out, "Thank you, Papa. I love you." She put her arms around him. He patted her shoulder gently as he urged her away and moved toward the door.

"I've gotta go now, Flo. I'll look into the legal matter, and I'll see you at the launch Tuesday mornin' bright and early. I'll also speak with Bill soon as I see him." She tried to say more, but he went out the door before she could utter another word.

She yelled through the screen door. "Papa, would you bring me a few things from Everglades?"

He paused on the steps and waited for her. She went back into the room and came out with some change. "Here's fifty-eight cents. Get me a piece of ice, a gallon jug of milk and a loaf of light-bread." He took the money and went down the steps.

Flo picked up a bucket, went out the back door and walked to the two water cisterns between her house and Papa's. Papa had built these cisterns in 1915 and they had served the Harrison clan well ever since. There weren't many places she knew of that

127

had city water that ran through pipes into the house. Most every place, even the city, had a well of some kind with a hand pump that always had to be primed to yield its water. On most of these islands there was no fresh water to be pumped. The only way to have water was to catch it from the rains and store it. There, etched into the cement on both cisterns, were the words, E.J. Harrison, 1915. She opened the trap door on the small roof over the cistern, dropped the bucket with the rope into the water, dipped it to secure the water, pulled it up and emptied the contents into her bucket. After closing the hatch, she returned to the house and took the water inside. Francis and Junior were still outside playing down by the shoreline and the baby was fast asleep in the bedroom.

Without hesitation she went directly to the big seagrape tree in the backyard and sat in Buddy's favorite chair – content to just sit all alone staring at the mangroves and the bog on the lee side of the key. All her thoughts were of Buddy and the life they had shared on this island.

Her house had been built on the high windward part of the key, as were the other houses that faced the beach. The house had been built in 1926, shortly before she and Buddy were married and was the last one built on Wood Key. Papa had it built for Buddy as an inducement for him to stay put for a while. There were now five houses on the key, spaced about 100 feet apart from one end of the key to the other, all facing south. Papa's house sat at the eastern edge and was larger than all the others. All the houses were built on pilings about three feet off the ground, with steps leading up to a porch, with entry through a screen door at the front of the house. Only hers had a screened-in porch. Construction rarely varied from wood frame covered on the outside with one-by-six boards placed together in the ship-lock method to prevent intrusion of hard-driven rain. Sometimes tarpaper was applied to the outside for better rain prevention. The flooring inside, and what walls were in place, was fashioned with tongue and groove one-by-fours about eight to ten feet long. In some cases, such as Lucy's place, which was the second house down, there were no walls at all. The bedrooms were separated by canvas or bedspreads hung on a line across the room. King and his boys had built that house and he didn't think it necessary to waste his hard-earned money for walls. The main thing, to his way of thinking, was shelter from the weather. He was rarely there anyway, so why should he give a tinker's damn. He figured Lucy was a hardy woman and Ricky and Albert were old enough at nine and five to build walls if they were needed – he'd said so many a time.

The baby's cry roused her from her daydreams. Mosquitoes were all over her and she hadn't been bothered too much by them. *Must be getting used to them again.* She hurried inside and found little Warren soaked to the skin. The soiled diaper, she threw out on the back stoop to be rinsed out later. A bottle of milk would be handy for him, but she knew none was prepared because there was no ice for the box – no need to even look. She placed her left breast against his face. He grabbed it with his tiny hands and after some wallering, got the nipple in his mouth. Papa would bring ice later tonight. Francis and Junior were playing with Albert and a few of the other children down by the net-spreads. She stepped out on the porch and called for them. Francis came right away, but as always, she had to threaten Junior with a strap before he came very reluctantly and mumbling to himself. He knew better than to talk where she could hear what he said.

The sun was just setting on the Gulf as she took down the kerosene lamp and shook it to see if it was full. She heard nothing and silently cursed herself for not seeing to those chores before now. The lamp was dry as a board. Dark was coming on fast and she hoped the kerosene can was not also empty. She had to get used to living in this country again. Out here you're always prepared – if not, you die. The liquid sloshed in the can she retrieved from the back porch – there would be no begging this night.

It was already dark and the baby was crying again. Junior and Francis were raising Cain, wanting supper. Just barely able to see, she removed the shade and filled the lamp with fuel, turned up the wick a little and reached to the shelf over the stove for the matches. They were not in the usual place and her heart skipped a beat. Her fingers scrambled frantically along the top of the shelf and when her hand touched the familiar box, she let out an audible sigh of relief. She lit the wick and replaced the shade and the room suddenly filled with a dim light. The other lamp, when filled and lit, provided all the light needed. The children's noise quieted down.

With the baby on her left hip she began to peel potatoes to go with collards and johnnycake. She vowed to stock the house better next week. A little piece of fish would satisfy her craving, but there was none to be had. Lucy probably had some, but this meal would have to do for tonight. She ordered Junior outside to gather more firewood for the stove, put the baby on a pallet on the floor and encouraged Francis to entertain him. She finished with the potatoes, chopped the collards and began sifting the flour for the johnnycake. Junior came in with the wood, placed it in the stove chamber and got the fire going again. By the time she had the food ready the stove was hot enough to do its job. Soon they all sat down to the simple meal, and since they had no fresh milk, their drink for the evening was rainwater. She was glad that she at least had the foresight to draw the water before dark.

# CHAPTER 18

As he went down the wooden steps into the front yard, Jim fingered the coins Flo had given him. *Bet she's countin' her pennies about now.* With his thoughts again heavy with Buddy, he strode down to the water's edge and walked out on the net-spreads. Buddy's net had been removed and piled up in his back yard and no one used the spread, out of reverence to him. Probably wouldn't as long as Flo lived in the house.

His gaze fell across the open stretch of water south of the farm and clearly projected Shark Point in his mind. They had searched every inch and hadn't found much to support a case for murder. There was the blood, but that was so contaminated it was inconclusive.

He should've told Flo about the rumor that Buddy had been sighted in an Indian Village east of Ft. Myers – that he had actually gone there and questioned some Indians back in September and again in October. There had been so many rumors that hadn't come to anything during the last nine months, he hated to mix that little bit of hope with her needs for somebody to support her and the kids. Sure be a shame if she ups and marries Bill Parkins and Buddy does come back – what a mess that would be.

He stared long at the freshly painted wooden house with screened porch. Buddy had painted it just two weeks before he left on the final trip. The three other houses to the west, all in various stages of needing paint, were all the same design. Jake's house at the western edge of the island hadn't been painted in years. Lucinda, and King Alvarez now lived in the house next to Flo's. King was a likeable sort, but what a rascal. He was not about to paint the house or fix it up.     Jim had loaned Buddy the money to build his house and the boy had done a good job. Since neither Buddy nor Flo had paid the money back, the house

131

now belonged to him and he wondered what to do with Flo. She could live in it for free or he could charge her rent. The business thing to do, of course, was to charge rent. Maybe it wouldn't be necessary to mention it to her if she married Bill Parkins and moved away. A deep sadness pervaded his soul – how could he even think this way – time to go home.

The screen door to his own house didn't squeak a bit. He would oil Flo's tomorrow. His sister Miriam was in the kitchen and motioned him to the table as she grabbed a cup off a hook over the sink and poured coffee for him. The linen sack dress she wore concealed her weight. A good woman, Miriam – strong as an ox – didn't go in much for appearances – not necessary she said. Eight years older than him and never married, she had been living with him since his wife, Harriett died three years ago. "You goin' into Everglades this afternoon?" She sat the coffee on the table in front of him, went to the oven and took out a platter of fresh biscuits.

He watched her move and smelled the bread before he saw it. She brought the platter to the table, sat it on a dishrag before him, went to the icebox and came back with butter and a case-knife. Nobody, but nobody, could bake biscuits like this woman. They were all just about the same size and wonderfully brown on the top and sides. He cut a biscuit in two, laid butter in between and closed it up to let the butter melt throughout. Melted butter showed at the cut and dripped down the sides. "Yeah, I ought to be leavin' right soon. Two now, take a good hour there. May stay over tonight and get back here before first light in the mornin'. You fix me some grub to take?"

"Right here in this paper sack, old man. Flo goin' back to work at the farm?" Miriam pulled up a chair and buttered a biscuit then wiped her hands on the apron.

Jim bit half the biscuit and washed it down with a half cup of coffee, wolfed down the other half and buttered another. "Said she was. Wants to start again on Tuesday. Bill Parkins's been makin' a play for her. She's beginnin' to take him serious. What do you think about that?"

"Did you tell her about the sighting of Buddy over at that Indian Village?"

"For God's sake, Miriam, we don't know it was Buddy there. No call to get her all het up before we know for sure. I questioned the Indians four different times and can't get nowhere with 'em. The man they said was there has disappeared off the face of the earth. Hard-headed, closed-mouth bastards." He removed the pipe from his top shirt pocket, tapped the dead ashes out into a tin ashtray on the table and, with his pocketknife, cleaned the bowl.

"Just the same, she ought to know what you know. If there's a chance that Buddy's alive somewheres, she'll want to wait for him. I know that woman better'n you do. If she's thinkin' about marry'n somebody else, it's just because of them young'uns and her knowin' that Buddy ain't comin' back. That woman truly loved that man." Miriam got up, walked to the sink and came back with the coffeepot and a cup for herself. She refilled Jim's cup and poured one for herself.

Jim opened the Prince Albert can, poured tobacco into the cleaned pipe bowl and tamped it down tight with his middle finger. "What if Buddy is alive, but has run off to get away from here and his responsibilities of marriage and young'uns. Ever thought about that?"

Miriam looked at him with shock and disbelief on her face. "Pure out-and-out hogwash. That man loved Flo and them kids with all his heart and soul. Ain't no way on God's green earth that he'd run off that way. If he's alive somewheres, he's either too sick to come home, or don't know who he is." She got up, went to the sink and busied herself with things there.

Jim scraped a wooden match on the leg of the table and lit the pipe. He puffed hard on it until a good stream of smoke went into his lungs. The exhaled smoke hung a long time over the table. "Guess I better get a move on if I'm to get my business taken care of." He stood, reached for the brown paper bag that contained his supper, and picked his hat off the table. At the door he turned and, with an apologetic tone and look,

133

said, "Why don't you go over and see if you can comfort her some if you get the time. Where's Jimmy?"

"He went down to Lostman's with Ray. They're due back before nightfall. You be careful. That rowdy bunch in Everglades always lookin' for some excuse to jump on you about one thing or the other."

"Don't worry none about me." He stepped through the door and went down to his launch tied at the net spreads to the side of the house.

# CHAPTER 19

King Alvarez, from the vantage point of his front porch, had seen Jim leave his sister Flo's house. Lucy, just a moment or two before, had told him that Jim was planning to go into Everglades City this afternoon. Being cooped up on this island was driving him crazy as a bed bug so he decided he would go into town with Jim. His excuse – needed a part for his boat engine. Really did need a balance wheel, but it wasn't crucial right now. Hadn't been out fishing in two weeks for one reason or another and itchy as hell to be on the move. No one could accuse him of being a homebody – had to be into something all the time – been that way all his life, but particularly since the Great War. He and Buddy used to get into a few scrapes when he was alive, but that's all gone now. Even Buddy had settled down too much. Life was boring as hell around here. Running hooch between Key West and Havana was the better life. Well, so much for the good old days. *Right now I got to hitch a ride with the old man.*

King watched as Jim left his porch and head for the net spreads near his house. *That big man hasn't got over Buddy's death yet – wouldn't believe it then and won't now.* Except for the weathered face, the man still looked like he wasn't much more than thirty. Heavy man, six foot tall and hard as a rock – just as mean, too – a man to keep on your good side. You learned that quick. He was just as tough on his kin as he was on outsiders. "Make a man out of you. Need to be strong in this country," he always said. He had been especially hard on Buddy at times. That may be why he's taking Buddy's disappearance so hard. Probably wishes he had been a little easier on him.

King made it to the boat about the same time as Jim. "Papa, I hear you're goin' into town. Mind if I tag along?"

Jim had just stepped onto the Donella and turned around at the sound of King's voice. He studied the man who had married his oldest daughter, now ten years and near three children ago. Damn, time flies. King was a fair-skinned wiry little man, not more than five foot seven and 150 pounds soaking wet. A daring-do, kind of like his nephew, Robert, ready to fight at the drop of a hat – about the same age as Buddy. He looked hard at King. Them damned Portuguese and their names. Named Juaquin, called King – called that all his life. Kind of favored his mama some.

Jim thought of that hard woman – now Mildred Patavia. Rarely saw her first husband Francisco Alvarez any more – kind of a standoffish sort. He got along right smart with her new husband, Joe Patavia. The missing whiskey, he attributed to King back then, and still did. Figured King and Buddy stole it from the yacht owned by the two men he was guiding for at the time. The fact that the two boys were in the area at the time and that they had been sick as a dog right after had whetted his suspicion. Unusual for Buddy, but King, you couldn't put anything past that boy. "Likely won't be comin' back till late, King. Maybe not even till tomorrow. Got to stop by and see old man Richard on the way for a few minutes. You're welcome, though. What you goin' in for?"

King jumped on board. "Need a balance wheel. Looked like a good time to go in and get it. Pick up a few more supplies, too. Need to stretch out some, too. Know what I mean? Young'uns drive me crazier'n a loon."

*Yeah and going in for a little more than that I suspect.* Jim stored his things in the cabin, moved to the steering wheel and turned the key. The big Ford engine came to life, roaring for a brief moment, then purring gentle as a cat in a lap. The time was 2:45 by his pocket watch and the dashboard clock. King saw to the lines and they cast off. King came into the canopy area and stood looking through the windshield next to Jim. The weather couldn't have been better, the sky, crystal blue with not a cloud anywhere and little or no breeze.

136

Looking straight ahead, King asked, "When you reckon the pompano will start hittin' again? Been a long dry spell for me. You?"

Jim turned the Donella hard to the left around the sandbar at the eastern end of Wood Key for the short run to Mormon Key and his daddy. He filled and lit his pipe. "Near the end of November now, weather startin' to cool. I'd say next week or so we ought to start doin' some good. You gettin' along all right? Money-wise I mean."

"Been tight as a tick these past three months. What little mullet there's been ain't brought no money. With what little Lucy makes at the farm and my crabbin', we've been able to make do." King dug into his pocket and brought out a crumpled pack of Wings and lit one, shielding the match with both hands, then flicked the match over the side.

"Times been tough all around. Maybe this Roosevelt feller will turn things around. There's Mormon Key just ahead. We'll stop there for a minute or two." Jim pulled back on the throttle and the big boat slowed quickly. "Guess you heard Flo's got ideas about marryin' up with Bill Parkins. What do you think about that?"

The fog-horn blast shattered the calm air and caused King to flinch. "Woman's gotta live. Can't keep on hopin' Buddy's gonna come back. Be good if he did, but it ain't likely, I don't reckon. Been about ten months now and no word you can sink your teeth into. Woman's got them three young'uns to look after. Bill's a pretty good man and about as good as she'll get in these woods, I reckon." King ducked into the cabin and came back with a tin cup full of water, drank about half and offered it to Jim, who declined.

"Yeah, I reckon you're right on all counts. Buddy's probably gone for good. She's got to look after herself and them kids." Jim didn't press his thoughts and hopes that the lead from the Indian Village would lead to something positive. The boat came to a stop well out from the sandbanks. King scampered up on deck and dropped the anchor. Old man Harrison put out from the shore in a small dingy.

The old wood-frame house, nestled way back among the scraggily trees and mangroves, was just visible from the boat. The water cistern over to the right was well above ground level and visible at the high end of the beach and near the raised wooden plank walkway. Richard Harrison, at eighty-four, still spry as a chicken, talked non-stop as they walked single file up to the house along the plank walkway which was barely wide enough for one person. The mangroves brushed against them as they walked. The cool breeze kept the mosquitoes at bay.

They stepped through the screen door quickly to keep out the mosquitoes and Mary welcomed them with a fresh pot of coffee. This old unpainted two-room shack had been on the Key for going on fifty years. Jim had no idea who actually owned it or who had first settled in it. The house belonged to whoever was living there at the time. Probably no one ever owned it legally. Mary was near twenty years younger than Richard and just as spry. They had lived among these islands since 1872 and raised a family of seven children. They were still trying to make it on their own – didn't believe in living off anyone else – fiercely independent. That was the lesson the old man had taught Jim as a child and what he was trying to teach his own family. Richard had lived with Jim in the early part of the new century, but had gone off on his own again about 1913. Jim looked out for him without Richard knowing about it. The old man was a proud bugger.

"Saw you coming. Figured you were going into Everglades City. Mary made up a list. When are you due back this way?" Richard turned to King. "Long time no see, Juaquin. How've you been? Lucy and the young'uns okay?"

Jim took out his pipe and tobacco and answered Richard's first question. "Probably about ten or so. That okay?"

Before King could answer, Mary said, "You're damn tootin' we'll be up. If not, take the things on to Wood Key. We'll pick 'em up tomorrow." She tried to refill Jim's cup, but he waved her off.

"Mama, we gotta get goin'. Gotta see Tom Riggs before five. Daddy, will you take us back out to the Donella?" Jim stood and King followed suit. They headed for the door and Richard followed.

They were half-way to Everglades and King was antsy, something obviously bothering him. Jim ignored him. Knowing King, whatever it was would be coming out soon enough.

Finally King came out with it. "Papa, I just gotta ask you. I've asked you before and you never say anything, but I figure I got a right to know what kind of blood is flowin' in my young'uns veins. It's about old man—"

Jim cut him off sharp, "All your kids got fair skin? Got blue eyes? Think they got all that from old man Francisco? Don't you think if there was some tainted blood, it would show up somewhere?" Jim looked straight ahead. *Good God, I don't need that talk today – got enough on my mind.*

"How about Uncle Walter? He's damn near black. Most of his young'uns are dark, too." Lucy's got dark skin, too. Buddy could pass for a breed." King was close up to Jim and getting excited like he always did when this conversation got underway.

The word 'breed' reminded Jim of the Indian village and the old man he confronted there. The man had said a breed was living with him. This kind of talk agitated Jim and now he had quite enough. "Goddam it, King, what do you want from me? Believe what you want to. Now leave it be. Let sleepin' dogs lie, why don't you."

"Just wish you'd tell me the old man's story. Where he came from, his folks and all that. It don't mean a hell of a lot, but I got a burnin' itch to know, that's all."

Jim gladdened at the sight of the fish-house and marina when he turned into the channel leading between the mangrove islands guarding the main island of Chockoluskee. Just around the easterly shore was the river leading up to Everglades City. In a minute or two he would be shuck of King Alvarez for a little while. He could think of his business, maybe have a little relaxation with the boys and a good game of poker. Maybe a couple swigs of a good belly-warming whiskey. "I don't know much about the old man either, but I'll tell you what I'll do. On the way back, I'll tell you what I know if you'll give me the straight skinny on what happened to the whiskey stolen from the Kennedy yacht back in '28." He looked straight at King and fixed him with his best 'King James' stare.

King stared back bravely, but backed off some. "What makes you think I'd know anything about that? I told you back then I didn't know nothin' about that damn whiskey. Don't now." He took out a cigarette and lit it, as if to say the subject was dead.

Jim, himself now again curious about the old man's past, edged the Donella around the east end of Chockoluskee and cruised alongside the small airstrip, then turned east into the Barron River leading up to Everglades City. The airstrip had been built during the great land boom of '24 when speculators and buyers by the drove flocked to the area. It was all over by '26 and all the people had left and things were back to normal again, except now work was scarce as hen's teeth. Mostly crop-dusters used the field now. He slowed the boat to a bare crawl so it wouldn't produce any wake to disturb the boats and lighters tethered to the cement seawalls lining the south side of the river. There were four offshoot canals dug off from the river mostly filled with houseboats and sailboats. Tourists still came down at this time of the year and some boats belonged to normal folks who had no better place to live.

As they passed the Rod and Gun Club, Will Curry, the manager for the last ten years, waved from the outside patio. Will was a good family man and commanded a lot of respect from the out-of-town guests as well as the townsfolk. Jim gave the familiar signal to let Will know that he would be back in a little while for his usual poker game. Will always set the boys up in the gameroom on the first floor just inside the street-side entry door. The room was exclusively theirs for the rest of the night – even had their own bar and bartender. Jim cherished those Saturday nights whenever he could get loose.

Jim took the northern turn of the mirror-smooth river and stopped at the Riggs fish house, an unpainted wood-frame building girded by a plank dock. He spoke to old Raymond Griffin as he maneuvered the Donella next to the dock. "Howdy, Ray. You all right? Fill her up before you leave tonight, will you?"

King tossed a rope noose over the nearest piling, then went to the stern, fixed the rope to the rear piling and jumped onto the dock.

Raymond, black as the ace of spades, and almost as old as Methuselah, showed his broken, rusty white teeth through a wide grin and continued his work cleaning fish at a weather-worn wooden table without missing a beat. "Yessuh, Cap'n James, ah'm jist fine. Ma woman jist fine and ma chillun and ma granchilluns, too. You been all right, suh? How you been, Mister King?" Deftly he slit the fish from gills to tail, cut the guts loose at each end and tossed them into the water. A pelican, sitting on one of the pilings, swooped down and just as expertly plucked the guts out of the water and paddled away from the dock to dine in peace. A toss of the head and the guts were gone. Effortlessly it glided across the water and back to the dock to await another morsel.

Jim hoisted himself up to the dock, grunting a little with the effort and anxious to get his business over with. "Yeah, Raymond, I'm fine and all my people are, too."

King stuffed his crumpled khaki-colored shirt into his pants and tightened his belt. "Ray, right now I'm in powerful need of a good stiff drink of likker. Know what I mean?" Old Ray chuckled aloud, but didn't otherwise respond.

Jim turned and looked at the two men. "King, you ought to be back here by nine. I'll be leavin' then with or without you. Understand?"

"Understand. See you then. If I ain't here just don't wait for me. I'll get along later somehow." King turned and headed towards town. Jim headed for the office.

# CHAPTER 20

Tom Riggs, busy with the never-ending paper work at his desk, glanced at the clock on the wall over the door just as Jim entered the office – four-thirty. Marge had gone home twenty minutes ago – normal procedure for a Saturday afternoon. He had the two glasses and whiskey sitting on the shelf just back of his desk – ritual, too. Jim would produce his receipts for fish brought in during the week, together they would determine the charges and credits, settle up and then have a stiff drink of Old Grand Dad. They would have some small talk then head for the Rod and Gun Club to see who would walk away with the pot tonight.

Tom, just two years younger, had known Jim all his life. The Harrison family had been trading with Riggs Fish Company since 1889. Jim was an astute businessman and the best known fishing guide in the whole area.

After their usual drink which they both quickly downed, Tom poured another for both of them. Jim leaned back in his chair and let out an audible sigh. Tom asked. "That bad, huh? How's the family?"

Jim filled and lit his pipe, took a deep drag, let the smoke escape slowly and watched as it trailed upward to the ceiling, then disappear out the window. "Aw hell, Tom, there's always a lot goin' on, you know that. Nothin' really new. Just wished people would start buyin' again. Got stuff to sell and nobody to buy. Yeah, all the family's fine. Miriam sends her love to you and the family."

Tom took a sip of the whiskey and made a wry face. "I know just what you're talking about. The paperwork mounts, but the dollars don't. Roosevelt said he'd be doing something about it when he takes office next year. Well, let's see just what he can do."

143

Jim toyed with the glass, turning it in his fingers. "In the meantime poor folks with no jobs are starvin' to death. We're kind of lucky down here in the swamps. Just need enough cash to buy the staples – flour, material and stuff like that, you know. Everything else we catch or grow. But cash gets harder and harder to come by. Can't understand how them damned idiots up there in Washington let the country get in this fix anyhow. Just can't understand it."

Tom agreed, "The Goddamned Republicans and their puppet, that no-good Herbert Hoover. That bastard just sat on his hands and watched the country go down, down, down. Makes me madder than a wet hen everytime I think on it. Be glad to see him go. Anybody would be better than him. Lesson number one, don't ever elect an engineer. Too damn technical and tied to the straight and narrow." He downed the rest of his whiskey, poured another and motioned for Jim to drink his, offering to pour another.

Jim waved it off and took a sip of his. "Newspapers say twenty-five percent of the people are out of work. It's no wonder we can't sell anything. Nobody's got any money. No jobs, no nothin'. If it wasn't for the sheriff's pay and the little bit of guide work I do, I'd be flat broke, far as money's concerned. Always got a dollar or two for the game, though." He grinned.

Tom stood and walked to the window overlooking the east canal that went all the way to Highway 41 and then farther east right on up to Port-of-the-Islands. He'd been there once in the heyday of '24. Even thought of putting a little money at risk in the project back then. It had been a bustling resort until the bust in '26. Glad now he hadn't put any money into it. His daddy had warned him and he had been right, as usual. He turned around and gazed at Jim. "If we can believe any politician, and specially Roosevelt at this time, we can expect some government-made work pretty soon. He said he would put the men back to work. I believe him. I voted for him. You?"

Jim tapped the tobacco out of his pipe and cleaned it with his pocketknife. He pulled a piece of paper out of his pocket and handed it to Tom – it was the list given him by Flo. "Would you have old man Raymond fill this order and put it on the boat before he goes home?" He looked at the clock, downed the rest of the whiskey and stood. 5:20 – time to go. "Yeah, I made it a point to vote for him. Didn't vote for nobody last time and look what we got. Republicans will just let us sink in our own misery before they'd let the government get involved. Think their policies are out-dated as hell. Our business done? Let's go relax some."

At the Rod & Gun the poker gang was already sitting at the large round table when Jim and Tom entered. Sitting next to Billy Walker on the right was Sam Perkins. He had a big glass of whiskey in front of him and looked like he'd been into it, and much more, for some time. Sitting next to Sam was Griffin Pardue, dressed in starched and ironed khakis, talking loud and wild to 'Gator' Ramsey who acted like he was enamored with the story. How could these men drink so much and still hold their own in a poker game? Habit, Jim reckoned.

Randy Wade, the last of the bunch, stood next to the bar. He spoke first, "Hey, Jim, Tom. You all ready to shed some of that cash? I'm in mighty bad need of some."

The others looked up as Tom and Jim entered, and when Randy greeted them, everyone started talking at once. Jim went straight to the table and Tom went to the bar. Jim spoke to each of the men and took his assigned place next to Billy Walker.

Maybelle came into the room and spoke with the bartender. All eyes turned to her, including Jim's. The jabbering stopped. She was dressed in a floor length pink-colored gown opened at the top all the way down to her shoulders. Her tanned skin, smooth as a baby's bottom, gleamed under the glare of the lights and reminded Jim of the last time he'd held her close. Her body smell, sweet and lingering, returned to his nostrils and he longed to hold her again. That last time had now been almost three months ago. Where does time get off to? Her eyes swept the room, settled on his and remained for the longest moment, but not long enough for others to notice. Jim paid attention to her and got the message loud and clear – she missed him and definitely wanted to talk with him before he left again. She breezed out of the room as effortlessly as she had entered. The jabbering began again.

Jim removed his brown felt hat and laid it on the table in front of him. "Billy, you reckon you ought to be out after that nasty accident last week? Figured you'd be laid up for at least a week or so."

"I ain't about to miss the chance to take some of your money, Jim." They all laughed.

Three hours later the pile of chips in front of Jim were no bigger or smaller than when he first started. He had just thrown in his hand when Robert Calloway from the Ft. Myers Sheriff's Office motioned for him to step outside. He excused himself from the table and followed the uniformed officer out to the covered porch overlooking the river and well away from the other guests. "What've you got, Bobby?"

"Don't mean to bust in on your game like this, Jim, but thought you'd like to hear the news right away. The Indian boys you're looking for have been found up in Savannah. Sheriff's office there thinks you ought to hot-foot it on up there soon as you can."

"You have an address for 'em?"

"They have all that up there. You just call and tell them when you'll be there and they'll take you to the Indians. Here's the telephone number." He handed Jim a small folded piece of paper.

Jim took the paper, unfolded it and looked at the number a long time. His hopes moved skyward once more. He had not heard anything now going on two months. "By God, this is good news, Bobby. Maybe I'm gonna finally get a solid break in this case. If Buddy's alive, these boys'll know. We'll get to the bottom of this, once and for all. I'll call them the first thing in the mornin'. Much obliged for bringin' me the news."

146

Back in the poker room, Jim picked up his hat and belongings, cashed in his chips, said his good-byes to the boys and walked through the lobby, past the dining room, to the wooden plank walkway near the river. Maybelle was nowhere to be seen. His thoughts turned to the Indians and the hope of finding Buddy as he walked along the lighted way towards his boat. His heightened elation upon first hearing the good news had quickly dampened. So far, every 'Buddy sighting' had been false. Maybe he ought to give it up and go on back to his own life. Since February his life had been in a fog – had to get out of it and soon. But yet, his senses told him that his boy was alive out there someplace and unable to get back home.

Suddenly a beautiful and familiar smell swamped and disrupted his thinking. There she was, now dressed in slacks and shirt, leaning against the rail just out of the light where several small yachts lay tethered in the mirror-smooth water. Without a thought of anyone else, he strode to her and took her in his arms. She came willingly. Her smell overwhelmed him. They kissed and held each other for a long while without talking. Finally she spoke. "Where've you been, Jimmy? Normally, I get to see you at least once a month. It's been over three long months now."

He put his arm around her waist and guided her farther into the darkness off the pathway near several large coconut trees. They sat on a bench beside the water, well off the beaten path. "I know. I've missed you, too, very much. Tryin' to keep up with all my operations and followin' up on all the sightings of Buddy has kept me in a tight ball, and I'm almost done in from it. Now, tonight, I hear of another chance that might shed some light on the mystery of how Buddy disappeared. Got to go up to Savannah soon as I can."

"When can you spend some time with me? I need you, too, you know. Ever since that first night last year I can't seem to get you out of my mind, and when you don't come around for a while, I think I'll just lose it. I almost lost it tonight when I walked into that room and there you were, sitting at the table. I hadn't been expecting you. Jim, I need you very much."

Jim felt a strong urge to take her in his arms and love her right there and then. Reason won over his emotions. King would be at the Donella at 9:00 and he had to be at Morman Key by 10:00 or so. "Belle, I got too many things to do right now. I wish to the man on high that I could stay here with you for a while tonight, but I've got a number of people waitin' on me. Tell you what, though. Why don't you plan to come to Savannah with me? We can make it a three or four-day trip – make up for lost time. How about it?"

"What about my kids and . . . Mama? When are you planning to go?"

Jim looked deep into her eyes. If this gal wanted something, she'd find a way to get it. He could almost see the wheels turning now. "Look, this is a great chance for both of us. I can follow up on a lead to Buddy and we can both have a good time while I'm at it. You think on it. I've got to go pick up a yacht in Miami and bring it around to Chockoluskee on Monday – be on a cruise all next week. I'd say we ought to be on our way no later than a week from this comin' Thursday. You figure a way. I'll pick you up at the bus station in Ft. Myers that Thursday at twelve noon. If you're not there, I'll know you couldn't make it. Got to go now."

"You sonofagun, you . . . ." She threw her arms around his neck and kissed him long and hard. He kissed back.

Jim arrived back at the Donella just a little after nine. Only a little light at the end of the dock gave him any aid in finding his way to her. He stepped down into the boat and began preparations to leave – no sign of King. After another ten minutes passed and still no King, he undid the ropes and shoved off. *Reckon I'll never find out about that missin' whiskey.*

His thoughts stayed on Buddy and his need to go to Savannah to question the two Indians. He recalled that day back in September and how excited he had been when that tall, skinny

Indian over near Lake Okeechobee had told him an injured breed had been staying with him for several months. Although he had tried to convince the old Indian that the man he was looking for had done nothing wrong, the Indian had clammed up completely. Seems the Indians won't hardly even talk to a white man, much less cooperate with him, but with persistence, he had managed to learn that the Indians he was looking for were somewhere in Savannah. The call to the sheriff's office in Ft. Myers had paid off. Hope of finding them had just about gone until tonight. Probably his last chance to find Buddy if he was, in fact, still alive. The Indians were his last hope. *Hope the Georgia police don't scare them off. Question is, though, where'll I find the time to go up there and still do all the other things I gotta do? When it rains, it pours.*

Jim slowed the boat to idle just off Mormon Key and looked to see if Richard or Mary were on the beach. Neither were to be seen. Damn, this seemed to be his night to wait for no-shows. The fog horn blast lingered in the air and echoed among the trees along the beach. He circled for twenty minutes and finally turned the bow towards Wood Key and a good bed. His thoughts and problems to resolve had worn him down.

He set the throttle at a comfortable pace and settled in for the half-hour home. There was just a slight breeze and the seas were unusually calm. Except for the running-lights and a few scattered stars, the night was moonless and almost black. His thoughts turned to King and his curiosity about Richard. Jim reckoned he knew more about the old man than he really wanted to.

He recalled the day many years ago when the old man shared with him the history of his life. He still found it hard to accept the fact that Richard had actually been a slave, living under the rule of a master, even though that master was his father.

Jim relived for a moment the remorse he had felt that day, but that moment was quickly replaced with the feeling of gratitude for his own life when compared to Richard's. He had heard the rumors of colored blood but placed it aside because most of the family, including Richard, had rather light skin. *Now he knew where the rumors came from.* He thought of Buddy, who was a bit darker than the rest, and his features did have some resemblance to coloreds.

He rounded the east end of Wood Key and soon had the Donella docked at his net-spread. There were no lights on at any of the houses except his. Miriam would still be awake. He looked at the clock before turning the cabin light out – it was 11:30. He threw his gear up on the dock, packed and lit his pipe. He thought about Richard and his life, and he thought about his own life. He hadn't paid much attention before, but the old man's manner of speaking was different from most others. Seemed more educated. There's more to his background. One of these days . . . .

*It's sure not easy living down in these islands, but it's the life I know and I wouldn't have it any other way.* Why had Buddy been so fired up all the time about moving away from here? Miriam would be happy to hear about the Indian boys in Savannah. She still had high hopes that Buddy would be found alive, even if she did pooh-pooh the thought. He was her first nephew. Jim looked forward to the trip to Savannah.

# CHAPTER 21

Flo was lying on her left side facing the window when her eyes finally opened. They had been ready to open for an hour or more. Light from the three-quarter moon, about two o'clock high, and a sky full of stars, filtered through the screened window and lightened the morning and the room. Mangroves, a good fifty feet away, and back-lit by the light of the moon, were about eight feet high on that side of the house and grew all the way down to the water, their long, tangled tentacle-like roots continuing out into the water. She lay peacefully staring at the big moon and relishing the cool breeze. It finally dawned on her why everything appeared so clear through the window. The top pane was propped up and the screen without oil. She would have to remember to paint it with oil in the spring to keep the sand flies out. Buddy had always taken care of such details before. Her eyes watered over with the thought of him. She would have to learn a lot if she was to stay in this country without a man.

Everybody had been so kind to her, but somehow they were all different since that awful day in February. She felt alone – somehow not part of the family anymore. Everyone seemed to be trying right hard to make her welcome, but she had a deep-seated feeling that they really wanted her to go and take the bad memories with her. Even her brother, King, sometimes seemed to blame her for Buddy's disappearance. She knew she would have to move on soon, but where to go? She could go and stay with her mother on Captiva for a while, but that likely wouldn't work for very long. Any reminder of the Harrisons was enough to set that woman off. The thought of going back to the drudgery of farm work caused her to shudder, but almost anything would be better than laundry work. Ironing clothes at Mama's house had begun just two days after the baby was born and she had started back at the laundry within the week. She continued there right up to the day before leaving to come back here to Wood Key. *Damn that kind of work anyhow. One day I won't do that slave work anymore.*

When Buddy was alive she had worked at the farm, but only because they needed money so desperately. Now it was worse — her money almost gone. She choked back a sob. Decisions would have to be made right soon, and they never came easy for her. She felt so terribly alone. She stared out the window for another long moment before shifting her eyes to the baby's crib. Through the mosquito net she could see Warren sleeping peacefully with his thumb in his mouth and all his bedclothes kicked off. The cool breeze coming in off the porch from the west didn't seem to bother him. *Buddy, you'd like this little boy. He'll be like you. Papa said he would be something special. Lord God, why oh why did you take my love from me? I need him so much now, and my children will have such a hurtful life because you took him away from us when we needed him the most. What is your plan for him and these children anyhow – and me?* She immediately regretted laying the blame on God. She had been raised in the church and highly respected its teachings even though she hadn't attended service that much in the past. She vowed to start going regularly if she moved to town.

In the single bed on the other side of the room, Junior, at the head was covered entirely with the blanket and Francis, almost off the foot, was bare except for his pajamas. Both were sleeping soundly under the mosquito net. Mosquitoes weren't all that bad at this time of year, but it always proved wise to use the nets for the children – they would be up all night otherwise.

Flo got out of bed and slipped her nightgown on over her pajamas. The wooden floor squeaked. She froze and looked nervously at the children, desperately wanting a moment or so to herself before they woke, demanding most all of her time. If it wasn't one thing it was something else, all the time. She took another step – it squeaked again. None of them moved. She

152

made her way out to the kitchen by the light of the stars and moon. Still a good two hours before sun-up.

She lit a kerosene lamp, turned the wick down real low and put it on the kitchen table. With the few pieces of wood left in the tub, she started the morning fire and put a fresh pot of coffee on the stove. She would have to remember to chop more wood before dark when she returned home this afternoon. Out on the back porch she poured icy cold water into the wash basin that caused her to wince when she splashed some on her face. The water felt refreshing, though, and seemed to give her some vibrancy. She dried with the towel hanging on the back rail and walked the few steps to the toilet, which was partially hidden amongst the bushes, but just barely visible in the glow of the moon. When she pulled on the door it almost broke loose from the single hinge at the top. With any luck at all, Papa would get someone to fix it this week. The normal stench would soon need a good dose of lime powder – another good reason for a man about the house.

The smell of coffee filled her nostrils when she re-entered the kitchen. That smell had to be the best part of early mornings. She especially loved the smell before sunrise when camping on the beach. The thought brought to mind the last time she and Buddy and the kids had gone into Everglades City and spent the night on Rat Key.

It was in November of last year and seemed only yesterday. Buddy had turned a turtle and stole a few of its eggs, which they boiled over the open fire that evening. He would've killed the turtle, but had no way to preserve the meat. She had thought at the time, "How lucky you are, Miss Turtle", and how happy she had been. She didn't have a problem cleaning and cooking the dead critters, but could never bring herself to kill one and could never quite get used to the continual slaughter of living things. She laughed to herself as she remembered Junior and Francis each eating a raw turtle egg and, after they were told that it was raw, how they had run down to the water's edge and scooped salt water into their mouths and ran around making gagging sounds for a half-hour or more. She could sympathize with them because it was hard to tell a raw one from a cooked one – they both looked like little white balls.

After the kids were asleep, she and Buddy had held each other close for a long time and watched the moon and stars move in their path across the heaven. In her mind, she could still see the shooting star which had begun in the south and flew northeasterly toward its destination. It had come out of nowhere as a speck, blossomed to the size of Venus, grew a long tail and disappeared as quickly as it had begun. Nothing could ever equal the thrill she felt that night. Ursa Major hung high in the east – the dipper part at the top. She had awakened that morning to the smell of coffee and Buddy bending over her with a cup of the wonderful brew. She couldn't even imagine then that this beautiful man would soon be taken from her.

Flo turned up the wick in the lamp and poured a cup full of coffee. The light was barely enough to see her way around the room. She sank into the chair and lit a cigarette, inhaled and took a big drink of the wonderful brew. The exhaled smoke, no match for the slight breeze, quickly disappeared. It was 4:36. At six, before sun-up, they would be on their way to the farm. *What will Papa have me doing today?*

The cane fields were definitely not to her liking. Men swung the big sharp machetes and the women toted the cane stalks to the storage and mashing house. She had carried many a cane stalk during her three years at the farm. Ten eight-foot stalks bound together weighed about twenty pounds and she had learned to carry one on each shoulder about one hundred and fifty yards. She cringed a little when the men took swipes at the stalks with the big blades.

They would grab the stalk with their left hand and, with their right, take a mighty swing with the machete. The men were powerful and the blades extra sharp. The swung blade would bite clean through the cane stalk slick as a whistle. They would toss the stalk to the side and move on to the next one. They worked side by side, each working a separate row. Sometimes there would be men working in front of others when they were in a hurry to make a shipment.

She remembered one time in particular when Leonard's darkie took a mighty swing and, for a reason that was never explained, lost his grip on the handle and the blade flew out of his hand and hurtled toward another darkie working about thirty feet ahead in the same row. She had been bundling stalks two rows over and stood dumbfounded as she watched the blade going end-over-end at great speed. The blade moved as if in slow motion. She watched in horror as the darkie in front grabbed onto a stalk with his left hand and raised his right for a swing just as the flying machete reached the same point. Her fist, balled up and stuck in her mouth, prevented her scream from reaching the man. The blade sliced clean through his wrist and continued on for another ten feet before crashing to the ground. The man turned to look at his hand and blood spurted all over him. His hand fell to the ground before he could fully understand what had happened. That was when she realized that the ear-piercing screams she heard at the time were coming from her mouth. The man had looked stunned and unbelieving for a moment, then, holding his wrist, ran screaming back toward the dock. The darkie that had thrown the machete picked up the fallen hand and went running after him. She had felt so powerless. The poor man never came back.

She cared not a whit for making liquor at the still either. If revenuers came, they would take everybody working there. There had never been any revenuers to her knowledge, but some said they had raided the still before and had taken several people away. Her only job there was to haul the pails filled with corn liquor back to the packinghouse where others poured it into gallon jugs.

She liked no part of farm life and dreaded going at all. Looking after the children and housekeeping and cooking for the workers she didn't mind too much. Working in the syrup mill was okay, too. There she would be assigned to one part of the process. She would either be feeding the cane stalks into the

155

grinder, taking the kegs filled with liquid sugar to the boiling pots, tending to the boiling pots or pouring the syrup into jars and sealing them up.

Bill Parkins was surely an escape out of the farming life. His offer may have to be taken for that reason alone, if for no other. She knew she couldn't make it alone very much longer. A tinge of fear rippled through her body and she shivered. The last she'd heard from him was the letter in Key West. Somebody said his mother was sick or something. If he continued to show interest, she would make up her mind before Christmas. If only she could believe that Buddy was still alive – if there were only some real reason to believe. If he were, he would have to be more dead than alive to stay away this long. She just could not and would not believe that he had run off deliberately.

Her thoughts turned to her conversation with Jim yesterday.

It was early Monday and she had been washing the dinner dishes and the kids had been outside playing when she heard his footsteps on the porch. She waited for the knock on the front door, then walked there and held it open.

"Flo, the Indians have been found in Savannah and I'll be goin' up there in a few days to find out what they know about Buddy. Don't get your hopes too high yet, but don't make any hasty decisions either, at least until I get back." He stopped at the door and squirted oil from his can into the hinges and moved the door back and forth a few times. The squeak was gone.

"Hasty decisions about what?" She returned to the sink and dried her hands on the dishrag.

He looked at her understandably and at the baby on the pallet next to the kitchen table. "You know, about marryin' Bill Parkins."

She reached for a cup. "I haven't had much time to think about that, Papa. These young'uns are about to drive me crazy as a baboon. This baby cries all the time, think he may have the colic. Did you ever find out about that law about missin' people and when they're declared dead? You want some coffee?"

He walked to the table and sat down. "Yeah Flo, I reckon I will have a cup. You gotta wait seven years unless you can prove Buddy's dead."

Flo flared up, spilling some of the coffee from the cup she had just poured. She sat the cup with the rest of the steaming coffee before him. "What in the hell am I supposed to do in the mean-time if he don't show up soon. I got young'uns to raise and don't have a pot to pee in." The words broke and tears welled in her eyes as she turned back to the sink hoping he wouldn't see her weakness.

Jim didn't say anything. She dried her eyes on the dishrag and turned to face him. "I'm sorry, Papa. I didn't mean to get riled up like that. I know you're doin' the best you can. It's just that I'm runnin' out of time and I don't know what I'm gonna do." She almost broke down again. The baby started to cry and she went and picked him up.

Jim took out his pipe, scraped the bowl with his pocketknife and knocked the ashes into the saucer. "Flo, try not to get yourself so het up about these things. Everything'll work out all right. I'm not gonna let you starve. You can count on that. You might want to go stay with your mama some till things get a little more settled."

Flo, still visibly agitated, rocked the baby in her arms and walked back to the end of the table opposite from Jim. "Papa, I don't want to leave here. This is my home. This was Buddy's house. Now it's mine. I couldn't leave it." She looked at him and saw his right eyebrow cock up. She read the shock and dismay on his face. He looked as if he had been caught at some dark secret. Normally his face was as unreadable as a rock. Something was dreadfully wrong – her concern deepened. "What's the matter, Papa?"

He looked away and fumbled in his pocket for his tobacco. He extracted it finally, stuffed his pipe and took his time lighting it. He still had not returned her gaze. Fear welled up inside her.

He was hiding something and it had to do with her staying. All of a sudden she was a very scared little girl, all alone in a situation which she could not control.

Finally he looked straight at her. "I've been meanin' to talk to you about that. Time's never been right and it ain't right now. You're in no condition to talk about this now." He stood as if to go. "We'll talk more about it in a few days. Perhaps when I get back from Savannah." His unreadable face had hardened again.

"No, damn it. Tell me now. Is it about Buddy? Is it about the house? You want me to leave?" Her voice got louder and louder. She was losing control again. The baby started to cry. She realized she was squeezing him. She relaxed. Tears welled again and overflowed onto her cheek.

"You're all het up, Flo. Calm down some. You're in no condition to discuss these matters now. I think we best put it off till I come back." He started toward the door. She rushed around the table and grabbed his shirtsleeve.

"Whatever it is, we gotta talk about it now." Her voice broke up again.

He stopped just inside the door, looked painfully at her and said in a measured tone, "This house didn't belong to Buddy and it don't belong to you now. The house is mine and I need to get rent on it to help pay for the lumber and materials. You . . . ."

She clutched his arm. He didn't resist. "But Buddy built it. You said if he did the work it was his. I don't understand. Are you telling me I have to leave if I don't pay rent?" She knew the agony in her face and voice was visible to him and she felt a tinge of regret for baring her feelings, but damn it, she had to find out where she stood.

"I told Buddy then the house was his as long as he lived in it. I didn't mean that he had the title, but just that he could live in it until he left."

Now she understood. She let go of his sleeve. This had been his way to try and keep Buddy tied to the land — under his thumb. His way to maintain control of Buddy. He was so afraid that Buddy would up and leave one day. He had no one else to take over his business when he got too old. "So, what am I to do, Papa? Should I leave tomorrow? Should I . . . ?" She seemed unable to keep from losing control again.

He put his hand on her shoulder. She saw tenderness in his face. "No, Flo, you don't have to go anywhere. You come on over to the farm tomorrow and go back to work. In a few days I'll go to Savannah and see if I can learn anything about Buddy. By the time I get back I ought to have more information. We can make some decisions then. Try to put it out of your mind for a while. You think you can do that?"

Junior tore through the door with Francis crying at the top of his lungs and hot on his heels. The screen door swung back hard against its hinges and then shut again with a loud bang. She thought it might even fall off the hinges. Junior grabbed onto her legs and started going round and round with Francis trying to catch him, all the while yelling for her to stop him. Both boys' mouths were going like a bell clapper.

Jim raised his voice against the din. "I'll see you in the morning, Flo. Bright and early, all right?" He stepped through the door.

She stopped Junior and placed her hand over his mouth to quiet him. Francis caught up. She held the two apart. "Okay, Papa. I'll be ready."

That was yesterday. The news had left her weak and feeling very vulnerable and alone. First she had been overjoyed with the prospects that Buddy might be found, only to learn that she might soon be out on her ear. She had fretted most of the day and had hardly slept at all. Now it was morning and time to go to the damn farm, and she felt like the dickens. Even the coffee and the cigarette hadn't changed things. She poured another cup and lit another cigarette. The inhaled smoke she kept in her lungs for a long moment then released it and idly watched it rise slowly to the ceiling.

Her calm nerves shattered into pieces when Francis let out a blood-curdling scream. She jumped involuntarily, then realized the source and ran into the bedroom. Junior had taken all the blanket for himself and had kicked Francis out of bed. Francis was still screaming as he pulled the blanket off of Junior, who now joined in with his powerful lungs. The baby joined the chorus and the household was now awake and normal once more. She sent Francis into the kitchen and quieted the baby. "Junior, wash your face then take out the chamber pot. While you're at the toilet, put some lime in the hole. The stink is bad enough to stop a mule." She went into the kitchen and put the baby on a pallet near the stove.

Junior followed her into the kitchen. "Why do I always have to empty the pot? Why can't Francis do it sometime?" He sat in a chair at the table and stuck out his bottom lip.

Flo turned on him. "You get in there and get that pot and empty it and don't give me no back sass. Boy, you better learn to watch that mouth or you'll get a good smack in the face." He put his elbows on the table and his face in his hands. She started for him and he jumped up crying and went into the bedroom. In a minute he came out with the pot and went out the backdoor.

Flo sifted flour into a bowl, made the mix for johnnycake and poured it into the hot frying-pan on top of the stove. The water in the pot began to boil and she poured in a measure of grits and added salt. Junior came in and joined Francis at the table and she gave them each a bowl of grits and a slab of johnnycake. She poured hot fish grease over the grits and stirred the mixture. Warren seemed content with his bottle of warm milk. The house was quiet again for a while. She smoked a cigarette and made ready for the ride to the farm.

# CHAPTER 22

Before sun-up, the Donella, loaded with all the women-folk and young'uns, rounded the east end of Wood Key and made its way across the bay to the farm. Stars faded in the dim glow of the sun, which still hid below the horizon far to the east. The Big Dipper, bright and pretty as ever, was still not too high in the east. As always, when she looked to the heavens she thought of Buddy and wondered what he could possibly be doing today, if he was indeed alive. She tried to form a picture of him somewhere else and couldn't. The only picture of him she could bring up was the day he left. That was a picture she could not get out of her mind. The moon, still in all its splendor from earlier, was three o'clock high and slightly to the south. The bay was mirror-smooth except for the wake provided by the Donella as she plowed her way along.

Flo leaned against the stern and held Warren close to her bosom. The slight breeze out of the north was hardly enough to ruffle the thin jacket she wore unbuttoned. She shivered, though. The cold seemed deep-seated within her body. She tucked the blanket closer around the baby. Junior and Francis were strangely quiet, sitting on the floorboards near her booted feet. Francis snuggled up around the cloth bag of dirty clothes to be washed at the farm. Lucy and Adele had brought bags, too. She wondered who would be chosen to do the laundry today. In a way she hoped it would be her. Anything would be better than the farm jobs. She looked long at the children. They seemed cold, too. The thought of that night last November on the beach with Buddy filled her to overflowing. The Dipper was almost in the same position. Her upper lip quivered as she fought to hold back the inaudible sobs and quickly looked away from the others.

Jim's broad back stood out plain in the dim light of the cockpit as he held onto the helm and steered a course to the edge of the mangrove on the eastern shore. Lucy stood next to Flo with her two boys holding onto her legs. Adele stood next to Jim and clutched her baby boy to her chest as if to shield him from the cool air. The baby, a dark skinned boy, was just a month younger than Warren. No one had spoken a word since they pulled away from the dock – still too early and too near the weekend. Tuesdays, like Mondays, were always like that, especially this one. It had been close to four months since she had worked on the farm.

Flo broke the silence as Jim maneuvered the Donella through the channel between the mangroves on both sides and made a sharp turn to the north to keep from scraping against the felled pine lying at the shoreline. "Lucy, what you reckon Papa will have me doin' today? You all been real busy since I been gone?"

"We been clearin' mostly. Gettin' ready to plant the winter crop. Been makin' a good amount of hooch. Some syrup, too. Corn's ready. So's the cane. Alligator pears about picked out. 'Nough work to go around, though, I reckon. You feelin' up to workin'?"

"Yeah. I'm good, but how about you? That baby looks like he's ready to come right now."

"Won't be long now, any luck at all. I'm all right. Do get tired a lot quicker than I used to, though. Papa understands and is always on to me about workin' too long without rest."

The Donella stopped short and Flo and the others had to hold on to keep from being thrown forward. Jim brought her around and docked with the bow to the south. Jimmy jumped to the dock with the tie rope.

Flo nudged the boys with her toe. "Where's King? He go fishin' with Jake?"

"Don't get me started on that bastard, Flo. I know he's your brother and all, but if I could get my hands on that sorry no-good today, I'd choke the life out of him. That sorry bugger went into Everglades with Papa Saturday and hasn't come back

162

yet. Don't know where he is and don't really give a damn at the moment." Lucy pouted her lip and reached down for her things, which she had wrapped in an old blanket, and pulled at Albert at the same time. Ricky had already jumped up onto the dock. Then she laughed aloud, showing the whitest and the most even front teeth Flo had ever seen. What a beauty this gal is, she thought. No telling what kind of a man she could've caught in town. "I love that rascal, though. Wouldn't trade him for nothin' in the world." She laughed with the familiar cackling sound and moved to the side to climb onto the dock. Flo shook her head, but said nothing as she gathered her things.

Jim cut the engine and Jimmy secured the bow. Flo woke her boys and climbed up on the dock. The boys walked along the clearing through the mangroves near the water's edge and wandered towards the frame houses. The dock was old and rickety and higher than the boat. Papa had been promising to fix it for years. She reached down, pulled Albert onto the dock, grabbed Lucy's hand and helped her up. Papa gave Adele a boost.

They all walked to the farm buildings without further talk. The others would be here soon. For now they would get the young ones settled and get prepared for the work at hand. It would likely be a grueling day – the days here always were – usually long and hard.

There had to be a better life than this. How would she ever know? The life of fishermen and farmers seemed to always be the same, generation after generation. What person in his right mind would bring his family down into this God forsaken country to live this kind of life? She knew her daddy's family were grape growers and wine makers back in Portugal. Why did he become a fisherman in the first place, and why did he come to this country and produce a bunch of young'uns to carry on in the same fashion, who in turn produced young'uns to carry on the same way? When she saw her mama again she would ask that very question. Where was her daddy, anyhow. She couldn't remember ever seeing him since the divorce when she was only about eleven. Mama was from Mississippi and her family were not fishermen. Didn't know much of anything about their backgrounds. Maybe they were farmers. Grandma Young was descended from Samuel Peterson, who came from New Market, a small village near Cambridge, England. Grandpa Young was a sailor from Bristol, England and she knew nothing more about that family. She momentarily had a strong longing for Buddy. He had promised to take her out of these woods. God, she missed him so much.

"Flo, Flo." She looked up and saw Jim yelling at her and waving for her to go to him. He stood by the building used for gasoline storage. She looked to see that Junior and Francis were all right, then walked over to him. She would get her orders now.

"Flo, I think it'd be a good idea if you'd look after the nursery and help Lucy with the cookin' and housekeepin' chores today and the rest of this week. Give you a chance to ease back into the routine. I'll be on a cruise the rest of this week and part of next. I'm thinkin' about goin' up to Savannah Thursday after next. Should be back by Sunday, the 4th. Hopefully, I'll have some good news by then. That okay with you?"

"It's all right by me, Papa. Sure could use some good news. Will the schoolmaster be here today?" Might be better to work the cane fields than have to tend to all the young'uns.

"Yes, Mr. Roberts should be here any minute now. You won't know him. He's the young feller that took over for Mr. Wimberly right after you went to Key West to have your young'un. He started the new term in September and seems to be doin' a fair enough job. Don't think he can hold a candle to Mr. Wimberly, but I reckon we're lucky we got anybody to come way out in these woods. Better than goin' all the way down to Key West, though. Anyhow, you know what to do. Ray'll probably make the run tomorrow. If I don't see you this afternoon, I'll see you when I get back." He turned and walked towards his office in the far building next to the packinghouse.

She nodded to him as he turned to go, but her mind stayed on old Mr. Wimberly. He was a wonderful teacher. He knew so

164

much and had such a way with all the students, young and old. He taught all grades, kindergarten through twelfth. Where had he gotten all his know-how? Buddy had gone to his classes every chance he had and was Mr. Wimberly's prize student. Buddy couldn't get enough learning. At one point, Mr. Wimberly had told her that he had taught Buddy everything he knew and couldn't teach him anymore. Buddy just absorbed everything like a sponge, he had said. Buddy had finally stopped going, but he continued to read all the books Mr. Wimberly got for him. She sometimes wished she had the same desire for knowledge that Buddy had. With a few exceptions, she was content to simply live her life for the time being. There were no desires burning holes in her at the moment except to get far away from this darned farm. She thought about her long-ago itch to gain knowledge in archeology and go digging for old relics. Maybe if Buddy came back . . . .

Flo walked past the long east/west building where packing crates were made, rounded the produce-gathering building and headed to the long building that housed the nursery, kitchen and school. The sun had just broken over the tree tops and glints of the bright stuff brushed the tall cane stalks as far as she could see. It was already warmer than out on the boat. She noted the drabness of the unpainted wood buildings and the darkies milling around, waiting to get started. They looked at her as she passed, but said nothing. She called to Junior and Francis who were still running in and out of the cane field with several other children their age. They came running and met her at the door to the nursery. Lucy was there, as was Adele. Others were beginning to trickle in. She would probably have five or six little babies to tend to as well as some little hellers. Most of the children would be in school. Junior and Francis would go, too. That would be some relief. He and Francis would not be fighting under her petticoat all day.

The room, bare with unpainted walls, contained a pot-bellied stove in the middle, three straight-backed wooden chairs and one cane rocker. A bucket near the stove contained wood cut up in small pieces, ready for the first sign of cold weather. On a large shelf at the rear of the room were several small blankets that served as pallets for the children to sleep on. The room was a little chilly, but not enough for a fire. The sun would soon warm it.

Flo nodded at Lucy and Adele and went directly to the blankets, chose one and spread it on the wooden floor not too far from the stove. She placed Warren on it and gave him a nipple to suck on. With any luck he would be asleep in a minute or two. Adele had already placed her child there, too.

Flo said, "I'm supposed to help you some in the kitchen today, Lucy. Got to watch the kids and do the wash, too. How about you, Del? What's he got you doin' this week?" Flo liked Adele. She was a dark-skinned beauty – had a little mole just at the top of her lip on the right side. About five feet five and a hundred and fifteen, she reckoned. She could probably get any man she wanted, but she had chosen Jake from amongst them all. A proud woman who stood up to the best.

Adele stood up from tending to her baby on the pallet. "Papa put me at the still again. Been there near on a month now. Lucky I don't drink the stuff, I'd be a sot for sure."

Lucy broke in, "I'll be doin' the cookin' the rest of this week. Guess he thought I needed a break from the heavy work with this young'un due any time now – expect next month at the latest. Wouldn't it be a cat's meow now if it was born on Christmas day? Sure hope it's a girl. King really wants one."

Flo stepped to the door to check on Junior and Francis. They were playing some kind of chasing game in the dirt road getting filthy dirty. Some folks headed towards the cane fields. She noticed some other women with small children heading in her direction. "Looks like I'll be in the nursery for the rest of the week anyhow. Figured since I've been off for so long he'd ease me back into it."

"Good. You and me work good together in the kitchen. I reckon I'll mosey on over there and get things started. Flo, you come on over when you get things settled here." Lucy went through the door and disappeared.

Flo watched through the open wall separating the kitchen from the nursery until Lucy entered the kitchen and waited for the other mothers to show up. Adele bent over her baby and straightened his blanket. "Flo, what you gonna do? You gonna stay around here or go be with your mama? I been worryin' about you some, gal, ever since Buddy went off."

"I don't know, Del. Don't really want to go live with Mama. She means well, but she's too old-fashioned, don't know what goes on in a young woman's head. Know what I mean?"

"Well, you and me are both twenty-three and your mama's about sixty or so, I reckon. Guess she is a little out-dated, but this is a mighty hard country for a woman with three young'uns and no man to look after her. I heard some talk about Bill Parkins. Anything to that?"

"Some. He's as much as told me he wants to marry me. He's written me several letters, but that's all. I keep waitin' on some word from Buddy." Her voice quivered and her eyes filled and overflowed onto her cheek. She smeared the tears with the back of her hand, then removed the bandanna from around her neck and wiped them away. She tried hard to smile and looked away from Adele as her mouth quivered and distorted from the near-cry. "I know in my heart Buddy's not comin' back, Del. I sure do hope he is, though, and Papa keeps that hope alive, but deep down, I know. He's gone." Could Adele really understand her predicament?

Adele brought her close and patted her shoulder. They were both about the same height and build. "There, there, Flo. I've never had such an experience, but I can imagine what you're goin' through. Know the pressure's on, but I've got a feelin' that you'll do what's right when the time comes. I've heard that Bill is a fine man. Know he's sure a looker, and you could do a lot worse." She laughed as she headed out the door. "Try to give Buddy a little more time if you can. I'll see you around dinner time."

Flo watched Adele walk across the road and disappear around a stand of cane. She dabbed at her eyes. Other women came in with their babies. The school bell rang. She yelled for Junior and Francis to get on over to the schoolhouse.

Flo was outside getting ready to take the clothes out of the pot with her jobbing stick when Bill Parkins came through the back door of the nursery. She saw him from the corner of her eye. Strains of "How Deep is the Ocean" filtered into her ears from the radio in the kitchen. The image of his flaming red hair, straight and neatly trimmed, stayed with her long after she turned away from him. The sun was just overhead and a little to the south – about an hour before noon, she reckoned. The children would be getting out of school for their dinner break soon and Lucy would be looking for help any minute now. She lifted some clothes from the pot on the end of her stick and let the boiling hot water run off into the pot. She swung around and laid them across the clothesline and came face-to-face with Bill.

"Hey, watch out there, gal." He jumped out of the way to keep from being scalded by the hot wet clothes and grinned, showing a mouth full of pearly white teeth.

Flo acted surprised. "Bill, you startled me." She took his measure quickly. As Adele said, he sure enough is a handsome-looking man. Lean and muscular, about five foot ten. Although she had not seen him in several months, she was surprised how fresh and recognizable he was. He had begun paying more attention to her even before the discussion of Buddy's disappearance died down. She had noticed him, too. Who wouldn't? He was a quiet man, but he stood out in a crowd. "Where'd you come from?"

"I been tryin' to track you down. Thought you was still in Key West. When'd you get back? You get my letters?"

"Been back about three, four days. Tryin' to get myself back into the swing of things. First day on the job today. How you been? I got your last letter just before I left Key West." She continued with the clothes she had laid on the line. With the

168

stick she separated them on the line so they could dry better. She looked at the sun again and moved back to the pot to pick out another stick full.

"I want to talk serious with you, Flo. Can't you stop workin' long enough for that?" He moved away from the dripping clothes she hefted from the pot to the line.

"Bill, I'd love to talk to you, but I've got to get these clothes hung out and get these others started. School will be lettin' out in just a few minutes and I've got to get in there and help Lucy in the kitchen and tend to them young'uns in the nursery. Papa don't cut nobody no slack around here. You know that. A day's work for a day's pay, he likes to say." She began to wring out the clothes that had cooled down some, leaving enough dampness to help with the ironing to come later.

"When can I come callin' so we can talk? I've got to run down to Cape Sable for a few days. Should be back by Friday. Maybe we can have a drink then, too." He moved around so the clothes wouldn't get between them.

"Might be better if we could meet in town. I'll be goin' in to Ft. Myers with Lucy on Saturday. Maybe we could meet in front of the Edison Theater then go get somethin' to eat in the Arcade. I'd like that. I can get Lucy to watch the kids for a little while." She wondered what he had going at Cape Sable. Dressed in pressed khaki pants and shirt, he surely wasn't dressed for fishing.

"Okay, look, if I get back across here before Saturday, I'll drop by your house. If not, I'll see you in town about noon time." He came to her and took her hand in his. "Flo, I want us to get married, and I want to do it right now. You've put me off long enough, gal." He looked deep into her eyes.

She looked into his pale blue eyes and saw the sincerity in there. She felt a strong urge to accept his offer there and then – and almost did. The school bell rang and the clamor and din of the children's shouts drowned out whatever thoughts she harbored. She squeezed his hands. "I guess I'll see you on

Saturday, if not before." The children came running around the building towards the kitchen yelling at the top of their lungs.

Bill's face lit up with a big grin and he said, "See you Saturday." He turned and walked off.

# CHAPTER 23

Buddy watched from his vantage point at the side of the road as Andre made a U-turn in the middle of Highway 441 and headed back to Liz's place. Andre seemed grave.

He waved and tried to smile as he drove by and yelled something, but the wind carried it away before Buddy could hear it plainly. Buddy yelled, "See you in a couple of weeks," and wondered if the words would overtake the speeding car. Andre gave no indication that he heard.

Andre had been sad on the drive out and had hardly spoken at all. Buddy felt sad for him and wished he didn't have to leave. These people had become family to him and he cared for them deeply. He and Andre had become very close over the past several months and he felt a special sadness for Liz, too. He had come to love and respect her as he figured he would a mother. The parting had been heart-wrenching for both of them. They had tried unsuccessfully to shield their tears from the other. Finally, they had hugged for several minutes and then unashamedly wiped the tears away with their bandannas. She told him there would always be a place there for him, no matter what, and there would always be a special place in her heart for him. If, for any reason, he was unable to find his other life, come on back and take up the one he began here. They made a good team and understood each other.

When he went through the door this morning and started down the steps, she had come up to him and placed something in his shirt pocket that looked green like paper money. She said, "I've been saving for you a piece of every dollar earned in the salvage yard. This is your share. Go with God." He had come damn near crying out loud. He had turned away abruptly and said over his shoulder, "See you in a few weeks, Liz." She stood on the porch, sporting her ten-gallon hat, until he and Andre

171

were out of sight. He could still see the sorrow in her eyes and face. The tears came into his eyes again. He wiped them away with the back of his hand.

The weather looked promising and bode well for a good trip to Savannah. Where he was, just north of Okeechobee City, the sky was almost completely blue with just a few low white puffy clouds drifting lazily towards the northeast. The sun was almost straight up, but a little to the east and to the south. He reckoned it to be about eleven. There was just a hint of a breeze.

He stood on the east side of the highway, just north of a dirt road that intersected it on both sides. At the northwest corner was an old unpainted ramshackle building with a roof that came out in front to cover what once were gas pumps – a filling station. The gas pumps had long been removed. There were unpainted, wooden vat-like affairs sitting on benches that could once have been used to hold produce for sale. That activity, too, was long past – the wood rotted and barely held together. High weeds grew up alongside the building and into the runway beneath the overhanging roof. Three crows sat perched on the edge of the roof, either just relaxing in the sun or waiting for some action to occur which might provide food or some other interest. One flew off and headed south. The others promptly followed.

A pick-up truck approached and Buddy stuck out his thumb. The truck, the back stacked high with crates of vegetables, slowed and turned west on the dirt road running alongside the old building. The old, grizzled-looking man did not acknowledge Buddy standing there. The dust, kicked up by the tires, drifted his way, settled on his white shirt and the denim jacket he carried under his left arm. He tried to brush the dust off the shirt, dirtying it more. Wearing that shirt for the trip was a big mistake. He breathed in some of the dust and coughed aloud to prevent the dust from entering his lungs. Some of the dust settled on the blue colored bag on the road by his feet. All his possessions, except what he wore, were in that bag – not much. Another clean denim shirt and pants, two pairs of socks, tooth brush, comb and his old brown felt hat with the floppy brim. That hat belonged to his other life. Toby had saved it for him. No other cars were in sight from either direction.

Buddy picked up the bag, crossed the highway and went into the old building. Inside, dark long shafts of sunlight played with and against each other on the dirt floor as the loose boards shivered in the slight breeze. A little heavier wind would surely end the building's life. Apparently somebody had been there and removed all the floor planking and the four by fours. From outside, the building had looked rather solid, but now he noticed gaping holes and large separations between the boards. The smell of rotting wood was everywhere. Scorpions scattered and disappeared under a pile of rotting boxes when he entered.

He removed the white shirt and replaced it with the denim, carefully folding and packing the white one in the bag after he removed his old hat. It had turned quite warm so he put the denim jacket in the bag and removed the white Stetson Liz had bought for him when they went to the fair a month or so ago. He brushed off the dust that had settled on the brim with his hand and placed it in the bag on top of the jacket. He placed the old hat on his head and pulled the brim down low on his forehead, almost hiding his right eye from view. With the bag in hand, he crossed the highway just in time to put his thumb out for a truck with high slat sides full to the brim with winter vegetables. The truck slowed and pulled over just north of the intersection.

Up on the wide running board, Buddy pulled the door open, climbed into the cab and placed the bag at his feet. A big hairy hand shifted the gear into first and the truck lurched forward. "Where you headin' fer, young feller?"

Buddy looked up from his bag and took serious note of the man. He couldn't judge his age, but the face was thin and well sun worn. Thin and finely engraved lines went from his eyes to the back of his neck. No doubt his had been a life long in the sun and hard to the labor. The hand shifted the stick again and then again, finally settling with the highest gear. The hand stayed awhile on the big black knob of the gearshift. The fingers with stubby blondish hairs above and below the joints were long, the fingernails dirty. Buddy glanced at the dashboard. The speedometer read forty-nine and the gas indicated almost empty. The temperature gauge was climbing up to the red mark. The man spat a dark brown liquid out the window and wiped his mouth on his shirtsleeve, leaving a dark streak there.

Buddy said, "I'm headin' for Savannah. Goin' there to meet kin. Much obliged for the lift, mister."

"No need to thank me, son. Been in your shoes before. Hiked these roads a many a time when I was a young'un like you. 'Course, back then weren't many a car on the road. Lucky to catch the back of a hog wagon." He spat again. "Ain't goin' fer. Just this side of Yeehaw. About thirty mile, give or take. Be some help to you, though, I reckon. Where you haulin' from? You been standin' out there long?"

"Reckon I been out there about an hour or thereabouts. Much obliged for however far you can take me. Glad to get in out of the sun. Breeze feels good. Been livin' on a farm south of Okeechobee for the past few months." Buddy removed his hat and held it in his lap.

The old man looked at him longer than he should have and ran off the side of the road. He slowed down and quickly corrected. Buddy, a little unnerved at the experience, looked intently at the man. "Somethin' wrong, mister?"

"Don't get me wrong, son. I ain't got nothin' aginst Injuns, but I ain't seen too many of 'em up north of the lake. Had a run in with a bunch near Moorehaven when I was a shaver and ain't cottoned to 'em much since. Keep 'em at a distance. Cain't trust none of 'em, you know. No offense, understand." He glanced at Buddy then back at the road. He showed no indication of stopping.

The experience at the tavern during the fair in Okeechobee came rushing to mind. Those men simply had no like for Indians and definitely didn't want them in their hangouts, no matter who they were or how well off they were. If they were Indians, they were not worthy to be in the same company with a white man. He had tried then to understand the hatred he saw in the faces of those men in the tavern and later on at the fair when they knocked Andre to the ground and started pushing Consuela. They probably would've killed Andre had he not stepped in. He couldn't understand either why none of the men in the crowd offered any help to the old man. He had a flashback of a dark-skinned man being taunted the same way. A man was calling him 'boy' and trying to make him pick up something on the ground. The crowd there was yelling, "Kill the goddam nigger." He had a momentary glimpse of the separate water fountains in a department store somewhere. The memory left and he felt flushed and fought to control his anger. He stared intently at the man. His eyes felt so hard and strained he thought they might pop out of his head. His lips had compressed into a sharp thin line and he knew his body was getting ready for action. "I'm not Indian, but I'll get out right here if you'll stop."

The man glanced at him then stared straight ahead. "Forget it, son. It ain't nothin' personal with me. Grew up that way. Taught from a boy that niggers and Injuns just ain't the same as white folks. They're a different breed. Branched off from a common stem long, long time ago. I never did take to that teachin' one hundred percent, but you do have to wonder why they look so different from us. Would've taken you for Injun with that long hair hangin' in one braid way down your back. Didn't notice it till you took your hat off. Can see now it's not coal-black like most Injuns. See a little curl to it, too, now that I take a closer look. See your eyes are green with just a hint of blue, not like the dark eyes of a Injun. You got some Injun in you? You live with Injuns down south there? What they call you?" The man smiled.

The smell of danger faded away. Buddy's muscles relaxed and he felt the tension drain off a mite. "Don't know if I've got Indian blood in me or not. Been called a breed sometimes. Picked up by some Indians who said I was more dead than alive when they found me. Shot in the back of the head with buck shot from long range. Their kin nursed me back to health.

175

They're like my family now. I owe 'em my life. They call me, Curly." They both laughed – the spell broken.

"That who you goin' to see now?"

"Yeah. The shotgun blast to the head caused me to lose my memory. Know next to nothin' about my past life. Hopin' I can talk them into takin' me back to where they found me and hopin' more that somethin' there will trigger my memory back to normal."

The man looked straight ahead at the road. "What's the matter with your voice? Kind a hoarse like."

"Been like that about a week now. Had a cold a while ago. Thought the voice was clearin' up. Still a little scratchy, huh?"

The old man looked long and solemnly at Buddy. "You know, ain't it the truth, just look around you and there's always somebody that's worse off than you. Man ought to be happy with what he's got. Ain't it the God's truth now?" He pointed to a dirt road to the left and said, "That's where I turn off, but I'll go ahead and take you on into Yeehaw. Better chance of gettin' another ride from there. You know that name Yeehaw brings to mind a strange quirk among white folks. They come into this country and fight and kill off the Injuns to push 'em off the land they held first, then, after they take it away from 'em, turn right around and name towns, rivers and lakes after 'em. Don't make no sense, do it?" Buddy shook his head.

Yeehaw was just a small bend in the road and Buddy left the old man and the truck where 441 crossed 60. "Thanks a plenty for the ride and the talk. You're okay, mister. I reckon you could get along with Indians if you gave it a try." He slammed the door and the truck pulled away. Steam came out from under the hood. That truck wouldn't go much farther without adding water to the radiator. A small flock of white heron feeding and milling about across the highway, started to run away from the loud, hissing, moving truck and slowly and gracefully lifted into the air. They never seemed to get startled – move just enough to stay ahead of possible danger. Man didn't disturb them too much along the highways and fields, so they generally felt safe.

Buddy stood at the northeast corner in the short grass just off the highway, bag at his feet, hat pulled low to fend off the glare of the afternoon sun, which was almost directly overhead, but leaning just a little to the west. On the northwest corner directly across the road was a dilapidated filling station. A faded metal sign at the top of the overhanging roof said to the world that it was Ryland's Texaco Station and Store. The price for regular gas, 10 cents a gallon, was marked in bright red letters on a small sign hung on an A-frame at the north edge of the clearing – Diesel 6 cents. The once white paint was peeling in most spots on the building.

An old rusted tractor with huge tires with heavy treads came lumbering east on Highway 60 and turned onto the dirt driveway in front of the store. The man drove it in front of the two pumps, circled around, came back on the inside and stopped between the pumps and the building. A young boy in overalls came out of the screen door and spoke to the man driving the tractor. The boy walked to a pump, removed a hose and stuck it into the side of the tractor and began turning the crank to build up pressure in the pump. First one way then the other. The driver went into the store.

Buddy looked at the large billboard far back off the road on his side. It, too, was old and faded. An animal with a large hump on its back and a man smoking a cigarette covered most of the sign. He could barely make out the message. 'I'd walk a mile for a Camel', it looked like. He reached in his pocket, brought out the makings, rolled and lit a cigarette. A 1930 Chevy came along, pulled off the road in front of him and stopped. He ground the cigarette under his heel, ran to the car and got in. After the pleasantries, they rode mostly in silence all the way to St. Cloud, a good piece in just over an hour. The man let him off on the other side of the city.

He was not so lucky here. There were not many vehicles on the road at this hour. He could either go back to St. Cloud and spend the night or start walking for Kissimmee, about twelve miles away. In the darkening sky he saw rain in the near future.

Dark clouds hung close to the far horizon, occasionally brightened by a flash of light. Still to early to turn in so he decided to walk.

After an hour of walking the first car came along, passed him by and turned off at a farmhouse about a half-mile up the road. Trees grew right up to the edge of the long, narrow road. Most of the time he walked in the short weeds along the side of the road. Finally an old rusty truck stopped for him and he climbed in the back and sat among a bunch of old tires, gas drums and pieces of rusted iron pipes.

Buddy beat on the cabin of the truck to get the drivers attention when they passed the intersection of 441 and 17. The truck finally stopped three long blocks beyond. He thanked the man, walked back and went into the men's room marked 'white' at the filling station on the northeast corner, a block north on Highway 17. In the restaurant the smells reminded him that he hadn't eaten since early morning. His stomach growled for attention, but he settled for a cup of coffee to go and took up a position just north of the station, planning to continue on until he was really hungry and tired. He figured he could go on for another four hours or so.

CHAPTER **24**

Jim parked the roadster on 1st Street and walked across to the Fort Myers Greyhound Station keeping his eyes peeled for any sign of Maybelle. Should be a lot more traffic for a Thursday at this time of day. The plan had been to meet her about noon in the parking lot. He was already an hour and a half late. There were a number of people milling about or just sitting on their luggage awaiting the arrival of the bus from Naples for points north.

He strained to pick her out, but saw no sign of her. Probably left by now, he thought disgustedly. Shouldn't have let those damn Yankees hold him up Monday afternoon - caused him to be late getting the yacht into Cape Sable for the fishing in the Gulf on Tuesday and Wednesday, which, in turn, caused delay in catching the boat out from there to Lostman's today. The fishing had been good, though, and next week he would guide another group on the same yacht. This was the kind of work that had built his reputation with the big-wigs in Washington and all along the East Coast. Anyone wanting to fish in southwest Florida was told to contact Jim Harrison first. There was a waiting list for his services. People came from all over now to fish and tour with King James – some mystery about him didn't hurt his reputation either.

His shoulders squared and he strutted a little as he wandered into the Arcade Plaza hoping to bump into Maybelle – hope she would understand. Hoped he hadn't missed her, be a long, lonely trip without her. The cool air inside smelled good. The Arcade, with its blue, highly polished marble floors, curved from 1st Street around to Edison Avenue. There were probably fifteen stores on both sides of the floor. His heart skipped a beat when he saw her in front of the Arcade Theater looking at the billboard of coming attractions. She turned, saw him, and in soft

179

moccasin-like footwear, ran toward him. She threw her arms around him and hugged him tightly.

"I was so afraid something had happened to you. I didn't know what excuse I would use if I had to go back to Everglades. What happened to you? I was so worried." She started to cry softly.

Jim held her close and massaged her back between the shoulder blades. "Everything is all right now. Got hung up in Miami. I had no way to let you know that I'd be a little late." He gently moved her back a bit. She took her hanky out of her purse and dabbed at her eyes. The long chiffon, powdery blue dress with a large collar was buttoned tight at the neck. The belt, pulled tight, accentuated her small waist. Her blonde hair hung down below her shoulders. He fought the overwhelming urge to take her in his arms right there and then. "Come on, let's get on the road. Where're your bags?" Hand-in-hand they walked towards the bus station.

She scampered to keep up. "It's at the ticket counter."

A little before two o'clock they crossed the Edison Bridge and started north on Highway 41. He would take 17 north at Punta Gorda. It was a long trip to Savannah, but it would be a pleasurable trip with Maybelle along, though. He felt easy and comfortable when he was with her and glanced at her now. "Figure we'll drive about six, seven hours today. Stop just this side of Jacksonville." Their eyes locked knowingly.

Just south of Arcadia the steering wheel began to jerk in his hand. The sound and rumbling came from the right rear tire. Dammit, a flat. He slowed to keep from ruining the tire and inner tube. He fought the wobbling steering wheel and pulled over to the side of the road. No other cars were about. Dammit, he had told Ray to check everything on the car to make sure there would be no problems like this. If he had him here now, he would strangle him. Jim started to kick the tire, but thought better of it. He extracted the jack and other tire tools and set to the task of patching the tube. Two cars passed without slowing down. He didn't really expect them to. Cars on the side of the road fixing flats were a common sight these days.

"Maybelle, honey, you better step out of the car so I can lift it up. There's some whiskey behind the seat. Fix us both one and throw me that old rag there, too. Don't want to get myself all greasied up."

The culprit that caused the flat was a big screw. Must have picked it up just outside of Arcadia. He scraped around the hole in the tube with the lid from the patching can to get it good and clean. Pre-cut patches would not fit the gaping hole. He had to cut a large patch to cover it. The sun beat down on him causing him to sweat from the exertion. He applied glue to the tube and pressed the patch on with the patch lid. The tire easily went back on the rim, now ready for air.

He stood up to retrieve the pump and Maybelle thrust the drink into his hand - whiskey cut with water in a tin cup. She had one, too, and clinked her cup on his. "Here's to us and the day when we can be together always." She looked into his eyes.

He looked into hers, too, seeing the desire hidden there and knowing the meaning behind the words. They had been over that topic many a time, and he was still unable to completely forget Harriet. He'd been with that woman through thick and thin and her memory seemed unerasable. Maybelle was a convenient and comfortable spot in his life, but if push came to shove, he would simply have to move on, at least at the present time. He and Maybelle had a good thing going, he hoped she wouldn't push it to the breaking point. Why couldn't women just leave well enough alone, anyhow? With the hand pump, he pumped the tire full of air and they were soon on their way again. The flat had cost them a good hour.

As they passed a large lake to the east the sun lay low in the west, forcing a red glow through to the edge of dark clouds at the horizon. They crossed U.S. 192 and headed out of the tiny town of Kissimmee – looked a lot like rain. A flash of lightning outlined the tops of a group of large dark clouds hugging the horizon. The windshield wipers responded correctly when he switched them on. Switched the headlights on and tested the horn, "auugaa, auugaa." Maybelle was startled at the horn blast. She looked at Jim and he at her. They both laughed. They should be in Orlando in another thirty minutes or so.

At the next block he stopped to fill up with gas and check the oil and water. While the man serviced the car he and Maybelle stretched their legs. Maybelle went to find the girls' room. Jim found the mens' and, on the way out, noticed a tall gaunt-looking man standing just north of the filling station. The man wore blue denims and a long sleeved denim shirt buttoned at the wrists. Long hair with one thick braid hung down his back out from under an old brown hat, pulled low down on his forehead. The man stooped and pulled a denim jacket from the dark blue travelling bag next to his feet. A car approached him and he stuck out his thumb. The car didn't stop. There was something about the man, but Jim couldn't put his finger on it – looked Indian. *Wonder where he's from.*

Jim was deep in thought about the man when Maybelle came up next to him and placed her hand on his arm. "Can we get something to eat while we're here?"

He turned at her touch, laid his arm across her shoulders and drew her close to him. Her smell engulfed him – he squeezed her waist. "Would like to hold out for another couple of hours if we can. Stop then, have some supper and call it a night. Can you make it that long?"

The filling station attendant came towards them wiping his hands on a dirty rag. She said, "Sure. We ready now?"

Jim paid the man and they got into the car. He started the engine and turned to her. "Mind if I give that man there a ride? Looks like rain but not for an hour or so. He can ride in the rumble seat for a while anyhow." She shook her head 'no'. He pulled over and stopped just next to the hitchhiker. Buddy had just started to stick his thumb out.

Maybelle stuck her head out of the window and spoke to him. "We're heading north, mister, want to ride with us for a spell? Open the rumble seat and climb in."

"Much obliged, ma'am." Buddy opened the seat, threw his bag in and climbed in behind it. He paid scant attention to the occupants of the car except to note that the woman was a real looker and had a very pleasant voice – must be a northerner. Her smell was pleasing, like soft flowers pent up in close quarters – it stayed with him for a while. Dark clouds were forming to the west with the smell of rain in the air. He wondered if he should take this ride or stay put so he would be near shelter in case of rain. The car pulled away. No need to think of that now. He could only vaguely make out the people inside the car through the dirty rear window. The woman sat close to the driver even though there was lots of room on the seat.

# CHAPTER 25

Buddy thought of Liz and wondered what she would be doing at this time of day. It was about an hour before dark. The sun had already settled behind the dark clouds in the southwest and light was fading fast. He thought of the green paper Liz had placed in his pocket and reached his hand there to find it. The paper was not there. He panicked. *Know she put it in that pocket.* He could see her face as she put it in his pocket. He felt again – it still wasn't there. Then he realized that he had changed shirts. It must still be in the white shirt. He reached for the bag and spoke out loud to the wind, "Goddam, if I've lost that money, I'll . . . ." He pulled out the white shirt and felt in the pocket. The relief he felt was instant when he touched the familiar packet. He pulled out the folded paper in the dimming light. It was thick and green and folded several times. One twenty, two tens, one five and four ones – forty-nine dollars. He couldn't believe his eyes. That woman had been saving this money all these weeks and hadn't let on a thing about it. This amount, with the nine dollars he'd saved on his own, gave him a whopping fifty-eight dollars and change – a small fortune. He refolded the money, placed it in the denim pocket and gave it a small pat.

The money caused him to think back on last Saturday and the party Liz had put on for him. He wondered what would've happened between him and Laura Mae had they been left alone. He certainly was taken by her and knew she had deep feeling for him, too. What about his other life, though? He had to find that before anything else.

The flash of light outlined the dark clouds close to the ground far off to the west and brought him back to the present. The deep rumble echoed across the landscape and seemed to rumple the air next to him. In a moment the air felt fresh and cool. Rain would be coming soon – likely within the hour. *Wonder where they plan to stop for the night?* Full darkness would be on the land in less than an hour. They were passing quietly through the peaceful countryside with barbed wire fences on both sides of the road as far as he could see. Three lonely cows wandered far off from the wire near a three-stand of cabbage palms in an otherwise wide-open range of short, well-grazed grass.

He had done nothing with Laura Mae and he was glad. Her words had struck a cord and had stopped the whole thing dead in its tracks. Her words now came back to him, *"Curly, what if you do have a wife someplace? What about her?"* He tried to light a cigarette, but the fire of the match wouldn't last long enough.

Buddy set to thinking about how he would go about convincing Toby to take him back and wondered just what kind of a man Toby really was. He hadn't known him that long and had been sick and weak most of that time. Best he could remember, Toby had always been kind and understanding to him, but that Marty was another story altogether. Marty had always seemed to resent him being a part of Toby's life. *If it had been up to Marty, I would've been left where they found me.* Andre spoke highly of Toby and respected him a lot. *Hopefully, he'll take me to where he found me and tell me blow-by-blow what it was like that day.* Maybe seeing the whole picture will cause the mind to remember. The doctor said the memory could all come back in a flash, with the right trigger.

It started to drizzle at the same time there was a knocking on the window of the cab. He could barely make out the woman motioning to him as the car slowed and pulled off the highway. The car was not completely stopped when the woman yelled back at him, "Leave your things in the rumble seat and close it tight, then come on up to the front before you get soaking wet." They were out in the country side and the only light was the car's headlights cutting a swath through the blackness and rain drops and the rising mist from the water hitting the warm pavement.

185

She shivered when his slightly wet clothes brushed against her bare arm. She reached back of the seat for her light jacket and put it on before they started off again.

The driver spoke for the first time as he shifted the gears from one to three, "We'll just drive a little longer tonight. Maybe stop over in DeLand. Might take less than an hour. About 7:30 I reckon. Okay with you?" The little Ford engine purred like a kitten. The sound was pleasing to Buddy.

"Yes sir, it's sure all right with me. Thanks for gettin' me out of the rain. It'll be rainin' cats and dogs in no time. Right warm in here. Hope I'm not crampin' you too much, ma'am." He tried to squeeze farther toward the door, but there was no more room. His thigh lay right up against hers, which felt soft and warm. He thought of Laura Mae. The rain beat against his face through the open window. He rolled it up near to the top.

The woman squirmed a little and he was well aware of the flesh-on-flesh through the clothes. "It is a little tight, but it won't be for long. I can stand it if you can."

He could feel her looking at him, but knew she would not be able to see much in the darkness. The only light came from the faint glow in the instrument panel. Beyond the woman he could barely make out the outline of the driver from his position. He could tell that the fellow was a big man just from the space he used.

"Reckon I can stand it, ma'am. Just don't mean to put you good people out no more'n necessary. I'm much obliged to you." He fingered the brim of his hat in his lap. "You mind if I smoke? I been tryin' to light one up out there in the wind for some time with no luck."

The driver's voice was deep and authoritative as if it was his practice to command. "You go right ahead and smoke, young feller. Crack the window a little. Might just join you with a bowl full myself. Maybelle, you hold the wheel for me?"

Buddy removed the pack of Chesterfields from his pocket and first offered one to Maybelle, then took one himself. He struck the match with his fingernail, lit hers and then his. The match light was flickering and feeble, but out of the corner of his eye, he saw the shotgun in the rack behind the seats, stock to the driver's side. There was something else hanging there, too, but he couldn't make it out before the match burnt his finger and he had to put it out. He took a satisfying drag and blew the smoke through the small space at the top of the window. The smoke was worth the rain that came through the space and pelted his face. The smoke Maybelle blew towards the windshield was quickly drawn to the crack in the window and siphoned off to the outside.

With the light from the match the driver used to light his pipe, Buddy saw, hanging from the shotgun rack, the polished handle of a pistol jutting out of its holster. The backside of the man's head and shoulders were also illuminated enough to make out some detail. Buddy had a seemingly innate knack for cataloguing details almost at a glance for instant or later use. He had no idea where it came from – a survival instinct maybe. The shoulders were broad, depicting a strong and solidly built man. His head was big, too, with coal-black hair neatly trimmed but far down on the neck. The body, at least what he could see of it, matched the voice. Buddy was unable to guess the man's age. The woman seemed young so the man must be, too, he reasoned.

Rain swept the windshield and kept it solid with water even though the wipers beat it off with each stroke. The blades were unable to keep pace with the rain – drops thick and big as quarters. Buddy could see ahead only during the time when the blades scraped the water away. Before the blade could start the return sweep, the windshield was fully covered again. Even in the clear period, the headlights seemed to be stopped by a solid wall of water and did not reveal much of the road ahead. The headlights looked like big bright shafts poking through the darkness. He wondered how the driver could see and how he could tell where the edge of the road was or if he was even on the right side. There were no marks in the road to get a position from, but the driver kept the car moving ahead at a slow, but steady pace. Every now and then the steering wheel would try to turn the car one way or the other, and the car would slow suddenly when the tires caught in a large puddle of water in a low spot in the road. Buddy threw the butt of his cigarette out the window and closed it. The woman put hers out on the floorboards.

The man spoke again. Sounded like through clinched teeth. "Never did ask you where you were headed for, young feller." A puddle of water tried to pull the steering wheel to the right. Jim fought for control and kept it.

"Headin' for Savannah. Goin' to meet some kin." Buddy mopped the rainwater from his brow and hands with his bandanna.

Jim stuck his head around Maybelle briefly to see his passenger, but couldn't. "Well I'd say you were one the luckiest fellers around, cause that's exactly where we're headed. Should be there by early tomorrow afternoon. Goin' to see kin, are you?"

Buddy thought about the guns hanging up back there. It wasn't unusual for a rifle or shotgun to be there – everyone around these parts were hunters of one sort or another. But a holstered pistol – that's another matter. This was a pistol worn on the waist. Maybe some kind of lawman. He thought about the lawman that had come looking for a Buddy back at Andre's. That man drove a car something like this one and wore a gun with a polished wooden butt like the one hanging up back there. With his survival instincts working over-time again, he said quietly, "Unh hunh." The man didn't follow up right away. They drove in silence for several miles before anyone spoke again.

The rain had begun to let off some and Buddy could make out faint lights far off to the northeast – houses he speculated. The lights streaked from the source as if across a body of water. Soon the large lake was visible under the abundance of lights and a roadside sign indicated they were coming into the City of Sanford, pop. 4,500. Another sign said the lake was called Lake

Monroe. It was as wide as the eye could see from his vantage point.

The deep authoritative voice filled the cab again. "Rain's let up quite a bit. Another twenty-five miles into DeLand. 7:00 now, ought to be in there before 8:00. Get somethin' to eat there. Try to make it into Palatka by 11:00. Get a place there. Get an early start in the mornin'."

The woman had not spoken for some time. "Jim, I'm cramped and tired out. Can't we stop for the night in DeLand? I don't think I can continue for much more and I'm starving to death." She squirmed in the seat and murmured, "Besides, this trip was supposed to be part vacation too, wasn't it?"

"We need to go on, but I reckon you're right. No need to kill everybody. Got plenty time to get there. How about you, young feller? You spend the night there and ride with us in the mornin? By the way, what they call you?"

Buddy was cautious. He had to measure his words until he could figure out who this man was. "I need to go on, but I'm plumb tuckered, too. Maybe I'll stop there, too. Decide when we get there. I'm called Curly."

"Well, it won't be long now and we'll all get a good night's rest. Be up early, Curly. I'll pull out at the crack of dawn. You can ride with us if you're by the car when we're ready to leave."

The rain had all but stopped, nothing left but a slight drizzle. Jim tried to get a look at his passenger, but Buddy stayed in the shadow of the woman. "Don't mean to pry, Curly, but where you comin' from?"

Buddy knew now he was up the creek without a paddle. He didn't rightly know how to answer. He didn't know enough about any other place other than around Andre's and could easily be caught lying if he tried to say he came from somewhere else. Damn, damn. "I been livin' down south of Okeechobee on a farm with friends."

Jim tried to look around Maybelle again. "That's Indian country around there, ain't it? Kinda figured as much. With your hair worn that way, kinda figured you to be Indian." He paused

189

for what seemed to be a long time. "You wouldn't happen by any chance to know a young Indian named Toby Cypress would you?"

Buddy almost choked. The darkness closed in around him and almost stifled him. He could hardly breathe. He fought to keep control of his senses. This man was, without a doubt, the sheriff who had come looking for a Buddy. He thought of the guns hanging behind the seat. He moved his right hand to the door handle and gripped it and started to push downward. The hand froze there. If he left the car at this speed he would roll head over heels down the highway. He planned to jump out and run the next time the car slowed. *Hold on, hold on. Get a hold on yourself. Take it easy. The man doesn't know who you are. He's looking for a name for some reason.*

Buddy cracked the window to let fresh air in, wanted to smoke, but was afraid of the light. In his mind he could see the man, exasperated, drying the inside of his hat brim with his bandanna, questioning Andre about this Buddy and about Toby. He could see him running eagerly toward the old sleeping quarters at Andre's. The man had never said just what it was he wanted this Buddy for. But Buddy had known that the name was his, even if he was not the Buddy this man was looking for. The man was on his way to Savannah to find Toby to get out of him whatever he knew about this Buddy. *Wonder what the man would say if he knew that Buddy was, at this very minute, riding in the same car with him?* He grinned to himself knowing the smile would not be seen by either the man or the woman.

Calmness returned as it always did when confronted with grave danger. He formed a mental picture of where the pistol hung. He would grab for it if the situation called for it. He was ready for action now. But he would play it out for a while longer. "No sir, can't say I ever heard of a Toby Cypress. Don't know nobody by either of the names."

The man spoke to the woman, but the words were indistinguishable to Buddy. They chatted among themselves for a few minutes. Buddy thought he was out of it. Then the man said, "Where 'bouts did you live down there?"

Buddy felt self-assured now and ready for action. He responded immediately. "Lived with an old woman name of Elizabeth Russell. Helped her get her place back in shape. Just finished the job and movin' on, lookin' for work. Hear there's work in Savannah. Hope so anyhow." He saw a sign on the side of the road that said DeLand, 1 mile, then, right after that, another sign, DeLand City Limits, Pop. 2,340. There were no streetlights on in the town. Up ahead on the left a bunch of electric lights provided a glow over the entire intersection and lit up a sign that read, "Palmetto Cabins, Vacancy". The little Ford slowed, pulled in and parked in front of the cabins. Just to the left was a filling station and a diner all lit up with a big sign in the plate glass window which said, Worley's Cafe.

Buddy got out before the others did, opened the rumble seat and removed his things. He moved around to the far side of the office and stood in the shadow of the building next to the entrance. The light flooding out of the office window lit up a rectangle of a parking lot in front of the Ford. Maybelle got out of the car, walked over to the driver's side and placed her arm around Jim. They walked together toward the office. Buddy stayed in the shadows, with his hat pulled low on his forehead almost covering his right eye. Just before they reached him, the man turned back to the car for something and Maybelle spoke. "Curly, are you going to spend the night here?"

"I reckon not, ma'am. I did want to thank you all for the ride, then I'll just mosey on. Will you tell your husband thanks for me, and that I surely do appreciate the lift. The best of luck to both of you." Buddy turned and walked off into the shadows. Out of reach of the light that illuminated Maybelle and the light from the diner, which also blazed through the window, the surrounding area was bathed in a dim light from the single street light on the corner to the south. A gust of wind brought chilly air, and he shivered. He looked up at the sky and had to strain to see a lone star far to the north. The smell of rain and freshness was still in the air. To the south he saw lightning flash and heard the low rumble of thunder. He predicted better weather ahead.

It was just after 10:00 before any vehicle at all came by. He finally flagged down the Greyhound Bus and paid $1.20 for the ride into Palatka. The bus was dark, but he could make out about seven riders. It wasn't hard to find a whole seat for himself.

It seemed that he'd been asleep for not more than a minute when the driver was rousing him. His stomach started growling again, but he was too tired to look for a place to eat. Near the bus station he found a hotel room for $1.25 and was soon fast asleep.

He dreamed about wild things as he wandered lost in the woods. Every way he turned something tried to get at him. He saw an opening in the trees and, as he reached sure freedom, a panther, black as the ace of spades and bigger than a boar hog, blocked his path and charged at him with jaws wide open and dripping with saliva. The fangs were as long as any blade he'd ever seen. He ran back into the woods only to be confronted by a twelve-foot gator, big around as a full-grown man. The gator, with two-thirds of his body out of the water, stared at him with eyes that seemed to be popping out of his head. When Buddy tried to go around, the gator opened its mouth so wide its whole body was hidden from view, and with teeth whiter than his shirt, lunged straight at him. Buddy fell back quickly, but it was too late. The gator crashed down on top of him – the big gaping mouth just ready to take his head off.

Buddy sat straight up in bed, flailing his arms in every direction and struggled to catch his breath. He tried to scream, but no sound escaped his throat. His brow, chest and shoulders were shrouded in sweat even though a slight cool breeze blew the curtains out of the way and entered the room. He got out of bed, went to the window and leaned down with his hands on the sill. He looked out and up to the sky, trying to judge the time. A milkman was delivering milk to a shop down the street. A light went on upstairs over the shop as the milkman went back to his truck parked in the middle of the block. A kid on a bicycle with a big wooden basket clamped to the handlebars came down the street towards the milk truck and threw papers at the bottles just placed there. He missed them all.

*Time to get back on the road.*

# CHAPTER 26

Toby Cypress wiped the sweat from his brow, pressed the kerchief against his neck on both sides and slipped it into his coveralls. How could it be so damn hot on the first day of December? Should be cool this time of year, especially in Savannah. He eyed the door to the jewelry store across the street as a man with a large leather satchel came out and went off down the otherwise empty street. That man had gone into the store two hours ago with the same satchel. Toby, still staring at the store, jumped involuntarily when Marty got in on the passenger side of the 1926 Model-T Ford and slammed the door shut.

"What the hell took you so long? You've been gone an hour," Toby said, reaching for the bag Marty had in his hands.

"Naw, been gone twenty minutes, that's all. You getting edgy?" Marty took a big swig of the Coca-Cola he had in his hand and flipped the last of the cigarette he'd been smoking out the window and onto the sidewalk.

Toby opened the bag and removed a hamburger wrapped in a white napkin. Farther down in the bag he found the French fries in another brown bag and fished those out. He handed the bag to Marty who retrieved another bottle of Coke from deep in the bag. Marty reached under the seat and found a bottle opener, opened the Coke and passed it to Toby.

"Where's the salt?" Toby asked. Marty's hand went back into the bag and came out with a napkin, which he opened to reveal the loose salt. Toby took a pinch and sprinkled it on his hamburger.

"How long do we watch that goddam store? This heat's getting the best of me." Marty opened his hamburger, salted it and took a big bite.

194

"Another hour or more. We have to stay here till five. Mr. Branbury says we must know who goes in and out and when, between one and five every day this week." He took another bite of the hamburger and poked several French fries into his mouth.

"Well, thank God it's Thursday. One more day. I'd rather be working under the torch than sitting in this hot sun with no breeze."

Toby eyed the big man sitting across from him. Martin Tucker had eaten one too many greasy hamburger in his day. His belly hung so far over the fancy cowhide belt that neither the big silver buckle or the belt could be seen. The striped blue shirt stretched at the buttons, trying to make room for the belly. They had been good buddies all the way back to the village and the white man's grade school. A simple man that seemed to always rely entirely on someone else for most of life's daily decisions. He could never be mistaken for anything but a full blood Miccosukee. That's all he was and all he ever would be – proud of his heritage.

Toby was proud to be part of the Miccosukee race, too. "Don't know for sure, but I think we'll likely hit it Monday or Tuesday. Mr. Branbury says it'll be a cakewalk if the customer action is as it has been the past three days. We'll be in the money then, Marty, old boy. What will you do with your share?"

"You know better than to count your chickens before they hatch, Toby, but I'm thinking about going home for a while. Been up here too long. Want to go fishing back in the Glades again. Miss that a lot. Want to go see John Henry down on the Tamiami Trail, too. How about you?"

"John Henry. Hadn't thought of him since we've been up here. I love that boy like a brother. We've all had some times, haven't we? You suppose he's still wrestling alligators and running the swamp buggy? Get his arms bit off one of these days. The more I think about it, the more I agree with you – time to head for home. Need to see my Mama and see how she's doing. Need to see how Uncle Andre is doing with Curly, if he's still around. Kind of feel bad about leaving Curly with him for so long, and him sick as he was. Promised I'd be back in two weeks, now been three months." He finished the hamburger and fries, gulped the remaining Coke and tossed the bottle and napkins behind the seat.

"I told you long time ago we should've left that damn weakling Curly to die where we found him. He was damn near dead anyhow. What a royal pain in the ass he's been. I'm glad to be rid of him." Marty took the last bite of his hamburger and the remaining French fries, then stuffed everything else into the greasy brown bag and put it behind the seat.

"Can't just leave a man to die like a wild animal in the swamps, Marty. Have a hunch that Curly'd do the same for me . . . you, too, for that matter. We've only seen him in a weak condition, but you know he was once a big strong man, and damn good with the traps, too, judging by the number of skins he had in the boat." Marty looked out the window and offered no more argument.

Toby's eyes were on the jewelry store when a man's hand showed from behind the curtain on the door. "There goes the 'closed' sign. Five o'clock. Let's go." Marty got out with the crank. Toby turned the ignition switch, advanced the spark and the accelerator. Marty turned the crank in the engine a couple of times and the little engine came to life. Marty climbed back in.

In another thirty minutes they drove onto the grounds at Broadhouse Heavy Equipment, all the way across town. Mr. Branbury stood in the shade outside the administration building waiting for them. He came to the car as Toby stopped in the parking lot next to the big tin building. The building had originally housed the machine shop as well as the main office. Now, the half on the far side away from the office housed the Parts Department and in between, autos used for the sales force were parked at night.

"How'd it go?" Branbury asked as he opened the car door for Toby.

Toby threw his legs out first and placed both feet on the running board, then stepped down onto the marl-covered parking lot. "Nobody came after one o'clock and nobody left after three – just like you said. Been the same all week." He thought Branbury looked uneasy. He slammed the car door and he and Branbury walked towards the car barn. Marty followed along.

"If it's the same tomorrow, we'll move in at 4:55, just before he puts the sign out," Branbury opened the big door to the building. Toby was looking at Marty and what Branbury said didn't register.

When they entered the tall one-story building, Toby looked to the stairs off to the left that led up to the owner's office high up near the ceiling. His eyes followed the stairs to the office, and sure enough, Mr. Copolla was at the window looking down at them. Toby glanced at Branbury and saw him nod his head at Mr. Copolla. Toby thought, you smart sonofabitch, you think I don't know you're not the brains behind this heist. Thurgood Branbury has a lot of brains, but not what it takes to plan a job like this. Lots of connections required, too, and you, Mr. Branbury, just aren't the type. He wanted to confirm this thought with Branbury, but held his tongue. It was none of his business. Toby winked at Marty. Branbury proceeded across the large room around the cars parked for the night, and entered a small room at the back. Toby and Marty tagged dutifully behind. Branbury held the door for them, looked again at Mr. Copolla and closed the door behind them.

Marty grabbed a chair and pulled it up to a large round table in the center of the room. Toby remained standing next to the table. Branbury went to the icebox, came back with three open bottles of beer and handed one to each of them. He pulled up a chair and sat his large frame in it. Toby drew up a chair, putting the back towards the table, sat in it and leaned his arms on the back with his chin on his arms. He looked steadily at Branbury. About sixty, Toby thought. How long has he been doing this for Mr. Copolla? He must be looking for his retirement. If he weren't careful he would end up on the Georgia chain gang. That would be plenty bad for an old man.

Branbury took a long pull from the bottle. "Let's go over the plan again. Must be sure everybody knows what he's doing and is locked into the timing for the whole thing." Toby looked at Marty who was leaning back in his chair fashioning a cigarette from the makings. Marty held the paper with his left thumb and two fingers, poured tobacco into it from the pouch, pulled the string tight on the pouch with his teeth and put it back into his top shirt pocket. With his other hand he rolled the concoction into a round cigarette, licked the edge of the paper with his tongue and lit it. He took a deep drag and waited for Branbury to continue. They had been through this routine every day this week. Toby knew the procedure by heart.

Branbury continued, "Park around the corner until just before you're ready to enter the store, then pull around to the front and park so as not to attract any attention from people on the street. Leave the engine running. We go in at 4:55 on the dot. The moment you enter, hang the "closed" sign on the door. There'll only be one man on duty and he'll be expecting you. He'll have a black bag for you. Be sure to get it. The vault will be open. Fill your satchels with the jewels and cash in the safe and under the counter. You then hit the man on the head with your gun butt, tie him up and tape his mouth. Be sure to always wear the gloves provided to you while inside. Toss them away later in separate places."

Marty spoke up, "I'll do that job of hitting the poor slob. That's the kind of work I like."

"For God's sake don't hit him hard. Remember, he's on our side. Tap him just hard enough to break the skin and make it look real to the police when they come." Branbury looked hard at Marty and then to Toby for support.

"Marty's just kidding, Mr. Branbury. He knows what to do. You sure the man will be working with us? What's he look like?" Toby looked at Branbury, took a long swig of the beer and lit the cigarette he'd just made.

"You can't mistake him. He's a small man with horn-rimmed glasses, which he wears low on a bulb-shaped nose and a handlebar mustache spattered with a lot of gray. He'll likely be wearing a vest and have armbands on each arm. Just say, 'Hi, Charley'. He'll take it from there." Branbury looked at the old round clock on the wall and seemed anxious to end the meeting.

Toby felt the effects of the beer and glanced at Marty who still had his chair tilted back. He wanted another beer, but knew Branbury was anxious. He would get some hard stuff after this meeting. To Branbury he said, "Okay, after the bags are filled, we walk across the street to the car and drive to the old marl pit off Highway 21. After we transfer the goods to our car, we run the getaway car into the pit. Then we drive to our house where we wait for you to show up to pay us."

"That's exactly right. Don't run any red lights and be sure no one sees you dump the car. Are you sure there's enough water in the pit to completely cover the car forever?"

"That old pit is sixty feet deep if it's an inch. No worry there."

Marty spoke up, "How we get paid, Mr. Branbury?"

"As we discussed before, you keep whatever cash you find in the cash register. There ought to be five to ten thousand in there, I imagine. I'll bring the rest in small bills for each of you – a total total of $10,000 apiece." The emphasis placed on the amount was not lost on Toby. Probably said to whet their appetites and make them the more eager. "I'll give it to you when I have the jewels and the black bag in my possession." Branbury eyed both men and finished his beer.

Toby rolled and lit another cigarette. Being extra cautious, he asked, "What happens if everything don't go as planned?"

"Nothing will go wrong. It's all been carefully planned. If you guys do what you're supposed to do and don't lose your nerve, you'll both be wealthy men. Monday you come back to work as usual. Nobody's the wiser. Okay, any other questions?" He stood, pushed his chair back and looked first to Toby who nodded 'no' and then to Marty who didn't answer, one way or the other. "There's just one thing more. We go in tomorrow."

Marty brought his chair back flat to the floor. Toby sat straight up and looked hard at Branbury. "Friday? What the hell's goin' on here? Why weren't we told about these plan changes? I thought you said Tuesday."

"Plans have been changed. Do you have a problem with tomorrow?"

Toby tried to think fast for any reasons he might have and tried to look forward to the actual robbery, but was unable to concentrate on it. He felt a tinge of fear and looked to Marty for help. Marty's face remained blank, showing no emotion or concern. "No, I guess I don't have any problem with it. How about you, Marty?"

"No, I don't have a problem. Sooner the better for me."

"Okay. You don't come into work tomorrow. If anybody asks, I'll tell them you all went directly to a job in north Savannah. You all go straight to the site as planned. Get a good night's sleep and don't get drunk tonight. Any more questions?" Neither man said a word. "All right, go on home then. I've got a few things to look after before I leave."

Toby and Marty stood up and headed for the door without a further word. Marty opened the door and went out. Toby started to follow, then hesitated. He realized now that he had been slow picking up references to date changes and wondered how much more he missed. He turned to face Branbury who had followed them to the door. "What's in the black bag, Mr. Branbury?"

"That's not your concern, Toby. Just do as we planned and you and Marty will be rich men tomorrow. Any more questions?"

Toby stared at him for a moment seeking enlightenment, shrugged and stepped through the door.

# CHAPTER 27

Branbury locked the door and returned to the table. He grew thoughtful as he cleaned the table, threw the empty bottles in the trashcan and cleaned the ashtrays. For some reason he placed a lot of trust in Toby Cypress. Except for the scar on his right cheek and his deep copper-colored skin, he kind of reminded him an awful lot of his only son. The thought of his son and his early and untimely death last year brought a pang to his heart and a tear to his eye. He wiped the tear with his handkerchief. Toby, at thirty-five, was about the same age his boy would have been, had he lived. Toby was a bigger man at 5'10" and 185 pounds and, of course, Toby was a full-blood Miccosukie Indian from a reservation down in Florida. Like his Billy, he suspected that Toby was one mean son-of-gun when riled – looked the type. Billy had almost killed a man in a barroom fight a couple of years before his death. He'd never seen Toby in a fight, but he had bailed him out of jail twice for fighting. He always said it wasn't his fault and, if the truth were known, it probably wasn't. Now Marty was mean to the core, but not likely to make a decision without first checking with Toby. Probably kill somebody if it wasn't for Toby.

Branbury went to the door, looked back and surveyed the room to make sure everything was in order. He stepped through the doorway, switched off the lights and locked the room. Robert Copolla was standing outside the upstairs office looking down at him.

Without yielding any recognition, Branbury threaded himself through all the parked cars and started up the stairs to report to his boss. He had never particularly liked that man too much, but never let on. Copolla trusted him and invested him with a lot of responsibility, but not nearly the necessary authority to do his job properly. The man constantly questioned his decisions and judgment. It wasn't like the old days when Copolla's father, Julio, was alive and running the business.

The thirty-five years he'd worked for old man Julio had been pleasurable ones. He started as a runner and did every job there was to do in the early years. He learned them all and rose up the ladder to be the lead supervisor of the entire company. The old man had not only trusted him, but gave him almost a free rein to operate the company on a day-to-day basis. *The good old days.* Now, this boy, about the age of Toby, wanted to run everything and everybody. He had been doing it that way since he took over from his father ten years ago and simply would not delegate authority to anyone. That would be his undoing one day. The other thing was his penchant for underworld activities. Definitely a brilliant man with connections throughout the South and the Northeast. Branbury was sure Copolla had obtained his contacts while racing sailboats all along the Atlantic coast and in foreign countries as well as his memberships in the country clubs of the world.

Branbury wanted out, but first he had to make enough so he could retire properly. The pension he would get from the company when he turned sixty-five, a year from now, would not begin to support him and Mary. That smart ass Copolla knew that and had lured him into the shady business of the underworld.

He climbed the wooden stairs and studied Copolla, standing at the top patiently waiting for him. The man was short, about five feet, seven inches, and extremely fit physically – a specimen of the active sportsman and athlete. He loved sports and played tennis almost every day at his club. This was the third robbery Branbury had participated in with Copolla and, hopefully, it would be his last. He had been promised twenty percent of the take on this one and expected to net more than $200,000 when it was all said and done. Nowadays, that kind of money would make him a rich man. He and Mary could have the really good life for a while. He looked forward to that – probably travel all over the country and just relax.

202

When Branbury reached the landing, Copolla retreated into the outer office and held the door for him. Branbury entered the spartan office with two desks and several filing cabinets and typewriters. Everyone had left for the day except the cleaning woman and she continued with her work as if they had not entered the room. He followed Copolla through the door at the back of the large room into the rather large office, which was not quite so plain. There was the familiar huge mahogany desk with in and out baskets, both filled with papers for someone to deal with. Over on the left wall was the bookcase with a few books, but mostly filled with trophies from Copolla's many sporting accomplishments. Every wall in the windowless room held a painting depicting his sporting prowess. Behind the desk hung his pride and joy, a thirty by forty painting of the "Becky Sue", the sailing yawl in which he had won the coveted Southern Cup.

Copolla sat on the edge of the desk and motioned Branbury to the sofa to the right of the desk. "Are we on for tomorrow?"

Branbury settled himself on the sofa and crossed his legs. "Yes. The boys are ready. We've been over the plan every day this week. They've surveilled the shop every day and it's always the same, just as you said it would be. Is Charlie ready?"

"Charlie's ready. I talked with him Tuesday. Should be a cool million in everyday bills in the store tomorrow afternoon." Copolla strolled over to the bookcase and stood staring at the trophies, his back to Branbury. He turned, "I know your boys have pulled some small jobs for us from time to time, but do you trust them completely? Can we rely on them one hundred percent? They are Indians, you know. That Martin seems like a loose cannon that can blow up at any time."

"Marty is a bit risky, but he's totally under Toby's control. He won't make a move without Toby's okay. He talks like he'd love to do everybody in, and probably would if Toby wasn't around."

"Why do we need him? I have a phobia about weak links." Copolla walked around the desk.

"He's strong as an ox and absolutely fearless. We need two men for the job and Toby won't go without Marty. Believe me, Toby can control him. Marty will not be the weak link. I'm more concerned about Charlie." Branbury walked over to the bookcase. This Charlie could get cold feet or not even be there when the time comes. It was not always smart to trust someone you knew, much less a complete stranger. He had not questioned Copolla about him before and wondered if he was on shaky ground questioning the boss this way. Copolla was well-known for his hot temper.

Copolla said, "Look, don't worry about Charlie. I've known him for years and I guarantee he won't let us down. Now, let's get down to business. The plans, tell me how you see it." He sat again on the edge of the desk and stared at Branbury.

"The boys will get there at three, in time to see the man leave with the bag. They'll enter the shop at 4:55. They'll switch to their car after disposing of the getaway car and drive to their apartment. I'll meet them there and give them $5,000 apiece – $10,000 if they didn't get enough cash from the register. I'll then meet you here at 6:30." The procedure rolled off his tongue almost without conscious thought.

"Now what is the plan if something goes wrong?"

"If they're unable to go to their apartment and if they are not being followed, they're to drive here and park the car in the usual manner and contact me. If they are followed, they're on their own until they can find a way to make contact."

Copolla removed his watch from his vest pocket, flipped open the cover and looked at the time. "Okay, very good. I predict it will all go smoothly. Tomorrow, Thurgood, you'll be a rich man, 200,000 smackaroos and your share of what the jewelry brings." He seemed very pleased and a little excited. "All right then, it's a quarter of seven. I have to meet my wife at the club tonight and I'm already late. Let's get out of here." He replaced the watch and went behind the desk. Branbury headed for the door and entered the outer office. The cleaning woman had gone. He went out the door and waited on the landing outside the office.

Soon Copolla stepped through the door and turned the key in the lock. The telephone rang. He unlocked the door and started to push it open, but hesitated. He said, "To hell with them. They can call back tomorrow." He locked the door. They left the building and went to their cars.

# CHAPTER 28

Toby and Marty were leaning against the bar talking with the waitress Evelyn when the three men entered through the front door to the far right of the room. Toby held his cue stick in his right hand and his heavily spiked Coke with the other, while waiting his turn at the table. He turned and saw the men – they were loud and mean-looking and their voices garbled the tinny country music coming from the jukebox. Marty stared at Toby with a quizzical expression. Toby growled, "Good Christ, not tonight. Don't need this tonight. Be ready Marty, this looks like trouble."

Toby gave the outward impression that he was paying attention to the game, but watched the approaching men out of the corner of his eye. As they made their way across the room they seemed to be heading directly towards him. They gave him and Marty the once over as they passed by on their way down to the end of the bar. The big one, with a full curly beard and paunchy belly that hung over his wide cowboy belt, said something under his breath as they went by. It sounded something like, "Them damned Injuns." They went to the far end of the bar on Toby's left and in loud voices called for chasers from the bartender. They sat small bottles of whiskey on the bar.

Toby's opponent at the pool table finally missed a shot and racked the balls. Toby broke the rack and the balls scattered. The thirteen went in the corner pocket nearest the three men and the cue ball came back to the other end. He lined up on the one ball for the same pocket. The three men were at the bar directly behind the one ball. He quickly sized them up. The big one with the beard was the loudest and looked the meanest. The man was huge – bigger even than Marty. Probably 6'4" and 250 pounds. He was looking directly at Toby, as if sizing him up for the kill.

The one on this side, tall and skinny as a rail, looked a little sickly and down on his luck. The third man, probably the drunkest of them, had a medium build and a thick handlebar mustache. Likely Mexican or Cuban – maybe a breed. They all wore Levis with colored shirts, black leather vests and motorcycle caps crushed in the middle with a black double cord – black boots with gaudy beads decorating the straps. They stood with their backs to the bar and their heels hooked on the rail. They talked among themselves, but loud enough for everybody to hear.

The one ball went easily into the corner pocket. The cue ball held at the spot where it had hit the one. The two lay at the opposite end. Toby looked at Marty. Marty looked at him as if awaiting orders to kill. Marty looked the Indian he was. Black denim pants held up with a broad leather belt with a large buckle, flower-colored long sleeved shirt, corduroy vest, pointed-toe cowboy boots and a wide brimmed white cowboy hat. Toby was dressed the same, except for the broad red bandanna around his neck. They always dressed this way when out on the town. It had drawn fire before and he sure expected the flames to flare tonight. He wondered how they could get out of this place without a fight, but Marty, he knew, would be looking forward to a good rough and tumble.

Toby thought of tomorrow. How stupid to come out drinking tonight. They should be home in bed right now, getting a good night's sleep. He shifted his eyes from Marty to the men and back to Marty and looked for recognition in Marty's eyes – it was there, as he knew it would be. He straightened up, chalked the end of the cue and walked slowly around the table. He avoided looking directly at the men, but he saw enough of them to detect any menacing movements. They all looked at him and laughed among themselves. He looked at Evelyn who was still with Marty. She looked back – the look, concerned and scared. He had his back to the men. Marty would protect his back. He lined up behind the cue ball, expecting them to come at him at any moment. Let them come, he was ready.

"Go get 'em, Injun. Pow wow, pow wow." A roar of laughter erupted behind him. He hit the cue ball, which proceeded true to the two ball which, when hit, went straight into the far corner pocket. At the other side of the table he lined up on the four, shot and missed. He held onto his cue stick and walked back to the bar.

"What's a matter, Injun? Not so good tonight, huh? Seems nervous, don't he?" More uproarious laughter. "Only good Injun is a dead Injun." More laughter.

Toby looked their way and decided it best not to answer them yet. He drank the rest of his coke, winked at Evelyn and nodded at Marty. In a subdued voice, "Be ready, Marty. They'll get braver any minute now. You know what to do." Marty nodded that he understood.

Toby pulled Evelyn to him and whispered, "Ev, why don't you go play the juke box." He put three nickels in her hand. She hesitated, then understood and moved away.

The Spaniard came down the bar and stopped in front of Toby. "Don't look like you're worth a damn at pool. Wanna shoot a game aginst me? Or are you afraid I'll whup your ass, Injun? Never knowed a Injun I couldn't whup."

Toby leaned his back against the bar acting as casual and unconcerned as if some child had come to talk with him. He looked the Spaniard in the eye. "Don't talk to me about that drivel – don't want to hear it. Go talk to that 'Injun' over there. He'll listen to you."

"Don't wanna talk to him. Wanna talk to you." The man inched closer.

"Marty, talk to this man. He understands your language." Marty moved. The man stepped toward him and started to say something. It never got out of his mouth. Marty hit him full in the face. The fist mashed the nose against his face and blood spurted. The man went backward over one table, into another and bounced underneath a third. The patrons scattered. Marty followed. The big paunch-bellied man came at Marty from the side. The skinny one followed behind. Toby rammed the sharp end of the cue stick into the big man's gut. The man grunted and doubled over. Toby brought the Coke bottle he had in his hand down hard on the man's head. The bottle shattered and blood flowed from the man's head onto the floor. The man didn't go down – Toby panicked. The man came erect and charged with head down like a bull straight at Toby and knocked him backward against the bar. Toby felt a rib give. A sharp pain tore through his body. The big man sprawled all over him. Toby kicked him in the groin and the man fell back with a roar. Marty hit him with a chair from the back and this time the man went down on his knees. Marty broke a cue stick over his head and the man flattened out on the floor and lay there, out like a light. The skinny one backed away and held his hands up when Marty turned on him.

Toby held his side, and using the bar rail, pulled himself up. He looked to the bartender and knew right away the police were on the way. Marty came to his side. Toby said, "We've got to get out of here. Out the back way." They moved towards the door.

"Nobody move. Everybody freeze." A big burly policeman burst through the door, followed by three others. Toby and Marty kept going towards the back.

"Goddam it, I said freeze. Stop where you're at or I shoot."

Toby turned and saw the policeman with his gun pointed directly at him. He stopped and Marty did, too. Two of the policemen rushed to them, handcuffed them roughly and dragged them to the middle of the room. The skinny man had backed up against the bar as if he was merely a bystander watching the whole spectacular event in awe. The policemen pulled the big man and the Spaniard to their feet. Both men were bleeding.

"All right, let's have it. What's going on here?" He looked at Toby. "Just can't stay out of trouble, can you? Take them to the wagon." He motioned to the policemen who started out with them.

The bartender spoke up. "These boys didn't do any wrong. They came in here minding their own business. Them three," he pointed to the two in custody and the skinny man down the bar, "came in here with trouble on their minds. They didn't let up on these boys and finally provoked the fight. These boys were only protecting themselves."

"Put the cuffs on that one, too." He motioned to a policeman who moved to cuff the skinny man. "Take them to the wagon and be sure they don't get to one another." He walked over to the bartender. "I'll have to take them all in now and get their statements. If it's as you say, and you come down to the precinct and give your statement, we can set these boys free. Figure up the damages, too, when you come. Maybe we can get it out of the guilty ones." He turned and left the room without paying the least attention to the whiskey bottles still in plain view at the end of the bar. The other policemen followed with the prisoners.

Toby had been here before. As they were led into the long room, he recognized the sergeant behind the long counter that extended from one end of the room to the other. The hall at the right led to the police bullpen and other offices. To the left was the hall to the jail cells – a long hall with cells on either side. He'd been in there, too. He looked at Marty who shook his head, then to the sergeant who nodded in his direction. The sergeant appeared to be writing and talking on the telephone at the same time. Toby looked at the clock on the wall behind the counter – ten minutes to one. If he had been smart he would be in his bed right now getting a good night's sleep for the caper tomorrow. *Dumb, dumb, dumb.* They were led down the left hall and he and Marty were put into one cell and the other three were placed in a cell farther down the hall.

"Yes sir, that's the way it happened," Toby said in answer to the plain-clothes policeman sitting across the table from him in the small interrogation room. They had been in this room for about twenty minutes now and he had been asked the same questions over and over again. The whiskey was wearing off. He needed a good stiff drink to make himself right again. He wished the bartender would get here to verify the fight wasn't his fault.

"Okay, make your mark here." The policeman shoved a hand-written sheet of paper across the table. Toby picked it up and read it. He had no trust in cops. He'd been stung by them one time too many. The policeman was visibly agitated. Probably didn't even think he could read. Toby signed his name and pushed the paper and pen back to the officer. A guard came in and led him back to the cell.

"Did he tell you when we were getting out of here?" Marty asked.

"Naw. I need a drink. How about you?"

"Yeah. I damn sure could use one. Let's go back to the Purple Derby and have a couple before we turn in."

Toby stretched out on the cot and closed his eyes. "Yeah, we can do that. That's a good idea. I can get a pool game going and get my money back. We better not stay long, though. We'll play hell getting up in time for the job. You feel good about smacking that guy? You sure racked him up good, huh?"

"Yeah, I caught him just right. Feels good when you get it just right. That big guy scared me for a minute, though. I didn't think he was going down." Marty smacked his right fist into his left palm.

Toby opened his eyes and looked at Marty, then closed them again. "A good fight every now and then is good for your blood. Gets it boiling good and proper. Feel good after, ay?"

Toby had started to doze off when the guard rattled his nightstick on the cell bars and he jerked awake.

"All right, you two, on your feet. You can't stay here all night." The guard unlocked the barred door and swung it open. "Out you go. Stay out of trouble for awhile, okay? Don't want to see you down here any more tonight. My advice, go home and sleep it off."

Toby grabbed his hat and followed Marty out the door. "How about a ride to the Purple Derby?" He grinned at the cop.

"Get outta here."

At eight o'clock in the morning, both drunk as a skunk, they crawled into bed fully-clothed. *What a night.*

"Tomorrow we'll be rich, Marty." Toby pulled the covers over his head. Marty heard nothing.

# CHAPTER 29

Just inside the door of the dimly-lit diner, Buddy, still dressed in blue denims and cowboy boots, paused and removed his hat. Besides the waitress who came around the counter with a tray of food in her hands, there were three other diners in the place. An older man in khaki pants and shirt sat in a booth near the front door. The waitress, heading in the man's direction, stopped short when she saw Buddy then continued on. A patch over the man's shirt pocket had letters that said Atlas Van Lines. Buddy had seen the big rig parked outside before he came in. The man's face was sun burnished with the lines of time etched around his mouth and eyes. He looked at Buddy standing in the doorway. Two young men dressed in denim coveralls sat at the counter, about center ways, talking with hands and mouths while they waited for their food. Local workmen he figured, maybe about twenty years old or so. Both had light hair worn long and shaggy down onto sunburned necks. They turned, stared at him and kept their eyes on him as he moved toward the counter. Buddy took a stool near the far end of the counter.

The woman looked confused as she approached him from the other side of the counter. She looked to her right through the opening to the kitchen behind the counter and to the back of the diner as if seeking help from some unseen benefactor. From Buddy's vantage point he could see the others without turning on his stool, and he noted that they were all staring his way as if awaiting a happening. The woman stood before him and started to speak, but before she could, a man with a big nose and thick lips stuck his bald head through the opening and said, "He's Injun, Millie, cain't you see his hair? Ain't no law aginst feedin' Injuns. Take his order and get on with your work."

Buddy sat bewildered at this exchange. Milly took out her pad and stood in front of him. "I'm sorry, mister, but I got my

213

orders, and I just knew you didn't look like no white man. What'll you have?"

Buddy ordered from the menu. "Let me have three eggs fried over easy, bacon, grits, toast, a half of grapefruit and coffee. Let me have the coffee first." He looked at the other men. They turned away and went back to whatever they had been doing before all this took place.

Buddy finished breakfast and was lighting a cigarette when the man in the khakis got up to leave. Buddy paid the woman twenty-nine cents, left a nickel tip on the counter and went out to the yard. The sky was just lightening up to the east and the air smelled fresh and clean. The big diesel came to life and black smoke spouted out of the exhaust pipe sticking above and behind the cab. There was a light on in the cab. The man inside revved the engine a couple of times and smoke jumped from the overhead exhaust and disappeared into the growing light. Buddy walked over and spoke to the man. "Mornin' sir. I'm tryin' to get to Savannah. Wouldn't be goin' that way by any chance, would you?"

The man appeared to be studying his map, but put it aside at the sound of the voice and looked hard at Buddy who was bathed in the dim light from the restaurant. "You Injun?"

Buddy stared at the man. Here we go again, he thought. He said simply and with no hint of inferiority and with just a tad of bravado, "Yes."

The man studied Buddy. "Where you hail from?"

"Indian village down near Okeechobee. You got room for an 'Injun' who'd be mighty grateful for a ride?"

The man skipped over the pun and said, "Climb aboard. I'm runnin' up to Jax. Take you that fer. I've done some tradin' with Injuns down near Miami from time to time. Got along right smart with 'em." Buddy moved to go around the truck. The man spit tobacco juice right where he'd been standing.

After a long silence the man spoke. "I reckon you put up with that kind of thing all the time, huh? Goddam shame, but that's the way it is in this country."

Buddy took out the pack of Chesterfields and shook one out. "Mind if I smoke?" The man said he didn't. Buddy offered the pack to him and he took one. Buddy lit both cigarettes and tossed the spent match out the window. "Only one other time that I remember. Most of my time is spent in Indian country with other Indians. Don't run into any other kind all that much. They keep some people from eatin' in diners?"

The man looked Buddy's way, then back to the road. "Reckon you been kept away from the real world. Colored folks not allowed." He made a few remarks about their history, then clammed up.

Buddy thought on what the man said for quite some time, looked at his own skin, and puffed on his cigarette. A picture formed in his mind of dark people working on a farm somewhere.

It was 7:15 when the driver pulled into a truck stop and parked on the far side. He kept the engine running. "I turn off here. You'll be stayin' on 17 you goin' into Savannah. I'd like to drop you on farther out on the other side of the city, but I gotta deadline to meet. Good luck to you, feller, and watch your back."

Buddy gathered his things and stepped down from the big rig. "Much obliged, mister. I'm learnin' fast about this world out here. Good luck to you, too."

He shut the door and walked to the rear of the truck as it started to move, crossed the street and followed the sign that indicated Highway 17 North. After near an hour of warm sun beating down on him and no one stopping to offer a ride, he decided to start walking. Seems the only way to get a ride is to get on the outskirts of town. He walked. The sun, canted to the south, was getting hotter and hotter. The sky was a perfect blue with only the slightest trace of clouds. The tall buildings were now behind him so he had nothing to ward off the sun's rays. As he got farther from downtown the business establishments changed into mostly houses and apartments, with an occasional filling station or grocery store on a corner here and there. He was now passing old unpainted houses not much better than shacks, some resembling Liz's place when he first arrived there with all the junk piled around. The only people he saw were what others had called colored. They seemed to bunch in groups in front of houses or stores or in vacant lots. It was Friday and he wondered why they weren't at work. Maybe there was no work to be had by anybody.

Finally the shacks and colored folks gave way to open and apparently fallow fields with no people about. He was alone in the sharp rays of the overhead sun. It beat down on him, giving no quarter. Even the cool air was no match for it. He simply had to get out of it for a while.

On the far corner was an old dilapidated unpainted store with one gas pump in the front. In faded and worn out letters the sign at the top said that it was Johnson's Food & Gas. The sign was worn out, too, like the letters and everything else about the building. The roof extended from the main house out over the gas pumps and would provide some relief from the unrelenting sun, though, so he ambled under it.

Buddy removed his hat and sat down on an upturned wooden keg, well within the shade of the roof. With his head down toward the ground, he mopped the sweat from the back of his neck. The slight smell of a chicken coop hung heavy in the still air and he turned and peered through the gaps in the well-worn and unpainted fence behind him. A Dominecker hen, unconcerned with the sun, pecked determinedly at something on the ground. The screen door gave out an awful screech – rusty metal on rusty metal. He raised his eyes in that direction and saw a woman who must have been a hundred if she was a day. She was skinny as a rail and her skin, the color of light chocolate, didn't have one place free of a wrinkle. Her mouth was closed, but any sign of a tooth, at least in the front, was long-gone. There didn't appear to be much hair underneath the bandanna that was tied to her head with four tiny knots. A few thin strands of brownish hair fell out and lay close to her temples. The thin grayish linen dress hung loose on the frail frame and almost reached to the ground. Her feet were bare. She took her time coming down the one wooden step, holding on to the side of the door the entire time. Buddy watched her, but she concentrated on getting out the door and paid him no mind.

When safely on the ground she looked directly at him. "What kin I git fer ya, young feller?" She walked over and sat on the keg next to him.

"Thank you kindly, ma'am. I'm just passin' through here on my way to Savannah. Just needed to get out of the sun for a spell. Hope you don't mind me usin' up a bit of your shade." He didn't even attempt to rise.

"You jist sit all you want to. Don't git a lot uh traffic stoppin' off here nowadays anyhow. You look plumb tuckered out. You walk all duh way from downtown?" She spread her legs, which resembled long sticks underneath the ruffled dress, out in front of her and leaned her bony frame against the fence extending from the side of the building – it groaned and bent a little. The chicken let out a squawk and fluttered away. She mopped the top of her lip and her forehead with the kerchief she carried in her hand. "You Injin? Never seen one m'self. Heard tell about 'em afore. Hear tell some of my folks run off from the plantations way up north and come down here to Floridy and joined up with Injins a long, long time ago, long time before the war. Don't mean you no harm, but you favor what I would picture a breed ta look like. That long wavy hair and dark coppery skin like dat. You reckon you got a little colored hidin' in you someplace? Maybe we kin, huh?" Her laugh sounded more like a cackle. She didn't seem to have any reservations about saying whatever was on her mind. She fidgeted with the kerchief in her hand. Beads of sweat built up on her lip.

He heard someone in his head arguing something about 'colored' blood. A picture materialized of colored men working in the cane fields somewhere, swinging machetes. The image was gone in a flash and he didn't try to retrieve it. A breeze came up out of the northwest and cooled the shade under the roof. "No offense taken, ma'am. I don't rightly know just what I'm made

217

up of. Lost my memory from a gunshot wound some time back. Been livin' with Indians way down near Lake Okeechobee for the past six, seven months. Haven't hardly been away from the area so don't know much about what goes on out here. This is a whole new world for me. Reckon you'd be what some folks call a colored. The white folks don't seem to take kindly to the likes of you, Indians neither for that matter." Since that incident at the restaurant, he had taken an interest in the history of the coloreds and just why everybody hated them so much. This seemed to be his chance to get some information. He knew he had to get going, but he may not get a chance like this again anytime soon. "You got any idea why?"

She turned toward the door to the store and yelled for Lulamay, and a little brown thin girl about eleven or so screeched the door open and said, "Yes, Granny."

"Git me and this young feller here a R.C. apiece and bring it over here." The girl disappeared and was soon standing in front of them with two ice-cold Royal Crown Colas and a device to take the tops off. She popped them right off, slick as a whistle. The old woman scarcely paid her no mind. "Are you sittin' right here tellin' me you don't know nothin' about the great war, or slavery or any uh dat?"

Buddy rubbed the cold sweat off the bottle between his two hands then took a big drink of the ice cold liquid. "Aaah, that's mighty satisfyin'. Thank you, ma'am. I heard mention of things like that just a little bit this mornin'. Other than that, don't know a thing yet. Aim to find out, though."

The old woman took a big swig of soda. The cooling breeze blew steady in the cloudless sky. She shifted her weight on the keg. "Where to begin? The whites started bringin' Africans into America over 300 year ago. Other dan dem what escaped, dey lived in slavery till '65, when old man Lincoln turned 'em loose. We was free all right, but we warn't people like duh whites. Most of us had no book larnin' a'tall. Didn't even know how to talk proper. Duh whites hated us even more oncet we was free. Free ah say, why we ain't never been free. Wan't then, ain't now. Jist like now, we had to go to dem fer what jobs we could get. We had ta go ta dem for housin'. We had to go to dem to get our bodies seen to. We had ta go ta dem fer everthing. We had ta do what dey said and stay in duh places dey set aside for us, or look out. We couldn't eat in dere places. We couldn't vote in dere elections, and don't even think about holdin' uh job of any kind in duh gu'ment unless dey was a wantin' you to. It was plenty bad in '65 and it ain't changed much since then. Gu'ment tried to change things, but it ain't done no good. I seen many a hangin' black man in mah day. Clan comes and takes 'em out and strings 'em up to duh nearest tree where everbody can see 'em. Burn houses, beat you up, rape duh women and duh chillins. You learn pretty quick-like to do what you been told. Ain't no different from duh old days. Dese old eyes done seen it all, yes suh." She took another drink from the bottle and wiped the tears that had formed in her eyes. Her lips quivered some, but she continued.

"When my ole pappy, God rest his soul, wanted ta come ta Floridy back in nineteen and leb'm, he had to sneak away in duh middle ob duh night – and he worked fer hisself. He was sharecroppin' just outside Savannah, and somehow he'd heard about a good chance to make a better livin' in Floridy. Duh owner ob duh fawm didn't want Pappy ta go. Said he didn't have no right ta up and move and vowed ta sic de Clan on him if he tried to go traipsin' off. Pappy sent all us on down ahead. He stayed ta work duh place. Month or more later he run away at night. Conditions no better here. We come to work for ole man Johnson on dis place and bought it from his daughter over in Charleston right after he died. Been here ever since. Jist me and Lulamay and John Mitchell now. Dere momma died some time back."

"Beggin' your pardon, ma'am but all this you tellin' is kind of hard for me to understand. You're tellin' me that you were actually owned by somebody? Like cows and hogs and the chickens back there?" He pointed toward the chicken, which had returned and resumed pecking at the ground. She glanced at the chicken.

She seemed pleased to be recalling her experiences, like she hadn't had an adult to talk to for some time. Lulamay came out the squeaky door and sat at her feet. She had been listening at the door and wanted to hear the story of the slaves.

The old woman began again, "Cain't tell 'bout everwhere, but ah do know 'bout duh plantation ah lived on near a little town in Georgia named Dover, not too fer from Statesboro. Warn't no real plantation like you see in duh pitcher shows, jist a big ole fawm with a bunch ob buildin's clustered around duh workin' and livin' places. White folks, duh massa and his folks, lived in duh big house sittin' fer off frum all duh rest. It always painted real fresh-like – a clean white with light blue trim 'round de winders and dohs. Lots uh winders and dohs, ah 'member real good. Big porch all 'round de house with railin's what come nigh up to duh waist. Rockin' chairs and a porch swing at one end in duh front.

"Some coloreds worked in dere and sometimes we'uns'd hear about duh insides and what went on in dere. Dey get uh mite persnickity and high falutin' now and agin', though. Got ta thinkin' dey be better dan duh workin' folks. Cain't member ever settin' foot inside uh duh place m'self. While ah's on duh place, dere was duh massa, duh missus, three daughters about two year apart and one son about two year older dan me and who was gone off to duh war when we was set free. Ah never seen him again after he went off to duh war. Don't know if he lived or died in dat God awful war." She worked her old gnarled fingers through Lulamay's kinky hair, not giving any thought to what she was doing. Her eyes stared far off to the woods across the road. She drank more soda.

"We'uns lived in a log shed built up like a hawg pen out behind duh massa's house. Ain't had no floor to it – cept'in duh dirt – sot plumb on duh ground. We'uns lived in one of duh six rooms in duh shed – everthing happened in dat room – birth, sickness, death. Ain't no winders to it, jist a hole with uh swingin' doh. Flies in duh summer and bitter cold in duh winter – no light get in when duh doh shut. Slept on bunk-beds made out of forked saplin's drove inta duh ground. Chilluns sleep on top 'cause dey can climb – mos time dey slept on duh floor."

Buddy caught himself staring at this old woman who had actually lived as a slave. It was hard to believe that people would actually own other people just like owning cattle. She was caught up in the story now, and he wondered if she would ever come to the end. Maybe there was no end. The slave life was burned permanently into her soul. He had a dozen questions to ask, but kept his silence and waited for her to continue.

He heard before he saw out of the corner of his eye, a rusty faded black flatbed truck, driven by what appeared to be a short and stocky middle aged colored man, turn into the yard and stop on the outside of the gas pump. Steam whistled as it escaped in a plume from the radiator cap. The man, black as tarpaper, shut the engine down and opened the door. The back of the truck had a canvas tarp covering something bulky underneath.

The old woman stopped talking and looked toward the man. Agitation showed on her weathered face. She squinted to see who it was. "Johnny Lee, dat you?" Lulamay sat up and looked at the old woman.

"It's me, Miss Orlie." The man came around the front of the truck, bent and picked up a spout can with water and poured it on the cap. The water hissed a loud whistle, turned quickly into steam and joined the rest. He removed a dirty rag from his back pocket and, with it wrapped around his hand, slowly unscrewed the cap. Steam gushed out and was swept away in the wind. Johnny Lee jumped back and away from the scalding mist. The denim overalls he wore fit him loose all over and the black brogans without strings were worn down on the sides – he seemed to be walking on the sides of his feet. There wasn't much life left in the shoes. He removed the ragged and torn straw hat, mopped his brow with the dirty rag and walked slowly toward the old woman he called Miss Orlie. He glanced at Buddy, nodded and spoke directly to the woman. He held the hat by the brim in his left hand and patted it against his leg. "Got to go up to Brunswick, Miss Orley. Got some plumbin' supplies to deliver. Make fifteen dollar. Need some gas now, though. Reckon I could pump out five gallon and pay you back first thing when I get back?"

She looked hard at him and drew her legs up to the keg. "You owe me, Johnny Lee?"

He stood rock solid and just a mite proud, Buddy thought. "No 'um." He shuffled a little, but looked her straight in the eye.

She studied him for a few seconds, looked to the door as if wondering if she should go in and check the accounts, then said, "You go right on and pump duh gas, Johnny Lee. I'll mark it in duh book when I'm done here." She looked at Buddy. "What'd you say your name was, young feller?"

Buddy looked first at Miss Orlie then at Johnny Lee. "They call me Curly, Miss Orlie."

Her wide smile created another million wrinkles and showed, as he had suspected, no teeth at all. "Miss Orlie is all right. What Johnny Lee calls me. Name, though, is Orelia. Orelia Alexia Edwards to be particular 'bout it. Johnny Lee, meet Curly." The men shook hands and nodded at each other. "Curly is on his way to Savannah. Mebbe you could do him a turn and give him a lift?" She looked at Buddy, then at Johnny Lee.

Johnny Lee looked at Miss Orlie and knew he had no choice, but to say yes. No ride, no gas. He looked at Buddy and placed his hat squarely on his big head. "Yes 'um. Be glad to do that. How 'bout it, Curly? You game to ride apiece with me?"

Buddy stood up. Johnny Lee was shorter than him by about a foot. He wanted to hear more about the slave business, but knew he had to get on with his own business. He would have to learn more about it later. "Yes sir, I'd be much obliged to ride with you."

"Sit fer a spell, Johnny Lee. I was just tellin' Curly here 'bout slaves. He never heard tell 'bout 'em afore. Can you believe dat?" She stretched the skinny legs out in front of her again.

222

"I sure do have to be movin' powerful bad, Miss Orley, but I reckon I can stay for a minute or two if you'll tell first about the breedin' nigras. Cain't hardly believe them stories." Johnny Lee sat on the ground in front of Miss Orley with one leg crossed under the other. Buddy looked at both of them and sat again on the upturned keg.

"It likely hard to believe, but it sure am duh truth. It happened jist like I tell it. I neither add or take away frum duh truth."

Before she could continue, Buddy broke in. "Breedin'? What you mean? Cattle?"

Johnny Lee blurted out. "Not cattle, Curly. Colored folks breedin' colored folks. They shore 'nuff treated 'em like cattle, though." He looked at Buddy then at Miss Orley for confirmation.

"It sure 'nuff duh truth. My Pappy am duh breedin' nigger on duh massa's plantation. I had near ta fifty brothers and sisters. Hear tell dat massa hired Pappy out ta other plantations as a breeder, too. So I reckon I had some more brothers and sisters around dere, too."

Buddy broke into her talk. "You tellin' me that your pappy was put out like a he dog or horse or bull to breed with women to make babies that would be slaves?"

Johnny Lee grinned broadly and showed his two broken teeth in the front of his mouth. "I'd a liked to'uv lived in them days and been duh pappy. Man-o-man, wouldn't that've been somethin', Curly?" He slapped his palms on his legs.

"Pshaws, Johnny Lee. You think you got it bad now. Boy, you don't know nothin'. Duh massa don't jist pick out jist any ole body to be duh breeder. He lookin' ta better his herd. He only breeds duh best wit duh best ta give him good strong workers. Duh breeders don't have nothin' a'tall to say about it. If dey don't do what dey told, dey get a good hidin'. And I can tell you dis, when duh Massa or his man laid duh cowhide whup ta your hide, it come off in bloody strips. I seen dat many a time in my day, and never could take a likin' to it. 'Course, Massa don't

223

like to whup. Not good fer his bizness. Marked slaves don't bring so much on trade. Buyers look over duh slaves like dey do duh horses dey buy. Ain't no picnic bein' a slave, I can tell you dat much." She called for Lulamay to bring more RC colas for everybody.

Johnny Lee stood up and began backing towards his truck, nervously twisting the hat brim in his hands all the while. "Beggin' your forgiveness, Miss Orley, I shore do wish I could stay and hear some more of them stories, but if I don't get these goods up to Brunswick, I'm in a heap of trouble. I shore do thank you for the RC, but I better get it another day. Curly, you wanna ride with me, you gotta come on now."

Buddy looked sorrowfully at Miss Orley. She seemed to be just getting warmed up and he was going to miss it, but he, too, had to get going if he was to get to Savannah before nightfall. He stood and took the RC Lulamay handed to him and also took the one meant for Johnny Lee. He reached into his pants pocket and brought out some change. It was fifty-three cents he handed to Miss Orley. She waved it off, but he insisted and placed the coins in the palm of her hand. "Miss Orley, I'll not soon forget your tale. I only wish I could spend more time with you to get more of it, but I need to get movin', too. Already been here too long now. I'd sure like the privilege of droppin' by on another day, if I could do that." He stood looking down at her frail frame and wrinkled face with sad, but twinkling eyes.

She drew her legs to her. "You feel free to come on round any time duh bug bites, Curly. I'll be right here."

Johnny Lee stood at the front of the truck. "Let's get on outta here, Curly." He got the crank and started the engine.

# CHAPTER 30

I t had been two hours since Johnny Lee let him off on the northern outskirts of Brunswick and the sun, almost directly overhead, baked him. The smell of cattle hung heavy in the still air. He pinched his nose with two fingers to try and block it out. Just off to the east, behind a barbed wire fence, two cows, far removed from the rest of the herd and grazing farther to the north end of the pasture, were busy chewing the new grass close to the ground and flicking flies away with their tails. The pickings they were chewing at seemed awfully slim to him. They seemed no better off than the human folk he had met. The grazing land appeared to be just a narrow strip bordered to the east by swamp and marshland and on the west by the highway.

Buddy started walking north alongside of the road to get away from the smell. Patches of grass and weeds grew tall among the litter strewn about. Out from a stand of live oak appeared a mighty black bull strutting along like he owned half the world. Head held high, and black and white horns curved outward and upward, ending in what appeared to be sharp points – moving towards the cows who seemed to be paying him no mind whatsoever. Buddy stopped to watch – to see what the bull had in mind. So absorbed with the animals he didn't see the car approach and stop just ahead of him. He turned toward the car at the toot of the horn and stopped dead in his tracks. There, in front of him, was the Model A Ford of the sheriff, and getting out the passenger side was Maybelle. There was nowhere to run. He was trapped. He pulled his hat low down over his brow hoping to avoid recognition. Maybelle said, "Curly, come on boy, hurry up, hop in the rumble seat. You can ride into Savannah with us." She opened the back seat and waited for him to come up to the car.

225

Buddy had no choice but to take the ride. The sheriff looked at him through the rear window, which was still as dirty as before. If he acted suspicious, the sheriff would surely question him more about Toby and about this man Buddy he was looking for. "Much obliged, ma'am." He climbed into the rumble seat and, with head held low, looked through the rear window. Jim waved to him. He waved back. *Good God, how do I manage to get myself into these fixes?* As the car began to move, Buddy looked back at the bull, which had almost reached the cows. *Your day seems to be going all right, Mr. Bull.*

The sun's position, in the southwest, told Buddy it was about one-thirty when he saw the first sign of Savannah. There were only a few scattered white clouds far out to the west. He was not surprised when they entered colored town on the southern edge of the city. It was no different than all the rest he had seen on this trip. Off to the left, just past a large drainage ditch control structure, a group of colored boys were trying to get a ballgame together. As they got farther into the town, he could almost reach out and touch a small group of men near a pool hall on the left. There on the right near a movie theater, young boys lolled about in front of a drugstore. Not many others were out at this time of day.

Buddy had no idea where he should get off. He only knew that Toby worked at Broadhouse Heavy Equipment Company on Montgomery Street and that he lived not far from there on 52nd Street near Highway 17. He would have to get a map of the city once they stopped. He had to make a quick getaway before the sheriff cornered him with more questions. They stopped at a traffic light and the stuffiness of the air and the heat from the sun caught up to him. At the green light the car turned left onto Montgomery and pulled over. Maybelle stuck her head out of the window and said, "Curly, where do you want to get off? We're going on into town. We'll be going back to Ft. Myers Sunday morning. If you're on the road, you're welcome to ride with us."

Buddy hopped out on the passenger side with his bag in hand, kept his hat pulled low and tried to stay out of view of the sheriff. "I'll just get out right here, ma'am. I think I have to go the other way on Montgomery. Thank you all a whole lot for the ride and thanks for the invite for another ride. With any luck at all, I'll be stayin' for a while." Jim said something as Buddy turned and headed in the opposite direction. He moved fast and did not turn back. His hands shook uncontrollably. He rubbed them together. What else can happen to me, he wondered as he headed south on Montgomery.

CHAPTER **31**

In the back of Jake's launch Flo leaned against the right bulwark and held Warren on her left hip. She kept Junior and Francis close to her legs with her right arm. Her eyes absentmindedly surveyed the shore of Wood Key as the boat crossed the bay from the farm. After three days working in the laundry, nursery and kitchen, and the last two at the still, she felt bone tired and looked forward to a quiet Friday evening at home. On Thursday, Jake had put her at the still – said one of the women fell sick and they needed to get the crop out before the weekend. It had been near two weeks at the farm and she knew for sure she would never want to return. With the kids in bed she could just lay back and relax all by her lonesome. Papa wasn't due back from Savannah until tomorrow or Sunday. After he left Thursday she'd been too tired to think much about his trip to Savannah. Now, though, she wondered if he had made contact with the Indians and if there was any word about Buddy.

She remembered her meeting with Bill in Ft. Myers the previous Saturday. They had, as planned, had something to eat in the Arcade, and he had proposed formerly. Said he wanted to get married before Christmas and that we could all spend Christmas at his mother's house in Ft. Myers. Bill said he understood the agony she endured over the possibility that Buddy might someday come back, and of her fear of marrying before she was sure that he wouldn't. No way he could possibly understand – nobody could.

Her mind returned to the present and just how bone-tired she was. *Don't think I'll go back to work on that farm ever again.* She scanned the net-spreads along the shore line.

Her eyes came to rest on a thin, white haired man standing on the dock in front of her house. The nets had long been removed from the spread and had just recently been sold to her brother. The money from that and from the laundry work in Key West was almost gone. She looked closer at the man as they neared the shore. He looked older than Methuselah. The ends of a bushy mustache, white as his hair and eyebrows, reached down to the edge of his chin on either side. There was a vaguely familiar look about him. His closely cropped hair gave his big ears the appearance of being larger than they probably were. His nose was long and thin. The shining eyes illuminated his face, old and lined with fine wrinkles. His blue denim jacket was a perfect match for the eyes. Her heart leapt as his identity sank in. *It's Daddy*. She could hardly contain herself.

He had been back a few times since the divorce but she always seemed to be somewhere else when he came. She often recalled that day when he walked down the old shell driveway at Bokeelia, got into the old Ford and drove away forever. He had brushed away her tears with his thumbs and promised he would come back often to see her. He remained deep-seated within her memory for many years.

She turned to Lucy who was busy gathering her things, getting ready to get off the boat. "See that old man over there on the dock?" She pointed with her finger. "That's Francisco Alvarez – my daddy. I haven't seen him in near thirteen years. I was only . . . ."

Lucy stared in the direction of the old man. The light was dimming and she strained to recognize him. "I remember him bein' around when I was a little girl, and I remember the talk about him, but I can't for the life of me place him now."

They passed the dock. Flo waved at him. He waved back, but showed no recognition. "Where's King, Lucy? I know he'd want to see Daddy."

"King should be home by now. What's the old man doin' here? I hope he's not bringin' bad news. I don't need no more of that. You still plannin' on goin' to your mama's tomorrow?" The boat neared the dock. Lucy gathered her things and yelled for her boys to come to her side and hold on.

"Yeah, then over to Dot's on Ky Costa. You all come down after supper. I know Daddy'll want to see King, too." Flo collared Junior and made him pick up her bags. He complained and gave one to Francis to tote. Francis screamed and she forced Francis to take one, too. She held on to the side of the boat as it slowed and stopped at the dock. Junior and Francis, along with Lucy's boys, scampered up onto the dock.

Francisco was sitting on the steps to the porch as she left Jake's dock and headed home, down the wide shell-rock pathway between the shoreline, the houses and net spreads. The mangroves had all been cleared way back from the houses. Only a few mosquitoes were about. With the excitement of the moment under control, she wondered how she would start the conversation with him. As she neared, he arose from the steps and took a few steps toward her. She still carried Warren on her left hip and a bag of clothes in her right hand. Junior and Francis ran past Francisco and slammed the doors as they went into the house – one door after the other. He was a very small man, about five feet four inches and not more than 150 pounds soaking wet. She smiled at him.

He came quickly toward her now with his arms outstretched. "Flodeenda, Flodeenda Marie. My flower." He pronounced Florinda with the distinct Portuguese accent she remembered. He rolled the 'r' so that it became a 'd'. He wrapped his arms around her and squeezed mighty hard for such a small man. She dropped the bag and threw her right arm around his shoulders. She towered over him and smelled his manliness. What about her own odor from working at the still all day? A tub with some good hot water and lots of soap was what she needed now. He didn't seem to notice. He was still a muscular man to be so old. She struggled with her mind for his birthday. April 24, 1855. He was seventy-seven. The baby let out a cry. He relaxed his hold on her.

She choked up, unable to speak without crying. Finally, "Daddy," was all she could get out.

He backed away, held her at arm's length and looked at her for a long minute. She felt a little embarrassed at the attention he gave her. "Flodeenda," he said again. "Look how much you have grown. I can't ride you on my knee any more, can I? Flodeenda, you were always my favorite. My beautiful little flower. I did not want you to ever grow up. I wanted you to always stay my little girl. Now you are a grown woman with little babies of your own and as beautiful as I expected you to be. What is a father to do?"

She blushed at all the attention and especially the beautiful part. She knew all too well that she was not even pretty, much less beautiful.

His accent hadn't changed a bit. It was just as she remembered. Flo said, still unable to speak in her normal voice, "Daddy, oh Daddy, I'm so glad to see you, we've got so much to catch up on. Where've you been? Have you seen Mama? How long you staying?" She grabbed onto his arm and led him toward the front porch. "Come on, let's go in." She felt like the little girl and the times that they both remembered and so cherished.

Once inside, she introduced the kids to him and he took them each in turn into his arms and gave them a big hug. He had a piece of candy for each. They began to ask him a million questions. "Who are you? How old are you? Are you my daddy's daddy, too? Will you go with us tomorrow? Are you comin' to live with us now?" He took a chair at the table. Flo put the baby on a pallet, got the stove going, put on a pot of coffee, then turned her attention to fixing something to eat. She lit the lamps in readiness for the fast-approaching darkness and sent Junior out for more wood and water from the cistern.

Flo shooed Francis away and when Junior came back in they drifted outside to play some before it was too dark to see. She continued with her chores. "I know you've been around a number of times and each time I happened to be somewhere else. But where've you been staying? I haven't even heard about you now for quite a few years."

He sipped the hot coffee and puffed at the corn-cob pipe he had lit after the kids went outside. She studied his face and the thin lines etched into it and thought he looked worn out. He said, "I have been all the way over to New Orleans and up and down the Flodida coast. Been back to Portugal several times, but things have changed over there, too. Feeshing mostly up around Steinahatchee. Hard to get way down here and, as you say, even when I do, I can't seem to get to see everybody. Follow the feesh down this way sometime. Spent quite a bit of time at Bokeelia and even stopped at Captiva a couple of times. Time seems to get away from me. I have seen some of you from time to time and learned something about what is going on. I know that you have been married about five years and that your husband went off hunting and never came back. Murder suspected."

Her back stiffened. She hoped he didn't notice.

He continued, "No I have not talked to your mama in all these years. Have seen her a couple of times from a distance and heard some about her from one of the kids on occasion. I suppose she is all right and just as ornery as ever."

Flo turned from the stove, wiped her hands on the apron, lit a cigarette with a wooden match, shook it out and threw it into the trashcan. She took a deep drag and watched the exhaled smoke blur his image then drift out the back door. "Mama's been ailin' some. She's over at Captiva now. Daddy Joe's runnin' a farm there and does some fishin' out of Ky Costa with Dot's Walter. Plannin' on goin' over there tomorrow for a few days. Dot's fixin' to have another young'un pretty quick now. She'll need somebody to help her. This will be her fourth." She turned back to the stove and readied the meal for serving. As she was setting the table she yelled for the kids to come in and wash their face and hands to get ready for supper. Darkness had set in. She turned the lamps up.

"Your mama and I had nine, you know. Times were better then, though. Feeshing was better and brought a better price and I was able to earn commissions from setting up wine buyers in the Americas. Everything seems to have dried up now. Maybe it is the age that is getting to me here lately."

Flo checked the kids' face and hands, made sure they had dried off proper and set them at the table. She brought the food to the table and told them to dig in. She gave the baby a bottle to keep him occupied.

After supper and the kids finally off to sleep, she cleaned the supper dishes and put them away. Francisco lit his pipe and settled back in the chair. From the counter and with just one lamp now burning, Flo could just make out his features as he sat relaxing at Buddy's place at the table. This was probably her only remaining chance to learn his side of the divorce story.

She poured them both a cup of coffee and sat in the chair next to him facing the door. "Why'd you come way off down here? I hope it was specially to see me." She looked at him and grinned.

He grinned, too, then looked solemn. "Actually, I came down for two reasons. I am going to Portugal next month. Not sure I will be back this way again. Getting old you know. Don't know how much time I have left. Wanted to get to see all you children before I go. I heard Waukeen lives around here someplace."

"King lives just two houses down from me. He'll be glad to see you, too. How long's it been since you seen him?" She leaned back in the chair and rested her feet on the chair on the other side of the table.

"Have not seen Waukeen in many a moon either. Heard that he had married, but do not recall ever meeting her. Heard she was a Harrison, too. Your husband's sister?"

"Yes. They've been married about ten years, I reckon. Got two young'uns and one ready to be born any minute. She was on the boat with me when we came over from the farm today. She's a couple of years older than me. Good woman. I like her a lot. She's just the match for King."

"What is Waukeen doing now-a-days? Still feeshing? Some word he has been running liquor. Any truth to that? Would not surprise me at all, knowing that boy."

Flo figured she'd let King answer that question. "When you plannin' to go and how did you get here? You want some more coffee?" Flo lit another cigarette. He nodded. She went to the stove and returned with a cup of coffee for both of them.

"The mail boat brought me. I will catch it when it comes back, Tuesday or Wednesday, and ride to Chokoloskee."

"I sure wish you could stay longer. This has been such a thrill for me. I haven't been as happy since you used to ride me on your knee so long, long ago. Remember that? You can sleep in my bed if you can put up with the boys fightin' durin' the night. I can make up a pallet on the livin' room floor. You mentioned two reasons for comin' down here. What's the other one?"

"I most definitely will not take your bed. I am not too old to sleep on a pallet. Slept on many a one in my day. Slept on the bare floor many a time, too. If it is all right with you, I will stay here until I catch the boat."

"Whatever you want to do is okay with me. What was the other reason?"

"Oh, yes. He died before you were born, but you have likely heard stories about him – most of them wrong, I imagine. Old man Juan Gomes, also known as John or Juan Gomez, who used to live around here long time ago, was my uncle, and the real reason I came into this country to begin with. It has been said that he was 122 years old when he died in 1900. Actually he was only 113, born in 1787 on the Portuguese Island of Madeira. He was throwing his cast net when it tangled in his foot and pulled him overboard. He could not free himself and drowned. A passing fisherman found him a day or two later. We buried him near his old palmetto shack on Panther Key. I loved that old man and wanted to come down and pay my last respects before leaving this country, perhaps for good, and look to his grave . . . if I can still find it. Hopefully, I can rent a boat to take me there."

She remembered some of the story from hearing her mama tell it, but here was the chance to get it direct. "You say you came here lookin' for him many years ago. How did he happen to be here to begin with?"

"That is an interesting story, too. The story begins in Oporto when he was but twelve years. He had the habit of hanging around the docks. He loved to go down to the wharf and see all the ships with different flags of countries from all around the world. My father, the youngest of the lot, was not yet born when a Spanish merchantman sailed into the harbor at Oporto that year. Fate would have it that the Captain's cabin boy had taken ill and died a few days before, and his replacement was to be young Juan who just happened to be at the docks on that fateful day. Juan – he later changed it to John Gomez – was shanghaied that day and served as cabin boy on the Villa Rica until it was looted and burned in 1801 by Jose Gaspar, the feared and world-renowned brigand and buccaneer. Gaspar, for some still unknown reason, took a special liking to young Juan and his was the only life spared that day.

"In 1851, fifty miles west of Pine Island, Gaspar fought his final battle. In that fateful battle against the United States Navy, Gaspar not only lost his last ship, but his life as well. Juan watched in horror as Gaspar wrapped chains around himself and jumped into the Gulf waters rather than be captured. Before he did so, he told Juan to get the map case, gold and jewels from the cabin safe and flee for his life. Juan had just turned twenty-four on that day when he jumped over the side and made his way to Sanibel, then on down into the Everglades where he stayed hidden and anonymous on Panther Key until I found him in 1877. I was but twenty-two and he then ninety. I stayed several years with him until I made my way to Captiva where I met your mama. Captiva, by the way, gets its name from Jose Gaspar. That's where they housed their women captives while their fate was decided. Juan and I got on famously over the years and I grew to love him as I did my own father. I was crushed when he died. He still had surprising agility for a man so old. Who knows how long he would have lived, but for that tangled net."

Flo sat transfixed as Francisco related the tale of John Gomez. "When did you meet and marry Mama? Why had you gone to Captiva and what was she doin' there? I thought she was from Mississippi." Before Francisco could answer there came a knocking at the screen door and Lucy and King came into the room.

Francisco turned in his chair and studied the two. "Waukeen, you have not changed so much that I would not recognize you. You were a handsome young man when I last saw you, and still are."

King, with a stubble of blond hair on his face, was barefooted and dressed in old dungarees and a long sleeved khaki shirt. He hurried across the room when he saw Francisco and took the outstretched hand and squeezed it.

"Let me see," Francisco continued, "you must now be about twenty-seven – eight, huh?"

"Yeah, Daddy, I just turned twenty-eight in January." King seemed genuinely happy to see the old man. Flo had worried somehow he would react because he was known to have spoken some harsh words against Daddy for leaving Mama with all the kids to raise by herself. King turned to Lucy and drew her forward. "This here's my wife, Lucy. She's a Harrison, the sister of Flo's husband."

Lucy, dressed pretty much the same as she was when they came from the farm this afternoon and also barefooted, took his hand, mumbled something then moved to the chair at the opposite end of the table. They all sat. Flo stood, put more wood in the stove, and started a fresh pot of coffee.

King lit a cigarette. He didn't seem to be his usual confident self – looked a little agitated.

Flo hoped he would contain himself and not start a fight or anything with the old man. You never knew with King. He could be friendly one minute and in a fitted rage the next.

King said, "Where you been, Daddy? I heard once you were up to Steinahatchee. Some said you had gone back to Portugal. We missed you a lot after you left. What you doin' down this way?" King looked at Flo then back to Francisco.

"Just telling Flodeenda I am thinking about going back to Portugal soon and wanted to try and see all of you before then. Also wanted to look after old John Gomez's grave. Have you been over there to see it lately? Maybe, if you have the time, we could go over there together. Would like to talk to you some." Francisco's deep blue eyes drilled straight into King's, which were the spitting image of Francisco's. They seemed to be sending out a demand to King.

King looked quickly at Lucy, then at Flo and then back to Francisco. Flo remembered the stories about the treasure maps and jewelry. Those stories were the great mystery that everyone wished to resolve. King and Buddy and some of the other boys had dug up near all of Panther Key looking for that treasure. Maybe the old man was finally going to share the secret with him. King was likely already spending the fortune that would soon be his.

Finally, after an interminable silence, King said, "When you want to go? Tomorrow? Lucy and Flo goin' into town then. Good a time as any."

Flo brought the coffeepot and cups to the table and poured a cup for everybody. "That's a great idea. Give you all a chance to get to know each other again. You all were real close at one time, if I remember right."

"What have you been doing with yourself, Waukeen? Feeshing much?" The old man probed as he studied King.

King took the coffee offered by Flo and put in two teaspoons of sugar and a measure of cow's milk. "Fishin's been okay, but they ain't payin' no money for 'em. Damn near a waste of time. This time of year better than summer, though. Pompano bring a better dollar. People don't seem to want mullet too much. 'Course, we keep our bellies full of 'em." He backed his chair away from the table and crossed his legs.

Francisco shifted in the chair and rubbed his legs and rump. He tamped out his pipe and began to refill it. "These damned old bones are not what they once were. Getting old, Waukeen. You know, I hear this Roosevelt's going to end prohibition when he takes his seat in January. Harm you any?" He struck a match against the table leg and lit his pipe. The smoke billowed toward the ceiling. He gazed over the match at King. Flo watched King's face for his reaction.

Lucy blurted out before King could respond. "If that son-of-a-gun stops our whiskey flow we're gonna starve for damn sure. It's one thing to give us some vittles and the measly jobs he's promised, but they ain't gonna make up for the money lost from makin' whiskey legal." She tried to go on, but King's look stopped her cold.

King said, "Yeah, I reckon I've turned a pretty good profit durin' prohibition, but I sure paid the price for it. Blowed out of the water and given up for dead once. Chased through the swamps by dogs several times. Robbed by thugs too lazy and scared to run their own hooch." He lit another cigarette and poured more coffee. He looked hard at the old man.

Francisco pressed on. "I heard you were doing all right at it, but never heard that you were blown out of the water. How? Where did that happen?"

"Me and Patch Wilkins used to run to Cuba in my old run-boat out of Pine Key. Make it in four hours. She'd hold a hundred cases. Come back in around Bay Hundy right at Spanish Harbor. Coast in of a night. Done it time and again. Revenuers never got wind of us. Six months ago . . . . " King looked at Lucy for confirmation. She nodded in agreement. He continued, "Six months ago, one beautiful, calm black night, we were on the way back, taking her real easy when a Coast Guard Cutter come alongside and ordered us into the water. Did let us get in a raft we carried. Didn't even see him comin'. Kind a slipped up on us, real easy like. We must've been asleep or somethin'. We watched as they moved all the hooch from her to the Cutter, pulled away and then blew her clean out of the water. The bastards even waved at us as they sped away. We drifted for three days and damn near died from hunger and thirst. Finally we drifted into Whale Harbor and made our way back to

238

Marathon and then on home. Thought I was a goner for sure that time."

Francisco looked astonished and sat up straight in the chair. "My God, man. I never heard such a tale. What are you doing now? I mean, I suppose you have another way to make a dollar, haven't you?"

"Oh yeah, sure. I now run it by car from the upper Keys down to Key West. Somebody else takes it from there. Don't make as much as I used to, but no need complainin'. Ain't had no trouble yet, knock on wood." He rapped his knuckles on the wooden table.

Francisco studied King. "What are you going to do when they make liquor legal again?"

King looked at Lucy and she looked at him. "That's a damn good question. Go back to fishin' and grubbin' for a livin' I reckon. Maybe this Roosevelt feller will make some better jobs for us."

Francisco turned his attention back to Flo. Filled his pipe again and lit it. "What are you going to do, little flower? You have been without a man around the house going on ten months. You have anyone in your sights? Like Waukeen says, hard for anybody to make it and stay legal, much less a woman alone." He took a deep drag and held his cup up for a refill.

Flo went to get the pot and filled up all around. She took the pot back to the stove and leaned with her back against the counter. "I've still got a few dollars left and Papa ain't kickin' me out of here for a while yet. I been—"

King cut her off. "Papa's talked to you about leavin' here? That bastard ain't got no right kickin' you out of here. Me and Buddy practically built this place with our bare hands. If he tries, I'll—"

"Take it easy, King. He did talk to me some about it, but he said not to worry about it now until I decided what I was gonna do. I'm waitin' now for him to get back from Savannah. Should be back tomorrow or next day. He went up there to talk to a couple of Indians that maybe helped Buddy escape from the swamps after he'd been shot."

"What the hell you talkin' about?" King pushed the chair back from the table so hard it almost fell over. "I ain't heard no talk like that. He told you that? That old man just ain't gonna give up, is he?" He was now standing, towering over everybody. Francisco just sucked on his pipe and listened, a frown on his face, apparently all new information for him.

Lucy put her arm on King's hand and pulled him back to a sitting position. "Take it easy now, King. Let Flo tell it." He sat and lit a cigarette. He was getting madder than a wet hen, Flo could tell.

Flo walked back to the table, but remained standing behind the chair. "Papa went to an Indian village over near Lake Okeechobee and talked to an old Indian who told him about a half-breed that was brought there by his nephew and another Indian several months ago. Papa learned the Indians were in Savannah and he went up there to find out if there was any truth to it and if the man could possibly be Buddy. Once I get the news from him, unless it turns out to be a real sighting of Buddy, I plan to go and spend some time at Ky Costa to help Dot deliver her new young'un. She needs some family to be with her."

Francisco stood and walked over to the stove, tamped out his pipe and put it in his pocket. He came back and stood with his hands on the back of the chair. "But Flodeenda, what are you going to do about a man? You need a man to help you raise the little children."

"There's a man that's been courtin', so to speak. Been comin' around and writin' letters and sayin' he wants to marry me. Saw him last Saturday in Ft. Myers. Haven't decided yet, though, just what I'm gonna do. If there's no chance that Buddy is still alive, I'll likely marry the man."

King stood up abruptly and said in an angry loud voice. "God damn it Flo, you know Buddy ain't alive. If he was, he'd be here now. No way in creation that man would've run off and left you and the kids alone in this God forsaken hell hole of a place." He pushed the chair seat under the table and motioned for Lucy to come along.

Lucy lugged herself erect with a big groan. "Yes, it's time I was headin' home. My bones are gettin old, too, Papa Alvarez," she cackled.

Flo placed her hands on the back of the chair. King's outbursts had shaken her considerably. "I know all that, King. I don't want to believe that Buddy's dead and gone, but I also know I have to agree with what you said. What possible reason could keep him away from his kids? Papa Jim told me not to get my hopes up too high, but there was a chance that somethin' bad happened to Buddy and he's been unable to get back here by himself."

King had already reached the door and spoke directly to Francisco. "Daddy, I'll go with you in the mornin' to visit John Gomez's grave. You get up early?" Francisco nodded. King's voice still had a bit of an edge to it. "Flo, if I don't see you in the mornin', I'll look you up when you get back from Bokeelia." He went through the door and Lucy followed.

Flo watched them go and looked sadly at Francisco. His face was expressionless. He sat motionless and puffed on his pipe. She banked the stove fire, cleaned the cups and coffeepot and tidied up the kitchen. She went into the bedroom, came out with a blanket and pillow and made a pallet next to the table. "Daddy, I'm plumb tuckered. You goin' to be all right out here on the floor?" She went to him and they embraced for a long moment.

"I will be all right, little flower. See you in the morning. Maybe we can have a few moments together before I go south."

Just as soon as she closed the door to her room, she realized that she never did get the answer to the question of divorce – maybe she could get it in the morning.

CHAPTER **32**

Toby's eyes snapped open. He sat up in bed and swung his arms in a punching motion, trying to hit the thing that came at him – or was it a person. He couldn't remember now. It had slammed through the door and caught him unprepared. His back was to the wall. The only defense was to come out swinging. He looked around and saw no one. There it was again – the banging at the door. His arms were still in the defensive up position. He looked to the other bed and Marty lay sprawled long ways in his shorts with no covers on and not moving a muscle. The banging at the door continued and went right on into his head, bouncing from one side to the other. He lowered his arms and looked again to the door, then to Marty. Who the hell could be at the door at this time of the morning? The sunlight played out in an oblong pattern on the floor. His eyes followed it as it climbed to the top of the table. Somehow it was all wrong. What was the sunlight doing in the room now? He tried to focus his eyes on the round face of the clock on the table. It looked like a clock, but it had no hands. He rubbed his eyes, but still could not see any hands. What kind of clock is that? There was a knock on the door again, but more gentle than before. A woman's voice called his name. He looked again at the sunlight and again at the clock. The fuzz was lifting from his brain and all of sudden, he was wide-awake. The sun meant it was afternoon. The clock bore him out – three o'clock. Good God, the job is set for four-thirty. They were supposed to be in position by three. They had just about an hour and a half to get all the way across town. *Good God-all-mighty.* He jumped out of bed and his head felt like it would come right off.

He reeled, caught the edge of the bed and sat down on it. He composed himself, reached for his pants draped recklessly over the back of the chair near his bed and pulled them gingerly on.

The knocking on the door continued and the voice called his name again. A key rattled in the slot. Marie opened the door at the same time he reached for the knob. She stood outlined by the light from the hallway. He studied her for some time. Not a bad looking woman and a pretty good shape, too. Thirty-five or so maybe. He thought about asking her in for a little fun, but somehow it didn't ring right. Wait, who was that with her? He strained to see clearly. A tall dark-skinned man in denim clothes with a brown floppy felt hat pulled low over his right eye stood just behind her a little to the side. The man was just in the shadows and his hazy features offered no identification. Toby moved back to the bed, sat on the foot railing and held on with his hands. Marie moved into the room a couple of paces and the man stood behind her. She looked at Marty sprawled out on the other bed.

She stepped to the side, half turned and pointed to the man. "Toby, what are you doing sleeping so late? Aren't you supposed to be at work?" Before he could answer she grabbed the man's sleeve and pulled him forward. "This man says he came all the way from Florida to see you. He couldn't get you to answer the door, so I came up to see if you all were dead or something."

Toby straightened up as the man inched forward into the light. He almost fell off the bedstead. Could this man be Curly? Could he have recovered so well? He composed himself, still holding on to his forehead. "My God, Curly, what the hell are you doing up here, boy? How'd you get up here? I was planning to come down and see you in a few days. I was . . . ."

Buddy moved toward Toby and shoved out his hand. He looked to the other bed when Marty stirred, turned over and snorted through his nose. "Toby, you all right? You don't look so good. You sick?"

Toby looked over at Marty, then at Buddy, then at Marie. All this going on seemed beyond his comprehension. He struggled to bring it all together. Marie started backing towards the door. She said, "Look, Toby, I've got work to do. Will you be all right?"

243

"Yeah, I'll be okay. You go ahead. Thanks for waking me up." Marie nodded, turned, and strode towards the door. He admired her body movements as she went through the door and pulled it shut behind her. The smell of her stirred his soul for a brief moment.

Toby stood. The pain in his head almost sent him down again. He braced himself on the bedstead. "Put your bag down over there by the table, Curly, and take the load off. I need some coffee. You had breakfast?" He motioned to the table in the middle of the room, now fully covered by the sunlight he had so recently been trying to figure out. As he moved towards the small kitchen just beyond the table, he realized that breakfast time was long gone. It was afternoon and he had to get a move on. "Wake Marty up, Curly." He thought about that before Buddy could get up to obey the order. "No, on second thought, you better not. Marty don't like just anybody waking him, and he don't particularly like you too much anyhow. I better do it myself." Buddy didn't move.

Toby started the coffee and came back to the table with a jar half full of a white watery-looking liquid then went into the bathroom on the far side of the room. When he came out the smell of coffee hung heavy in the room. He went into the kitchen and came out with a cup filled to the brim with coffee.

Buddy crossed over to the one window and cracked it a little. The air felt fresh and crisp. He lit a cigarette and sat again at the table. Marty groaned and sat up on the side of the bed. He scratched his head and looked at the stranger at the table. Toby stood next to Marty. "Know who this is?" Buddy turned to face Marty and Toby.

Marty growled, "Good Christ, what's he doing here? You realize what today is? What are we gonna do with him? I told you we should've shot him a long time ago." Without waiting for an answer he rose and headed straight for the bathroom.

Toby walked to the table and sat down. "Give me one of your cigarettes, Curly." He took the offered cigarette, lit it and blew out a big stream of smoke. "I told you he didn't cotton to you too much." He grinned, drank about a third of the coffee, filled it up with the white liquid and stirred it with his finger.

Buddy put the cigarette out in the ashtray on the table. "I never done nothin' to him. Don't know why he don't cotton to me none." He got up and headed for the kitchen. "Mind if I have a cup of that coffee?" Toby waved him on into the kitchen.

The coffee and the whiskey settled Toby's nerves and his mind started to work full time on the robbery and the fix he was now in with Curly here. What to do with him? He couldn't take him on the heist and he didn't feel good about leaving him here until they came back. Copolla will kill us all if we take him on the job. Outside of the four of us, nobody is supposed to know except the inside man. If I leave him here and something goes wrong, he'll lead them directly to me. He was deep in these thoughts when Marty came out of the bathroom and bumped into Buddy as he came out of the kitchen. Marty growled something under his breath and Curly came back to the table without saying a word. Toby wondered if Curly had much spine. Even though he looked strong and healthy he didn't have much to say and seemed a little timid. Marty would likely test him one day if he stayed around long enough. "What've you been doing, Curly? Are you still with Andre?"

Buddy sipped the coffee and lit another cigarette, offering the new pack to Toby. A sullen Marty came and sat at the table with his coffee and filled it up with whiskey. Buddy ignored him and spoke directly to Toby. "No, I left Andre's back in September and went to stay with Liz Russell, way over on the south-side near the lake."

Toby cut in, "I know where Liz's place is. I love that woman more than I do my own mama. What are you doing over there?"

"A sheriff came lookin' for me. Didn't know what he wanted me for, so I ran into the woods. Andre told him that you'd brought me there and that you were in Savannah. He's in Savannah now."

Toby cut in again. "The sheriff's in town? How do you know that?"

Buddy put out the cigarette. Marty drank his coffee and said nothing. "I rode part way here with him."

"You what?" Toby flung his arms wide and knocked his cup over. Coffee spilled across the table and onto Marty. Marty jumped up and Toby stood. "How the hell could you ride with him and he not know who you were if he was looking for you? What did he want you for?"

"I don't know what he wants with me. I've racked my brain, but can't come up with nothin' I know of to give him cause to go huntin' for me. I tried to keep my face and features from him. It must've worked because I'm here and not in some jail. I thought he had me when he asked if I knew you. But it passed and somehow he never found out who I was. I've searched all the memory I've got and ain't been able to come up with a reason."

Toby went into the kitchen, came back with another cup of coffee and again filled it with whiskey. He reached for the pack on the table, took another cigarette and lit it. He looked at the clock – three-thirty. They had to get a move on. What to do with Curly. Marty looked too sick and tired to do anything. Maybe Curly could come and drive for them. "You never got any of your memory back?"

"Not much. A little here and there. That's why I'm here. Want you to take me back to where you found me. Maybe when I get there somethin' will spark the memory. Will you do it?"

Toby stood with his hands gripping the back of the chair and ignored the question. "What does the sheriff want with me?"

"Wants you to lead him to me, I reckon."

Toby looked again at Marty. No reading his face except for the scowl and the hatred he had for Curly. Probably the only reason Marty didn't kill Curly was because he wouldn't do anything without Toby's okay. Toby couldn't understand how people could hate one another like that. "Look Curly, me and Marty have to go and do a job. Got to get going right now. We really tied one on last night and neither of us is in any condition to drive. We can talk about going back down to the Glades when we get back. Okay? You want to come along? Maybe you can drive for us."

Marty sat up at that and spoke for the first time. "Toby, you're not serious? You gonna have him come on the job? Bran . . . uh, the boss gonna be mad as hell at us if we bring anybody along. You know that." He scowled at Buddy.

"No choice, Marty. Time to go now. Can't leave him here. Besides, he can drive for us. Won't be a problem. Trust me." Toby stood and headed for the clothes closet. "Come on, let's get ready. Curly, are you game? You can drive right?" It was a quarter to four.

Buddy looked a little bewildered, glanced at Marty then back to Toby. "Sure, why not. Yeah, I can drive."

CHAPTER **33**

The plainclothesman came into the room and handed Captain Clark two files, said something unintelligible and left. Jim Harrison gazed through the huge window which covered almost the entire side of the room facing the bull pit. Uniformed and plainclothesmen were coming and going, busy at their work. He watched their arms and mouths move, but couldn't hear a sound they made. Very interesting to watch people's gestures from a distance without hearing.

Clark opened the files and studied them for a few minutes then laid them on the desk on top of other files and loose papers. Randolph Clark, a large man with a white shirt and tie loosened at the neck and pulled to the side, mopped his face and neck continuously. The big, smelly cigar went from his fingers to his mouth regularly. The ash dropped onto the desk and was lost among the papers there.

Jim waited patiently, eager to get out of there and return to Maybelle who was waiting at their cabin on the north side of town. They would go out to dinner before they retired for the night. The big round, black clock hanging over the door indicated four-fifteen.

Clark said, "These boys have been in a few scrapes with the law during their short stay here in Savannah. Mostly petty, fighting, drunk and disorderly, that kind of stuff. Spent a couple nights in jail on two different occasions, each time bailed out by their employer. He must think highly of them. Just last night they were brought in again and held at the station house until the manager from the Purple Derby came in and vouched for them – said the fight was not their fault – said they should not be held liable for the damage to the bar." On its trip to his mouth the cigar dropped another ash into the pile of papers. Clark didn't seem to notice.

Jim said, "I know boys like them. Will I be able to talk with 'em tonight? Got to be headin' back to Florida no later than Sunday."

"Shouldn't be a problem. My officers have kept tabs on them ever since we located them. They usually get home from work about six and head out to the Purple Derby about seven-thirty, eight, then back home about eleven or so. Sometime bring girls back with them. Little strange behavior today, though. They usually leave the apartment about seven-thirty in the morning. Their car hadn't moved at two this afternoon. When our officers went back at four, the car was gone. For some reason they didn't go to work today or, at least, didn't take their car in the morning."

Jim was getting impatient. It sounded like these Indians were just normal young men to him. "Where they work?"

"On the other side of town on Montgomery. Place called Broadhouse Heavy Equipment Company. Been around a long time. Fine reputation. Economy don't seem to be bothering them too much. The owner, a man named Robert Copolla, inherited the company from his father about ten years or so ago. I understand the company was suffering some financially then, but picked up considerably after the son took over. He's a pillar of Savannah society – member of Bell Isles Country Club. Only the top of the barrel belong there." Clark picked up one of the files and flipped the pages. He paused on one, then said, "Toby Cypress works as a machinist. I imagine the other does, too."

Jim stood and turned the brim of his hat in his hands. "Well, okay, Captain. I won't take up any more of your time. Much obliged for your time and your cooperation. Shall I come back over here tonight to go out to their apartment?"

"No need. An officer will pick you up at your cabin at six and take you right on over there. He'll be instructed to wait as long as it takes to get what you want. Let me have the name and address again, just to be sure. By the way, I understand you just want to question them about what they know about your missing son, that right?"

249

"Yes, that's right. It's the Great Southern Motel and Lodge on Highway 17 just past Bay Street on the right hand side. Cabin 106."

The Captain stood, came around the desk and started for the door. "What happened down there, Jim, if you don't mind me asking?"

"Appears to have been foul play. Some think my son and his cousin were killed down there while campin' way down in the islands. Others hold he's still alive. I followed up on a rumor that he was seen at an Indian's place over near Lake Okeechobee. That's southern Florida, mid-way between the coasts. That's how I came up on this Toby Cypress in the first place. Rumor has it he brought a very sick white man into the area and left him with an uncle. I found out Toby was in Savannah and that's when I contacted your office. You all have been a great help and I'm much obliged for it."

Clark opened the door and, as Jim stepped through, put out his hand. "Good luck, Jim. I hope this exercise will lead to your son. If I can be of any more help to you, don't hesitate to call. Maybe I'll come down your way some day and you can show me around."

"You come on down, Captain. You can stay with me. Just let me know when you're comin' and give me a little warnin'. Gone off a lot. Most any time, though, is okay." He grabbed Clark's hand and squeezed

CHAPTER **34**

Toby pointed to the car parked down the street from the apartment and on the same side. Buddy remembered the car. He had worked on a similar one before somewhere. The engine had caught on fire and spread to the body and interior and he was called on to put it back in condition which entailed completely rebuilding the engine. The car, a 1924 Hudson four-door sedan, had a tall chrome angel with outspread wings capping the radiator.

Toby spoke when they reached the car. "Curly, you ever drive one of these before?"

"I know this car like the back of my hand." Buddy moved to the driver's side and climbed in. Toby and Marty got into the back seat. They were still moaning, but not as much as before. The whiskey in the coffee had done its job. Buddy turned on the ignition, set the spark, grabbed the crank and inserted it into the front of the engine. Two full turns of the crank and the engine sputtered for a moment then purred like a kitten. He got under the wheel and turned to Toby. "Where to, boss?"

"Go straight ahead to 17 and turn right, then left on Tremont. Stay on that until I tell you where to turn."

After a number of turns Buddy headed northwest on Highway 21 and had only gone a short distance when Toby directed him to turn left onto a dirt road then told him to stop on the far side of what appeared to be an abandoned barrow pit, filled to the top with water. He noted another car parked just west of a dirt track which lead down to the water's edge. At Toby's direction, Buddy parked the Hudson next to the car. Toby opened the back door, "We'll change cars here. Take the keys, Curly, and lock up.' Toby went to the boot, removed a bag and took it to the other car.

251

Buddy backed the new car out onto the dirt road and headed back out to Highway 21. Without looking back he asked to no one in particular, "What kind of car is this? Never seen one like it before. Why we leavin' the Hudson?"

Marty spoke for the first time since leaving the apartment. "It's a '27 Studebaker." You could almost read the word 'stupid' into the answer.

Toby crossed his arms on the headrest of the front seat. "No questions now, Curly. All will be explained in due time. When you come to Highway 21, turn right. It runs into Bay. I'll tell you where to park." He stared out the windshield and became silent. No one spoke.

Buddy stared straight ahead. He had a funny feeling in his bones. Something was not exactly right here. Toby seemed uptight and all business. He'd never seen this side of him. Why had they left the other car in exchange for this one? Something was going on and he felt sure he would not be any too happy with the outcome. Here lately he had been in some tight spots, but he felt that somehow this was going to be quite different. He also wanted desperately to find his other life. Toby had mentioned the Glades. He'd heard some about the swamps down there in South Florida. If Toby wouldn't take him soon, he would head out on his own. Somehow he would find that other life.

Around a bend in the highway a sign said, "Savannah City Limits" and the highway widened and became Bay Street. Suddenly they were in the familiar colored town with its run-down buildings and people milling about, then out of it just as quickly. Buddy stopped for a red light at Highway 17 and Toby spoke. "See the three-story gray building just before that next street? Turn right on that street and you can turn around in a lot just behind the building." After they turned around and drove back to the edge of Bay, Toby spoke again. "Marty, get the bag." Marty got out and moved to the rear of the car. Toby still leaned on the seat and now looked at Buddy, "Curly, take this pocket-watch and in five minutes pull out onto Bay heading west and park directly across the street from this building. Keep the engine running and don't move from there until we're back in the car. Understood?"

Buddy turned in the seat and stared at Toby. "What the hell's goin' on, Toby? I don't want to get myself involved in no tom-foolishness. I just want to find my memory. I can't—"

"Too late now, Curly. You've got to do this one thing for me now, then we'll head for the Everglades and your memory. You won't get into any trouble. Trust me now, boy. Besides, you owe me your life. You can do this one little thing for me." Toby got out of the car as Marty came up to his side. They walked west to the gray building and disappeared inside.

What in the hell are they going to do? There was a jewelry store on the first floor of the gray building. Were they going to rob it right here in broad daylight? Buddy looked at the watch. It was 4:53. Hardly anybody about, but there would be plenty in just about ten minutes. What was their plan? How long had they been planning this? The questions jumbled up in his head and no satisfactory answers came. He looked up and down the street from his vantage point in the alley. The engine purred. He looked at the watch. One minute to go. Then what? Toby said not to worry – he had sounded confident. Buddy would do what he was told and hope for the best.

At exactly 4:55, Buddy drove the car out onto Bay and parked across from the gray building. He studied the building. There was a door to the left and one farther to the right of the building with a large plate glass window facing the street. The door near the window also had a small window and hanging in it was a "Closed" sign. It still moved slightly as if it had just been placed there. Big white letters painted on the window spelled out the name, P. Sher, Jeweler. Underneath was the address, 311 E. Bay Street.

The moment Toby entered the store he knew something was not right. A young man with dark hair, dressed in a white shirt with sleeves buttoned at the wrist and a tie knotted tight around his neck, stood behind the glass counter. He seemed very uncomfortable. The man was supposed to be older with grayer hair, big nose, handlebar mustache and large horn rimmed glasses. Should be wearing a vest, too, with armbands. Marty entered behind him and turned the door sign around to show that the store was closed. The store was bare except for the counter that ran almost the width of the room and a small desk and chair to the right of the door. Behind the counter an open door led to another room behind. Toby looked at Marty who came up behind him opening the bag. Did he notice the difference in the man, too?

The man, who had just stood up from under the counter, had a quizzical look on his face. His mouth pursed to say something, but before he could, Toby strode to the counter and placed his hands on it with palms down. "Hi, Charlie." He looked straight into the man's eyes and knew instinctively that the man would not know what he was talking about. He wondered what he was to do now. What happened to Charlie?

The young man looked bewildered as if he hadn't expected any customers so near to closing time. "I beg your pardon. My name is not Charlie and, I don't even know a Charlie. Do you wish to see a particular piece?"

Toby backed away from the counter as Marty came along beside him. "Sorry, but we were expecting somebody else to be here. Where's the person who would normally be here?"

"I don't know the whole story, but I do know that Mr. Echley, the man who normally works here, is in the hospital and, as I understand it, is in the Intensive Care Unit. I was called in to replace him until he's back on his feet. Never heard him called Charlie, though. Are you a friend of his?"

Toby thought fast. If 'Charlie' called Copolla to cancel the plans because of his illness, why hadn't Branbury called? Did they miss the call? Did 'Charlie' not call? There was a considerable amount of jewels in the case and probably more in the safe which was supposed to be open and ripe for plucking. Through the glass case he saw a satchel sitting on the floor next

254

to the man's feet. That must be the bag Branbury said to be sure to get. He suspected the bag held pure cash, probably brought in by the man that came and went every day. Missed seeing him today. He needed more time to think. "Yeah, you could say that we were friends. Charlie is my nickname for him. Big joke between us, you know. What's the matter with him? When did he go to the hospital?"

"Far as I know he went in soon after he closed up yesterday. I'm sorry, mister, but I've got to close up here and be across town in just a short time. Might I suggest that you go over to the hospital and see him. I know he'd be happy to see you. Moultrie General Hospital."

Toby knew if the play was to go forward it had to be done now. He patted Marty's foot with his and Marty looked at him knowingly then reached his hand into the bag. Toby said, "Mister, I don't know who you are and I'm sorry as hell you had to get mixed up in this, but we came in here for jewels and that satchel by your feet and we mean to have them before we leave." Toby reached for the man's shirt, but he was too quick and immediately ducked down behind the counter. Marty, in a flash, vaulted over the top of the counter with the pistol in his hand. The man came up with a pistol of his own and grappled with Marty. Flame shot out of the barrel with a terrible roar. The man relaxed in Marty's arms and looked at Toby with an expression of disbelief. Another gun blast shattered the counter in a million small pieces of glass that seemed to be held suspended in mid-air for a long time. Toby looked dumbly at the crumbling counter as the bullet tore into his leg and exploded with unbelievable pain. He fell to the floor and grabbed his leg to try and run off the pain.

Marty let the man fall to the floor and came to Toby. A big shard of glass stuck through Toby's bloodstained shirt into his stomach. Blood flowed out onto the floor. "Toby, Toby, you hit?" Marty looked like he had seen a ghost.

"Feels like my whole leg's been blown off. Get the bag over there by the man, then get the hell out of here. If I'm not out there in five minutes, take off." Marty hesitated. "Get going, damn it."

"What about the jewels and loose cash?"

Toby writhed with the pain in his leg, the glass shard still sticking out of his stomach. "Forget everything but the bag – get the bag. Not much time. Now move, man."

Marty went around the counter and looked through the open door and saw the safe. Jewels and small boxes filled the shelves. He hesitated for a brief moment. Glittering jewels were in a jumble in the shattered case. He stepped over the man and grabbed the bag. With the two bags in his hands, he stopped by Toby and tried to say something to him. Toby waved him on and he went out the front door.

Toby took hold of the glass and eased it out of his stomach. Surprisingly, it didn't hurt at all. He stuffed his bandanna into the gash to stop the flow of blood. With his knife he opened his pants just above the right knee. The bullet had passed through the fleshy part of his leg close to the knee, but must have torn a ligament because the leg wouldn't move an inch. Blood was everywhere. He looked for a long moment through the broken glass at the unmoving body on the other side. The guy looked dead. A sudden unfamiliar fear crept through his body. *I know I've been a bad boy at times, but I don't deserve this kind of payback. This is surely the end of the line for me.* He ripped off his shirt and tied it the best he could around his leg to try and stem the tide of blood. At the door he tried again to stand – no go. He crawled through the door to the sidewalk and disinterestedly watched his blood ooze down to the gutter at the edge of the street. He yelled for Marty, then fainted.

The first shot sounded like a dull pop, way off in the distance, but Buddy recognized it for what it was. Before he could zero in on the location, there was another, followed by a faint sound of tinkling glass. The sounds came from the jewelry store. Good Lord, what now. He looked around to see if anybody else heard it, but the few people on the street paid no attention at all. He noted the time – 4:57. He saw Marty tear out of the store, running for all he was worth, and dive into the back seat of the car.

Buddy turned in the seat and shouted. "What happened, Marty? Where's Toby?

Marty was hysterical – out of his mind. "Toby's dead. Get outta here." He babbled uncontrollably and curled up in a fetal position on the seat. "Everything went wrong. Get moving, dammit."

"Marty, get hold of yourself, boy, and tell me what happened. How you know he's dead?" Marty didn't respond. Buddy shook him hard, "Come on, Marty, what happened in there?" Nothing. If Toby really was dead then Marty's life was over, too. Just at that moment Buddy heard a call from the store and turned to see Toby crawl out onto the sidewalk. He saw the blood run down the pavement and into the gutter. *Good God Almighty. What am I going to do now? Not supposed to be any trouble. Now here I am being dragged into this thing and no way to control it. If I go to Toby's aid, I'll be as much a part of it as he is. There were two shots, which meant somebody else was shot, too. Maybe dead. I'll be charged with murder for sure, probably go to prison and be locked up for the rest of my life. One thing for certain, if I don't go and get Toby, he'll die for sure. Toby did save my life and I owe him for that. I don't want to leave this earth owing anything to anybody. I'm here now and this is as good a time as any to repay my debt. Besides I'm already in up to my eyebrows, whether I like it or not.*

Buddy opened the car door and got out. A big man far down the street to the west was yelling something to someone. The man turned and ran off the other way. Without another thought, and with the adrenaline now pumping strongly in his veins, Buddy sprinted across the street to Toby's side. There was no fear or forethought now, only decisions and action. He was back in his element again. A man and a little boy, walking toward them on the sidewalk, stopped and stared. Another man ran from across the street to help. Buddy brushed him off, picked Toby up in his arms and calmly walked back to the car. Pockets of people began to gather and stare. One man went into the store. Buddy put Toby in the backseat, forcing Marty to get out of the way and sit up. When Marty saw Toby with his eyes open and breathing, he snapped out of his stupor and helped comfort him.

Toby's voice sounded weak. "Curly, let's get out of here. Head straight west on Bay and retrace the path back out to the barrow pit. We'll ditch this car there and pick up the other one. Don't get a speeding ticket on the way. Let's do it now, boy." He grinned at Marty and put his hand on his arm.

Marty grinned big. "Damn, Toby, it's good to see you made it. I thought you was dead, for sure."

The man came out of the store yelling for someone to call the police. Said a man was dead inside the store. Buddy engaged the clutch, shifted to first gear and roared away.

# CHAPTER 35

J im had just changed his blue shirt for a fresh white one when he heard the pops. He stepped outside the cabin and walked to the edge of the highway, buttoning his shirt as he went. He saw nothing that would indicate the firing of guns, but yet, the sounds were definitely gunshots – he had heard many in his day. He walked the one block to Bay Street and looked first to the east. He saw a man get out of a gray car parked in the westbound lane and trot across the street. The man looked oddly familiar, but he couldn't place him. What was it about him? Jim looked in the direction the man was running and saw another man lying on the sidewalk and other people gathering around. A robbery, he thought. He ran back to the motel office and yelled at the old man reading a newspaper, with the radio blaring. "Call the police. There's been a shooting on Bay, one block east of Highway 17. I'm a Deputy Sheriff. Tell them I'll be there." His voice was authoritative and commanded respect. The man sat up straight, looked at Jim, then grabbed the phone.

When Jim reached his cabin, Maybelle stood in front of the open door. She was excited. "What's going on down there? What are you doing?"

He pushed by her and went into the room. She followed. He went to the closet and pulled out his traveling bag. He removed the holster and pistol and strapped it to his waist and pinned the sheriff's badge to his shirt. "There's been a shooting down the street. I've got to go see if I can help. You stay inside until I get back. Could be dangerous outside. Lock the door behind me." She tried to say something, but he brushed by her and ran outside. He stopped at the car, got his shotgun and shells, and loaded it as he ran.

The getaway car passed by as he reached Bay Street. It moved fast towards the west. He could not recall ever seeing one similar. The fleeting glimpse of the driver told him that it was the same man he'd seen running across the street at the robbery site. Again, he thought there was something strangely familiar about the man. The only thing he could tell about the man in back was that he was young, big and had coal-black hair. They looked into each other's eyes as the car passed. Both men in the car had dark complexions. He drew his pistol, cocked it and aimed at the back tire. People came pouring out of buildings all along Bay Street. Somebody could easily get hurt if he fired now. He wasn't sure if it was even legal for him to carry a firearm in Georgia. He uncocked the pistol and reholstered it. The car was now too far away to clearly read the license plate, which looked to be smeared with dirt.

The wailing of sirens several blocks away came to his ears as he trotted toward the store. People were standing around in front, talking among themselves and gawking at the blood. One of the men started to go through the door but stopped when Jim yelled at him. He started to protest, saw the badge on Jim's shirt and the shotgun in his hand, then backed away. Jim stepped to the door and opened it. He hesitated and turned to the people. "You folks ought to move on now. There's nothin' you can do here. The police will be here in a minute and you need to give them room to do their job. Go on now. Go on home." He went inside without waiting for their response.

A pile of glass lay in a pool of blood on the floor in front of a shattered display case. Through the case he made out the body of a man. Little pieces of glass were strewn all over the room. He made his way around the pile of glass, went around back of the counter and knelt next to the crumpled body. He felt a trace of a pulse in the man's neck – none at all in the wrist. The bullet had entered the man's belly at the lower ribs. Blood seeped from the exit wound at the back. Unable to do more for the man, he went outside to wait for the police. A good many people were still hanging around. They moved back when he came out and leaned

260

the shotgun against the wall. He motioned for a young woman in the crowd to come to him. The sirens were louder now. They would be here any minute. "Ma'am, would you please get to the nearest phone and call for an ambulance. Tell 'em there's been a shooting and the man is still alive. They ought to get here quick." She turned and hurried off.

The sirens turned the corner to the east, followed immediately by three squad cars, one after the other. Sirens faded as the cars pulled up to the curb. Rotating flashing red lights strobed buildings on both sides of the street in the fading light. The sun had moved far to the west and had taken its heat with it. The cool wind, coming out of the northeast, strengthened as it rushed through the alleys between the buildings and caused him to shiver. Police officers, armed to the teeth, poured out of the cars and took up positions around the building. Jim stepped away from the building and flashed his badge to the first officer to debark. The sergeant faced Jim while two other officers had their guns trained on him. The sergeant barked, "Who the hell are you?"

"Jim Harrison, Special Deputy from Monroe County, Florida. Happened to be in the neighborhood and came to offer my assistance."

The sergeant looked around at all the people and then back at Jim. "Have you been inside? Is it all clear?" Officers stood now at both sides of the door waiting for orders to enter. Sirens continued to wail throughout the city.

"Yes, I've been in and it's all clear in there. There's a man dyin' in there and needs medical assistance right now."

At a nod from the sergeant the officers entered the building. "An ambulance is on the way."

A loud siren quit its mournful wail as the ambulance pulled up and parked in the middle of the street next to a police car. Two men in white uniforms jumped out. One went up to the sergeant and the other went around the back of the ambulance and came out with a stretcher. "You have a man dying here?"

An officer stuck his head out the door and yelled to the sergeant. "It's all clear in here, sir." The sergeant motioned for the cameraman to go in for pictures.

"All right, Corpsman, you can have him as soon as we get pictures. Don't move anything else." He took Jim by the arm and guided him toward the door. Jim picked up his shotgun and removed the shells. The medics followed and went directly to the dying man. At the door, the sergeant grabbed onto an assistant. "Jody, get this crowd dispersed. I don't want to see them within a hundred feet of this store when I come back out. Understand?" The officer moved away. As they entered, the cameraman came out from behind the counter and signaled that he had the needed pictures of the dying man. He continued taking other pictures of the room. Plainclothes detectives arrived and talked briefly with the sergeant and the cameraman. After looking at the dying man, one of the detectives came back to the sergeant and pulled him toward the desk and chair in the far corner of the room. "What can you tell me, Frank?"

"This here is Jim, uh." He turned to Jim, "what'd you say your name was?"

"Harrison. Jim Harrison."

"Uh, okay. Jim Harrison is a Special Deputy from Florida. He saw part of what went on. Let him tell it." The detective turned to Jim and nodded.

"I was in my cabin around the corner on Highway 17 when I heard the gunshots. I got to Bay Street in time to see a big man pick up another who was on the sidewalk just outside the door and take him to a car parked on the other side of the street."

The detective interjected, "What kind of car?"

"Don't know the make. Never seen one like it."

"Okay, go on."

"I ran back to call the police and to get my guns. When I got back on Bay, the car with the two men I could see passed by goin' like a bat out of hell."

"Heading west? Did you get a look at the men? What color was the car? Tag?"

"Yeah, headin' west on Bay. The car was a gray four-door sedan. Tag was muddy. Both men had kind of dark skin."

"Colored men?"

"No, I don't think so. Didn't see their features. The car sped by too quick. Color more like Indians or Spaniards, I'd say. The driver had one long pigtail, couldn't tell if the other man had long hair. It was coal-black, though."

The detective's assistant came up to him and whispered in his ear. "Got to go now. Jim, will you be around for a while? May want to talk with you some more."

"Plan to leave here Sunday. Will hang around if you need me, but I really do need to get back home. Matter of fact, I've got to get back to my cabin. I'm supposed to meet with an officer from Captain Clark's department at six."

"It's five of, now. You better get going. I'll get hold of Clark if I need you. Thanks for your help." He turned and went off with his assistant.

Jim shook hands with the sergeant and went out the door. As he walked back to the cabin, he went over the day's events in his mind. The thing that troubled him most was the lingering image of the man driving the getaway car. He knew he had seen that man somewhere before. He went over the description he gave the detective. The detective had asked if the men were colored and he had replied no, they were more like Indians. By God, that's it. The long hair braided into one pigtail and the light coppery skin. It was Curly, the Indian he had given a ride. Naw, couldn't be – too much of a coincidence. Could it really be Curly? Just who the hell is Curly anyhow? He started to turn around to tell the detective of his thoughts. The other officer who was to take him to interview the Indians would be here in just a few minutes. *Maybe my suspicions are all wrong anyhow – I'll tell him later.*

# CHAPTER 36

**B**uddy had to fight himself to keep his foot light on the accelerator. His urge was strong to get as far away from this town as possible in the shortest period of time. Night was coming down fast. In a minute it would be completely dark on the highway. Sirens wailed all over the city, it seemed. Although they were all far away for now, he suspected the cops would be closing in on them pretty quick. Right after passing through colored town he pressed his foot down on the accelerator and the big car lunged forward.

Toby sat up and looked all around before he spoke. It was now dark outside and only the faint glow of the dashboard lights provided a light inside the car. "Where are we? Put your lights on, Curly. How fast are you doing? We don't want to attract any attention."

Buddy flipped a switch on the dashboard. The light from the big head lamps sliced a clean hole through the night and illuminated the highway out in front for two hundred feet. No other cars were about. The sirens sounded like they were getting closer. "We just passed through colored town. Another five miles or so to the turn off. Just took her up to sixty-five. This thing'll do ninety, I bet."

Toby lay back on the seat and said nothing. Marty had not uttered a peep. Buddy saw part of both of them in the rear-view mirror.

He thought about the man who yelled at him just before he picked up Toby. The man was too far off to make out, but there was a certain familiarity about him. The glimpse of him as they roared up Bay Street strengthened the notion that he had seen him somewhere before. "Marty, did you get a good look at that man on the corner, right after we left?"

264

Marty grunted something, but went no further. Toby leaned forward from his seat. "What about the man, Curly? What's he have to do with us?"

"Don't know that he has anything to do with us, but he did look like somebody I've seen before and I haven't seen too many people off from Liz's. Know he held a shotgun in his hand. Didn't get to see him too good and just wondered if Marty did."

"A shotgun huh? Well, Marty, did you see the man? Might be important."

"Yeah, I looked him dead in the eye and he looked right back."

Toby's interest in the man had deepened. "Can you describe him?"

"Big man. Maybe six feet and about fifty, I reckon. Had on blue pants and a white shirt buttoned at the sleeves. Wore a holstered six gun around his waist and toted a shotgun in his hand." Marty paused as if thinking about what he had seen. "He had a policeman's badge on his left chest. I ducked down when he pulled the pistol."

"Marty, I'm always taken by you. Never met anyone else with a memory like yours. How do you remember things like that?"

"Don't know. It's like somebody took a picture and left it in my head. Just see the picture all over again. Everything's right there."

Toby groaned and held his stomach as he leaned against the front seat. "Well, Curly, did that description help your memory any?"

"I'm scared of what I remember. That description, when mixed up with my own memory, paints a pretty good picture of the sheriff I rode up here with, the same sheriff that came to Andre's lookin' for me and you . . . the same sheriff that came to Savannah lookin' for you. You reckon he could be one and the same?"

Toby leaned back against the rear seat and still had not responded when they came to the dirt road turnoff. Buddy

265

turned left and soon pulled up alongside the old Hudson. He switched off the lights and the blackness engulfed them. For an instant they might as well have been blind. "Don't turn off the engine, Curly, but go and unlock the Hudson. Marty, you help me out of here and be damn careful about it. Put me in the Hudson and make sure you bring the bags."

Buddy opened the driver's door to the Hudson and held the back one open for Toby. Marty was careful as he put Toby in the back seat, but even so, Toby let out a scream as he settled on the seat. "Get the bags, Marty. Curly, you take the Studebaker and run it in the water. Be sure the lights are off."

Buddy started to question the order then understood the reason for the two cars. He backed the Studebaker out and lined it up on the dirt ramp going into the water. His eyes were now accustomed to the dark and the headlights weren't needed. He shifted to first gear with the clutch engaged, advanced the spark a little to keep the engine accelerated some, gave it a little gas and released the clutch. The car moved slowly towards the water. He held the door open and jumped out just before the water reached him, slamming the door on the way out. He watched as the perfectly good car went out on the water and seemed to float for the longest moment, then start to sink. In less than a minute the car was gone. He wondered how far out it would settle and how deep it was there. Would it ever be found? Toby yelled for him to hurry. The sirens seemed close out on Highway 21.

Toby leaned against the front seat as Buddy started backing out. The headlights shone on the water. There was not even a ripple where the Studebaker had just been – no sign of it at all. "Let's go home, but this time, Curly, we'll go out the other way. Follow this dirt road until you come to a paved road and turn left on it. It'll get a little muddled out here in the dark so take it easy. The police won't be looking for us way out here."

The night was pitch-black and getting colder. Once on the paved road, Buddy rolled his window up and almost ran off the road trying to roll the other one up. The headlights cut a strange looking swath through the blackness and the road seemed to roll under the car as they sped forward. Soon they crossed Highway 21 and headed south on Tremont. The sirens sounded very faint farther to the north. At Toby's direction Buddy turned west on Highway 17 then south on Liberty and came to a full stop at the intersection at 52nd Street. "Cut your lights, Curly. I want to ease up to the house without Marie hearing or seeing us. I don't want her to see me in this fix. We'll be turning left at the next corner. Give your eyes time to adjust to the dark before we move."

Buddy switched the lights off and the night consumed them – the quiet pervasive. He eased the car forward until they reached the corner and began a slow turn to the left. From there they could clearly see the apartment. The front porch light bathed the porch and part of the street in front. They were easing their way around the corner when the headlights of a car entered the street at the other end. Buddy stopped.

Toby ordered, "Back around the corner, Curly." They watched as the headlights came to a stop in front of the apartment. Toby cursed, "Goddam, it's a police car. What are they doing here? How could they know that we pulled the job?"

Before he could continue, the car headed in their direction and, just as quickly, did a U-turn and headed the other way, then parked on the other side of the street in the darkness on this side of the apartment. The headlights went off. The street lay in darkness except for the apartment light and a house light farther to the east.

Marty popped up, "What's going on? I can't see anything from here. Did you say the police are there?"

Buddy backed around the corner and kept the car in reverse, ready to make a quick exit if that was called for. "Looks to me like they're on to us already. They're gonna nab us soon's we pull up."

Toby cut him off. "What I can't figure is how they got on to us so fast. You say the sheriff was looking for me. Suppose he's in cahoots with the police about that? Well, no matter. We can't take a chance now. Need more time to think. We'll sneak in the apartment the back way and get some of our things in case we want to take off right quick. Curly, back up to the alley just behind us and go down it to the east."

Going without lights, they pulled up past the apartment and parked at the edge of a vacant lot on the far side. "Marty, you and Curly go up to the room and get as much of our clothes and stuff as you can carry. Get something for my cuts, too – bandages, iodine and stuff. We don't want to stir Marie so go quiet as a mouse, and be quick about it." A sharp pain in his right rib cage caused him to wince – his hand went there automatically.

They felt their way across the lot in the dark and Marty started to open the wooden gate to the backyard of the apartment building – it creaked. He stopped. He inched the gate open until they could squeeze through. Marty trotted toward the back porch and ran headlong into a low clothesline full of damp clothes. Buddy, following too closely, almost suffered the same fate. Working their way through the wet clothes they made it to the doorway leading to the front of the house and the stairway to their room. The floor creaked as they stepped through the door. They froze and listened for movement from Marie. Nothing stirred. Rousing music from the radio in Marie's room filtered out into the hallway. Buddy recognized the tune – Play Fiddle Play. The squeak of the rocking chair on the front porch indicated that Marie was out there. They tread softly to the foot of the stairs, climbed to the landing and went into the room. Without light, other than the moonlight filtering through the window, they began to gather the things they would take. Buddy walked to the window, moved the curtain a dab with his forefinger and peered down to the street. The police car was still there.

# CHAPTER 37

Jim opened the car door and stepped out onto the sidewalk into the chilly air. The windbreaker he wore didn't ward off the chill. He stuffed and lit his pipe, keeping the car between the glow of the match and the apartment building. The police officer got out onto the street and came around to where Jim was. "Mr. Harrison, it's almost seven. Think we might've missed them?"

Jim looked at the young officer over the glowing pipe bowl and thought to himself, we wouldn't have missed them if you'd been on time. Can't stand incompetence or tardiness. "Your captain told me they usually get home about six, then go off to a pool hall somewhere. They could've come and gone by now. Maybe we can drive over to the pool hall. You know where it is?"

"Yes sir. It's the Purple Derby on Montgomery, just a few blocks from here. You want to go over there now?"

"We'll wait a few more minutes." He sucked the final mouthful of smoke from the pipe and tapped the spent tobacco out on the heel of his shoe. He opened the car door, hesitated, then re-closed it. "Let's go over and see if we can talk to the landlord. Maybe he might know where they are."

They walked across the street and had started up the steps when they were startled by the woman's voice coming out of the darkness at the far corner of the porch. "What can I do for you gentlemen?"

The officer stepped towards the voice and identified himself. "Ma'am, I'm Officer Jeffery Oglesbee with the Savannah Police Department. This here is Deputy Jim Harrison. We need to ask you a few questions about a couple of your guests, if we might." Jim came and stood by the officer.

Marie resumed her rocking with the squeak squeak of the chair on the wooden floor. "I only have two at the time, so you must be talking about Toby Cypress and Martin Tucker. What do you want to know about them?"

Jim spoke for the first time, "It's very important that I speak with Mr. Cypress, ma'am. Do you know if he came home tonight? I'm told that he usually gets home about six or so. Reckon we missed him?" He held his hat in his hands and looked down at the small woman in the rocker.

"I haven't seen them this evening at all. Far as I know they haven't come home from work yet. Sometimes they go straight to the pool hall."

"Have you seen them at all today?"

"They busted their routine today. They didn't go out until almost four in the afternoon. Wouldn't of then, I reckon, if that Indian boy hadn't come by."

Jim jumped to high alert, but kept his voice calm. "What Indian boy? When did he come? What did he have to do with them?"

"I directed him to Toby's apartment about two o'clock today. I heard him banging on the door and after a while he came down and said nobody answered. I hadn't seen Toby or Marty leave so I went up there with him, thinking that maybe something was wrong. I banged on the door for a while, then when no one came to the door, I opened it with my key. Found Toby drunk as a skunk. I left them, and in a little while they all came down and the Indian boy drove them away in Toby's car. That's the last I seen of them."

Jim's mind reeled. All this was too much to sink in correctly. The information formed a jumble in his mind. "What kind of car this Toby own?"

"1924 Hudson sedan – black."

The robbery car was gray and definitely not a Hudson. Jim continued the questioning. "Can we look in their apartment?"

"I don't know that I ought to do that. Don't you all need to have proper permission to do that?"

The officer spoke up, "Yes, ma'am. We could go and get it done up all proper, but then the detectives and all would be coming around asking a lot of questions. Could be bad publicity for you. We could be in and out in a minute and cause you no trouble at all. You come with us to see we don't pry into anything. Just want to get a look-see."

Marie stopped rocking and seemed to be thinking this thing through. "Well, I don't know. I sure don't need the police crawling all over my place. Come on, I'll take you up for just one quick peek. You promise me you won't touch nothing?"

"Promise."

CHAPTER **38**

Marty and Buddy crept down the stairs without making a sound and stopped at the foot to listen for Marie. The rocker had stopped squeaking but they heard men's voices on the porch. Marie was talking to men. Police? They hurried silently down the dark hallway and went through the backdoor. Avoiding the clothesline, they went through the still-open gate and got into the car.

Toby was up and anxious. "Well, what happened? Did you see Marie? Were the cops still there? Did you get the medicine?" Buddy held his tongue and gave Marty the first shot at answers.

Marty said, "Marie was on the front porch in her rocking chair. I didn't check for the police." He turned to Buddy. "Curly, did you think to look for the police on the outside?"

"Yeah, I looked through the window and they were still parked at the same place."

Marty continued, "When we came down the stairs, Marie was talking to some men, probably the police. We could hear their voices. We didn't stick around to hear what they were saying. Got what medicine we had. It's in this box. I'll get it for you." He went around the car to the other side and got in. Buddy got in the driver's side.

"Curly, let's ease on out of here. Go out towards Montgomery. There's a little diner on Washington Avenue where we can get something to eat. Marty, you help me get some of this medicine on these cuts." Buddy let out the clutch and moved eastward with the lights off. "It looks like the bullet went clean through my leg. Let's try to pour some iodine into the hole and maybe it'll seep right on through. Maybe that's all that happened to it. I can move it all right now, but it still hurts like hell. First, though, put some on this belly cut and see if you can shut it up with some gauze then wrap it tight."

Buddy turned left on Montgomery and switched the lights on. Marty looked up from what he was doing. "Turn right at the next corner, then right again until you come to Washington, then right. Pull around back of Jackie's Diner. It'll be on the left-hand side." He went back to helping Toby.

At the diner, Buddy turned the lights off and killed the engine. Except for a small dim light over the back door of the diner, the night was pitch-black. Old wooden boxes were stacked near the building and next to them were three trashcans with the lids on. Another can lay on its side and a rough-looking dog rummaged through the spilled garbage. He had apparently found something of great interest because he paid no attention to Buddy as he got out of the car and relieved his kidneys against the building. Two other cars were parked on the other side of the lot.

When he returned to the car, Toby was sitting up, his chest wrapped in gauze. "Curly, you go into the diner and get us some hamburgers and French-fries. Get us a couple apiece. I'm starving to death. Get whatever you want to drink. I want a big cup of coffee. Cream and sugar." He handed Buddy a ten-dollar bill.

Marty grunted. "I want coffee, too. Same as Toby."

Buddy walked around to the front of the building, stood for a minute at the corner and surveyed the surrounding buildings. The area was built up with buildings and stores of one kind or another – mostly all closed now. Across the street, on the corner, a gas station attendant was pumping gas into a car. Buddy could just barely make out a man and woman inside the car. A car passed going north and all was silent. Street lights lit up the street around the pole and faintly illuminated the storefronts within the circle of light.

Buddy looked through the large plate-glass window of the diner. A young girl behind the counter with her back to him, was busy with somebody at the opening to the kitchen. Two men sat on stools at the counter with about five seats between them. At a booth under the window, a man and woman were busy talking

273

and eating their supper. The far end of the room was out of his view. He looked himself over and remembered the last cafe he had entered. *Hope these people will let me be.*

The music from the jukebox drowned out the sound of the door opening and no one paid him any heed until he stepped up to the counter between the two men. He felt their eyes on him and he glanced at one and then the other. Each one nodded a greeting and went back to their eating. The girl ignored him. After a long minute, Buddy said, "Ma'am, I'd like to make an order to take out."

She turned toward him, turned back to the person she was talking to, then came over to him. "What can I do for you, mister?"

"I want six hamburgers and French-fries and three big coffees to go." He laid the ten on the counter top.

"Want the hamburgers all the way?"

"All the way?"

She gave him a funny look, like 'Don't you know anything?' "You know, with ketchup, mustard, lettuce and tomato and onion?"

He smiled at her. "Yeah, all the way." He looked at the two men who were looking at him. They both quickly looked away.

The jukebox went off and the man nearest to it walked over and studied the labels. The door creaked and Buddy turned to see who had entered. He almost jumped out of his skin – two uniformed cops had entered and were walking directly toward him. They looked straight at him and didn't say a word. What to do? Did they know he was part of the stick-up? Did they already have Toby and Marty? *God Almighty. God Almighty.* He turned to look at the man and the jukebox as the music blared and filled the room from end to end. The cops passed right by. The one nearest Buddy looked past him and spoke, "Lindy, what's on special tonight? Not that same old meat loaf again, I hope." They both laughed.

"No, not tonight, Sam. That was real popular, it only lasted three days." They all three laughed at what apparently was their inside joke. "You're in luck tonight, though. This is the first night for some good old down-home cooking. Baked ham with new red potatoes and fresh picked green beans cooked down long with fat-back. Some three-day-old collards and okra, if you want it." They all laughed again.

The one called Sam said, "I'll have the special. How about you, Buck?"

The other one lit a cigarette and nodded, "That's fine with me." He blew the match out and exhaled the smoke across the counter. "Coffee, too, Lindy gal."

Buddy looked at the other people in the room. No one seemed to pay any attention to the cops or the conversation between them and the girl. She went to the window and called out to the person hidden there. In a minute she was in front of Buddy with a bag full of food. "That'll be three dollars and a quarter, mister." She put her hand on the ten – he nodded – she went to the cash register and returned with his change. "I put extra salt and pepper in the bag."

The cops were now looking his way. Buddy picked up the change and left a fifty-cent piece in its place. He felt all the eyes in the place boring into him. "Much obliged, ma'am." With his back straight and his face without emotion, he nodded at the policemen, strolled across the room and out the door.

They sat in the dark car and ate their fill in silence – each person to his own thoughts. The coffee, except for the first warming sip, was kept until last to enjoy with a cigarette. The glow of the match lit their tired faces and the fire lit all three cigarettes. They sipped their coffee and smoked. Even with the windows down, the car quickly filled with smoke. They were used to smoke-filled rooms. Toby threw the butt out the window, looked longingly into his empty cup and it followed the cigarette. "Marty, strike a match." The flame lit up the cab. He looked at his watch. "Twenty-five to nine. Branbury and Copolla will be jumping through their butts by now. We better get on over there and settle up with them. Then we've got to find someplace to stay. I'm plumb tuckered. You all ready to move out?"

Marty threw his cigarette and cup outside on the ground. "We can get us a room on  Brunswick Highway just south of the airfield. I remember a group of cabins over there set way back in a grove. You reckon they'll give us anything even though the job was botched?"

Toby reached for the full bag and placed it on the seat between him and Marty. "Yeah, they'll give us our share all right." He patted the bag with his right hand. "I wonder how much cash is in this bag. We've been so busy we haven't even counted it." He reached into the bag.

Marty's high-pitched voice stopped him cold. "Cash? How do you know there's cash in that bag? We were supposed to get jewels and loose cash. You told me to leave them be. I didn't take anything except this bag."

Toby lit another cigarette and threw the match out the window. "That bag was mighty important to Mr. Branbury. Always figured that it must've been loaded with cash. Let's see what's in there." He unzipped the bag and pulled out four bundles of bills strapped together with paper tape. Underneath that bundle was another and another and another. He let out a low whistle. "Must be a million dollars in here." He shoved one bundle under Buddy's nose and tossed another one to Marty. "Curly, have you ever seen anything like this?"

Marty whistled softly, almost to himself. "What do we do with these, Toby? Do we keep it for ourselves? Those bastards done us dirt. We shouldn't give them a damn thing."

Toby retrieved the bundle from him. "We'll see, Marty old pard, we'll see."

Buddy could barely see the bundles, but from following the conversation, knew exactly what they were. He reached out and touched the money. He didn't want any part of this money – just wanted to get back down to Florida and get far away from these boys. If he continued to hang around with them he would likely end up in jail or face down in a swamp some place. He would just have to find another way to locate his memory. "Naw, I never seen nothin' even close to that much money. You reckon it's really a million? How much is a million anyhow? What's your share of that?"

"I don't know exactly how much it is. They never did tell us how much would be in the bag. Our share is $10,000 apiece."

Buddy was curious about the word 'they' and if 'they' were getting all the rest. "Is 'they' Branbury and the other feller? They the ones that planned the whole thing? How much they gettin'?"

Toby stared at Buddy as if in deep thought about the question, before he took the money and put it back inside the bag. "Okay, boys, that's enough BS for now, let's get on out of here, then find a place to turn in. Crank her up, Curly, and head back the way we came." He lay back against the seat. Marty looked at him for assurance. Toby patted him on the knee.

# CHAPTER 39

It was 8:13 when the special gatehouse phone on Copolla's desk rang. Branbury, sitting on the other side of the desk, answered it, "Yes?"

"There are two police officers down here wanting to speak to an officer of the company."

"Put one of them on. Did they say what they wanted?" There was a pause at the other end, then the guard came on again.

"I'm sorry sir, they want to speak with you in person."

Robert Copolla came into the room through a door at the back with a quizzical look on his face. Branbury spoke into the telephone, "Hold on," Then to Copolla, "Police at the gate. Want to come up and talk. Don't know what they want."

Copolla walked behind the desk and lowered his frame into the padded leather chair. He studied Branbury still holding the phone, obviously very concerned. "Send them in."

Branbury relayed the information to the guard and replaced the phone on its stand. To Copolla he said, "Do you think they're on to the boys? Those sirens came on too soon after the planned time."

"Well, we know now they were thrown into a non-planned situation. We can only hope they made the right decisions. Guess we'll be knowing something any minute now. Just be calm and let me do the talking. You better go down and meet them at the door."

Jeffery parked the cruiser next to the door. Branbury, already waiting, led them up the stairs to Copolla's office. Copolla came from around the desk and held out his hand. "Hello, officers. I'm Robert Copolla, President of the company and this is Mr. Branbury, my assistant. How can we help you?"

They shook hands all around. Jeffery answered, "We're looking for Toby Cypress and we understand he works for your company. We tried his home, but he wasn't there. Thought someone here might be able to help us."

Copolla turned to Branbury, "Thurgood, you know this Toby Cypress? What does he do for us?"

"Yes, sir. He's a machinist and heavy equipment mechanic. Been with us about eight, nine months. Good worker."

Copolla motioned the officers to the two chairs in front of the desk, moved around behind the desk and sat in the chair there. Branbury pulled up a chair from across the room and lowered himself into it. The policemen moved near the chairs, but continued standing. Copolla, with a quizzical look on his face, looked at Branbury who was eyeing him intensely and said, "Do you know anything about his whereabouts?"

"They were scheduled to work on a broke-down dozer out on 17 South today. They—"

Jim broke in, "Excuse me, sir. You said, 'they'. Was someone else with him?"

"Yes. Martin Tucker was assigned to go with him. They work together a lot. I believe they also live together a little west of here. But I was going to say, I expected them to be in here this afternoon with the dozer, but I haven't heard a word from either of them. I drove out there earlier to check on them. The dozer was there, but they weren't."

Jim asked, "These two men, they Indians?"

"Yes, they said they were from Florida. Lived on a reservation down there somewhere. Both men are good workers, though."

Copolla broke in. "Why are you looking for these men? Did they do something wrong?"

Jeffery took the lead. He had been well taught never to explain anything to the public you're questioning. He was unsure how the sheriff would respond. "We don't know that they did anything wrong, Mr. Copolla. Just need to ask them some questions, that's all."

279

Copolla was visibly relieved. He sighed and lay back in his chair. He looked at Branbury who seemed relieved, too. He and Branbury had heard the sirens wailing all afternoon and felt sure the job had been pulled off as scheduled. It wasn't until an hour ago that they learned that Harold Echley, the man on the inside, had been hospitalized and had been replaced at the jewelry store by another man. No other news was available. These officers apparently were not associating Toby with the robbery at this time. He stood and came around the desk. "Officers, I'm sorry we can't be more help. Leave your telephone number where we can reach you. When we hear from these boys, we'll call you. I'm sure there's a reasonable explanation for their absence." He ushered the officers towards the office door. He glanced at the clock in the bookcase to the left of the desk – ten minutes to nine. Martha would be calling any moment now.

When Branbury walked into the office after directing the officers to their car, Copolla was pacing the floor in front of his desk. He stopped and whirled around, his face flushed with fury. "Thurgood, where the hell are those boys? Weren't they supposed to come straight back here after the job? You think they have the goods?" He backed up to the desk, shook a cigarette from the pack and lit it with the lighter on the desk. His eyes looked hot enough to light the cigarette.

"They were supposed to get here as soon as they could if there was a problem. I don't know where they are. If I know Toby, though, he'll be trying every way possible to get here. He's honest as the day is long. I'd trust him with my life."

Copolla jumped away from the desk almost out of control. "You'd trust him with your life? You know how much cash was in that bag? Thurgood, I don't give a good Goddam how the hell you do it, but you get out there and find those boys and report to me as soon as you find them. I don't care what time it is when you do. You understand?" He shook his finger right in Branbury's face – another inch and he would have touched it.

280

Branbury understood very well. Twenty percent of the contents of that bag was his retirement – his ticket away from Robert Copolla. "Yes sir, I understand. I'll see if I can find out what happened and see if I can locate the boys." He turned to leave.

"In any case, be here in the morning – 8:00 o'clock sharp. We've got to figure how to retrieve that bag, if they have it."

Marty flashed his badge at the guard and the big gate swung open. The trees and shrubs blocked the main buildings from Buddy's view. He passed a row of buildings on the right and turned into an empty parking lot. Other short trees separated this lot from the lot closest to a large metal building with a small light over a door. He saw a police cruiser parked just this side of the door. Instead of proceeding on to the smaller lot he drove on past the door to the far end of the large lot. The short trees partly shielded the bottom of the building from view. He could not see the cruiser now. "Toby, there's a cop car parked by that big building over there."

Toby sat up like a bolt of lightning. "What? Where?" He moved about in the car trying to get a clear view of the police car. "Back up a little."

Buddy slowly backed the car up until he could plainly see the cruiser. "There it is. Look right through there."

Toby stared long at the police car and seemed to be talking out loud to himself. "First they were at the apartment, now here. What the hell's gone wrong? I don't get it. All the planning and everything else that was supposed to go right has all gone wrong and that damn sheriff from Florida is right in the middle of the whole thing. I'll just have to find another way to contact Branbury." Then to Buddy, "I see it. Let's get the hell out of here, and be quick about it, but don't speed or do anything to alert the guard." He lay back in the seat and groaned.

As Buddy eased up to the gate it opened. He nodded to the guard as he went through and turned right on the paved road.

The headlights cut through the darkness. The half moon provided scant light. He reckoned they were headed south.

Toby sat up. "Curly, follow this road on around until you come to Highway 17 and turn south. We'll drive for a while until I can get my thinking cap on straight. How are we on gas?"

"About half a tank."

"Better stop first chance you get and fill up. Make sure you check the water and oil, too."

Just north of Brunswick, Buddy saw the faded sign of the Victory Motel and pulled into the parking lot. There was a diner with loud country music escaping through the door. Toby sat up rubbing the sleep from his eyes. "Where are we?"

"Just outside Brunswick. Maybe we can get a room here. I'm tired out. Gotta stop for a while." Buddy shut the engine off, stepped out of the car and walked up and down rubbing his legs to restore the circulation.

Toby ripped the tape from a bundle of the bills. "Marty, take this money and get us a room with three beds for the night."

# CHAPTER 40

Flo had been waiting twenty minutes when she saw the run-boat round the point at Hog Key. It was a welcome sight. Randy Wade, probably the pilot – always on time. Flo liked Randy. He was just a few years older than her and always seemed happy. He seemed to care about the needs of other people – about Buddy's age she reckoned.

A deep rumble from the southwest and a sudden gust of damp wind caused her to pay closer attention to the sky, now filled with heavy dark clouds close down to the water and far out in the Gulf. The normally blue sky had turned into a brooding gray, and she knew it carried just enough rain to make life miserable. The best the rising sun could do this morning was to lighten the clouds to a very pale gray with a coral tint at the tops.

Flo shielded the baby from the cold wind and looked along the shoreline for Junior and Francis. Lucy had them in hand and was talking with Adele at the edge of the dock. As usual the children were bare-foot. She looked down and saw their shoes lying by her bag. The boat drew nearer as Lucy came out on the dock with the two children in hand.

"Flo, I don't know how in this world you keep up with these two young'uns, but I reckon they'll sure pop keep you young. You sure do look slim and prim today. You still losin' weight? Is that the new dress you got in Key West? Let me get a closer look at the beads." Her hand touched the necklace and Flo shivered as the cold fingers brushed her neck. Lucy held tightly to the boys with her other hand as they tried to break free to get closer to the edge of the dock so they could watch the boat come in.

Lucy was dressed normally with a plain cotton dress hung loose and baggy down to her ankles, her feet as bare as the kids. Her loose brown hair blew freely in the wind. She was still big as a cow with the child that could be born any minute. "Lucy, I

283

don't know how you could forget this dress. You were at my wedding, and no, I'm not still losin' weight. I'm down to one hundred twenty-nine and plan to stay right there."

"Well I'll swan. That is your wedding dress. Where's my mind? I don't know either how I could forget how fancy you were that day. Neckline a little low for a proper girl, though, ain't it?" She cackled.

Flo fingered the neckline of the dress. She had bought the dress for the wedding five years ago particularly because of the brown embroidery around the neck and down the sides. She remembered, too, how nervous she was that day. She stopped Buddy's memory from entering her mind so she wouldn't break down. "I reckon you all ain't goin' in this mornin'. Good thing I decided to take the run-boat. Never get to Captiva if I waited till this afternoon to go in." She turned to look at the boat as it neared the dock.

"Reckon you were right smart on that count. King and your daddy were up before the crack of daylight, headed south. Ray's still asleep – hung over from last night's party down at Lostman's. Don't know if we'll even get into town today. We'll be a sorry mess if we don't, though."

The boat pulled up to the dock, and Randy looked down at the bags sitting by Flo's feet and called out as he continued forward, moved to reverse, then to stop, "Flo, you gonna ride with me today? Hello, Lucy, you goin' into town, too?" He looped the stern rope over the dock pole and ran to the bow and secured that line.

Junior and Francis finally wrenched loose from Lucy and ran to the boat, jabbering away and eager to get onboard. Lucy took the baby from Flo, "No, Randy, I'm not goin' nowhere today it looks like. Just come out to say hello and see if there's any mail." She turned her face into the wind so it would blow the hair out of her eyes.

"I do have a few pieces for old man Harrison. Reckon you can give it to him for me, Lucy." Randy stepped out onto the dock, careful to avoid running into the children. He handed

Lucy two letters. "Got one for you, too, Flo." He passed the letter to her, picked up her bags and climbed back onto the boat, ready to shove off. The children fought to see who could get on first. Randy picked Francis up and Junior jumped over the side and onto the floorboards, just missing an elderly woman sitting at the dock side of the boat. He rolled over holding onto his toes and screamed, then got up okay. Randy moved to undo the bow ropes. "Shake a leg, Flo. Gotta be on time, you know."

Flo turned to Lucy and the wind blew strands of hair into her eyes and mouth. She turned part way into the wind and took the baby from her. "Lucy, don't forget to tell Papa I'll be back Sunday night if nothin' happens and I can get a boat. If I'm gonna be late, I'll try to send word. If he needs to get in touch with me, I'll either be at Mama's or Dot's at Ky Costa. Tell him I been thinkin' about what he said and, besides, I had to go see if Dot needed help with that new young'un." She neglected to tell her she also wanted to get Dot's advice about marrying Bill Parkins.

"Don't you fret none, Flo. You try to take it easy the few days you're gone. Everybody'll be just fine here and the farm will still be here when you get back."

"Yeah. I bet it will." Flo stepped onto the wooden seat, bowed her head low to get underneath the canopy and moved to the stern where she watched Lucy turn and walk toward the beach. The wind had turned to the north and had become downright chilly as the boat rounded the east end of Wood Key. The choppy water slapped against the side of the boat. She still had the letter in her hand and looked to the bow where Randy had placed Junior and Francis on the console just behind the windshield. They played like they were steering the boat.

The boat was about thirty feet long and eight feet wide with wooden seats lengthwise on both sides. The canopy, supported by several wooden poles, ran the entire length and had canvas sides rolled to the top and tied there by small ropes. It would take just a small tug on the ropes to drop the canvas to keep out the bad weather she suspected was coming. The old woman, sitting on the right side, nodded her way. The woman was not known to her, but Flo nodded back and took a seat on the end of the bench at the stern with the baby on her lap and opened the letter. It was from Bill.

*Everglades Fla*
*November 18 1932*

*Dear Flo*
*I will drop you a line or two to let you know that I made it OK to Turkey Key and got me a man to fish with me. How is your cold and all of the boys. It has been blowing a gale down here. I come up here to vote but I didn't get a chance to – don't make no difference no how I reckon. I am going on to Sand Key tonight. Fish on the way down. Is your Mom down there with you? Flo I don't know how to tell you to send mail to me.*
*I guess you can send it to Punta Gorda or take it to the fish house and they will send it to me. Well Flo I don't know mutch more to write you, onely that I am in the Everglades. I think I could write more if I could spell or write better. But I guess you can read it. I am thinking of you all of the time and hope you are the same of me. When I see you again I hope you will be ready to marry me. I love you so much. I guess I will close for this time. With love for you only.*
*Bill Parkins*

Flo folded the letter and stuffed it in her handbag. She looked out over the horizon, sort of expecting answers to her many silent questions. That letter had been written on the 18th of November and here it was already the 3rd of December. She had already met Bill that day at the farm and again at the Arcade in Ft. Myers since the letter was written. Sometimes mail comes a few days after it's mailed, and at other times, like this one. Good thing she didn't have to make big important decisions based on letters. Bill was just going to vote then and already Roosevelt is president. She wondered if he was still at Turkey Key. She knew she would have to make a decision about him any day now. Bill was a nice man and she really thought that he could and would make a good father for the boys. He had sure been after her long enough. His romancing, when he came around, seem to get more serious all the time. The last time when she met him at his mother's in Ft. Myers was particularly troublesome. She had felt a long pent-up desire and had actually been a bit intimidated by his passes. It wouldn't be put off much longer. She knew that. Papa would surely understand her needs as a woman and as a mother with three small children. *Wonder what Papa found out up in Savannah?*

As Randy was maneuvering to dock at Plover Key, Junior grabbed onto the steering wheel when he jumped down from the console and, only but for the quick action of Randy, was a collision with the dock avoided. Junior hit the deck and was thrown off balance, skinned his knee and started to yell. Flo, jerked away from her thoughts, grabbed Junior off the floor. "Junior, what the hell you doin'? You want to get us all killed?" She whacked him with the palm of her hand on his rear end and sent him sliding across the deck to the stern where she had been. She reached for Francis who was still on the console. "Francis, get down from there before you fall and break your neck." He jumped down and ran to the back before he got a whack, too. She walked back to them, wagging her finger in their faces. They huddled in the corner.

An old woman she had never seen before got on at Plover and they started out again. The baby woke up coughing and wanting to eat. She turned in her seat to face the stern and unbuttoned her dress enough to get her breast out. She flinched as the baby's fingernails dug into her skin. He raised a ruckus until he got it situated in his mouth. The boys were getting restless again and she looked hard at them – they straightened up and acted like they had not even seen her look.

Just off Turkey Key, the boat slowed and tied up to the pilings of the old fish-house. The shade from the building felt good for a change. The old unpainted building had been there and used as a fish-house even before she was born. Randy climbed the wooden ladder nailed to the pilings up to the deck overhead and started talking to someone. The man's voice sounded familiar. She could not see the men, but now recognized Bill Parkins's voice. She yelled at the voices, "Randy, is that Bill Parkins up there?"

Bill stuck his head over the edge of the platform. "Flo, that you?" He recognized her and started down the ladder. "Where you goin'?" He climbed all the way down and hopped onto the boat. Randy came down behind him.

"Goin' to Mama's on Captiva, then over to Ky Costa to Dot's on Sunday."

He put his arms around her and squeezed lovingly. "Damn, I sure missed you, gal. I'm not goin' to let you go from me again." He held her tightly.

Randy butted in. "Come on, you two, I've got a schedule to meet." He moved to untie the line.

"I gotta talk to you, Flo. I'll see you over at Ky Costa." He kissed her hard and quick on the mouth and backed away to the ladder as Randy started to pull away from the dock.

With Bill hanging onto the ladder, the boat pulled away. The kiss agitated her innards and she blurted, "I'll look to see you there, Bill." She was immediately sorry for saying that. A decision about marriage was surely necessary, but first was the information Papa learned in Savannah. *If there is any chance at all of Buddy being alive, I've got to wait for him – will wait for him.*

They passed Mormon Key on the Gulf side and she saw old Richard Harrison down at the shore fussing with a skiff pulled half-way up on the beach. He must be ninety, she mused. Nobody knew for sure just how old he was. Some said he was born in 1840 while others said 1848. Randy tooted the foghorn and Richard turned and waved.

Behind Richard she could see the raised plank walkway disappear over and through the cutaway mangroves. At the end of it was the old house she and Buddy moved into so many years ago. God only knows how old the house is. The best part was the peace and quiet with no one else around. Over on the bay side where the mud was knee-deep in some spots, she could dig for clams in the late afternoon when the sun hovered far out on the Gulf. She could walk around the whole key in thirty minutes, even sloshing in the mud and mangaroots.

She and Buddy spent many a night watching the sun set on the Gulf side where the white sandy beach was once fifty feet wide and a quarter mile long. The hurricane of '28 took away most of the beach and now it looked to be about half as wide. The shoreline near the north end was now almost up to the old dead tree stumps, still stretching towards the sky. One half-rotted tree, uprooted from its position farther out on the beach, was now right at the edge of the water. It lay on the white sandy beach blocking the way to the north. Its roots still clinging pathetically to the sand, like it hoped to suck up a little nourishment. It was too late though – it's life was over.

So caught up in her thoughts, she was unaware that Randy had turned the boat into the Barron River. She looked down at the boys. They were sound asleep. The baby was sleeping with her nipple still in his mouth. Her love for the child was overcome with remorse for bringing him into such a harsh and unforgiving world. No matter what came, she would not bring any more into this world.

Just before reaching the Rod & Gun Club at the foot of Broadway, Randy pulled into the dock and secured the boat. Flo stood up and stretched. The baby stretched, too, but stayed asleep even when she removed the nipple and put her breast back inside the dress. With her foot, she nudged the boys. They both groaned, then came wide-awake. Randy helped Flo and the boys off and they walked the block to the Greyhound Bus Station in the Sundry Store in the old Everglades Inn. She bought tickets to Punta Rassa, where she planned to catch a ferry to Sanibel. *Hopefully, Mama will be at the Sanibel lighthouse on time.* Flo worried now about the mail and how she would get to Captiva if her mama wasn't there to meet her. She bought soda-pop for her and the boys and, at their continued pestering, a piece of penny candy for each of them.

289

They all went to the west end of the building and sat under a large, old oak tree with Spanish moss hanging almost to the ground. In no time Junior and Francis were at the cage trying to feed their candy to the monkey, their fascination understandable. As a small girl she, too, had been fascinated with the monkey in the cage at that time. She supposed it was not the same one as today. Could be, though. It hadn't been all that long ago since she was just a little girl. Now here she was a grown woman with three small children of her own to raise.

She spread the blanket out on the grass and, with the baby on her stomach, lay down on it. Soon she would have to resort to getting help from her family. She hoped it never came to that. Buddy always took care of all of that. Life was so simple then. *Here I go again, feeling sorry for myself when the big question should be, how do I get myself out of this fix I'm in. It's so peaceful here under this big old tree. No mosquitoes, no one hounding for anything, no crying babies or energetic young'uns, no dinner to fix, aaah, enjoy it while it lasts.* The serenity ended as quickly as it begun.

The bus passed by, went down to the end of the street, turned around, came back and parked right in front of her. The fumes from the exhaust pipe reached her nose as soon as the bus pulled up. The driver kept the engine running. The boys still clung to the cage. "Junior, Francis, let's go now." She gathered the baby and blanket and stood. The baby did not awaken. "Junior get these bags and lug them to the bus." She walked over to the bus. Francis went over and tried to reach the big leaping Greyhound painted on the side of the bus. He jumped up time and again, but the big dog was always just out of reach. Taken by his fascination and determination, she bent over, and with her left arm, lifted him so he could touch it.

# CHAPTER 41

Flo counted five people lolling about as she stepped outside the Punta Rassa grocery store where she had just purchased tickets for the ferry ride over to Sanibel. An elderly couple, obviously Yankee tourists down to search for shells; a young woman sitting alone on a bench; a young man at the opposite end of the building, pacing up and down, and a very old man dressed in a business suit, leaning on a cane and preoccupied with retrieving material from the briefcase he carried.

Francis and Junior ran immediately to the dock to await the approach of the ferry, which was nowhere in sight and not due for another fifteen minutes or so. All the people glanced at her as she came out, then went back to what they were doing with not even a nod in her direction. She counted the coins the clerk had returned to her from the quarter she had presented as payment for the trip – two nickels and four pennies. They had not charged for the children – thank God. If she kept spending at this rate, she would soon be flat-broke. She carefully wrapped the coins in a handkerchief with the rest of her meager coins and placed them in her handbag. The sun, now high in the north, had broken free of the dark clouds which still covered most of the sky to the south and west. There was just the slightest breeze amongst the buildings.

Flo followed the boys down to the wharf and sat on a bench under the porch of an old unpainted wooden building just to the left of the landing. Two cars were parked in line at the end of the road where the ferry would dock. She lit a cigarette and watched the boys nose into everything of any interest to them.

She had no recollection of ever actually being in Punta Rassa, but she had heard stories. The small town had once been the terminal for cattle being shipped to Cuba. Large herds were driven here from around Okeechobee and La Belle. Stories had it there were many a fight and killings back in those days. She'd passed it many a time in the boat on the way to the north islands or Ft Myers, but never had occasion to stop.

She looked back at the store where she bought the tickets. The people were still doing as before. The two-story building had a fresh coat of white paint with dark green trim. The new sign covered the entire front of the overhanging porch. It sported two red circles at either end that announced Coke could be bought inside. The other letters proclaimed proudly, "Punta Rassa Grocery, Sanibel Ferry Information". Three other buildings in various needs of repair fronted the street. One still had an old faded sign that said it had once been home to the Red Dog Saloon. The street between the buildings was a broad avenue of shell rock. She could picture the days of cattle and cowboys after a hard day's drive – could almost smell them.

A bell clanged out on Carlos Bay and brought her back to reality. There, coming from the north, was the ferryboat, its bow plowing through the choppy surf. She walked to where the children were playing near the landing. Over at a rundown dock a little to the south, an old grizzled fisherman in a small boat was getting gas from the pump near the outer end. His face below the nose bristled with a week-old beard and his mouth was sunken from the absence of teeth. From the looks of his dark and shriveled skin, he had spent his life on the sea under the unrelenting sun. The sky had darkened some and the wind had picked up from the west. It would be a rough ride to Sanibel. *This trip is getting tiresome and will get a lot worse if Mama's not there.* She began to wonder if she had made the right choice to come way over here all by herself.

The clanging bells drew her mind back to the ferry. White with a black bottom, it looked to be about sixty feet long and maybe fifteen feet wide. The cabin and control structure, sitting amidships, was a two-tiered affair, topped with a radio antenna and American flag. There was another flag with the large capital letter K. She assumed that had something to do with the ship's owner. She looked at her ticket and saw the words at the top in bold letters, 'THE KINZIE LINE'. With more clanging of the bell, the ship headed straight in and slowly nosed into the dock. The rattle of chains and the creaking of old, strained wood mingled with the clanging as the crew lowered a huge wooden ramp from the bow of the boat to the dock.

Pelicans roosting on old weathered pilings flew to the seaside porch of the old building to wait out the noise. Clamorous seagulls took to the air and headed out into the bay only to quickly return and swoop low over the ship, looking for a handout. Down on the beach near the dock, amidst thickly scattered seaweed, fiddler crabs scurried for cover among the debris scattered there, and into the sparse weeds growing above the water line. The ship's wake, washing high on the beach, sought them out. Most eluded the rising water, but one, intent on getting the morsel it was after, was bowled over and pulled into the retreating water.

Flo, a bit remorseful for the crab, gathered the children, moved off to the right side and presented her ticket to the man standing there. He told her to wait until the cars were loaded. The people near the grocery store now scampered to their cars and were directed by other workmen to move toward the ship. The old man with the briefcase strolled over, presented his ticket and was also told to wait.

Soon all walking passengers boarded and were shown to the lower part of the control tower, after which they were free to move about on deck, but were ordered to stay out of areas being worked by the crew. The ramp lifted with a loud clanking and rattling of chains as the ship backed out into the bay. The ship's bell resumed clanging. Flo moved to the bow with the children, who got a kick out of the tumbling water being produced by the big propellers at the stern now pulling full steam in reverse. The water seemingly boiled out from under the boat. She had to pull the boys away from the rail.

The boat made its turn and headed, bow first, out across the bay. The wind had picked up but the big boat cut through the choppy waves with barely a tremble. Salt spray misted as the bow cut deep into the frothy sea. She pulled her light jacket tighter and drew the children to her. Braving the sea was a challenge she had loved when helping Buddy fish and trap before she became pregnant with Junior. Standing with her face to the winds fury and tasting the salt spray offered her a certain solitude that she couldn't find at home. For a pleasant moment she was free from the confusion of her current situation.

The boys tugged at her dress and yelled at her. A pair of porpoises showing their backs and dorsal fins just off the bow had fascinated them. With the aid of a loudspeaker, the captain introduced the fish to the other passengers and soon the bow was crowded with people straining to see what they had only previously heard about. Flo felt a momentary fear the boat would tilt when so many people ran to one side at once, but the boat didn't budge.

Soon the lighthouse at Point Ybel rose up high above the mangroves, seagrapes and buttonwoods, and the shoreline grew larger. Seagulls flew overhead, squawking and sometimes lighting on the edge of the boat. The smell of land, trees and seaweed drifted out and mingled with the smell of the sea and the normal boat smells. The old man from the store came up beside her and cleared his throat. She jumped. He put his hand on her arm.

"Forgive me for startling you. I just wanted to remark how breathtaking the view is and wondered if you felt a certain awe, too. Did you know the lighthouse rises ninety-eight feet above sea level?"

She turned toward him. "That's all right. I was just lost in thought and didn't hear you come up." She put her hand out. "I'm Flo Harrison."

He took her hand gingerly in his two. They were old looking, but strong. He carried his briefcase under his arm. She looked at his weather-beaten face and stared into his heavily browed dark blue eyes. She was reminded of her father. He bowed slightly.

"I am Rutherford Bellmont at your service, ma'am." He switched his gaze toward the lighthouse and seemingly, far beyond. "Each time I come, I am more intrigued than before with the history of these islands and its people. I could stay here forever."

"Why don't you?"

"Fortunately, or unfortunately, I have a job I must attend to. I'm a Professor of Archaeology at Colgate University in upstate New York. I come here every year about this time to dig for artifacts and study the history of the place and the ancient people."

She perked up. She dearly loved history and had taken an archaeology course in high school. On Key Largo, she had participated in several digs with the science class. "Then you'd know the meaning of Ybel?"

He looked at her approvingly and smiled. "The island was named by Ponce de Leon, in honor of the deceased Queen Isabella, and subsequently shortened to Y Bel. It was also called San Y Bel. See, the derivation is Sanibel."

She grew very interested. She continued. "How about Punta Rassa?"

He seemed to be warming up, too. She could tell. This was his stage and he loved it. Maybe, just maybe, he could offer advice on how she could go back to school and maybe even get the long sought after degree in archeology.

He said, "Punta Rassa means 'cattle point'. McKay and Sumerlin drove cattle to Punta Rassa. The cattle were loaded on schooners in Carlos Bay and delivered to Havana. On return trips, contraband supplies were brought to Confederates living on the islands around Charlotte Harbor and up the Caloosahatchee."

The ship's bell clanged. They were getting ready to dock. A crewman came to her. "Ma'am, you and the children should go into the cabin to prepare for landing. You, too, sir." He turned and was immediately gone.

She turned to the old man. "Its been real good talkin' to you, sir. Never had chance to talk with a real live professor before. I wish I had more time to take advantage of it." She turned to go.

He hung back. "You can reach me through the Post Office on Captiva. They'll know where to find me. Ask for Hattie Gore, Postmaster. If you find the time and have the interest, look me up. I'll show you where I'm digging and some of the things I've found."

She put out her hand. He took it. She said, "Bye for now." She went to the cabin.

# CHAPTER 42

Toby drank the rest of the now-cold coffee and crushed the cigarette in the ashtray on the table. He had been silent all during breakfast. Curly had been quiet, too, and had hung off to himself. Marty had tried to get Toby to talk, but he would only give curt answers or explanations. Toby's mind was preoccupied with Branbury, Copolla and the money. He tried to retrace the events of yesterday and what it held for his future. Had the police connected him with the robbery or was their coming around just a coincidence? He laid a ten on the table and stood up. "Marty, I'm going outside. You finish your breakfast then pay up. Leave the girl a dollar." He walked out the door.

Toby stood just outside the door and lit a cigarette. Curly was standing close to the edge of the highway looking south, the wind blowing the hair around the edge of his hat. The one big braid hung down his back past the top of his shoulders. Over the last several hours Toby had developed a new appreciation for this Curly. At times he thought the man was just a big kid with not much spine. Just listened mostly, but seemed to have an ability to sort through all the talk and come up with the right questions and answers. Easy to misjudge a man like him. Now he owed Curly his life.

At 7:30 the wind was brisk and the sky generally overcast, with just a little blue showing in the north. The smell of the air foretold storm. He walked over to Curly. "You say, when the sheriff came to Andre's, he was looking for a guy named Buddy he'd heard was staying there. How'd he know that?"

Buddy turned toward Toby. "Don't rightly know how he came to be there, but Andre told him that you'd brought a half-dead breed there and that he'd been takin' care of him ever since you left. Sheriff wanted to talk to you. Guess he wanted to find out about me."

"You? Your name Buddy?" He looked deep into Buddy's eyes.

"Yeah. When he said the name, I remembered it as mine. Never did figure out why he wanted me, though." Buddy turned his face back into the wind.

Toby moved alongside Buddy. "I'm trying to figure out if the police were on to me back there in Savannah for the robbery or just looking for me because of you. If that's so, the sheriff would've contacted the police, and that's possible, I reckon . . . but even if he had contacted them as soon as he got into Savannah, they wouldn't have had time to track me down in that short time. No, I think he's only a coincidence, and somehow the guy Marty shot must've fingered me. But that guy damn sure looked dead to me. It's got me puzzled big time, Curly, ah, Buddy."

"You go right ahead and call me Curly. Kind've got used to that name now. That sheriff may be just a coincidence as you say, but I think he connected me to you and I think he recognized me as the driver of the getaway car. He must be the one that called the police. He knew your name and somehow the police found out where you lived and worked."

"By God, Curly, you just may be right. That makes sense. My name and address is on file down at the police station – fingerprints, too. With my name they would have all they needed to find me. What in the world have I got us into?"

Buddy turned and looked straight into Toby's eyes. "I don't know why he was after me before, but I know why he's after me now. Damn it, Toby, I don't remember ever doin' anything wrong like that. Now here I am right in the middle of a robbery and maybe even a murder, and I didn't have a damn thing to do with any of it. All I ever wanted was to find my memory and go back to it. Maybe I won't like what I find, but I have to go look. Now, I might not even get a chance to do that." He pulled his hat low as the wind blew in the first small spray of rain against his face.

"Curly, I know I drug you into this thing against your will and I want you to know I'm really sorry for that. If I ever have any say, I'll damn sure tell them that you weren't a part of it. I sure wish I could undo what happened yesterday, but I know, and you know, I can't do that. We've just got to live the best we can with what we've got. I've got to call Branbury and try to decide what to do from here." He turned and walked to the phone box on the outside of the cafe.

Branbury picked up the phone on the first ring. Mary Lou would not be in for another thirty minutes. Copolla was in the bathroom. The meeting this morning had not gone well. He had been unable to get a lead on Toby and Martin. Copolla was fit to be tied. "Broadhouse Equipment, Branbury."

"Mr. Branbury, Toby."

"Toby, where the hell are you? I've been looking all over the place for you. What happened yesterday?"

"Hold on, Mr. Branbury. I'll try to bring you up to date, but first, what were the police doing there at the plant last night?"

"They came looking for you. They wouldn't say what for, but they didn't tie you to the robbery either. What happened down there? Where are you?"

"Your man, Charlie wasn't there. The man that was didn't play along and was shot. Looked to me like he was killed, but I'm not sure. I was shot and got poked by a piece of glass. If Curly hadn't been there, I'd be dead, too."

Copolla walked into the office and, with his face forming the question for him, asked who was on the phone. Branbury placed his hand over the mouthpiece and mouthed 'Toby'. Back into the mouthpiece he said, "Who the hell is Curly? Nobody else was supposed to be with you and Martin. How did a Curly get mixed in?"

Copolla blurted out, as he walked around the desk with his finger poised over the intercom button. "What the hell's going on? Where is Toby? Tell him to get his ass over here on the double. Does he have the bag? Who's this Curly?"

Branbury listened to Toby in the mouthpiece. "It's a long and tangled-up story, but let's just say that he came at the wrong time and I had no choice but to take him with us. He drove the car for us."

Copolla's finger pressed the button down. Branbury asked into the phone, "Do you have the bag there with you? Were you able to get the jewels and loose cash?"

Copolla erupted, "Where the hell are you, Toby, and how come you didn't come over here like you were supposed to last night?"

Toby's voice sounded agitated. "I came over there last night, but the police were there. They also came by my house. You guys didn't keep your part of the bargain. Your man, Charlie, wasn't there like you said he would be. How come you didn't tell me before I went over there? I was damn near killed because of you." Toby sounded real shook up and sore as hell.

Copolla cut Branbury off and assumed control of the call, recognizing Toby's state of mind and the danger that posed to getting the bag of cash. His voice took on a soothing manner. "Hold on now, Toby. We didn't hear about Charlie until about 7:00 o'clock last night. He tried to call us Thursday night, but we didn't connect with him then. We would've called you if we had heard in time. Are you okay? Did you get the bag? Where are you now?"

"All I know is that the police are after me and if I hang around here much longer they're just liable to get me. I'm going down into the Everglades till I can decide what kind of trouble I'm in. I'll keep the bag with me till then." Toby sounded like he had calmed down and was now in full control of his senses.

Branbury almost screamed into the phone. "Toby, don't you dare do that. You tell me where you're at and don't leave until I can get there. We can split up the cash like we agreed on. We did our part. Now you've got to do yours. I've always thought of you as my son. Don't give me cause to distrust . . . ." The dial tone buzzed loud in his ear. The phone line was disconnected.

Copolla screamed, "That sonofabitch hung up. A million bucks down the drain. Branbury, you've got to do something. What are we going to do?"

CHAPTER **43**

The moment Flo stepped off the ferry she saw the black Buick sedan bordered by a jungle of mangroves and buttonwoods. Her mother sat behind the wheel – back straight as a ramrod. She had been a much kinder and gentler woman back when that car was first bought. Things were a lot better then when her hopes were higher. Now she seemed bitchy all the time. Nothing ever seemed to be right with her anymore. She had missed her chance and she seemed to hate everybody for it.

The car showed some rust now, but otherwise still in good shape. "Look there's Grandma." Junior and Francis broke loose from her grip and ran to the car. She looked around for the old man, but he was nowhere in sight.

Along the shoreline the birds paid scant attention to the hustle and bustle of humans and went about their business as usual. The seagulls, squawking as loud as ever, continued their flight out to sea, back over the boat then to the sandy beach on both sides of the dock, then back out to sea. Occasionally, they would land on a piling if a pelican was not already in occupation. The pelicans said nothing, but from the seagulls and the other small birds mixing it up, the uncoordinated music was a constant din. The white beach was broad on either side of the dock and covered with seaweed half-way down to the water. On the beach down to the right a fisherman worked with his knife on a swordfish that must have been twelve to fifteen feet long. The sword itself was a good three feet. A large skiff lay on the beach half way out of the water.

The lighthouse loomed high against the dark and brooding skyline to the west, towering way above the government buildings and lush jungle spattered with Australian pines surrounding it to the sides and back. Flo walked the short distance along the dock to the shore and over to the car. The old professor was climbing into another car. He waved to her – she waved back. A shuttle bus pulled into the clearing, likely transportation to the beaches. The children got in the back and Flo climbed into the front seat and gave her mother a hug. "Been waitin' long? How you been?"

Mildred seemed in a good mood for a change. "Just got here. Enjoyed the few minutes all to myself." She shifted into first gear and drove away from the landing. "Who was that old man you waved to?"

She never missed a trick, did she? "I met him on the ferry just a few minutes before we landed – a most interesting man. Says he's a professor at some college up north. Knows all the history of these islands. Digs for things from the past. He's stayin' somewhere on Captiva. Wish I could find somethin' like that."

"Damned Yankees. They're takin' over the whole place. I tell you there's not a shell left out on the beach for the regular folks no more. Every time a wave brings in a bunch of shells, the Yankees swarm down and scoop 'em all up. Yankees just ain't no good for nothin'. Wherever a Yankee squats, it rots all around there." She harumphed and spit a mouthful of snuff out the window.

"Aw, Mama. There must be some good to 'em. They bring money down here and buy things from the local folks."

"Don't 'aw Mama' me. I seen what them damned fools can do. Not one of 'em got sense enough to get in out of the rain."

Flo, at last, could breathe easy. She nestled the baby on her lap and leaned as far back as she could in the seat. She stretched her legs out in front of her and sighed loudly. Mildred looked at her. The sun came into her window and warmed the chill air coming in off the Gulf. About eleven o'clock, she figured. The trip so far had been a good five hours and now she was tired out. The pangs of hunger reminded her that she hadn't eaten in some time now. The boys must be getting kind of lunchy, too. The drive was scenic and peaceful. The shell rock road, about fifteen feet wide, made its way through high pines and massive coconut trees on both sides. Other vegetation came right down to the edge of the road and sometimes brushed the side of the car.

Mildred spat snuff again. "What you plannin' to do with your life, Flo? You heard any more from that Bill Parkins?"

"That's what I came over here for. Want to talk to you about what I should do. But I thought we could get somethin' to eat first and maybe take a nap."

"Comin' to me for advice? Hrumph. Young lady, you should've come to me long before now. If you had, you wouldn't be in the fix you're in now. And you sure as hell wouldn't be married into that damned Harrison family. You—"

"I know, I know, Mama, but we can't go back to then. I've got to go ahead now. And I need you to help me. You will, won't you?" The baby whimpered and she brought him up to her chest.

"I've always been here for you, haven't I?"

"Yes, you have."

They had been driving in silence about ten minutes when Mildred made a sharp left turn, slowed almost to a stop and approached a very old-looking wooden bridge. A sign on it said, 'Blind Pass'. Flo wondered if it could hold more than one person at a time. The bridge had railings on both sides made out of long unpainted boards nailed to upright two-by-fours spaced about three feet apart. The planks to drive on, laid crosswise, looked rotted, and some, on the ends, were not nailed down to the under-structure. Mildred eased out onto the bridge and it gave a mournful groan. Flo gulped, but guessed that Mama knew what she was doing.

Finally they were across and on the island of Captiva. Over low clumps of grass Flo could see the wide expanse of a pure white sandy beach in front of the car. A sharp right turn onto a much narrower shell road took them parallel to the beach which could be seen from time to time through the pines, buttonwood trees and gulf grasses. The journey lasted another bumpy six miles almost to the northern end of the island before they turned off onto a heavily rutted dirt road no wider than the car. There were no sounds other than the noise of the car engine and the grass scraping underneath and along the sides.

Off to the left were two unpainted houses, one behind the other, sitting way back off the shell road. Mildred pulled into the yard between two large coconut trees and stopped about fifty feet from the first house. The houses reminded her of Key West and Poorhouse Lane. They sat on big coral blocks off the ground about two feet or more. The house in front was built out of unpainted boards placed upright with two windows on the side fronting the road. The front part of the building rose to a peak then sloped down in the back. A wide front porch graced the front with three coral blocks placed in such a way to provide steps up to the porch.

The roof was made of tin sheets. The house behind was constructed with the same materials but had no design. It, too, had a pitched tin roof but otherwise just a long straight house with one window on the roadside. The yard that could be seen was covered here and there with green weeds and prickly-pear plants struggling to get out from under the shell which must have been laid down thick. Must have been twenty or thirty coconut trees with old coconuts in varying degrees of decay strewn all over the ground underneath.

Once inside, Flo fed the baby and put him to sleep in the room assigned to her. Junior and Francis pestered her constantly for something to eat. Finally, Mildred gave them each a biscuit with peanut butter on it with a promise of more later. They ran outside to play. Flo changed into a loose cotton dress and went barefoot into the kitchen. Mildred stood at the stove watching a frying pan melt the glob of lard she had placed there. The pan popped grease into the air. The smell of burning lard stirred Flo's senses.

"I'm starved. What are we havin'? Wow! Just look at this stove, would you. Buddy said he was gonna get me a gas stove just like this one someday."

Mildred turned as Flo came up behind her. "Thought we'd have tomato gravy and rice and johnny-cake for dinner. We'll fix somethin' more when Joe gets home for supper. Look there in the icebox and get the bacon and slice a few strips off the slab. There in the basket are tomatoes. Chop some up for the gravy. I'll get the johnny-cake on."

Flo diced up the white bacon and fried it brown, then put the cut tomatoes in with the bacon and cooked them down. The smell of bread mixed with frying bacon gave her a peaceful and satisfying feeling. She loved the smells of home – all of them. *Just plain good being here with Mama. Somehow all my troubles melt away when I'm with her.* She hadn't been this relaxed in some time now. Flo added water, salt and pepper and let it all simmer until it became a thick red gravy. She took a taste. "Uummm. The gravy is ready and the bread looks and smells ready. I'll call the kids in."

After dinner she took the kids into the bedroom and spread a blanket on the floor for the baby. Junior and Francis climbed up on the big bed. She pulled the light spread over them, bent over and hugged them both. She praised them for behaving on the trip and promised them a story from the storybook. Buddy would've been proud of them – her eyes watered. She removed the book from her bag and began reading. In a brief time both were sound asleep. They were such angels when sleeping. She kissed each on the cheek and wiped away the tears before they dropped onto their faces.

Out on the porch Flo sat down near the coral steps and leaned against a support pole. She lit a cigarette and let the smoke out with a contented sigh. The smoke left its smell as it drifted up towards the rafters before being blown away by the breeze coming off what she reckoned to be Pine Island Sound.

Mildred sat rocking in the big rocker crocheting, the big needles working with a magic rhythm and clicking their own special music. Flo took another drag on the cigarette and looked over at her. "Looks like a bedspread, Mama. You makin' it for me?"

Mildred kept on rocking or crocheting. She didn't look up from her task at hand. "Might be for you. Then, again, might not."

Flo gazed lazily out over the property at all the many coconut and pine trees. Not another house or person was anywhere in sight. "When will Daddy Joe be home? Who's he fishin' with now days?"

"Not fishin' with anybody. You forgot already? Not fishin' at all. Farmin' now. Growin' eggplants, tomatoes, peppers, squash, cucumbers, lettuce, cabbage and most everything else a body could want. Everything grows on this island. He won't likely come home till just for dark."

"How many acres is it on? You all still just sharecroppin', ain't you? I mean, you've got no intentions of buyin' the place, do you?"

"God no, girl. We ain't got that kind of money. Joe thought he might have some time to fish some with Walter over at Ky Costa, but he can't seem to find enough time just for the farmin', much less fishin', too. The owner, young Jeff Willis who's off to college in Virginia somewheres, don't want to sell the place anyhow, just wants somebody to get a farm started. Says he might come down here and run it by himself someday. Pretty good deal for us, though. Young Willis put up the start-up money and property and Joe put up the labor – they split fifty-fifty. Joe's been workin' it since he left Key West in October. Don't know how that old coot's gonna keep it up at his age. But he's up at the crack of daylight every mornin' rearin' to go, rain or shine. He acts like a man half his age. He loves farmin' so much better than fishin'."

"How old is Daddy Joe now, Mama?"

"Well. Let me see. Think he's about twelve years older'n me. That'd make him about seventy-two, give or take. He is gettin' on up there, ain't he? Me, too, I reckon."

Flo grew excited and wanted to go find him right away. She was just a little girl when her own daddy went away and she had taken up right quick with Daddy Joe when he first came around.

She always felt good around him. "Let's go find him. Maybe I can help him somehow." She stood.

"Don't know how you can help him, but we can't go nowhere till them young'uns of yours wake up. Besides, you wanted to talk to me about the mess you're in. What you gonna do with your life? How you gonna get these young'uns raised up?" Mildred wrapped the loose cord and the finished material around the needles and put them in the cloth bag next to her feet. "Let's go in and fix a pot of coffee." She rose and went into the house. Flo followed.

Flo lit another cigarette and cupped the coffee between the palms of her hands to savor the warmth. She loved the smell of freshly brewed coffee. "Papa Jim heard a rumor that two Indians from over near Lake Okeechobee had rescued Buddy. He went there lookin' for 'em for information. The Indians had left and gone up to Savannah. The police up there found 'em and he went up there Thursday to question 'em."

Mildred fumed, but allowed Flo to finish. Unable to hold it any longer, she cut in, "That damned Jim Harrison ain't gonna never let up, is he? Everybody knows that Buddy's dead as a door nail, except him. He keeps this act up and keeps your life in a mess all the time. I'd just choke that man if I had him here. You better just—"

"I thought I'd at least give him this one last chance, just in case Buddy really is alive."

Mildred overrode Flo, her voice getting louder and more agitated, "Just get over this idea that Buddy is still alive and find yourself a man to raise these young'uns. Gettin' a man to take on raisin' three kids ain't no easy job, you know – specially in these times. What about that Bill Parkins who's been writin' you all them love letters? You seen anything of him lately?" She picked an empty coffee can off the floor by the table and spit snuff into it.

Flo knew it would not be easy to keep her mama calm long enough to get some good advice from her. She kept her own tone even. "Anyway, Papa is due back on Sunday and we'll find out then if he has any new leads on Buddy. I'll try to get back by then, but in the meantime, I wanted to just talk about the problem so, when the time comes, I can have a good shot at makin' the right move."

Mildred walked over to the stove, poured more coffee and sat again at the table. The time spent calmed her some. "Flo, you gotta just forget Buddy. He's gone. Ain't no amount of mournin' gonna bring him back. You just gotta accept that, girl, no matter how much it hurts. Now what about Bill Parkins? That spark in him still there?"

Tears welled up in Flo's eyes. She went to the stove and wiped them with a dishrag. She stood there a moment to compose herself and leaned her back against the sink. "Mama, I know what you say is probably true. I, like Papa Jim, keep hopin' against hope that Buddy will show up someday. I know that time is runnin' out for me. I've got to make a choice now. That's why I'm here. When I leave here tomorrow, I want to go over and spend some time with Dot. I've always been real close to her. She and I understand each other. I can draw some strength and understanding from her, too. Bill Parkins still wants to marry me, or so he says. I think he'd marry me today if I'd just say yes. I think he's gettin' ready to really start puttin' the pressure on during the next few days. He said he would come to Ky Costa while I'm there." She walked back to the table and lit another cigarette.

"Well, It's settled. You'll marry Bill before Christmas. We'll take the boat and go with you to see Dot. I need to see her, too. Reckon that baby is due any time now."

Flo hadn't counted on Mildred going with her to Dot's. "There's just one small problem with me marryin' anybody right now. A missin' person ain't dead by law till he's been gone seven years. That means, I'm still married to Buddy. How can I legally marry Bill Parkins?"

Mildred exploded. "Where in the hell you hear that at?"

"Papa told me. He—"

Mildred pushed her chair back and virtually leaped up from the table, almost upsetting Flo's coffee. "Oh, God. That old man seems hell-bent on keepin' you from marryin' again. What am I gonna to do about this?" She emptied the dregs out of her coffee cup and poured it full again.

Flo tried hard to keep calm. She was tiring of this ranting and raving and not getting any solid advice. "When the question first came up, he said he wasn't sure, but that he would call somebody at the sheriff's station. He later told me he found out it was seven years."

"Hrumph. To hell with the law, lawyers and the whole kit and caboodle. My best advice is for you to get married as soon as you can. I'm sure your money must be gettin' low."

"Yes it is. Mighty low." Flo thought better about telling Mildred that she would soon have to leave her house on Wood Key. She sought to change the subject for a while. "By the way, Daddy came by to see me yesterday. Said he was tryin' to see all us kids before he left for Portugal. He asked about you. How you were and all."

Mildred, her temper now subsided, stayed by the sink. "I ain't seen that old coot in a hundred years. How'd he look?"

"He didn't look any different from what I remembered. Had a lively sparkle in his eyes."

Mildred moved back to the table. "Sometimes I've missed your daddy a whole lot. First man I ever really loved. Never really loved any other man like I did him. I was just a young sprout then." She seemed embarrassed and got up and went to the front door.

"What about Daddy Joe? You been with him a long time now."

She turned around at the door and walked back to the table. "Oh, I love old man Joe, and we have a good and satisfying life together, but it's different somehow. Maybe you can only really love hard when you're young. Kind of like you and Buddy maybe." She stood with her hands on the back of the chair.

The baby started to whimper. Flo got up. "Why'd you and Daddy get divorced, Mama?"

Mildred looked agitated and walked over to the stove then back to the table. "Flo, you not gonna start with that tom-foolishness all over, are you? What are you after with that question, anyhow? We all do things based on what we know at the time. Sometimes what we did is right and sometimes it's all wrong, specially when judged from lookin' back. But there's no way another person can ever stand in your shoes to make judgment on what you did. A good example is your decision on whether to marry Bill Parkins or not. What if you decide to marry him this month and next month or next year Buddy comes home? You've waited ten months with no real word that he's alive. You have three small children to look after. You have no way to make a livin'. You're just twenty-three years old. What are you supposed to do? People tryin' to judge you then would have to know everything you know now and they'd still have to stand in your shoes and have all the feelin's that's pent up inside you. I tell you nobody can ever stand in your shoes completely and that's why Jesus was so smart when he said, 'Judge not lest ye be judged.'"

"But, Mama I don't want to judge—"

Mildred cut her off and continued on. "In my case, I was just plain stupid. I thought I knew it all." The baby started to cry. Flo started to say something and began moving toward the bedroom. Mildred sat down at the table and continued, "Truth is, I was too damn ambitious for my own good. I wanted a better life for my young'uns as well as myself. Francisco was content to just be a fisherman. I harped at him all the time about it. His family was well-to-do back in Portugal, you know. Had wine farms in the family for generations – might even call them royalty. They went by the name D'Sa over there."

Flo disappeared into the bedroom and emerged with the baby. She poured herself another cup of coffee and sat at the table. The baby was fidgety and cranky. Her nipple calmed him down. The boys were still sleeping soundly. "You all were divorced when I was just a young girl. Did you ever go to Portugal?"

"Oh, sure. I went several times. Judith was born over there. That time we stayed almost a year. That's when I saw how they lived. I decided then, that's the life I wanted. I thought I'd get it someday, but it was not meant to be, I reckon. Francisco traveled all over South America as a sort of agent for the wine business back in Portugal, makin' contacts and all. But all he ever wanted was to be a fisherman. We argued a lot whenever he was home from the trips, which wasn't often back in them days. One thing led to another and . . . ." She got up, went to the stove and cleaned out the coffeepot. She kept her back to the table. "Well, enough of that stuff. You wanted to go see Joe? We better be goin'. When you expect them young'uns will wake up?" Flo detected a slight quiver to her voice.

"It's time for them to get up now. I'll go in there and rummage around some. That ought to wake 'em."

They walked the short distance from the back of the house to the farm. There were rows and rows of green plants and new sprouts. There, towards the back and off to the west side, was Daddy Joe and a mule working at moving a very large tree stump. He was not a big man and never gave the impression that he was old. She heard him curse as he gave the mule a mighty slap on the rump. The stump budged, but didn't give up its place in the big hole that had been dug around it.

Flo yelled, "Daddy Joe."

Joe turned, looked at them and waved. He removed the harness from the mule and walked toward them, wiping his hands on a big dirty rag.

He gave her a big hug. "Flo, it's good to see you. Been expectin' you. How you been? Millie, everything all right?"

His clothes were damp and he smelled of sweat. Flo hugged him back just as hard. "I've been just great, Daddy Joe. How about you? You got anybody to help you with this work?"

He backed off, still holding her hands. "Just that cussed old mule there. Couldn't do without her, though. Come on over here. Maybe you can be good luck for me to get that bugger of a stump out of there."

They all moved that way. The boys ran out ahead and jumped into the hole that had been dug around the stump. The sky had big patches of pure blue pushing out the dark, weakly-formed clouds. The weather was turning good for the boat trip to Ky Costa tomorrow. Things were looking up. Flo ran the boys out of the hole.

Joe dug more around the stump and took an ax to some stubborn roots. He hooked up the rope, which was tied around the stump, to the mule. "Flo, you take the mule by the halter and guide him away from the stump. I'll stand by here with the ax and whack any roots tryin' to hang on."

Flo handed the baby to Mildred and pulled at the mule while Joe stood in the hole chopping with the ax. She saw the stump move a little then topple over. Joe waved for her to stop pulling. He got out of the hole and took over for her. With him leading, the mule pulled the stump out of the hole and off to the side of the cleared field.

Junior and Francis jumped back into the hole. Flo saw something that resembled a long slender doll tangled up in the cut off roots that remained. She told Francis to fetch it for her. The item still had chunks of mud clinging to it. At a pump nearby she washed off the mud and discovered a dark-colored stone a little larger than the palm of her hand. The excitement of the find overcame her. She remembered the professor back at the ferry. He was looking for artifacts about the early inhabitants of the islands. Could this be one of them? It appeared to be a statue of something. The thing's head looked like that of a cat of some kind with a long nose. Its ears stood straight up from its head. The long slender body with its arms tucked in close was kneeling on oversized legs. She showed the statue to Mildred. "This looks like an artifact the professor was talkin' about. You remember that man I waved to at the ferry?"

313

Mildred took the doll in her hand and looked at it for a moment and handed it back. "Don't know nothin' about artifacts, as you call it." Flo started to explain, but Mildred waved her off. "See what old man Joe has to say about it."

Flo walked over to the hole where Joe was working on a stubborn root poking out of the ground near the edge of the hole. He stopped what he was doing when she handed the doll to him. "Looks like it might belong to some old Indians who used to live here. You reckon?" He handed it back to Flo.

"That's what I think it is. We can find out tomorrow from that professor I met on the ferry. He knows all about such things. It belongs to you, though." She held the statue out to him.

He pushed her hand away. "No, Flo. You keep it. You brought me luck gettin' this stump out of here. I'd a never got it out without you pullin' on that damn old stubborn mule. You want it, you got it. I got no use for such as that anyhow."

"Thank you very much, Daddy Joe." She clutched the doll to her and gave him a big hug. "I've always had a great interest in the past. This is all very exciting. I hope I can find the professor tomorrow."

"Flo, you want me to take you over to Ky Costa tomorrow, we're gonna have to leave early – likely before the crack of dawn. The landowner's comin' in tomorrow afternoon and I've got to be here when he gets here. You may just have to wait to see this professor friend of yours till another day."

Flo promised herself she would leave Dot's early enough so she could come back to Captiva with enough time to visit with the professor. This doll was surely a true artifact and belonged to some long-dead Indian. Probably some kind of religious totem or something equally exciting. She had to find out and she was sure the professor had the answers.

CHAPTER **44**

Buddy stared straight ahead, seeing nothing but the road stretching endless miles, as it had been for the past two hours. Mile after boring mile of black road running under the front of the car and out from under the back. The rearview mirror reflected road as far as he could see. He was oblivious to the chill wind streaming in the windows. The sun, a bright reddish orange color, hung far out to the southwest and low on the horizon. Rays streamed in the passenger side and lay bright and warm on his clothes. It would be dark in an hour. The jumbled voices of Toby and Marty in the back seat, sometimes loud and dangerous, sometimes low and consoling, commingled with his private thoughts. He paid scant attention. The two had been at it ever since Brunswick, more than eight hours ago. Home was close by now, but for some reason that provided little or no gratification.

His mind would not let go of yesterday. He reviewed the events over and over, trying to sort it all out. How had he managed to get caught up in the middle of a robbery and possible murder? He probed in his memory for his early life and any hint that he might have ever even mildly considered anything like that. Revelation seemed right on the brink of discovery, only to be lost just as quickly. He could grasp a snatch of memory but nothing else – unable to penetrate the mist. It was like trying to remember the words or the tune of a song. He knew the song, but couldn't identify it. Then came a few words, but no tune would fit. The song kept coming back to the front of his mind, but would not yield the full song or title. A few more words, then the tune, then, like a dam bursting and flooding the whole countryside – the total song – in full bloom. A miracle. It had happened like that several times since he started playing the guitar at Liz's house. He knew his full memory would soon crash through the same way. He just had to keep working at it, adding a little more each time and keeping what he had out in front. If he could just get back to where Toby found him and pick up a few more clues, the full memory would be wide open in his mind. He tried mightily and continually to unscramble and organize the memories recalled since he woke up in the hospital. It seemed so long ago but was less than seven months. Toby never seemed to be in the right mood to share what information he had. Buddy would press him more when they stopped again.

Toby seemed to be reading his mind, "Curly, we've got to stop right soon. This side of mine is killing me and the bandages are sopping wet with blood. I'm getting a mite hungry, too. How about you? Maybe we ought to spend the night up this way somewhere. Ought to be some cabins or something for rent. Where are we, anyhow?"

Marty chimed in right quick. "I'm tired riding. Need to get out and stretch if nothing else."

Toby's voice brought Buddy back to the present. The cool wind sent a shiver up his arm and down his back. He rolled the window part-way up. "Just went through St. Cloud five minutes ago. We can look for somethin' along the way, but not much between here and Yeehaw Junction – about sixty miles or so, if my memory serves me. Hour and a half – about seven, I reckon."

"That's a good time to stop. Hope we can find a place to stay there. I'll shut my eyes till then. How we fixed for gas?"

"We probably should get some when we stop." Buddy had enough riding, too – bone-tired from driving all day long. They had only stopped twice during the whole trip. Toby's condition prevented him from driving and Marty never even offered to help. Maybe he didn't know how. Reckon if he could, Toby would've ordered him to. Marty seemed a great big baby anyhow. *One day I reckon I'll have to have it out with him. Don't know why he hates me so much.*

They reached the intersection at Yeehaw Junction about seven and pulled into the gas station and cafe on the southwest corner. A young boy came out to pump the gas. "Fill 'er up, son. Check the oil, too. Them cabins out back for rent?" Buddy opened the door and got out, stood by the door and stretched.

The boy stuck the hose nozzle into the tank in front of the windshield and lifted the driver's side of the hood. His head disappeared underneath the hood and when he emerged he held the dipstick up to the light. "You need a little less than a quart, mister. The cabins are for rent, but you'll have to check with the man inside to see if they're full up or not." He wiped the dipstick clean and put it back in the engine.

"Put in the oil needed and give me the rest in the can to take with me." Buddy bent down and spoke with Toby, then went into the front office.

When he came back to the car the boy handed him the change and the can of oil. Toby obviously had paid the boy for the gas and oil. Buddy handed the money to Toby. "Man had one cottage left out back, cost $1.25 for the three of us. Only two beds. One of us will have to sleep on the floor. He'll give us the stuff to make a pallet with. We can get vittles in the cafe. It closes at nine so we better get a move on." Toby nodded assent. Buddy got in and drove around the main building to the cottage.

They were all starving and did nothing but eat after the food was served. When it was finished, they all sat back with coffee and lit up. The plentiful smoke took its sweet time dissipating. None of them seemed to mind. Toby looked refreshed and renewed after his bath and change of bandages. The jagged cut in his stomach was swollen and had an ugly color – poison maybe. Consuela would know what to do when they arrived there tomorrow.

Buddy inhaled the smoke, took a big swig of coffee and let the smoke out over the table. "Toby, you were gonna tell me how you happened to come up on me down in the swamps last February. Feel up to it now?"

Toby looked at Buddy for a long time, as if studying what story he should tell – what story Buddy wanted to hear. Finally, he said, "Yeah. Not really much to tell except that two men were hot on doing you in when me and Marty came along. We heard the shot that hit you in the back, and we came into view as these men were running towards you ready to fire again. You were laying face down in the beach sand. I fired my gun at the man just a split-second before he fired again at you. I caught him with the edge of my buckshot and he stopped dead in his tracks. He looked at us coming in off the water like he was seeing ghosts. Marty had his gun up to his shoulder ready to fire when both men turned and high-tailed it. They must've had a boat over on the creek beyond the point. We heard them crashing through the woods, then they were gone. I went to see about you, and Marty scouted around for any sign of the men. You were still alive, but had been back shot, and it looked like a piece of the side of your head had been blown away. Marty found what we figured to be your buddy. His chest was ripped open by buckshot at close range. We took you to the settlement over near Ochopee and then to Miami. You know the rest from there."

Buddy struggled with his memory – trying to find a piece that fit with something else. The vision of a man running, and straining to breathe clouded his eyes. Somebody yelling. Then the quietness. Nothing else. "Where did all this happen at? Could you tell what my buddy and I were doin' there? How did we get there? Did we have boats?"

Toby looked at Marty then back at Buddy. "We found you at Shark Point. There were two twenty-foot skiffs piled high with coonskins. You all had been trapping for several days, I reckon."

Buddy lost his cool a little and his voice rose. "Where the hell is Shark Point?"

Toby's uneasiness with this conversation showed in his face, but he kept his calm. "It's the end of some high ground down in the Everglades, in the swamps, near the Gulf of Mexico. That's the best description I can give you, Curly. I'll try to take you down there in a few days. Let me get healed up a little first, okay?"

A moving picture built up in Buddy's mind. *He was standing by a boat pulled up on a beach. He heard a shotgun blast and saw the body of a man being propelled backwards and falling into the sand. Two men had guns leveled at him. He was stunned and scared.* The vision was gone. "Sorry, Toby. I didn't mean to get hot under the collar. Don't usually do that. Usually pretty good at controllin' my temper. Just seem so close sometimes to rememberin', only to have it slip away as fast as it comes in clear. Where're the boats now? What happened to the skins? Did you find guns that belonged to us?"

"We sold the boats and skins to pay for your stay in the hospital in Miami. Still wasn't enough. You still owe me some for that."

*The body of the man flashed again. It was lying flat in the sand. Grains of sand and dust were suspended in the air.* "What happened to my buddy's body? Did you bury it somewhere?"

"We didn't have anything to dig with there. We hauled it out into the Gulf and slid it overboard. Nothing else we could do."

Buddy could see the body slipping over the side with a splash into the water. What a way to be buried. Didn't make a difference, though. When you're dead, you're dead. Everything you once had is gone. He wondered what he and his partner were doing there with the skins. Had they camped there?

The picture of a large bladed knife with the body of a snake twisting around the hilt flashed and was as soon gone. He tried to re-access the picture – nothing "Was there a knife? Did you find a large knife with a snake carved into the handle?"

"Don't know anything about a fancy knife. You, Marty?"

Marty shook his head, 'no', put his cigarette out and stood. "I'm going to bed. Which bed I sleep in?"

"Take either one you want. I'll be right behind you. Curly, I suppose it's you that's got the pallet." He grinned and started to get up. He held his side and the pain showed on his face.

Buddy didn't want the session to end. He felt close to remembering some important things that would help him. "What about the guns? You never did say. Don't think a man would go traipsing off to the swamps without a gun. You?"

319

Toby stood – the interview over. "There was a shotgun in each of the boats. Sold one, still have the other one. It's at Andre's."

Buddy stood, too. "If we was trappin', there must have been some knives. You didn't find any?"

"Yeah, we found a couple of knives, but none with any special markings I know about. There were camp goods that didn't amount to nothing – normal stuff. I'm plumb worn out, Curly. We can talk more later. I understand how important it is for you to get your memory back, but bear with me for a few more days. Come on. Let's go to bed. Get an early start in the morning." He dropped a few coins on the table and walked to the cashier.

Buddy got blankets from the owner and made his pallet near the front door. He lay long into the night thinking about Toby's words tonight and how they tied into other things he had learned about himself. The still of the night was broken now and then by the roar of a car or truck passing by on the highway not too far from the door. He forced his eyes shut, but there was no sleep in them yet.

*Finally he was running from two giants with small cannons under their arms. They yelled at him to stop. Fear tried to stop him, but he kept running with all his might. He was getting away from them when all of a sudden he started rising in the air and drifting right back towards them. He struggled and flailed his arms, trying to come back down to the ground where he could gain some traction, but he could not.* Buddy awoke with a start, happy to know that it had all been a dream. Soon he found himself back in the same predicament. He wakened again, just before he floated into the giant's arms.

He tried to concentrate on other things to put the dream out of his mind. He tried to focus on the rest of the drive home. It would be good to see Liz again and dig into her good cooking. Might even look up Laura Mae. He became a little antsy when he thought on her too long. The day before he left to go to Savannah was still fresh on his mind. He wondered what would happen if he found himself alone with her again. He drifted off to sleep again.

*A woman stood at the edge of the shore with her bare feet covered with water. At first he was far away, then he was right up close and could almost touch her. He could smell her scent, but even when close up he couldn't make out her face. He felt good all over. Two small boys played at her side. She held something in her arms. He strained to see what it was but was unable to focus on it. The wind blew her hair away from her neck as she strained to see something out on the water – or was it a sound. Small waves from an approaching boat washed her feet and encased her ankles. Her toes dug into the sand as the water ebbed. He yelled at her and waved his arms desperately to get her attention. She didn't seem to hear. He shouted louder as the boat got closer and closer to the shore. She looked to that boat and started moving towards it. The two little boys ran towards the boat yelling at someone. He strained to see who was in the boat, but couldn't make out anyone. He floated just above the water. She was right there. He called to her louder, desperately, but she did not hear or see. Why couldn't she see him? She moved faster now toward the boat. She yelled to someone.* When he awoke, frustrated and struggling with the impossible, a dim light at the far side of the room illuminated the outline of a body sitting on the side of the bed. "Toby, that you?"

Toby turned toward him. "Yeah, Curly. Let's get on the road. I'm itchy to get home. How long, you reckon?"

"Hour and a half." Buddy stood and gathered his pallet, put it on the bed by Toby and went to the dresser. He poured water from the pitcher into the washbasin and slopped water on his face. He used one of the towels to dry with, then walked outside to find the toilet. The tree-tops at the horizon were mere shadows against the sky, lit with a pale misty blue tint. The blue just barely peeking through between the shadowy palm fronds. The tint darkened as it climbed and finally was gone completely. The overhead mist muted the half-moon about two o'clock high and slightly to the south. With no breeze, the full sun would be needed to burn the mist off. About an hour before sun-up he reckoned. He walked to the car and started it with just one turn of the crank and set the gear on idle.

321

Toby and Marty climbed onto the back seat. Toby said, "Let's go, Curly. We'll have breakfast at Mama's. She can get me healed, too. Aah, I've missed village life with my own kind – slow, measured and easy. We can go over to the lake and fish some. You would like that, Curly. How about you Marty, want to go fishing?"

"Harumph." Marty turned on his right side and went back to sleeping. Toby laughed. He seemed happy. Buddy pulled out onto the highway and headed south.

# CHAPTER 45

Darkness still shrouded the island when they shoved off from the dock jutting out into Pine Island Sound. The cool, fresh breeze out of the west brought a faint hint of the sea from which it had just come. A half-moon almost directly overhead and a thousand stars, provided enough light to see the enchanting white beach of Captiva recede as they gained speed and distance. The light blue sky was speckled with myriad small cloudlets all grouped together like sheep herding in a pasture. The few large, scattered cloud formations far to the south were white and not predictive of bad weather. The wake of the boat spread out to the sides and glittered florescent as the boat cut through the calm waters.

Flo huddled the sleeping children to her. The baby, wrapped snug in a small blanket, she held close to her bosom, and the boys, also wrapped in blankets, slept near her feet on the bottom of the boat. Mornings were the best part of the day for her. Troubles and disturbances usually began soon after the sun came up. They all crowded under the canopy in the cockpit as Joe piloted the small launch out into the sound, picking up speed as he went. Mildred had decided against coming with them at the last minute.

This launch, about twenty feet or so, Joe had owned for over ten years. It was an old boat even then. He fished her out of Key Largo even when he farmed there. He loved this old boat and would probably keep her until he died.

The bowl of the pipe glowed bright red and sparks jumped into the air every time Joe sucked heavy on the stem. The sweet smell of tobacco smoke filled the cockpit and was as soon wiped clean by the sea breeze. Flo opened the thermos and inhaled the fresh fragrance of brewed coffee. The faint steam climbed from the top and disappeared in the darkness. She poured them both a cup. Only the purr of the engine and the cut of the water broke the peaceful silence of the open sea. Soon they were opposite the southern beaches of Cayo Costa which were as wide and white as those at Captiva – a beautiful and captivating sight. If only all of her time could be mornings like this one.

Flo used Joe's pipe to light her own cigarette. She inhaled deeply, took a large sip of coffee then exhaled the smoke, which quickly dispersed. "Daddy Joe, what can you tell me about Buddy?"

Joe remained silent for a long moment. "I fished with Buddy quite a bit before he disappeared. He was a damn good man. Best I've ever known. He had a lot of promise, too, Flo. If he'd lived, I reckon he would've gone on to do great things and taken you all right along with him. He had a mind like no other man I've ever known. He was always thinkin' up new ways to do things better. Put me to thinkin' of the likes of Edison. He told me about the trap and car distributor he made. Never seen either of them, but I did see him actually make a carburetor out of old parts while we were waitin' for the mullet to strike. I often wonder what he could've done if he'd had a better chance to get some real schoolin'. He loved you and the kids more'n anything else, I can tell you that. When he wasn't talkin' about one of his inventions, he was talkin' about you all. Flo, that man would never have run off and left you and them kids all alone in this country by yourself. He's either dead or out of his mind. That's all there is to it." Joe tapped his pipe on the side of the boat to clean it.

Flo looked longingly at the white beach skimming by. They were running fast just off the coast. The fire still sparkled in the wake. There were no other boats about. The stars were fading and the sky was still speckled with small clouds. They would reach Cayo Costa in a short while. She took a deep breath to control her emotions. She almost always broke down when others talked so glowingly about Buddy. "You think I'm a fool for not goin' ahead and gettin' married to Bill Parkins?"

His voice was soothing, but stern. "Flo, honey, I won't ever think you're a fool, no matter what course you take. I know you'll do the right thing when the time's right for you. It's just my belief that Buddy's dead, God rest his soul. I know, too, that you got three young'uns to raise in these worst of all times. I ain't never seen no tougher times to scrape out a livin' than these. A woman with small children got no chance at all. I hate to put it that way, Flo, but facts are facts. You gotta face 'em head on, honey. There ain't no easy way. I wish there was. Wish I could be more help to you."

That's what she liked about Daddy Joe. He could give you his opinion without giving an opinion. Usually, when he spoke, it was to state a fact or a presumed fact. He had already accepted Buddy's death as fact. And certainly, if it was indeed a fact, her decision was an easy one. But she still had her doubts and, above all, she still had her hopes. As Mildred said, what would she do if she married Bill Parkins and Buddy showed up. She had heard stories like that. Everything seemed to point to his death, though, but it was hard for her to sort out the facts from the emotions. They always seemed to get mixed up together somehow. Bill Parkins wouldn't wait forever. That was a fact, too. She would have to make up her mind this month and probably, before Christmas. The baby shuddered and Flo shivered. The wind had turned colder and had turned more to the northwest without her being aware. The boys slept on. The coast sped by.

"You're a big help, Daddy Joe, and I love you dearly for your care and understanding. These are tough times, there's no doubt about that. Daddy Joe, you know why Mama hates Papa Jim so much?"

"People are like magnets – opposites attract and likes repel. Jim and Millie are likes – both of 'em want to rule the roost – want things to be to their likin'. If your mama had been a man, she'd be just like Jim. Maybe that's why she hates him. He's a man and has more power and can do more things than's allowed

325

a woman. She resents it and fights against him ever chance she gets . . . ."

"Mama says I should forget what Papa Jim says about Buddy not being dead. She's probably right, but she says it with such spitefulness and hate that I'm prone not to take her advice."

Joe huddled down in the cockpit and lit another pipe full. The glow of the match lit his face. "What does Jim say?"

"He's followed up on several rumored sightings of Buddy since he went off and none of them have proven to be true so far. He's up in Savannah now trackin' down a couple of Indians who might know somethin' about a white man they found that had been shot and left for dead. Somebody said the man favored Buddy some. I won't know till I get back down to Wood Key late this afternoon or tomorrow. He just won't give up hope that Buddy's still alive somehow. I don't know what he knows about Buddy that gives him that hope. I've got hope, too, but I got to admit, it's weakening fast now."

"You gotta remember one thing about Jim, Flo. He had great hopes that Buddy would take over all his business interests someday. He simply won't accept what everybody else knows as fact. Buddy was cut down in cold blood and his body scattered to the four winds. Jim just knew that God had placed Buddy on this earth for some great purpose and he knows that God wouldn't take the boy till he'd realized the purpose. I agree with your mama, honey. Jim's once very logical and calculatin' mind is now completely overshadowed by his emotions. You've got to take what he says with a grain of salt when it comes to Buddy. Don't let it sway your decision one way or the other. Remember, you can't wait forever. I hate to say it, but Buddy's more likely deader'n a door nail."

Junior had been listening to them talk for some time. Now he started squalling like a stuck pig and yanking on Flo's dress. "My daddy ain't dead. I know he ain't dead. My daddy's comin' back. Momma, Daddy ain't dead, is he?"

Flo brought the child to her and smothered him with her arms. "Hush now, child. Of course, your daddy's comin' back home one of these days real soon." She looked at Papa Joe through the growing light – he looked saddened.

The boat slowed as they passed the schoolhouse on the point, turned into the cove and the docks straight ahead. The stars were all gone now and the sun peeked up above the dark mangrove shores, far to the south and east. Just up the coast from the dock Flo saw smoke rising above the trees. She could almost smell the bacon and eggs frying. Francis and Warren both woke up at the same time. It must have been the slowing of the boat and the change in the engine noise and rumble. The smell of rotting seaweed and dead fish wrenched at her nose. She pinched it shut and let the smell in a little at a time until she could get used to it. She slapped a mosquito and reached into her bag for the salve to spread on the children before the pests had a chance at their tender skins. The mosquitoes were thick as a hornet's nest when they docked. The wind had died down to almost nothing. Flo said, "But still, they never found any bodies, boats or anything. How can we be sure he and Robert were killed?"

Joe maneuvered the boat up to the dock near the fuel tanks. He would have to get gas before he made the return trip. Nobody was around this early on a Sunday morning. He looked at Junior who no longer paid any attention to him. "They did find one of the skiffs and lots of other signs. The bodies were dumped in the Gulf." He stopped the boat, grabbed onto a piling and threw a rope around it.

She wondered how people could accept something as fact without real proof, but she decided not to respond. Seaweed lay thick upon the shore, mixed with dead fish in varying degrees of decay and other natural and human debris. The natural stuff gathering along the shore she could understand, but simply could not understand how people could throw trash right in their own back yard. The awful stink would not go away. She felt better when they all started walking inland a ways to Dot's house farther up on the north point.

The two-story house, sitting far back from the beach, was completely covered with black tarpaper except for the roof which was sheeted with tin. The building sat on thick, square logs about two feet off the ground. It resembled a square box with a pitched roof. There was no porch, just two wooden steps leading up to the front door. Three windows on the side facing the yard and two in the front. The yard, made up mostly of shell with weeds here and there, was littered with the typical fisherman's gear; gill-nets in two piles and one hanging from a net spread; crab pots and crawfish traps stacked three high; an old skiff turned over on its back; a launch up on blocks, apparently being reworked in some way; two rusted fifty gallon drums and various other items used in the repair of things, and a couple of old bottles and empty cans, probably the result of some games the children played. Near the rear of the house were two large piles of oyster and clamshells.

A scruffy looking brown dog ran out from under the house barking, but with tail wagging briskly. It sniffed everybody for new smells, then started licking the boys in the face. They ran and gathered around Flo's legs and the dog came, too. A black and white spotted mongrel stayed at the edge of the house growling with bared fangs showing.

A boy about eight years opened the screen door, looked out and yelled, "Momma, company's come." He jumped down to the ground and ran toward the dog, waving his arms in a shooing motion. "Rusty, git away from them kids." He picked up a bottle and threw it at the growling dog, missing it by a mile. The dog, still growling deep in his throat, retreated back under the house. "Hello, Aunt Flo. Grandpa Joe." Two Rhode Island Red roosters got in the way and scattered, squawking, with wings beating frantically, much disturbed by the unusual activity in the yard.

Flo noticed the chicken-house, a long unpainted wooden shed with nests for the laying hens built up off the ground and completely enclosed with meshed wire fencing behind and to the left of the main house. She untangled the boys from her legs and began walking towards the front screen-door. She recognized Dot's oldest, "Hello, Cal, your mama's home, I reckon?" Daddy Joe didn't say anything and Cal didn't have time to respond before Dot stuck her head through the door and called for them to come on in.

Flo welcomed the warmth of the large long room. She hadn't completely gotten over the chill from the boat ride. Dot, big as a house with child, stepped aside and let them in, then gave them both a hug. The boys hung back, close to Flo's legs. Walter and the other Morales children stopped eating to stare at the intruders for just an instant and were back at it as the group moved toward the kitchen table at the far end of the room.

"Come on, Daddy Joe, you and Flo come on and join us for breakfast. Flo, you can put the baby on the floor there next to the divan." Dot took the boys by the hand and led the way to the table. "Grab some chairs out of the livin' room and pull up. Move over, Nancy. Make room for your grandpa and Aunt Flo. Cal, run out to the coop and rustle up six more eggs."

Walter was in the process of sopping the rest of the yellow egg yolk from his plate with the remnants of a biscuit. He paused, with the biscuit hovering just over his plate, and acknowledged the visitors. He remained sitting, "Flo. Joe, I thought you were gonna come over and fish some with us. Don't make much difference, though – not much runnin' now anyhow. A few pompano, that's about all. Not much of a market for 'em neither. You okay?"

Flo and Joe pulled their chairs up to the table and sat down. Joe said, "Been meanin' to run over here and talk to you about that, but been so damn busy with the farm, just haven't had time. Don't reckon I've got time to fish now anyhow. If you need somebody to fill in a spot, though, I'll make the time."

Dot served him a plate of three fried eggs sunny side up, grits piled high with a tablespoon of melting butter in the middle, four strips of fried bacon sliced thick with a crackly rind and two biscuits opened up, butter melting in the center with steam rising from the plate. Flo's plate was similar except the eggs were fried over easy with the yolk misted over with a whiteness. The aroma from the food overwhelmed her and hunger took control – she dug in. The smell of fresh brewing coffee filled the room. The boys had already finished their breakfast and were off playing with Dot's youngest boys about the same age.

Dot began clearing dishes from the table and cleaned them out in the trashcan. She filled a dishpan with hot water from the kettle on the stove and, with some chopped up Octagon soap, put the dirty dishes in to soak. When she finished, she poured everyone's cup full with fresh coffee, sat across from Flo and lit a cigarette. "Flo, I thought we could go clammin' this mornin' and have steamed clams for dinner today."

Walter pushed his chair back from the table and rose, "I've got to run over to Bokeelia to see Shelly. You gonna be around for a while, Joe?"

"No, I'll be leavin' soon's I finish with these eggs. Got to meet with the farm owner this afternoon. I'll get over this way again pretty soon. If you need me, send somebody over." Walter took his coffee with him when he left.

Dot arranged for Calvin to watch the children and she and Flo went to the boat docks to see Joe off. They pulled a twenty-foot skiff off the beach and into the water. Dot started the small stern kicker and soon they were on their way to a small key across Pine Island Sound. Dot said it was called Mundongo Key. The wind had picked up some and the waters of the Sound had small chops with a little white foam at the tops. The skiff cut through them, but the ride was still bumpy. They skirted around the southern point of the key and headed around to the side, away from Cayo Costa where the mud banks were. Flo tried to say something to Dot, but the engine noise and the slap of the boat bottom on the waves was too much competition. She gave up trying to talk. Soon they were around to the other side and the wind dropped off. Dot killed the engine, guided the boat onto a mud bank and secured it to a mangaroot.

330

Flo took advantage of the quiet and asked, "Dot, ain't you just a little bit scared comin' way off over here and takin' those bumps? That young'un could be born any minute. You wantin' me to be deliverin' it?"

Dot tossed a croaker sack to Flo and took the other one for herself. She stepped over board and into the water. "Come on, Flo. Let's get these clams. That young'un will come when it's good and ready. Besides, I don't expect it until sometime in January. Can't stop livin' just because a young'un's to be born. You remember the last time we did this? Then we were both full with child. Come on."

Flo stepped over the side. The slimy mud oozed through her toes and engulfed her legs up to the calf. The cold water came all the way up to her thighs. A tingling shiver ran up her spine. The smell, something akin to stale oil, offended her nose, but she soon became accustomed to it. They started to move alongside the shore, feeling for clams with their toes as they went. The mud was so loose she didn't have to lift her feet all the way out of it to move forward – sort of pushed through it. She shivered when Dot dipped the front of her body into the water and brought out a clam. Flo felt one and lifted it out of the mud with the top of her foot. She brought her foot as close to the water's surface as she could, but still had to immerse a portion of her body in the water to snag the clam. She shivered again when her body touched the water. They were both soaked to the skin in the front, but soon they had their bags filled and returned to the boat.

They both lit up, sat and enjoyed the smoke. "So, Flo, what are you goin' to do with your life? You goin' to keep on waitin' for Buddy?"

"I just don't know, Dot. One minute I'm ready to take Bill's offer and marry him and the next I want to wait for Buddy to return. What would you do?"

"You actually think Buddy's alive?"

"I don't know what to believe. If he's alive and left me with these three young'uns, I'm not sure I want him back anyhow.

What kind of man would go off and leave his kids behind? It's hard for me to believe Buddy had that in him, and nobody else does either. If he's alive, he must be mighty sick or somethin'. Only thing, I just can't understand what kind of sickness he could have to keep him away all this time. And, even though they didn't find his body, most everybody, except Papa Jim, says he's dead. And that brings up another point. With no body to prove he's dead, the law says he ain't until seven years passes. That means I'm still married to him and can't legally marry anybody else. Too much for my little brain, Dot, but I know I gotta do somethin' real soon. What little money I had is almost gone now and Papa Jim is talkin' about chargin' me rent for my house or he's gonna kick me out."

"What? Kick you out of your own house? I don't believe what I'm hearin'." Dot stopped trying to start the stern kicker and looked at Flo like she had just gone completely off her rocker. "Did he tell you that? What's he expect you to do? God help us."

"Well, he was nice about it and didn't want to get me upset or anything. Told me not to worry and that things would work out. Of course he believes Buddy's comin' back."

Dot gave the rope a pull and the engine started right up. "Tell you what I'd do if it was me. If I could at least stomach Bill Parkins, I'd marry that son-of-a-gun in a heartbeat. I wouldn't put it off another minute. You keep on waitin', he'll find somebody else, I guarantee you that. Then what you gonna do? Go live with Mama?" She undid the ropes, pushed the skiff off the bank with a long pole and headed towards the north end of the key. She shouted, "We'll go up to the oyster bar at the point and get a mess for supper tonight."

Flo sat silent, alone with her thoughts. No need to try and talk over the engine noise anyhow. Everybody except Papa, had advised her to go ahead and marry Bill and do it now. She absent-mindedly looked at the passing key. It was mostly just like all others in this area. Dense mangroves with their spindly legs all tangled together snatching up and building on whatever

332

happened to float by. Farther in, on the sandy part, buttonwoods and pines grew, grabbing for the sky and dwarfing the mangroves. The windward side always seemed to support white sandy beaches while the leeward supported mangroves and mud.

At the point, Dot anchored and took the long pole with a device with pincers on one end and set to gathering oysters from the bed beneath them. She reached into the water and, with the use of ropes on a pulley, operated the pincers and brought up oysters one at a time. After about thirty minutes, she had enough to satisfy her. She pried one open with her sheath knife and threw the top part of the shell overboard. Then she loosened the oyster with the knife blade and offered it to Flo with salt, pepper and vinegar. She opened another and prepared it the same way for herself. They ate several in silence then Flo asked, "Dot, if you had it to do over again would you change the way you've lived your life so far and what would you do from here on out?"

Without any hesitation Dot said, "I think I would do it different, but I'm not sure just how. I'm twenty-seven now and already have four young'uns and another one on the way. If Walter has his way, there'll be several more to come. The way we're goin' now, I don't see much chance of improvin' our way of livin' any time soon. God knows, Walter works hard enough, but we never seem to get ahead of where we're at. We get a little saved and somethin' comes along and takes it away. There's just not enough money to be made fishin'. One month we're in high cotton and the next we're lookin' for a handout. I think I'd go to school and devote my early years to learnin' and get as far away from fishin' as I could. How about you? What would you do?"

"I agree with you. Since Buddy left I've thought about it quite a bit. Education is the only way out of this kind of life, but when you're young you just want to be like your parents. You don't know any better. They might try to tell you to do things different, but you don't listen so well. Every now and then you have the chance to see a different kind of life, but it's far enough away that you don't get to really taste it – you never learn what it is. I met a friend of mine in Key West who finished high school and now has a good job workin' on the inside. She married a feller who also graduated from high school and he has a good job, too. They have a comfortable life and have money saved up, or so she said. I sure wouldn't have all these young'uns to look after. Don't get me wrong, I wouldn't trade 'em for the world now, but if I was doin' it over I wouldn't have them this early in life. No need to look back though – can't change nothin' now." She thought again about the itch to get better educated and become an archeologist like the professor on the ferry. But she thought such an idea was downright silly. How in the world could she even consider such a thing, with four mouths to feed and no money? Buddy had plans to get them out of the swamps and that, too, was now gone. Then, as if from nowhere, she shouted to the wind, "By God, I'm gonna do it. I'm goin' back to school. I can do better."

# CHAPTER 46

As they approached the docks at Cayo Costa, Flo saw a man dressed in coveralls standing by a launch moored at the end of the dock. As they drew nearer, she saw the red hair and her heart skipped a beat – Bill Parkins. She looked at Dot who just grinned. Dot drove the skiff right up on the beach, tilting the engine out of the water and shutting it off at just the right time to prevent it from chewing into the sand and shells. Bill walked over to them. The sun was almost directly overhead.

Bill had no sooner come alongside the skiff when one of the children let out a blood curdling scream and cried, "Mama, Mama." It was Francis. *My God, my God, what's happened now?* Flo jumped out of the boat and looked at Bill. They both ran towards the children gathered around in a knot over near the pile of nets. In the middle of them Francis lay on his side clutching his right foot. Next to his foot lay the jagged bottom of a broken bottle covered with blood. Blood poured through his fingers and ran onto the ground. He screamed at the top of his lungs. Her heart skipped a beat and pounded within her chest. She pulled his hands away from his foot and saw the blood gushing out of an unseen wound. "Bill, run up to the house and find some cobwebs to stop this bleedin'." She brushed away the blood, trying to see how bad the cut was, but as fast as she wiped it away, it renewed itself. The cut could not be seen through all the blood. Blood pulsed out of the wound and it had to be stopped quickly. Bill came back and put the cobwebs in her hand. She placed them into the cut and pressed down tight. Francis screamed louder. Soon the blood clotted and stopped flowing almost completely. She looked at the cut and almost fainted. The cut covered almost the entire top of his foot. When he stepped on the bottle bottom, one end of it must have come right over

335

the top of his foot and made the gash. The cut would need stitches and there were no doctors on Cayo Costa.

Bill stood by her side. She looked up at him. "Bill, I need to get this boy to a doctor at Bokeelia. Can you take me?"

"Let's go." He reached down, picked Francis up from the ground and headed for his boat. Flo went to the house and got the baby and her things. She yelled for Junior to follow and ran towards Bill's boat. Dorothy still stood by her boat, removing clams and oysters. "Dot, I don't know how long this will take. I may not make it back out here. You get in touch with me if you need help with that young'un. I'll come runnin'." She turned to leave.

"Flo, what are you gonna to do about Bill?"

Flo turned back to look at her. "Probably marry him." She turned and fled to the boat.

They arrived at the fish house at Bokeelia at 2:00 o'clock. Bill spoke to the woman on duty there and she immediately arranged for someone to drive them to the clinic. She said the clinic was the closest thing they had to a hospital, but they could handle all but the most severe cases. More serious cases had to go into Ft. Myers.

Within fifteen minutes the car stopped in front of the double screen doors. Bill picked Francis up, pushed through the doors and went straight to the front desk. Flo, with Warren on her hip, was hot on his heels and Junior hung onto her skirt. Her clothes were still damp from clamming. She imagined she smelled of raw oysters to the clinic staff. A young man and woman sat on a side bench. The woman was crying and the man kept trying to console her.

The nurse came around from behind the desk and looked at the foot. She grimaced when she saw the wound filled with cobwebs. She went back around the desk and spoke into a phone. Soon a corpsman was there with a stretcher. He took Francis from Bill and placed him on the stretcher and started

336

away. Francis bawled and mournfully reached for Flo. She followed and tried to console him.

The corpsman, continuing on down the hall, said, "Ma'am, I'm sorry, but you'll have to wait in the lobby. The doctor will speak to you after he has looked at the boy."

Flo started to protest, but Bill grabbed her by the arm and led her to a bench against the wall. She started to fight against him, tears welling in her eyes, the wails from Francis ringing in her ears. Now she understood why the woman on the other side of the room was crying. She must have someone being tended to inside.

Bill said, "Come on, Flo. The doctor knows what he's doin'. There's nothin' you can do. Just be in the way."

She knew he was right and went quietly to the bench, but kept shaking like a leaf. Junior went to the Coke machine down the hall and banged on it, trying to make one of the bottles fall out. Bill walked down, put a nickel in the slot and told Junior to pull on the knob. He did and a bottle fell down to the bottom. He opened it and he and Bill walked back to the bench.

Flo flinched when she heard a child scream. It was the same scream she'd heard from Francis earlier in the day. She knew it was him. The woman across the room flinched, too. Junior played with some toys he found in a box in the corner and sucked on the bottle of Coke. Bill went outside to smoke. Flo paced up and down. Finally the doctor came out with a small girl and approached the couple. Flo couldn't hear what was said, but she saw the relief on the woman's face.

At four o'clock they brought Francis out in a wheel chair with his foot swathed in white bandages, propped up on a footpad on the chair. He was sucking on a lollipop someone had given him. He looked like he had been crying a lot. He brightened up when he saw her. Junior ran over to him, started jabbering away and showed him his Coke. Francis said he wanted one, too. Flo got one for him. The doctor came over and said the cut took fourteen stitches, but should heal without any complications. She almost fainted again when she was told the charge was fifteen dollars – that left her with just over five dollars to her name – her choices were narrowing.

They caught a ride to the fish house just in time to see Daddy Joe's boat pulling in. What now? Daddy Joe was the pilot and Mildred stood next to him. Dot and all her kids were on the boat. What in the world? They tied up at the dock and Mildred left the boat first. She looked a sight. She looked like she had been up all night. Maybe she learned about Francis and was concerned enough to make the trip here to help. Flo stood next to Bill, holding the baby to her bosom. "Mama, what are you all doin' over here? Nothin' wrong, I hope."

"Your sister is dead. Killed . . . ." The words tore into Flo's head like a cyclone – her knees buckled. She fainted dead away and as she started downward, her arms loosened and the baby started to fall. Bill, quick as a flash, circled his arms around her and the baby, guided them down to the plank flooring of the dock and leaned her against a post. Dot scrambled up on the dock and moved everybody away to give her air.

When Flo finally came to, it took her a few seconds to realize where she was. She focused on Dot. "Did Mama say my sister died? What sister? How?"

"Whoa, gal, take it easy. Bill, would you get her somethin' to drink." It was more of an order than a question. "Edna was killed in a train wreck over on Michigan Avenue in Ft. Myers last night. Somebody got word to Mama today and she came to Ky Costa to let me know and hopin' you was still there. We're all goin' over to Edna's house in Ft. Myers. The funeral is tomorrow. Mama is about to blow a gasket. Edna was her pet, you know."

# CHAPTER **47**

L ester moved the stacked files on the desk out of the way with his right arm and picked up the phone. With the phone cradled on his left shoulder, he bent his ear to the receiver and laid the cigarette on the ashtray. He picked up a pencil, dabbed the pencil lead on his tongue, and retrieved a blank piece of paper from a desk drawer.

The receptionist at the front desk said, "Lester, a Miss Agnes Stimson from Moultrie General, regarding Billy Blanton. I believe you were waiting for this call?"

Lester's heart skipped a beat, his right hand poised to take the information. He hoped the call was positive. He needed a break in this case. If this guy Blanton died, any hope of a positive ID was gone. "Miss Stimson, Lester Johnston here. Thank you for calling. You have some good news for me I hope."

"Mister Johnston, Mr. Blanton has been moved from ICU and is off the critical list. If you can come over now, you can see him right away. If not, you'll have to wait until this afternoon or tomorrow. You can't spend much time with him in any event."

Lester gave the thumbs up to Earl who hovered over him. "We'll be right over and thanks, Miss Stimson." He replaced the phone on its cradle, stood up and grabbed his jacket off the back of the chair. "Blanton is out of ICU. Let's go."

Earl moved back to his desk and put on his jacket. They headed for the door. At the front desk Lester slapped the palm of his hand on the counter top and winked at Joyce when she glanced up from the pile of papers in front of her. He grinned, "Paydirt, baby." He followed Earl's broad shoulders through the door.

Earl's long six-foot four frame towered over his own five-foot eight. Earl's girth made Lester look almost like a dwarf. Earl had come to work for him in the Detective Bureau three years ago. Earl had proved to be a moxey detective, with a nose for scooping up valuable information. Lester himself had been on the force going on twenty years, with the last twelve in the Detective Division. His wife, Emma, says he's been on the force all his life. Matter of fact, it is his life. She didn't understand the love a body could develop for a particular work. This job provided exhilaration like no other experiences he'd ever been exposed to. When you brought all the key pieces of information together and they fit like a jigsaw puzzle, there just simply was no greater feeling, bar none. He loved the force, the job and the guys. With Earl's nose, and with his own devotion to detail, he would solve this case, too – in short order.

At the hospital, they took the elevator to the fourth floor, Agnes was waiting for them at the nurses' station. She motioned for them to follow and led them to a single room, at the far end of the hall, straight down from the Nurse's desk. "Remember, you can only stay a few minutes. Can't allow him to get too tired or upset. Be good, fellas. Please?" She turned to leave. "I'll be right down there if you need me." She pointed at the desk at the other end of the hall.

Lester spoke as he walked into the room. "Thanks, Agnes. We'll take good care of him." He noted the room number, 412. Earl jotted it down in his notepad.

The man in the bed looked like death warmed over. A large white bandage covering his chest showed through the hospital shirt, which was open half way down his torso. He opened his eyes when they entered and looked at them as if in a stupor.

Lester approached the bed and flashed his badge attached to a leather wallet. "Mr. Blanton, Lester Johnston, Savannah Police Department. This here's Detective Earl Griffin. We'd like to ask you a few questions. Feel up to it?" The man nodded his assent and motioned for the glass of water sitting on the table next to his bed.

"I understand you were on duty at the Paul Sher Jewelry Store on the afternoon of Friday December two." The man nodded. "Can you tell us just what happened when the robbers came in?"

The man tried to speak, but no words came out. He drank more water. Lester and Earl waited patiently. The man's voice was scratchy and barely audible when the first words came out. "I was just getting ready to close up when they came in the door. There were two of them. They looked like foreigners, maybe Indian or some such. They both wore hats and their hair was worn long." He hesitated and cleared his throat. He drank more water. "They asked for Charlie. I told them I didn't know a Charlie. The one doing the talking looked a little bewildered. Then he shoved a gun in my face and said he wanted the bag sitting by my feet. I reached down as if to get the bag, and came up with a gun of my own. The shot shattered the case and the man fell to the floor. In an instant the other man was all over me, and the next thing I knew I was on the floor clutching my chest and trying hard to breathe." He stopped talking and started coughing. Lester sent Earl for the nurse.

She quieted him down and he lay back breathing easy with his eyes closed. "Detective, you'll have to leave now. He's too excited to talk more."

"Just one or two more questions, Agnes. I promise." His face conveyed his best begging and pleading posture, designed to melt even the hardest hearts.

Blanton spoke. His voice seemed stronger than before. "Nurse, it's okay. I feel all right. I need to tell them what I know."

She looked hard at Lester. "All right, but if this happens again, that's it."

"Agreed, thanks again." That look could make ice melt. She turned and went out.

Lester turned to Blanton and continued, "You work at the store every day?"

"No. This was my first day at this store. I was called in to replace the normal guy who had taken sick the day before. Think he was hospitalized. Appendicitis or something like that, I believe. I came down from Atlanta."

"Was his name Charlie?"

"His real name was Harold . . . I'm sorry, I can't seem to remember the last name."

Lester didn't push it. "The robbers must've been expecting somebody else. You reckon it was the regular clerk?"

"Sorry, can't help you there."

"You say the man asked for the bag. What was in it?"

"Not sure exactly, but I'd guess close to a million."

"Whuwee! What the hell?" Lester looked at Earl who seemed just as shocked. "What was the million for?"

"The purchase of diamonds. It's not unusual. The store takes in diamonds from South Africa and other countries almost on a daily basis. Buyers come from all over the country almost as often."

Earl spoke for the first time. "So those boys got off with a cool million. My God, I wonder what a million looks like. How big was the bag?"

"Just a regular bag about the size of a suitcase. All hundred dollar bills. Listen, I don't know for a fact that they took the bag. I shot one of them. I saw him fall to the floor." He started coughing again and Agnes was immediately in the doorway urging them out of the room. They left quietly with the promise that they could come back in the future.

They waited for Agnes to come back to the nurses' station. Lester asked, "Agnes, if a person came to this hospital with a case of appendicitis, which ward would he be in?"

Agnes went behind the counter and busied herself with things on the desk there. She looked at Lester. "I'm not exactly sure, but I think it's either the third or fifth. Check with Admissions on the first floor. They can tell you, for sure." She dismissed them and continued with her work.

At the elevator, Earl punched the button to take them to the first floor. "Something don't strike me as just right. Could be some big fish swimming here. Much bigger than we can imagine.

We need to find out who owns this little store here in Savannah and why there's diamonds and so much money here. Should've asked him that question."

"You on to something?"

"Just a hunch. Think we ought to go back and ask him?"

The elevator came and they rode it down. "Never mind now. We find this other guy with appendicitis we'll get the answer there."

On the way to the Admissions Desk Earl asked, "Think this guy with the stomach problems is Charlie?"

The elderly lady behind the wrap-around desk spoke pleasantly when they approached. "Hello, gentlemen. Can I help you?"

Lester introduced themselves and asked, "We're looking for a man suffering from appendicitis who may have been admitted to this hospital on Thursday the first of the month. Right now we don't know his name. Can you possibly help us locate such a person?"

She fingered through some cards on a roller, rummaged through a file cabinet, then made two telephone calls. "Your man's name is Harold Echley, but he was discharged Monday."

Earl was getting the scent. He spoke. "You have an address for this man? Phone?"

"He lives at 347 Huntington. No phone listed here."

Two men in business suits in a black 1931 Buick sedan, parked down the street from the hospital entrance, watched as the detectives emerged through the door and walked the short distance to their car. As the detectives drove away, the men eased their car forward and parked in the parking lot across the street from the entrance. They had been on the fourth floor earlier and had overheard the nurse when she first called the detectives. They had decided to wait until the police left before visiting the patient in room 412. They walked the short distance to the lobby and took the elevator to the fourth floor.

# CHAPTER 48

347 Huntington was a white two-story wood frame house with railed porch along the entire length of the front. A solid green hedge hid most of the railing. A large oak tree with low-hanging Spanish moss was just to the left of the walkway and shaded half of the house and porch. They took the three steps up to the porch level, opened the screen door and knocked on the main one. Lester noted the three rockers and the swing at the far end. It would be a peaceful afternoon reclined in one of the rockers with a good book and a cool glass of iced tea. Just this kind of day with the waning sun at the back of the house and the soft, cool breeze would do just fine. An elderly lady opened the door and Lester introduced themselves. She invited them in and led them to the parlor just off the entry and the staircase leading to the second floor. Lester removed his hat. "Ma'am, sorry to trouble you, but we have to locate a Mr. Harold Echley. We understand he resides here."

"Yes, he does. Room 203, to the right at the top of the stairs. Nothing serious, I hope. The poor man was just released from the hospital and is having a difficult time getting around. He was so active before the operation. An avid golfer – played every weekend, I think. Can I get you something cool to drink?"

Lester spoke, "No, ma'am. We've got to be getting along. Mind if we just go on up for a few minutes? Avid golfer, eh?" He started towards the stairs. Earl followed.

"Sure, go right ahead. I'm sure he's awake. Hasn't been out even to take his meals since the operation." She trailed behind them.

A very thin man in a bathrobe with horn-rimmed glasses and several days growth of beard answered the door. He was white as a sheet. Lester mused, an avid golfer should be tanned. It's amazing how illness and hospital confinement can run off with your color in no time at all. Lester flashed his badge. "Mr. Echley, my partner and I are detectives with the Savannah Police. Need to ask you some questions. Can we come in?"

The man didn't seem surprised to see them. He pulled the door open farther and stood back as they entered. "I'd offer you something, but I don't have anything worthwhile. Been a little down the last few days. Have a seat. You're here about the Paul Sher Jewelry Store robbery?"

Earl looked directly at the man and said, "Hello, Charlie."

The man, about to close the door, hesitated and turned to face Earl. His face dropped and turned whiter, but he recovered quickly. "What's that?"

Lester followed up. "Mr. Echley, as you know, a man was shot at the jewelry store last Friday. The robbers asked for Charlie. Are you Charlie?"

Echley seemed flustered and sat down in the overstuffed chair across from the detectives. "I'm sorry gentlemen, but I don't know a Charlie. I can't imagine what they would be doing asking for a Charlie. There's no Charlie working at the store."

Lester had wandered over to the window and stood looking out. That was the signal for Earl to proceed with the questioning. "You the only one that works there, Mr. Echley?"

"Yes, I have the store open five days a week – Tuesday through Saturday – nine to five."

"What happens when you get sick?"

"Sorry." He looked sheepishly at Earl, glanced at Lester and back to Earl. "There is another fellow that works part-time and he fills in for me during those times. If I'm out for any length of time, they send someone down from headquarters. That's never happened, though."

"Was the part-timer the guy that got shot? What's his name?"

"Sorry, again. Guess you guys got me nervous. That was a fellow from headquarters. They send down a special courier every month to pick up accumulated cash and transport it back to Atlanta."

Earl pressed on. "What's the part-timer's name and where can we find him?"

Echley was now sitting on the edge of his chair. "Carl Watkins. Middle-aged man lives over on Jefferson."

Earl scribbled the name on his scratch pad. "The name of the company that owns everything? Their address and telephone number. Who's in charge?" He looked up from the pad at Echley.

"Euramco International. They're on Peachtree Street in downtown Atlanta. Don't have the telephone number here. Have it at the store."

"How much cash you usually accumulate for a courier to pick up?"

"Usually about a million."

"Was that the amount this time?"

"Yes, about that."

Lester joined them and interjected, "Was this fellow from Atlanta expected or did you call for a backup because of your illness?"

"He was due sometime Monday. I called the main office late Thursday and he came in and opened for business on Friday. He was supposed to run the store until we could contact Mr. Watkins to come in."

"What about the money? Was he supposed to take it back after you came back, or was someone else coming for it?"

"I don't know about that."

Lester walked around the room looking at pictures on the wall. He felt sure this guy was Charlie and definitely part of the heist, but didn't think he had planned it himself. There must be a connection to someone else. He gave Earl the look to continue. Earl spoke, "The landlady tells me you're a golfer. Where you play?"

Echley perked up at the mention of golf. "Yes. I love the game. Can't get enough. Play every chance I get. You play?"

"I play some. Don't get the opportunity often enough, though. Where do you play?"

"Belle Isle Country Club. You?"

"Bacon Park. Never played the country club. Don't make enough to play there. You're a member, I guess?"

"Yes, been a member since '27. I love it there. Maybe you could come as my guest someday."

Suspects were always trying to bribe a cop in one way or another. Lester listened more intently. Earl was trying to develop something. Could be the connection he was looking for. Earl continued, "I'd like that very much, but I imagine you've got your usual foursome."

"Yes. The same guys play every Saturday, but we could get together some Sunday if that would fit for you."

"Maybe I'll take you up on it someday soon."

Lester strolled over. He handed the man a card. "Mr. Echley, we'll have to be going now. I'd appreciate it if you would call me if you can think of anything that might possibly help us. We may be calling upon you again as the case develops. You're not planning on going anywhere, are you?"

They all walked to the door. Echely opened it and said, "No, I'm not going anywhere. If I'm not here, I'll be at the store."

The sun was completely behind the building when they left, the air busy and turning cold. Lester picked up the mike and called headquarters to let them know they were coming in. After a few minutes the chief came on. "Where the hell you been? I've been trying to reach you for the past hour. Billy Blanton is dead."

"Who?"

"Billy Blanton – the clerk that was shot. The one you visited in the hospital."

"What?" Lester controlled himself. He was shouting into the radio. He saw the positive ID going out the window. "What happened? What—?"

"I've got a man over there now. He should be reporting back any minute. Talk to you when you get here." The other end went dead.

Lester hung the mike up. "Earl, before you go home, I want you to go over to Echley's country club and find out who he plays with every week. Find out what kind of business they do. Get back to me at the station before you head home. Drop me at the station and hot foot it right on over there. Blanton is dead."

# CHAPTER 49

Copolla reached for his coat hanging on the back of the closet door. Branbury rose from the chair and was halfway to the door when the phone rang. Copolla, looking a little irked, with his coat held in one hand, walked to the desk and picked up the receiver. "Copolla."

The voice in the receiver, "Robert . . . ."

Copolla cupped the mouthpiece and whispered to Branbury. "It's Echley." Branbury stopped and returned to the desk.

The voice continued . . . "The police just left here. They asked a lot of questions. They may be on to us."

Copolla barked into the mouthpiece, "What kind of questions? How could they be on to us? What do you mean?" He frowned at Branbury. Branbury looked worried and started to say something. Copolla put his first finger to his lips as a sign to hold any questions.

Etchley continued, "They know about 'Charlie' for one thing. I think they suspect me as being 'Charlie'."

Copolla interrupted. "They can't prove anything. You weren't even there. How could they tie anything to you?"

Echley seemed agitated and nervous. He dropped the phone. It clattered to the floor. Copolla removed the receiver from his ear and grimaced. He waited. Echley said, "I don't know, but I'm scared. This was all supposed to happen so easily, but nothing has gone according to plan. I'm thinking about running away. If only you'd taken my call Thursday afternoon none of this would be happening."

"For God's sake, man, get hold of yourself." Copolla's voice was now soothing. He didn't want him to start spilling his guts to the police. He wished, too, that he'd taken that call. "How about Euramco, you heard anything from them?"

"I talked with them Monday afternoon, right after I came home from the hospital. I told them the store had been robbed and that their man had been shot and was in the hospital. They asked about the money. I told them it was stolen. They asked for details and I told them I had none at this time. They were to send someone down. As of today, I've not heard from any of them. Robert, I'm scared to death. If the police don't get me, I'm afraid Euramco will."

Copolla thought fast. He was good at that when the going got rough. That trait, together with his underworld dealings, had made Broadhouse Heavy Equipment what it was today. He always had been quick on his feet. A quick study, those that knew him said. "Got to get you calmed down. Maybe a good idea for you to disappear for a while. Do you feel up to a good stiff drink?"

"Yes. I could use something and I would like to talk to you right away."

"I'll meet you at the club in thirty minutes." He hung up the receiver, slumped down in his high-backed red leather chair and looked forlornly at Branbury.

Branbury stood at the edge of the desk. "What did he say? I take it he's very uptight."

"Yes. The police questioned him. He's thinking about running. Maybe that's best for us. He's the only one that can link us. I'll meet him at the club and try to calm him down so he can think straight – so we all can think straight."

Branbury said, "Don't forget about the Indian boys. They have a direct connection to me."

"Yes. I'm acutely aware of them. Their connection to you and their scooting away with the money." Branbury noticed the emphasis on the word "you". Copolla continued, "The police will play hell rooting them out of the Everglades, even if they are able to identify them, which I doubt they will. Those boys got away clean as a whistle, and with our money. The only person that could identify them, other than you and me, is the guy that got shot, and he's almost dead from what I hear. We keep our wits and we should be home free. Nobody's the wiser. Yes sir, the more I think about it the more I believe that Echley's running may be the right thing to do. Maybe a trip to Europe for a few months would do him good." He intertwined his fingers and bent them back. Most of them gave off a cracking sound. Branbury seemed overly contemplative. *Don't tell me he's going to crack, too.*

"That money had my retirement in it, Robert. Have you thought any more about what we should do to get it back?"

"I've been trying to figure the Indians. Do you think they tried to outwit us and took the money for themselves? Or are they just running scared like everyone else?" Copolla lit his pipe, took a big drag and looked long at the smoke trailing off the spent match, then put it in the ashtray on the desk.

Branbury sank his frame onto the straight-back chair in front of the desk. Copolla allowed only uncomfortable chairs for visitors so they would be inclined to stay briefly. "I always had the impression that these boys were not the greedy type. They were both just simple ordinary people who worked hard for a living and spent whatever excess they had on wine, women and song, as the saying goes. I think they're simply running scared and have no intention of taking more of the money than was agreed upon. $10,000 is a lot of money for one of them. I'd almost bet on it."

"You'd be willing to bet your $200,000 on their sense of fair play? Maybe I'll take you up on your bet." A big grin flashed across Copolla's face. He rose from the depths of the large chair, picked up the phone and dialed his house. When his wife answered he said, "Honey, I've got to take care of some business. I'll be late, don't know how long. You go ahead and eat without me." She started to protest and he hung up. To Branbury he said, "I should get to the club and meet with Echley before he does something drastic, which we probably won't like."

Branbury stood, too. "Those boys are running scared. They're not likely to come back this way any time soon, if ever. I think we ought to consider going down there to look for them. Perhaps I should go since they know me fairly well."

"I think you may be right. But if you go, I want you to take a strong arm with you in case those boys are not quite as fair as you think. If we're going to do it, we better start soon. Euramco will certainly be looking for that money, too. Probably already are."

Echley was waiting just outside the entry door when Copolla pulled into the driveway under the canopy. A boy was at the car door immediately and had it open, waiting for him to exit. Copolla took the parking ticket and moved towards the door. He spoke to Echley, "Been waiting long?"

"Just got here myself." He opened the door and held it for Copolla to go first, then followed close behind.

Through an office door to the left of the foyer, Copolla saw the manager at his desk facing a tall man in a business suit with a broad back. He waved, nodded when the manager waved back, then turned towards the lounge.

Earl turned slightly to see who the manager waved at. He caught the profile of Echley and another man's back as they disappeared into the dimness of the lounge. He turned back at the voice of the manager. "There goes two of the foursome into the lounge now."

Earl turned toward the lounge again as if he would still be able to see the men who had already entered the lounge, and immediately turned back. "I recognized Mr. Echley. Who was the other man?"

The manager rearranged the papers on his desk, turned and opened a file drawer behind the desk and carefully placed the papers in a file there. He closed the file drawer and turned back to his visitor. "Mr. Robert Copolla, a member for twenty years or so."

Earl thought all the paper shuffling was a lot of 'put on'. "What business is he in and where?"

"He's the president and owner of Broadhouse Heavy Equipment Company off Montgomery near 52nd Street. His father and mother operated the business up until about ten years ago when they turned it over to him. He's really made it into a regional operation, branching into many different sectors. Mom and Pop operation before he took over."

Earl wondered how this man could know so much about the members, but chose not to question him on his nosiness while he tried to extract information of a more important nature. He was chomping at the bit to get out of there and relate this new information to Lester. He knew Lester would still be at the station. No wonder his wife was upset with him all the time. When Lester sank his teeth into a case, he didn't let go until he had it solved. This case was looking juicier and juicier all the time. "Who are the two others in the foursome?"

The man handed him a piece of paper with the four names, their addresses and line of business. Earl walked into the lobby and picked up the pay phone. "Lester, you won't believe who I saw over here at the country club." Before Lester could answer, Earl continued, "Be there in fifteen minutes."

CHAPTER **50**

Flo kicked the covers off. Not a breath of air stirring in the room, but cool just the same. She was tired and weary from the long week of working in the cane fields and in the syrup factory. A major life change is an absolute must, she thought, and working on the farm any longer is out of the question. Just too much to ask, working like a slave all day and raising three children at the same time. Anything would be better than this life.

Buddy had always looked out for the future and took care of most everything. She stifled a whimper at the thought of Buddy and her dwindling hope for him. Papa hadn't brought back much in the way of hope from his Savannah trip. *I'm on my own now.* A shiver ran down her spine.

She looked out the screened window as she did every morning. The mangroves were a shadow against a dark blue sky with just a tinge of morning close to the treetops. A rooster crowed at the east end of the island to signal the fast rising morning. One of the children stirred. She held her breath, not wanting any sound to awaken one of them. This time of the morning was sacred. Lying in bed and allowing her thoughts to go wherever they wanted was heaven on earth. She instantly felt ashamed to be wanting things for herself. Poor little Francis hadn't slept well ever since he cut his foot. It seemed that every way he turned, the foot got in the way. The doctor would take the stitches out this coming week. How she would get to the doctor was another question.

Suddenly she had a strong desire to go to church and try to get closer to God. She hadn't been to Mass since Key West. Somehow, being in church during a service calmed her soul even though she couldn't understand a word they said. The choir and music were the best parts. She promised herself that if she ever moved to town she would attend Mass every Sunday and bring her children up in the way of the Church.

Her eyes focused on the window sill and the Indian doll she found on Captiva. *Missed opportunities.* Opportunities were everywhere if you could just get tuned into them. If only she could've had the time to meet with the professor to get his knowledge about the doll. He could probably write an entire book on just that one little item. She chided herself for quitting school and missing another opportunity for fulfillment. Life seemed so fleeting. Already twenty-three and most of the opportunities of youth missed – and now faced with the decision of a lifetime. Was Bill Parkins an opportunity or merely more of the same? No doubt, more of the same, but what other choice was there? *There's not enough money to move into town on my own, and even if I could, what do I know, no education and no experience except as a laundry worker. If only I could've met the professor again. Good Lord, is this the life you put me here for?* A slight breeze rustled the rag curtain hanging at the open window. A little more morning now showed itself over the tops of the trees. She got out of bed quietly, slipped her nightgown on and tiptoed out to the kitchen.

The light in the kerosene lamp was just barely visible. She made her way there and turned up the wick – light was immediate. She dipped water out of the bucket that she had thoughtfully filled and brought in last night, poured it into the basin, sloshed some on her face and dried off with a raggedy towel hanging on a peg at the end of the counter. A few fresh logs on top of the embers from the night before got the fire going in the stove. She poured water into the coffee pot, mixed some grounds in the water and set the pot on the stove. Outside on the porch she paused to allow her eyes to adjust to the darkness. Morning still had not arrived. She could just barely see the toilet through the trees at the back of the house. She made her way there. Mosquitoes were scarce.

The coffee was boiling when she came back in. After allowing the grounds time to settle in the pot she poured a cup of coffee, picked up the lamp and placed it and the cup on the table. From the sideboard she took out paper and pencil and went back to the kitchen table, lit a cigarette and started to write.

*Wood Key, Florida*
*December 11, 1932*

*Dearest Dot,*

*It's 5:30 in the morning here. All the children are still asleep and I'm all alone at the kitchen table. I dearly love this time alone. It gives me time to think, which here lately though, hasn't been all that great. I can only think about the decision I have to make about the future of my young ones and me and, I have to confess, it scares the living daylights out of me. I wish you were here to help me. I know that I have to make it by myself though. Actually I have already made it, in a way. At the funeral I told Bill that I would marry him and even set the date for him to come for me, but now I'm not so sure I should've done that.*

*It was a spur of the moment kind of thing, you know. I can't say that I love him or anything like that. It's just that I've got to, you know, look after my kids. And me, too. Just between you and me, I don't know what else to do. I'm really in a pickle.*

*Bill is a good enough man, I reckon, but I know I'm still going to be stuck down here in this mosquito-infested hellhole of a country, even married to him. He's just a plain old fisherman with no other interests in life other than living. He simply does what his daddy did who did what his daddy did before him. Seems like one big circle, don't it? At least I won't have to work at this damn farm anymore. Makes you wonder sometimes just what God has in store for us. Guess it's not right to blame our troubles on God, is it?*

*I wish you had been able to stay for Edna's funeral. It was pretty and the preacher said some beautiful words over her. When I die that's what I hope people will do for me. It was sad though when they lowered her into the ground. Mama just started bawling out loud and started screaming, "I'll never see my baby again." She kept saying it over and over again. She got me to crying and my kids clung to my coattails like they were afraid somebody was going to strike them down. Finally Bebo led her over to her car. Everybody was getting histerical (spelling). After it was over everybody went over to her house out at East End. That's where I found out what happened.*

356

*Edna had been visiting Judith out on Ballard Road and was going into town on Michigan Avenue. She was speeding in that old Model T of hers and tried to beat the train. The train tore the car in half. She never knew what hit her . . . Oh, well . . . .*

*I talked to Papa Jim on Thursday. He said he couldn't find the Indians he went up there to talk to. You remember I told you he had gone up to Savannah to talk with two Indians who had saved a white man in the swamps early in the year. The rumor was that the white man was Buddy. Papa didn't have much else to say. He seemed in a down mood and none too happy either. Then yesterday afternoon he came by and told me he had heard from the police in Savannah. They said the Indians had not returned to their work place and they didn't return to their house either. It looked like they may have left Savannah. He said he was going up to the Okeechobee villages again to see if they went back there. He tried to cheer me up but he was too down to do much good. I felt sorry for him. He had such high hopes that at long last he had found his son.*

*I told him of my plans to marry Bill on the 23rd. That saddened him even more, but he said he understood and that he would not think less of me for doing so. He wished there was some way that I could put it off, but he understood. He asked me to keep an open mind until he got back from Okeechobee. He still has a strong hunch that Buddy is alive, but he knows that time is running out for me. He hugged me and he turned away real quick, but I saw his lips quiver and the tears well up in his eyes. I almost cried out loud. It's all so very sad. Oh, how I wish things were different. I pray to God that I make the right decision.*

*Write to me soon and tell me when you want me to come and help with the baby. I will probably be at Mrs. Parkins's house on Fowler in Ft Myers for Christmas. I will get the exact address to you as soon as I can. I don't know where I'll be after that. If you can't track me down, send mail to the Everglades City Post Office with instructions to hold it. I'll check there every now and then.*

*If you get a chance, go by and see Mama. I bet she still hasn't gotten over Edna. She could use some babying, too. Write me soon.*

*Love always,*
*Flo*

357

Flo laid the pencil down and flexed her stiff fingers, poured more coffee and lit another cigarette. She walked to the front porch and looked out at the empty net spreads. The trees on the horizon were still just a dark shadow, their frame now a light blue turning to dark as the sun rose. Way out to the west dark clouds clung to the water on the horizon. High in the darkness the sky was awash with stars, the Big Dipper, about half-way up, almost due north. The sea around was a little choppy and the waves washed up and down on the shore. An empty beer bottle rolled back and forth with the waves. For a moment she was hypnotized by it. *Buddy was mending his nets and talking up a storm to Junior and Francis. He saw her and waved.* She started to wave back then realized she was dreaming standing up and wide-awake. She went back into the room and read the letter again, then sealed it up and addressed the envelope.

Francis came limping out of the bedroom and climbed up on her lap. He curled up there and she held him close. He stretched his arms around her waist as far as they would go and with big sad eyes looked up into hers. "I wish Daddy would come home again, Mama. Why won't he come home, Mama? He ain't sick, is he?" He buried his face in her bosom.

Her eyes welled over and tears streaked down her cheek. "Hush, child, your daddy'll come home, if he can. He may be too sick to come home right now. We have to be big for him." Her voice began to quiver and she quit talking. She wiped the tears away with her shoulder. She rubbed his back and began to hum his favorite tune.

# CHAPTER **51**

Buddy rose early. He planned to spend an easy day fishing at the creek. He hadn't been there in a month or more and was eager to try his hand at it again. He poured the basin half-full and doused his face three times with hands full of the cold water. When it was over and his face dried, he felt refreshed. He put a pot of coffee on to boil then stepped outside and lit a cigarette.

The wind, coming out of the southeast, was gusty and chilly and caused a shiver to run the length of his spine. It took a few minutes for his eyes to adjust to the dark. The outlines of the buildings and the big gates to the junkyard were just barely visible. There were no lights on at the main house. He and Liz had stayed up well past midnight talking about the future and the work he had done during the past week. She wanted to pay him for it, but he had refused. Sunday was her day. She would probably sleep in. She usually did. He couldn't blame her for that. He wished he could sleep in, too. Fishing would be just as relaxing, though. The smell of fresh coffee beckoned. He tore the cigarette butt and scattered the tobacco and the wadded paper and went inside.

The sky above the treetops was brushed a pale pink against a background of lightening dark blue as he strode down the dirt road toward the creek, south of the house and grounds. His casting rod rested on his right shoulder. The basket of fishing gear and the lunch, he carried in his left hand. The wind blew the dusty layer off the top of the road and out into the field. He had thought about bringing a gun, but had decided not to. An eddy of the dusty stuff curled up toward the sky in front of him.

The leisure of the moment allowed his mind to turn to his burning desire to retrieve his past. Toby had promised to take him back to where he was found half-dead. He'd only seen Toby once since they arrived back in the area a week ago, and even then had not had much opportunity to talk with him. He had kept his mind busy during the week working for Liz and that had worked wonders for him. Now, though, he knew it was time to leave, even if he had to go it alone. The vision of the woman and the children at the water's edge kept returning time after time. If there was such a woman waiting for him, how long would she wait? How long could she wait? It had now been close to ten months since he was shot. Surely she had taken him for dead by now. He told Liz last night that no matter what Toby did, he would have to go down around that country and see if somebody there might recognize him. Maybe his memory would someday come back on its own. If he did have a family down there, they could help him pick up the pieces that mattered.

After about a mile and a half he turned off the road and started down the gradual slope leading to the creek. The narrow path through the cabbage palm and pine forest was clear, as it was the first time he used it more than six months ago. Although rattlers didn't venture onto the pathway too often, he knew they lurked in the lush, thick palmetto scrub that lined the path. He had come upon one once, but at the sight of him the bugger slithered off in a hurry. They normally won't strike unless you intrude into their exclusive territory. No need to fear the snakes if he stayed on the beaten path.

The path twisted first to the north and then to the south as it descended toward the creek. On the other side, just back from the shore, the cypress trees towered toward the sky, trying to find the power of the sun which barely filtered down through the green thickness. Close to the water on both sides the young cabbage palms spread their huge fans, providing a wonderful shade for hot summer days. The sun would be welcome this morning, he thought as he made his way along the edge of the steep ground near the water. The water was crystal-clear up in the creek, around the bend from the main lake. Fallen and rotting tree stumps littered the water near the edge of the damp sand where the water had been just a little while ago. Right at the point where the land curved back to the west he took up his place against a young cabbage palm. From here he had a clear view of the opening to the lake. The lake beyond seemed endless. The water in this area was deep and tended to be muddy from the action of the lake. The sun had just begun to peek over the far horizon which, from his vantage point, was considerably above sea level. About six-thirty, he reckoned.

His rod was already equipped for the bass he planned on taking back to Liz. He brought the rod up about forty-five degrees and flicked his wrist. The lure flew across the creek and landed next to a fallen tree stump just out from the far shore. He jerked the line several times and the lure skipped across the top of the water and returned to him. He flicked it out again. When the lure skipped the second time a bass caught it and dove. Buddy jerked the line and immediately relaxed and let the fish take it for a while. He stopped it and the fish came toward him, then just as quickly turned and tried to shake free from of the lure. Buddy reeled the line in slowly. When the fish reached the shore he stepped into the frigid water, grabbed it by the gills and pulled it out. He ran a string through the gills, pulled it through the mouth and placed the fish back in the water. The other end of the string he tied to the palm tree.

Buddy was bringing in his fifth bass when he heard the breathing before he heard another sound. The hair stood up on his back and a tingle ran across his shoulders. He looked for his gun and instantly realized that he had not brought it – how careless. He turned ready for he knew not what.

Toby, standing with his right side away from view, spoke softly. "Liz told me I'd probably find you here when you didn't answer your door. A good morning, I see." Toby motioned to the fish wriggling under the water near the edge of the creek bank. His eyes followed the string from their mouths to the cabbage palm farther up the bank.

Buddy lay the rod down and reached for his thermos. "Ought not sneak up on a man like that, Toby. Might get shot one day."

"Wasn't sneaking. Just walking normal. Besides, you don't have a gun. I checked before I came up." Toby laughed.

Buddy laughed, too, took a sip of the coffee and passed the thermos top to Toby. "You feelin' better, looks like. Want to try your hand at the bass?"

Toby turned to face Buddy square on. The butt of a shotgun rested on the ground next to his foot with the barrel end under his palm. Buddy recognized the gun immediately. "Is that my . . . ?"

Toby lifted the gun and passed it to Buddy. "Yep. I told you I had one of them. Just figured you'd be the owner of this one."

Buddy's hands caressed the gun. He broke it open and looked down the dusty barrel. He blew into both barrels. A scene flashed across his mind. *He was talking with a man and laid the gun in a boat. The man came closer – he was shouting something.* The scene faded and was gone.

Buddy snapped the gun shut and smiled at Toby. "By God, I'll forever be in your debt." He handed the fishing rod to him.

Toby caught three medium-sized bass before he called it quits and lay the rod on the bank. The sun was now high up out on the lake, right at the mouth of the creek and came dead in on them. Toby joined Buddy under the cabbage palm just back from the water's edge. Buddy shared his lunch with him.

Buddy looked up and found Toby staring at him, his face somber, the scar muted. Toby was about seven years older than he was, even though they looked about the same age. Toby spoke. His voice, not much above a whisper, seemed grave and serious. "Curly, I never did get to thank you for saving my life last week in front of the store. I know I would've died sure enough if you hadn't been along. Andre told me how you took up for him, too, at the fair. Figure I owe you now. Don't know what happened to Marty. Just froze up. Never seen him do that."

Buddy poured the rest of the coffee in his cup, put the cap on the thermos and placed it in the paper sack. "Have to be straight with you, Toby, I thought twice about runnin' over there. I was real scared about gettin' mixed up in a robbery. Don't recollect I ever done anything like that. Couldn't just let you lay there and bleed to death, though. Besides, I owed you. Marty thought you were dead already. Reckon he was just lost without you and lost control. I love old man, Andre. These people here are my people now. I owe all of you plenty, not to mention my life."

"Marty's a good man and a good friend. Do anything for you. But he's really just a big kid. He don't like you worth a hoot, though, don't really know why."

"I don't neither. Never done a solitary thing to that man that I know of. Maybe he resents me comin' into your life." Buddy took a sip of the coffee, passed the cup to Toby and lit a cigarette. He leaned back against the tree and stared straight at Toby. "You see your way to take me into the swamps?"

Toby drank the coffee and threw the cup back to Buddy. He took his time fashioning a cigarette and lit it. He let the exhaled smoke emit from his nose. "Yes. That's what I came to see you for. Going on Thursday. You ready?"

"Ready right now."

Toby studied Buddy for a long time then stood up and strolled down to the water. He stared out towards the lake for a while then turned back. "Another thing, Curly. Me and Marty have decided to keep the money from the robbery. We're not sharing it with Branbury. We figure they didn't play fair with us. They didn't let us know that Charlie wouldn't be there. They damn near caused me to get killed."

"They?"

"Yeah. They don't think I know that Mr. Copolla is the mastermind behind the whole thing. They think we're just a couple of dumb 'Injins'. They don't care a damn about Marty or me. So I say to hell with them. By God, I'll show them. Let them come for me in the swamps." Buddy waited for him to continue. "I want to do something for you, too, Curly. I've set aside $50,000 for you. What do you think about that?"

"My God, Toby. You can't do that. That's a whole lifetime of wages. I don't know what to say. If I had that much money, I could pay Liz and Consuela and Andre for all they've done for me all these months." Buddy stood and started gathering his gear together, his mind full of all the things he could do with that much money. He could not imagine ever having that much money and couldn't really understand just how much money it was. Then something within him took control. It brought out in the open a part of him he was not completely aware of. That money was dirty and had blood on it. He was not a crook and he could have no part of stolen goods. Somehow he knew that even in his other life he would never take unfair advantage of anyone at any time. This was not money earned by him and he simply could not take any part of it. "Toby, I want you to know that I love you for doin' that, but I just can't take it."

Toby looked at him in total disbelief. "Are you crazy as hell? I'm offering you a small fortune and you're telling me you can't take it? You some kind of goodie-goodie or something? We just robbed the robbers. That's not doing bad."

"It's my upbringin' I reckon. Somehow I know it ain't right for me to take it. I'll no doubt live to regret it, but let's leave it at that for now. Maybe you can give it to them that took care of me. Let's get outta here." He started gathering his things.

"Never met anyone exactly like you, Curly. That money could put you on easy street for a lot of years."

*Buddy and another man about his own age were standing in a clearing, surrounded all around by thick woods. They were talking happily about going into town to celebrate striking it rich — about all the things the money could buy. Buddy had made something that brought in a lot of money.*

The walk home was much hotter than early morning. The sun had passed overhead and was heading west. Not one cloud in the whole sky.

# CHAPTER 52

Buddy breathed a sigh of relief when they pulled into the shell parking lot and stopped. Marty's carping was about to get the best of him. All the way from Okeechobee for the last three hours he had been on Buddy's case. Nothing Buddy could say would escape some snide remark from Marty. Buddy knew the time was fast approaching when he would have to face him. Marty seemed hell-bent on provoking a fight. Toby did nothing to try and stop it. He even laughed at some of Marty's goings-on. Only Buddy's willingness to take the abuse without pushing back had delayed a fight. He would have to keep on his toes, though.

Buddy got out of the car and walked back to the entrance. He stood under the big sign arching over the road into the area. A similar sign across the street read, 'Miccosukee Indian Village' and underneath in smaller letters, 'Airboat Rides', 'Alligator Wrestling'. Through the arch he could see chickees topped with brown palmetto fans and some brightly dressed Indian women and children milling around. He turned around and read the sign on this side. It read, 'Guided Tours. Canoes'. Out behind several chickees and a white, wooden one-story building, wooden docks extended out into the water surrounding the area. Canoes and small motor boats were moored there. Alongside the building were numerous canoes turned upside down and stacked one on top of the other. Pulled up on the shore were two airboats with large propellers encased in a metal framework. The sign on the building read, 'Café', 'Office'. He watched as Toby and Marty went into the building.

When Buddy entered, an Indian woman in traditional garb stood talking to Toby. Marty was nowhere in sight. She said, "John Henry is over in the Village across the street. He's supposed to put on a show this afternoon if any tourists show up."

"Still wrestling the gators, huh?"

"Toby, you know he'll never stop acting. He's been on the stage since he was born. One of these days either the gators or the airboats will do him in. Won't be a surprise to me."

"You all taken over this business yet?"

"Yeah, sure. We've been trying for years to get into something for ourselves but can't ever seem to scrape together enough to get started. These young'uns," she pointed to several small children playing out the back door on the docks, "and John Henry's love for hooch keeps us right on the verge of starvation all the time. This place is now owned by white people over in Miami. They check on us every now and then. So long as we send the right reports, they don't mess with us too much. Just can't make any money for ourselves, though."

"How's business? Don't seem to be too many tourists around this time of year." Toby motioned toward Buddy as he pulled up a chair and sat down. "This here's Curly. This here is Betty Mae Jumper, wife of the famous alligator wrestler, John Henry Jumper."

Betty nodded to Buddy and yelled at two of the kids who came running through the room. She chased them to the front door. "Here comes John Henry now. Guess there were no tourists for the afternoon show." She went behind the counter and busied herself with the day's business.

John Henry came through the door and started to say something to Betty Mae when he saw Toby standing at the table. He came up short, then bolted towards him. "By God, Toby, what're you doing here, boy? Last I heard you were in Savannah making your fortune. You said you weren't coming back till you made it big. Made it?" They gave each a bear hug and went back to the table. "You hungry? Betty Mae, rustle up some food for my boy here. Bring that bottle, too. Some celebratin' in store. You sure a sight for sore eyes, boy. How've you been?" He didn't seem to see Buddy.

"You son-of-a-gun, John Henry, you haven't changed one bit. Of course it's only been six months or so." They both sat down as Betty Mae brought the bottle and three glasses. "This here's Curly. You probably don't remember him."

John Henry studied Buddy as if he were seeing him for first time. "Should I?"

"Remember back in February when I came through here with a man all shot up?" Toby acted like he was presenting a major catch.

"Good God. That's him? I thought he was a goner at the time. I'd never have recognized him in a million years." He stuck out his hand to Buddy who grasped it and matched the squeeze applied by John Henry. "Boy, you was one lucky son-of-a-gun that Toby came along when he did. The way I heard it, that man was hell-bent to do you in." He poured the three glasses half full with whiskey, picked his up and held it out high over the table. "Here's to your health and full recovery. To yours, too, Toby, and to mine." He waited until they picked up their glasses and downed the entire amount with one big swallow. Both Toby and Buddy drank about half of theirs and gasped for air. John Henry called for water for them to chase with. He poured more whiskey in his glass and offered more to them. They both declined. Betty Mae brought a pitcher of water, shook her head and went on with her work. "What you doin' way off down here in these woods, Toby boy?"

"Curly here is still having some problems – can't remember who he is. Plan to take him back down to Shark Point and let him look around. Maybe he'll remember something. Need to rent a boat and some camping gear from you – two, maybe three days."

"Hell, that's no problem, but you all ought to stick around here a few days before you go traipsing around down in the swamps. We'll go off in the airboat and catch some snakes and gators and have a good old time like we used to do. I was planning on going out in the morning. What you say?"

367

"I'd sure like to do just that John Henry, but I promised Curly. He's hot to find his roots. Reckon I can understand that."

"Where's Martin? He's not usually far from underneath your coattails."

Betty Mae set three plates filled with fried fish and swamp cabbage on the table. The aroma engulfed the air around the table. Buddy dug in.

Toby said, "He's wandering around here somewhere. Probably out around the boats. He's had a big itch to get back down here. He'll be here in a minute, I expect."

When the meal was over they walked out on the dock, lit up cigarettes and talked about old times. Buddy looked at the boats. He didn't recognize any of them, but there was something about boats and docks and water lapping at the pilings that pulled at him. This is the kind of life he'd lived. Somehow, he knew boats and fishing. At long last he would get back to the exact spot where Toby found him. He fought hard to hold down the excitement. The time was near. He would find his past.

Toby spoke, "John Henry, what do you say. Can you fix us up? It's two o'clock now, only a few hours before nightfall. We need to be on down there a ways and set up camp before dark. Fix us up for three days. We'll have us a toot when we get back. Just like the old days."

The sun had passed its zenith when they entered the Gulf from the Harney River. The mosquitoes were bad and swarming up in the swamps, but now faded away in the cool breeze of the Gulf. Buddy felt good as he brushed the remaining mosquitoes from his sleeves. They turned to the south and in just a few minutes Toby pointed out Shark Point. Buddy kept his eyes glued to the shore, hoping to pick up some clues. They passed a few mangroves growing out into the water from the land then a long stretch of white sandy beach was revealed, broken only by seaweed and rotting remnants of once-proud pine trees done in by the encroaching water. Buddy hadn't heard a word from Marty during the whole trip. Maybe being down here in his home territory had softened him up a bit. They pulled into shore, beached the boat then walked along the shore a ways to the north.

Toby stopped and stood over a spot in the sand. "Right here's where you were, face down in the sand when we first saw you. We'd heard the first shot only moments before. Two men were running towards you from over there." He pointed along the beach to the south. "Me and Marty fired at the same time at the men, but were too far out of range to do much good and not soon enough to keep him from firing his final shot. I think some buckshot hit the man in front because he looked shocked and turned tail and ran like a scared rabbit."

Buddy studied the spot where his body had lain trying with all his mind to remember – nothing came. There were not even any wildlife sounds. He looked to the south where Toby was pointing. *Two men were running at him shouting something he couldn't understand. He couldn't see their faces. One was closer than the other and had a shotgun pointing his way. Fear overwhelmed him. He turned and ran. He was sweating and struggling to get away from the men when he heard the blast from a shotgun.*

Toby walked along the beach to the south. He stopped at the mouth of a creek running east. Buddy, now sweating profusely followed. "Right here," Toby pointed down to the edge of the beach just before they reached the creek, "This is where the skiffs were beached. They were both piled high with skins. Marty went looking for the men." Toby walked eastward away from the shore. He stopped, scraped his boot in the fine sand and uncovered some charred bits of wood. He pointed at them. "This is the leavings of a campfire – likely a spot used by many campers here – and likely used by you, Curly, and your partner. He was laying on his back between the campfire and the boats. His chest was torn wide open by a shotgun blast."

Buddy mopped the sweat from his forehead, his mind racing way in front of his conscious thoughts. *He was standing by his boat when he looked up and saw Robert fly through the air and land in the sand. The smoke rose from the man's shotgun and Buddy smelled the burnt*

369

*powder. His hand reached into the boat for his own gun. He touched the skins, they were soft – the smell of them reached his nose. The surroundings engulfed him. The water lapping at the boat bottom; fiddler crabs scurrying about in the seaweed half-way up the beach; the smell of the seaweed in the salt air; the rustle of the wind in the trees to the south and to the east; the constant chattering of birds way up in the trees.*

Toby's talking roused him back to the present. "Curly, you stay here and look around. Me and Marty need to go down south aways to look for something we left when we were down here at another time. We'll be gone just awhile. You okay?"

Buddy sat down by the old dead campfire. "Yeah, I'm fine. Some things comin' back. You all take your time." He took out a cigarette and lit it. Toby and Marty went to the boat, shoved off and headed south. Buddy noted the time on the old watch Liz had given him. Ten minutes to three.

He walked down to the shore and stared after the two men until he could barely make them out. They turned to the east and disappeared into the dense foliage. A momentary vision of a narrow creek with mangroves scraping the sides of the boat came to mind. He suspected they had gone down there to stash the bag.

Looking out onto the Gulf he let his mind wander. There was a memory of him standing in this very spot relieving himself early in the morning when only the stars were out. He turned and looked back towards camp. In his mind as clear as day, Robert was asleep, rolled up in his bedroll. His own bedroll was between Robert's and the woods to the east. He turned and walked to where he had seen the bedroll in his mind, stopped there and squatted down on his haunches. Over the chatter of the birds he heard a large twig snap. It was a sharp sound. He automatically reached for his gun. It wasn't there. It was in the boat. The memory of a breaking twig had caused him to reach for his gun. He'd heard the men coming and still let them get him and Robert. He strained for the reason.

Buddy was standing by the shore when he heard the boat motor approaching from the south and noted the time. Twenty-two minutes after three. They had been gone thirty-two minutes. Soon he could see Toby in the front of the boat and then they landed.

Toby said, "Curly, we'll spend the night here. Fish some tomorrow, head back in the afternoon. You okay? Get any memory back?"

Buddy took the bow rope and pulled the boat up onto the shore. "Yeah, some of it's comin' back."

"How about helping Marty bring the stores up to the camp? I'll get a fire started."

Marty grabbed the bedrolls and headed up the beach. Buddy took the bags of groceries and the water out and set them on the beach. The handbag was missing. It wasn't with Toby. He watched as Marty laid the bedrolls in three different positions – no black bag. He looked across the bay to the south and in his mind saw the boat turn into the shore and go directly to a stash. *By God, they've hid it some place up in the woods, just fifteen minutes away.* He picked up the goods and went up to the camp.

CHAPTER **53**

Captain Randolph Clark busied himself with papers and files on his desk, but closely eyed the small man slouched in the chair in front of his desk. He had known Lester Johnston for near on fifteen years and the man was a constant amazement to him. Lester was not an imposing man by any stretch of the imagination and to watch him at work was total frustration. He moved around like he had no pieces to a case, then all of a sudden, as if out of thin air, all the pieces fit like a well-worked jigsaw puzzle and the case was solved. Clark wondered if that was the case this time. He spoke for the first time since he uttered a muffled greeting when Lester had first come in. "Where the hell's Earl? And where the hell's the Commissioner? He was supposed to sit in on this meeting today." Clark put the file he had been toying with on the desk, stood up, went to his coat hanging on a tree in the far corner and rummaged around for something.

Lester muttered, "Earl should be here any minute. Must've got caught up in traffic." He looked up as Earl walked by the window separating Clark's office from the bullpen outside. "Here he is now."

Earl came into the room and dropped into the other chair next to the desk. To the captain who had turned to face him he said, "Sorry I'm late, Captain. Got stuck in traffic." He looked at Lester as if for support. Lester grinned. Clark frowned. The Commissioner came in, nodded to Clark and took a chair in the back of the room.

"All right, Lester, let's get on with it. You have this case solved yet?" He sat in the chair behind the desk and re-lit the half cigar he'd been puffing on earlier.

Lester straightened up in the chair. "Think we may have it solved locally, but there just may be implications that go far and wide. May be that much bigger fish might get snagged in the net before it's all said and done."

Clark puffed on the cigar and sent a barrage of smoke into the room. He leaned forward and rested his elbows on the desk. Lester rubbed his nose. "Get on with it, Lester."

Lester flipped through the pages of the yellow pad he had on his knee, stopped at a certain page and turned the others over, but he didn't refer to the notes scrawled there. "The jewelry store is owned by a Georgia corporation named Jewel Imports, Inc. The Registered Agent is one Tobias Lockhart, a local attorney. The corporation is owned, through layers of interconnecting corporations, by Euramco, a New York corporation whose headquarters is in New York City. Its main business is the importation of diamonds and other jewels from around the world, mostly from South Africa. It distributes them mainly through its local stores. It has at least one regional office in Atlanta and numerous local stores throughout the U.S., such as the one here in Savannah.

"The local stores sell to the general public and directly to industry. Several times a week jewelry, in one form or another, is delivered to the local store, and just as frequently, cash buyers come by for the industrial diamonds. After a substantial amount of cash is accumulated, Atlanta sends a courier for it. Mr. Billy Blanton was just such a courier, and if events had gone according to normal, he would have returned with the cash to Atlanta the same day he arrived here. But, as we now know, events didn't go as planned. The regular store manager, a Mr. Harold Echley, took sick and had to go to the Emergency Room. Mr. Blanton was ordered by Atlanta to stay put and fill in for Mr. Echley, pending the outcome of his hospital confinement. That happened late Thursday afternoon, the first of December. It was later learned that Mr. Echley made a telephone call from the hospital, but we'll take up the significance of that a little later."

Clark emptied the ashtray into the wastebasket under his desk and put the well-chewed cigar butt in it. "Just why the hell are we concerned with the organization chart of this New York corporation, Lester?"

Lester turned over a few more pages, studied the notes facing him and continued. "The relevance will become all too clear as we proceed with the facts. Now, as we know, late Friday afternoon the assailants entered the store and confronted Mr. Blanton with the utterance, "Hello Charlie". A tussle broke out and Mr. Blanton was shot and seriously injured. One of the assailants was also shot during the melee and may have bled to death had it not been for a third man, presumably the driver of the group. Mr. Blanton characterized the robbers as Asian or Indian.

"Mr. Jim Harrison, a Special Deputy Sheriff from Florida, heard a gunshot and ran toward the scene. He saw a man pick up another man off the sidewalk in front of the store and carry him to a car parked across the street. Mr. Harrison ran to his room around the corner to get his guns and when he came back the car was racing away from the scene. It passed right in front of him. He said, in his own words, "I saw two men in the car. They looked like Indians." Mr. Harrison took control of the crime scene until our own officers arrived." Lester was aware that Clark knew all this, but he went over it primarily for the Commissioner's benefit.

Clark interrupted. "It might be good to explain to the Commissioner what Jim Harrison was doing up here from Florida, anyway." He removed a cigar from a desk drawer and bit the end off it. "Back in September, Mr. Harrison called, asking for our assistance in locating two Indians believed to be in our city." He stopped short, looked puzzled then looked hard at Lester. "By God, are you saying there's a connection between the Indians he came to see and those that pulled this job? Is it possible?" He stared for a long moment at the cigar he was holding, then at the Commissioner and back to Lester. His brow creased as if he just couldn't comprehend what he had just deduced.

374

Lester looked uncomfortable. "Let's not jump to conclusions just yet. Let the facts play out first."

The Commissioner spoke up. "This Harrison. Why was he looking for the Indians in the first place?"

Clark lit the cigar and blew smoke across the desk. Lester frowned and Earl turned away from the smoke. Clark turned his gaze from Lester to the back of the room. "Mr. Harrison's son is missing from a hunting trip and presumed murdered. Jim heard a rumor that some Indians had found a white man half-dead and rescued him. Jim learned the Indians may be here in Savannah. Through the Lee County Sheriff's office, he sought our help. We subsequently located the Indians and he came up to interview them. He never could find them, though, and went back to Florida."

An officer came in, went to Clark's side and whispered in his ear. Clark listened and stared blankly at Lester and Earl. The Commissioner stood and went outside. Clark said to the officer. "Tell Lieutenant Bryerly I said to contact the Lee County Sheriff's Office and ask the Sheriff to call me directly on my private line. See if he can make contact with Jim Harrison, too." The policeman left the room. The commissioner re-entered with a cup of coffee and took his position at the rear of the room.

Clark spoke directly to Lester. "I'm told our people followed up on the Indians Harrison was looking for and determined that they have not been back to work nor have they returned to their apartment. There were no personal belongings left in the apartment. It appears these boys have left the area. I played on a hunch that Jim's Indians are the assailants in the jewelry store caper. Florida will be calling me soon. You need to get on with establishing your case. Go to it." He sat back and chewed on the wet end of the cigar. The room remained quiet while Lester readied himself to proceed.

"We suspect that Mr. Echley is the so-called 'Charlie' and an integral part of the originally planned heist. Additionally, we suspected that he had an accomplice. Following up on that suspicion led us to his connection with a Mr. Robert Copolla who is the owner of Broadhouse Heavy Equipment Company who is, uh, was the employer of the two Indians sought by Mr. Harrison. On Thursday evening, December one, Mr. Echley, while at the hospital, placed a telephone call to Mr. Copolla's company. On the evening of the robbery, Friday December two, another call was made from the hospital to the company." Clark tried to butt in. Lester held up his hand to ward off any interruptions. "We're not sure yet if there are others involved, but we're working on it.

"The Indians, apparently just a couple of good old boys from the reservation and, like most Indians, unable to hold their liquor, got into several scrapes with the law over the past several months. Nothing ever serious, fighting mostly. They were suspected of petty theft, but were never formerly charged. Our people fingerprinted them, and those fingerprints matched those found at the jewelry store. We've sent them off to GBI to confirm our in-house findings – expected back in a day or so. We think we can make a solid case against the Indians and, if we can get them to talk, a solid one against Copolla, too."

A whistling sound from the back of the room caused Lester to stop short. The Commissioner walked to the front of the room. "By God, man, you better be right and have all your ducks in a row before you even think about arresting Robert Copolla. He is damn near 'Mr. Savannah', a pillar of this town's elite society. We need to get the prosecutors in on this right soon. Randolph, you better call them in soon as we break up here." He remained standing at the edge of the desk.

Clark nodded at the Commissioner and turned back to Lester. "What else do you have, Lester?"

"Captain, you already know that Billy Blanton died in the hospital on December seven. Just stopped breathing. Agnes, the head nurse on the fourth floor tells us that she noted two men dressed in business suits leaving the floor shortly before Mr. Blanton's death was discovered."

"She didn't notice them when they first came onto the floor?"

"She said the other nurses were all busy looking after patients. She was called off the floor momentarily and didn't see the men enter." Clark re-lit his cigar and waited for Lester to continue. "We just found out yesterday that Mr. Echley has also disappeared. Earl, you tell what happened."

Earl sat up in his chair and spoke for the first time since he came into the room. "I called Mr. Echley to follow up on his connection to Mr. Copolla, but he was not in. I called back several times without positive results, then finally went over there yesterday and spoke with the landlady. She said that Mr. Echley went off with two men dressed in business suits on Thursday, December eight and, to her knowledge, has not returned. She has not entered his room."

Clark ordered, "Get a search warrant immediately."

Earl responded. "It's already ordered, Captain." Clark looked at the Commissioner and beamed.

Lester flipped the pages of his notebook and interrupted. "Only thing left now are the big fish, and they are completely separate from the Copolla group." The Commissioner sat on the edge of the desk and Earl had a smug look on his face. Job-well-done type of look. "We have reason to believe that Euramco, through all of its subsidiaries, has been smuggling narcotics, whiskey and illegal industrial diamonds into the country. The drugs and alcohol are brought in all along the southeast coast and distributed throughout the country. The diamonds are brought into the various local stores from strategic points around the country. The cash from the drugs and alcohol is used to *buy* the diamonds, effectively washing the money. When the *courier* failed to account for the money the local store had accumulated, they sent their hit-men down to find out what happened. They apparently determined, through their own mysterious connections, and through the threat of death, that Blanton and Echely were involved and, once they got the information they wanted, killed them. We know that Blanton is dead and I suspect the same fate for Echley."

Clark and the Commissioner looked at each other. The Commissioner whistled again. Clark put his cigar in the ashtray and leaned way back in his chair. He laced his hands behind his head. "They will likely be after Copolla and the Indians, looking for their money. You said it was close to a million bucks?"

"That's what Blanton told us. Poor Blanton was simply a courier and got caught up in a sinister plot. He paid with his life." Lester continued, "There's just one small hitch that's not completely tied yet." He stood and started slowly and methodically placing papers back into his briefcase.

Clark sat forward abruptly and exploded. "What the hell you talking about now, Lester?"

"In the jewelry store, after the robbery, there was more than fifteen thousand in loose cash in plain view and every kind of jewelry imaginable laying around and in an open safe and none of it was taken. Our accountants went over the books and accounted for everything. Only the black bag was supposedly taken."

Clark interrupted again. "What are you trying to suggest, Lester? Get to the point."

"Just this, Captain. The planners of this job would have directed the Indians to get jewels and small cash to direct attention away from the bag of big money. The Indians were small-time punks and wouldn't have missed the chance to pick up a lot of the small stuff. It just might be that the bag was gone before the Indians got there. After the mix-up and shooting, the Indians panicked and fled without getting a damn thing. It might have . . . ."

Clark came around the desk and sat on the corner right in front of Lester. "Goddam it, Lester, are you trying to say that Blanton and Echley double-crossed Copolla and pulled the big heist themselves?"

"I don't know that for a fact, but I just have trouble believing those Indians would've left that store without taking some of the cash and jewels had they not been so spooked. Also, why would Euramco have Blanton and Echley killed if they weren't somehow involved? We need to find those Indians and get their story. They may be simple dupes all the way around."

Clark stood. "My God. All right, guys, get out of here and back to work, and get your report into me by this afternoon. Let me know when you all plan to go to Florida so we can get the paperwork cleared." Lester and Earl stood and started towards the door. Clark continued, "And boys, just want you to know, you did one hell of a good job busting this case so soon. I'm proud of you."

The commissioner chimed in. "A mighty fine piece of work. Ought to be some commendations coming as a result of it. You've placed a good mark on the whole department. Keep up the good work." Lester and Earl went through the door and returned to their desks and the boring paper work.

# CHAPTER 54

"All right, men, listen up." The sheriff stood behind a wooden chair in front of the room. He was an imposing figure at six foot three and a clean 195 pounds. Anyone that knew him was well aware of the power contained in that lanky frame covered by his tan gabardine uniform pressed with the creases predominantly displayed. Richard Deakens was a proud man, but a no-nonsense sheriff who had promised that he would not tolerate any when he was elected seven years ago. He was fair towards his men, though, protected and stood by them unless they abused the power invested in them. He would not, under any circumstances, tolerate power abuse. His standard sermon was, "We are here to serve. Don't ever forget that, but don't ever allow anybody, and I mean anybody, to break the law we're charged with upholding."

"It seems that a couple of Indians, could be from one of the villages up around Okeechobee, maybe not, are suspected of armed robbery in Georgia, and they're now believed to be in Florida. The authorities there have asked for our assistance. A couple of their detectives will be here Saturday, but in the meantime, I want a couple of you to call on the headmen at each of the villages around Okeechobee and solicit their cooperation in locating the suspects. Another couple of you go to Big Cypress and villages along the Tamiami Trail, and another couple go over to Dania. I don't need to tell you that dealing with Indians is like walking on eggshells. We don't want to get them riled up at us or the whole damn State Department and the Federal Government will be down our throats in a heartbeat. We'll be searching the entire Everglades. Be thankful that it's happening at this time of the year when it's not so damn hot. Lieutenant Hanley will fill you in on all the details." He turned to

Hanley. "Jerry, I want you to get word to Jim Harrison right away. These are the same Indians he was looking for some time ago. Do whatever you need to do to find him. Keep me informed every step of the way." He turned and strode out of the room.

# CHAPTER 55

Flo came into the kitchen with a bucket of water she'd drawn from the cistern and poured some over the soapy dishes in the small tin dishpan. She busied herself with rinsing, drying and putting them away on the shelves over the counter top. The door to the shelves brought Buddy to mind. He had built the shelves and the counter top from pieces of plywood he had salvaged from other construction sites around the islands. Hours and hours had gone into sanding the pieces and getting them just right, before varnishing and installing them. None of the other homes on Wood Key had doors on the cabinets. He had insisted that his would have doors. The cabinets with doors were the talk of the islands for many months afterwards. A tear formed and dropped down on her cheek. She wiped it away with the bottom of her apron. Here she was just six days from re-marrying and still the deep and intense feelings of love for Buddy lingered and burst forth every time something reminded her of him. It would be better for her to leave this place. Bill Parkins was a wanderer and maybe that would be good for her soul.

She listened absentmindedly to Junior and Francis arguing about one thing or another. Night had begun to fall and the room was darkening. She dried her hands on the apron, went to the sideboard and lit a lamp, which brightened the room a little. Warren slept peacefully at the far side of the room. The pacifier he'd been sucking was lying on the side of the pillow. She fussed with the covers a bit and went back to the dishes.

Junior's voice stood out above the normal chatter going on between the boys, "We're gonna have Santa Claus at Gramma Parkins's house this time."

Francis, in a louder than usual voice said, "No, we ain't. Santa Claus is gonna come right here and he's gonna bring my daddy back."

Flo's ears perked up, but she decided not to interfere – she listened. Junior said, "Daddy ain't never comin' back, Granpa Joe said so. Mama's gonna marry Bill Parkins and we're goin' to live with Gramma Parkins in Ft Myers."

Francis slammed down his spoon and yelled, "Mama, tell Junior to shut up. He don't know nothin'. We're gonna have Santa Claus here, ain't we?"

She thought her heart would burst wide open. She turned around from the dishpan and dried both hands on the apron. "Now, boys, don't get to fightin' tonight. You'll wake the baby up and then you'll really be in for it." She knew what was coming and also knew that she didn't have satisfactory answers for Francis. Junior seemed to have accepted the idea that his daddy wasn't coming back. That extra year in age seemed to make the difference. Francis wouldn't let it go, though. He kept hoping to see Buddy come in on his boat any day. He even had recurring dreams where he saw his daddy coming ashore in his skiff, lifting him up and hugging him tight. She didn't know what she was going to do with him. Her only answer was to try and change the subject whenever it came up. She walked to the table with the pot of lima beans. "Who wants more beans?" She lifted a dipper full and held it over the pot so it wouldn't drip on the table.

Junior yelped, "I do. I do," and held his bowl up for her to fill. "I want another piece of corn bread, too, Mama." He stuck his tongue out at Francis.

"Mama, he's doin' it again. He's stickin' out his tongue and makin' fun of me. Mama, Daddy is comin' home again, ain't he? You said he was."

"You want some more limas and bread?" He shook his head, 'no.' She placed her hand on his shoulder and silently prayed for the right words to say. "Honey, your daddy's been gone now goin' on ten months – a very long time. I sure hope and pray

383

he's comin' back someday, but we've just got to try and understand that God may have a different plan for him than ours."

Francis jerked away. "It ain't fair for God to take him away from me. I love him, and I want him to come home right now." He started to bawl. "I want my daddy, Mama. Why don't he come home? God is so mean." He got up from the table and ran into the bedroom.

She started after him but decided to let him cry it out of his system. Time would heal things, she told herself. She went back to the table for the pot and scolded Junior. "See what you started. Why do you have to pick on that boy all the time?" Junior stared into his bowl of beans and kept right on eating. Flo went back to the dishes in the dishpan. Junior finished eating and went into the bedroom. Soon, she saw both of them head out the door for some adventure Junior had dreamed up. There were probably a few more minutes before night settled in completely. She would let them play for an hour or so.

Flo filled a bowl with beans and broke off a piece of cornbread. She looked in the icebox for butter, but there was none. The inside of the box was not even cold. In the top there was nothing but cold water and one very small piece of ice, no bigger than the palm of her hand. It would be Tuesday before the iceboat came again. She berated herself for not getting a bigger chunk when he was here before. Oh, well. She took an onion out of the box under the counter and started for the table. The familiar squeak of the front porch when someone was on it interrupted her step.

Lucy opened the screen door and poked her head in. "Flo, you decent?"

Flo continued to the table. "Come on in, Lucy. Just fixin' to have a bite of limas. Want some?" She set the plate down, turned back to the water pail and dipped water into a glass. She turned up the lamp, lit another one and set it in the middle of the table.

"I brought you a mess of pompano – all cleaned and ready for the frying pan, but if you'd rather have limas, then go right on. Don't mind me none." She came on into the room carrying four Pompano laying wide open in a big shallow pan.

Flo stopped in her tracks. "My God, I've been cravin' fish all the live-long day. What a God-send."

Lucy put the pan down next to the stove. "Ain't no God-send, it's King-sent. King just got in a while ago and said I ought to bring you these. He knows how you love 'em. They done right good down at Marathon. They'll go back down there in a few days. I'd go with him, but I expect this young'un any day now." She sat her heavy frame down into a chair at the table.

Flo poured the beans back into the pot and set about readying the frying pan. She brought out the jar of hog fat, scooped three tablespoons full into the pan, put cut logs in the stove then salted the fish on the meat side and dusted them on both sides with flour she'd taken from the barrel under the counter. She went to the table and sat while waiting for the stove to heat up. "That young'un comin' before Christmas? You're bigger'n all outdoors."

"Wouldn't surprise me none if I had it before I got back home. That young'un's been kickin' my sides down. He's kicked me from one side to the other, and when he gets tired of the sides, he kicks me straight in the belly. Never seen no kid kick like this'un."

Flo got up and looked at the fire in the stove. A drop of water on the stovetop hissed and turned instantly to steam. She put the frying pan on and moved the lard around to get it to melt quicker. Her mouth watered for the fish. "What you gonna name it if it's a girl?"

"Don't you 'member nothin'? Nellie Irene. After my little sister over in Key West. You met Irene, didn't you? We'll call her 'Little Nell.'"

"And, if it's a boy?"

"I tried to get a junior on the first two, but King would have none of it. Said he didn't want nobody named after him. Said it was enough for one person to go through life with such a name. But I aim to have me a junior. If it's a boy, his name will be

Juaquin and I'll call him 'Little King', and old man King Alvarez be damned."

"Who's gonna look after you when the time comes?"

"There'll be Adele there, I reckon, and I'd be mighty pleased and beholden if you'd be on hand to help out if need be."

Flo put two of the fish in the pan. The grease sizzled, and steam erupted out and up toward the ceiling. She stood watch over the pan and put water on for grits. "Lucy, I'd be right honored to look after you. I wouldn't mind givin' that young'un it's first spankin' for kickin' at you so much." They both laughed.

With the fish fried and the grits cooked, she fixed her plate and set a place for Lucy who refused to eat, saying she was full as a tick. Flo dug in with vigor and finally Lucy succumbed to the aroma and started to pick at a side of the fish. When they were finished, Flo went outside and called for the kids. It was pitch black outside. In a few minutes they came in and went into the bedroom. She told them to wash up some before they got into bed.

Lucy spoke, "Papa headed south Thursday on a charter. You talked to him lately about Buddy?"

Flo put the dishes in the tub and chipped up a few slivers of soap. She put the rest of the fish in the icebox then remembered she had no ice or butter. "Lucy, you got any extra ice? I'm plumb out. Need a tad of butter, too. You got any of that?" She fixed a pot of coffee and put it on the stove. The fire was still hot enough to make the coffee. Back at the table she lit a cigarette, leaned back in the chair, inhaled deeply and spoke through the exhaling smoke. "Papa's heard no further word from the Savannah police since the first message he got right after he got back here. You know he was unable to talk with the Indians up there and they hadn't gone back to work or back to their house. He keeps hopin' he'll hear somethin' more, but maybe there's nothin' more to hear. He's given me no more encouragement. He's a sad man, Lucy. Maybe he's finally givin' up and acceptin' Buddy's death like everybody else."

Lucy grunted and put her hands on her stomach. Her face wrenched and she tightened her lips. "You little rascal, stop that. Yeah, I can let you have a little of both. What happened to your ice?" Before Flo could answer Lucy went on. "You accepted Buddy's death yet, Flo?"

"I only know I'll never be sure of that, Lucy. Fifty years from now, I reckon I'll still wonder if he was out there somewheres, tryin' to find his way home. I've been over it so many times in my mind and talked with so many people about it, and still, I'm at a loss for solid answers. No need to beat it around no more. I'm just gonna do what I have to. Can't do no more than that, I reckon." The smell of the brewing coffee filled the room. She stood. "Want some coffee? How long will Papa be gone?"

Lucy stood, "I don't want no coffee, Flo. Just came down to bring you the fish and ended up eatin' half of it for you. I better get on home to my man. You been through a time of it, girl. I don't envy you none, and you're right, you got to look after yourself and your young'uns. Come on over for the ice. Maybe we can get King to go get us some more."

Flo came back with a cup of steaming coffee. "Where's Papa goin'?"

"He's takin' a charter off Cape Sable all the way down to Key West. Be gone about a week, he said. When's the big day for the weddin'? Where you gonna have it at?" Lucy headed for the door. She was big as the house. The floorboards groaned under her weight. Flo followed her to the door.

Flo's lips quivered. Her voice trembled. The decision, although made and agreed upon, was still fraught with doubt and uncertainty. She still loved Buddy deeply and nothing would ever change that. "Bill's comin' for me Friday. That's the 23rd. It'll just be a simple weddin' at the Justice of the Peace in Ft. Myers. Have Christmas at his mama's." They went out onto the porch and Lucy started down the steps. "Lucy, you send somebody after me if that young'un decides to come. Anytime of the night. You know that."

"Don't you worry none, I'll send for you, that's for darned sure." She walked away into the night.

Flo stood looking after her for some minutes. Their marriage was a rocky one, but they loved each other, she was certain of that. Theirs would be a marriage that would last a lifetime. Hers would have been that way, too, if God had not stuck his bill in. She went inside to Francis yelling at the top of his lungs.

## CHAPTER 56

"Sheriff Deakens, Deputy Bullard here. Just wanna bring you up to date on this Indian thing. You got the time now?"

"What've you got, Bullard?"

"We've been to all the villages and got nowhere. Nobody's seen hide nor hair of the two Indians. At Okeechobee, they think they're still in Savannah. At a village south of 29 on the Trail, we may have hit on a tiny bit of somethin', though."

Deakens tried to hide his impatience. "Go on, Bullard."

"Over at the village itself no one knew anything, but on the other side of the road at a boat rental and cafe, there's an Indian name of John Henry Jumper who manages the place. We talked to his wife. This John Henry has a party out campin' in the wilderness on an airboat. We showed her the mug shots of the two Indians and she said she'd never seen 'em, but a little boy who happened to be lookin' over her shoulder blurted out that he'd seen the big one out by the boats and over at the village. She ran the boy off with the excuse that lots of people come up around here for food and to rent boats and the boy had no idea what he was talkin' about. She couldn't remember 'em even if she wanted to. I didn't press the point with her, but I have a hunch she was lyin' through her teeth."

Deakens perked up. "Good job, Bullard. When will this John Henry be coming back in?"

"She said he's usually out for three days, more or less."

Deakens didn't speak for a long moment. Finally, "This could be it. I want one of your men there when they come back, but I want him in civvies. I want him to be taken for a tourist. Change the men as necessary so they aren't marked as a sheriff. I don't want an arrest there. I want to know immediately where they're

389

heading if and when they leave. Report to me when they come in."

Deakens motioned to the secretary outside his door and began to pace up and down. The phone rang. He frowned at the interruption and continued pacing. The secretary came in with the coffee and he motioned for her to put it on the desk. She picked up the phone and murmured into the mouthpiece. She turned, "Sheriff, its Jim Harrison calling from Key West." She held out the phone to him.

He strode to the desk and took the phone in one hand and the coffee cup in the other. "Jim, got a charter in the Atlantic? Been trying to reach you since Thursday."

Jim's voice was slightly muffled. "Yeah, I left then. Be finished here this Thursday. What're you after me for? The Indians?"

Deakens took a sip of the coffee. It was hot. He took another bigger one. "It turns out the Indians you were looking for are suspected of pulling the robbery in Savannah and the people they worked for could be a part of the whole thing, maybe put them up to it."

"Good God."

Deakens continued, "Savannah suspects they may've come back to this area and asked us to help. We've got the boys covering almost all of south Florida. We suspect they've been at an Indian village on the Trail south of 29. If we spot them, hope to tail them just in case they don't have the money on them. We're hoping they come back to the village, if in fact they've been there."

Jim's voice sounded anxious. "Deak, I need to talk with them boys somethin' serious-like. When you reckon they'll come back, if they're comin' back?"

"Deputy Bullard expects two - three days at the most. Don't worry, Jim, if we get them, we'll hold them at the jail till you get a chance to talk to them, I guarantee it."

"Thanks, Deak. I'm obliged." He hung up.

# CHAPTER 57

J ohn Henry eased back on the throttle and passed quietly under the bridge. He followed the creek to the west and slightly north. In a short while it turned all the way to the north and ran parallel to the unseen highway blocked by mangroves. After making the turn he switched the big engine off and the boat coasted to a halt. He took the long pole and began to propel the boat forward. There was no sound other than the water lapping under the bow. The sun, low to the south, had moved farther to the west and now darkened the vast mangrove swamp that grew right down to the water on the western shore. Only a few puffy and flimsy white clouds drifted lazily from west to east. The sun was still bright and hot, but the cool air contradicted it and provided a pleasing atmosphere. John Henry spoke directly to Toby. "We'll pole the rest of the way and come in real quiet like at the south docks, just in case somebody's still waiting for you. Less than a mile I reckon."

From his position at the stern, Buddy watched with detached interest. He knew something about poling boats and thought about mentioning that fact to John Henry with an offer to help. He hesitated as John Henry's words carried him back to early afternoon at the Indian village farther north on the Tamiami Trail and the old Indian that had frantically flagged them down as they approached. It was the same old man John Henry had talked with the first day out. He could still distinctly hear the old man's words as John Henry had slowed the boat to a mere crawl.

"John Henry, your boy was here yesterday and said to warn you that police were at the restaurant looking for you and your friends."

To Buddy that could only mean the Savannah police had tied the robbery to Toby and Marty and had tracked them here. It seemed that no matter how hard he tried to break away from these boys, he kept getting in deeper and deeper. Now the police had tracked them here and would be searching everywhere. His chances of getting away clean were quickly becoming slim to none. He had to make his break now. He would do it as soon as they returned to the restaurant.

Buddy idly watched as Toby got up and stood next to John Henry. He heard him say, "I need a boat to go back to Shark Point. Can we get a boat out of there without them seeing us?" Buddy took that to mean Toby was going back for the money. He looked over at Marty who stared straight at Toby, his scarred face a mask, without any sign of emotion. Scabs had already begun to cover the long shallow cuts made by the sawgrass. The showdown with Marty when it finally came on the first night out, was long overdue, but he had begun to think that just maybe he would get away from these two before the fight actually happened. That was not to be. Marty had kept his seething hatred bottled up as long as he could when he made his move. The attack had been sudden and unexpected. Marty had the upper hand early in the fight and may have won had it not been for the knee to his groin. That kick followed by two powerful rights to the jaw sent Marty face first into the watery and lethal saw-grass. It took Toby to pull him out and that was the end of the fight.

He looked away from Marty and stood up. "John Henry, I'll spell you at the pole if you've a mind to."

John Henry looked steadily at Buddy and nodded his head. A short time later John Henry turned the pole over and he and Toby returned to the front seat. Buddy poled from the bow. When they were about a quarter mile from the docks John Henry took the pole and nodded his approval. Buddy was sweating a bit from the exertion as well as from the sun which had moved still farther to the west.

John Henry spoke in a whisper. "Marty, how about you walking along the bank up to the docks. Go in the kitchen door and get Betty Mae's attention. Find out if any policemen are about, then hot foot it back here and we'll decide how to go from here." Marty stepped over the side and walked along the edge of the water.

Buddy was left to his own thoughts as Toby and John Henry chatted about one thing and another. After about a half-hour, Marty came back drinking a cool-looking RC Cola with beads of moisture clinging to the sides. He took his time and they all waited patiently. "Betty Mae said she hasn't seen a sheriff in the past two days, but there have been several single men who just seem to wander around looking at everything and asking questions about prices and so on. She figures they're police and waiting for you all to get back."

John Henry picked up the pole. "We'll ease on in to the south docks and load up another boat that you can take down into the islands. From there we can see without being seen unless somebody comes around there. Let's go, but no talking. Sounds carry easy up in here."

They had just finished with the packing; food and water for two days, tobacco, coffee, cooking utensils, bedrolls and tents, when Betty Mae came out the back door of the kitchen which opened up onto the dock. "The man that was wandering around here is nowhere to be seen. He either left or went over to the village. Come on in and have some food before you take off into the swamps. One of the kids can watch for the man."

They all went inside. The men sat at the table and soon Betty Mae put plates heaped with venison and vegetables in front of them. The warm aroma drove out any fears they might have had. Marty finished his meal first and went out to the boat to get it warmed up.

Buddy figured this was as good a time as any to make his break from these people. He made a cigarette, lit it and passed the makings to Toby. He spoke quietly. "Toby, I reckon I'll be sayin' goodbye now. I know I'll never be able to thank you enough for savin' my life, but I just gotta go try to find my past. Tell Liz and Andre I'll try to stop by and see them one of these days." He stood and put out his hand.

Toby stood, too. "Curly, I figure we're even, except I did promise you something when we were fishing up near Liz's place. You remember that? You come on and go with us down to Shark Point and I'll give it to you there. A promise is a promise." He grinned and gripped Buddy's hand powerfully.

Buddy thought about that $50,000 offer and figured he could sure use it. He also thought about the police closing in for the kill. "I sure do remember that and I'd like to take you up on it, but I just got to get goin' and I've got to do it now. You give it to Liz and Andre. I'll see you to the boat. John Henry, thanks for the trip." He took the man's hand and squeezed.

They had just started walking towards the boat when two men in business suits walked into the cafe and spoke to Betty Mae. The men asked in a loud voice if she knew two Indians named Toby Cypress and Martin Tucker. Without thinking Betty Mae looked quickly at John Henry and the others. The men caught the glance and started towards them. Toby bolted for the boat and Buddy, at first bewildered, quickly followed and jumped in. John Henry stayed, threw a block at the men and managed to delay them in the narrow doorway. They cracked him on the head and he sprawled out on the floor unconscious. Marty already had the motor running by the time Buddy and Toby reached the boat and was pulling out when the men rushed out onto the dock with pistols drawn. Marty cut a zigzag path away from the docks. The report of the pistols filled the afternoon and the bullets splashed harmlessly in the water next to the boat. In the next instant, Marty had the boat around the corner of the dock and into a side creek, shielded from view by stands of cypress and cabbage palms. The docks were now blocked from view.

After about ten minutes Marty pulled back on the throttle and the boat pulled up short. He shut the motor down. They all listened. Far off to the east a boat motor was racing and getting closer. It could be John Henry, but not likely. The men in suits, probably the police, had taken up the pursuit. Buddy wondered what the hell he was doing here. He should be gone by now.

394

Again he was caught up in a situation which was not of his doing. Already he may be held liable for the death of the store clerk, and now unlawful flight from authorities. He would be lucky if he got out of this alive. He could very well have been killed in the shootings of the past few minutes. Those people were in a serious mood. He was not going to get any more information from Toby. His memory was stuck in place and didn't reveal very much of his background or where he came from. He needed to break off from Toby and Marty and he had to do it soon – but how? Here he was in the middle of the swamp with no way out except with them. He shouldn't have gone on the airboat trip. He had no idea where to begin looking for his past. Maybe he would just start in some place like Everglades City and hope someone would recognize him and lead him back to his past.

Marty broke the silence. "This ought to be fun. We'll let them get us in sight then take them on a chase they'll never get out of. I'll wind them up so tight in these swamps they'll be damn lucky if they ever get out. They won't know if they're coming or going. They're playing in my game now." He looked to Toby and Buddy for their approval.

Buddy looked up at the bright blue sky just barely showing through the canopy of trees growing on both sides of the creek. He reckoned it to be four or five o'clock. Be dark in another couple of hours. He recalled playing games in the swamps trying to lose the other fellow or to get him hopelessly lost. In that game, though, he would always be sure the other fellow got out safely. Here, Marty planned to lose them for good. He wondered if this, too, would be murder. Their comrades would miss them and send out a party to rescue them, he reasoned. Toby looked at him as if seeking his concurrence to start the game. The adrenaline began to course through his veins and the excitement began to build. His worries of getting back to his past were lost for the moment. The sound of the motor was getting closer. He gave a thumbs up and grinned.

Toby said, "Let's do it, Marty. This is right up your alley. Just don't tempt the bullets."

Marty started and gunned the motor. The two men came into view about a hundred yards away with guns blazing. Buddy and Toby ducked down in the boat. Marty let the boat out with a lurch and the bow sliced through the mirror-smooth water causing a wake that ran to the shore on both sides. In a moment he turned to the left and was out of sight of the men. As they came back into view he turned right again, and once again was lost from view. The sound of the men's motor was constant, speeding up and then slowing down. They were inexperienced at this game now being played by a master. At times the sky was completely obscured by the trees and only occasional shafts of light would play between the branches. The sky was further darkened as curlew, stirred out of their afternoon rest, and squawking continuously, left the treetops in droves. A flock of white heron left the shore where they were enjoying an afternoon meal and flew across their bow just above the water, then disappeared down another watery avenue. The image of the trees in the smooth water was shattered time and again by the boat churning up the water.

Marty held the distance between the boats constant, luring the other boat deeper and deeper into the web of interconnecting creeks. He now turned to the left, then to the right, then to the right again and finally began to put distance between the boats. After awhile, when the other boat could not be seen and its sound far off, he shut the engine down and coasted to the shore with high ground behind the spidery legs of the mangroves. He put his finger across his lips to command silence and put a slipknot around a mangrove root. They sat and listened to the far off sound of the men's curses above the drone of the motor. Toby rummaged in the bags of stores and came up with a loaf of light-bread and made a peanut butter and jelly sandwich. He passed it to Marty, made another for Buddy, then finally one for himself.

Night was just a breath away when the motor stopped. The men's voices, muffled, indistinct and far off, were carried on a soft breeze of the otherwise still air. Marty motioned for the others to grab their bedrolls and make camp on the high ground. They satisfied their hunger with more dry sandwiches and water. Buddy craved a cup of coffee and a cigarette, but Marty cautioned against a fire or smoke. The night darkened. They heard the men's voices all night. They were hopelessly lost. If someone didn't come for them they would be dead of hunger and mosquito bites inside of two days.

Buddy drifted off to sleep and dreamed about a woman with a baby in her arms and two small boys wading at the shoreline somewhere. As always, he was unable to get her to hear him. When he awoke, a full moon, seen through the tree tops, provided enough light to read by if he wanted. The sky above the treetops was a pale blue – the sun not far behind. Marty and Toby stirred. There were no sounds except an occasional fish jumping far up in the creek. The images of the trees were now clear and distinct on the mirror-smooth water. He hadn't dreamed of a baby before. He wondered if there was a connection there somehow.

Marty whispered, "Curly, here's where your poling skills pay off. We'll pole for a ways, then we can light a fire and have some real vittles."

Buddy stood, ready to move on. Toby awoke and soon Buddy began poling, following Marty's instructions. Without Marty he would be lost, too. He was surprised at Marty. In his element, he was king. Even Toby didn't question him. Marty had taken charge and performed very well. Buddy started to congratulate him, but thought better of it. He knew Marty was still smarting from the beating he'd given him during the airboat ride. The beating had only strengthened Marty's deep-seated hatred. If they stayed together long enough, Marty would likely try to get even some way. Finally, Marty motioned for him to pull into shore. The trees had thinned out considerably and the sun now hung well above the trees in the east, the air a tad chilly.

Toby resumed control. "We'll camp here for a while and have some breakfast. Curly, you seem to be a pretty good fisherman. How about catching some for us. Marty can make a fire and put on some coffee."

After breakfast, they all laid back with coffee and cigarettes, enjoying the moment. Buddy sipped his coffee and spoke to no one in particular. "This is the life. Whatever I end up doin' with the rest of my life, I always want to be able to do this every now and then. When we get out of here, I plan to split company with you boys and go see if I can find somebody that knows me. What're your plans now, Toby?"

"Just as soon as we get the money, we're getting out of the state. Maybe go to California. Always wanted to go out there. What do you think, Marty?"

Marty stood, walked down to the water and relieved himself. He washed out his cup and came back to the fire. "I'll miss this place a lot, Toby, but I guess there's no way I can stay here with the police hot on our tails all the time. Probably some place like this in California, you reckon?"

"I reckon. Now here's the plan. When we leave here we go to Shark Point. Curly, you stay there while me and Marty go get the money, then we ease our way out of the swamps. Of course, you don't have to go with us, Curly, except I don't know how else you'll get out of here. You could wait for a passing boat. If you want to do that, we can leave you with some vittles. I think you might want to come with us out to the highway. Be much easier going from there and I have trust in Marty that he can get us there without the law finding us."

Buddy threw the remains of his cup into the fire, the fire hissed and the steam climbed in the still air. The sun was higher in the sky and getting warmer. The mosquitoes were light. One thing he knew for sure. He had to get back to Everglades City and see if anything stood out for him. The doctor's words at the hospital in Miami came to mind, *"One small thing could bring all of your memory back in a flash."*

"I think I'll go as far as the highway with you. I trust Marty's judgment there, too."

CHAPTER **58**

Flo put the bucket of water on the edge of the porch, and on a whim, went to the big seagrape tree and sat under its long wandering limbs. The sunlight, still hot for late afternoon, filtered through the big roundish leaves and splattered the ground with many varied shapes. She thought the leaves sometimes looked like hearts. Now there were many brown-colored ones all over the ground. She loved to pick the grapes and eat them on the spot, even though it took a handful to really get the taste – they were mostly seed with just a thin layer of meat. She equally loved making jelly with them and spreading it thickly over a freshly baked biscuit. The time was not right now, though. She would have to wait for the Fall. The coco plum tree was without fruit, too. It, too, would wait until far into next year to produce its crop. Unlike the seagrape, the coco plum, round and white like a green-turtle egg, was a mouthful in itself. Of course, you could never eat just one. They were so tasty, the kids would, time after time, be down with the bellyache.

The time was so peaceful, the air so perfect – neither warm nor cool. She stretched her legs out in front of her, leaned back against the tree trunk and let her eyes gaze out at the calm water of the bay. She wiggled her toes and picked up twigs with them. In her mind she could see Mormon Key far up to the north and wondered what old man Richard was doing today. *I'll sure miss his antics and his music this Christmas.* He could play the fiddle like nobody's business and when he teamed up with Buddy and Jake the music was as good as any she'd ever heard on the Victrola. She would miss Buddy a whole lot, too. Tears welled immediately at the thought of him. She bent and wiped her eyes on the edge of her skirt.

In just two days, Bill would be here to take her away. She knew life would never be the same, but she would make it work somehow. The Harrison clan would never accept her, as before – she would no longer be a member of the family. They would always treat her with respect, she knew that, but she also knew it would never be the same. That thought saddened her more than anything else. She had become one of them, and now it would no longer be.

She looked now at the house, the back porch, the steps up to it, both needing a nail or two to keep somebody from tripping and breaking their neck. Her eyes traced the steps through the path to the cistern. She had been to that watering hole many a time during the three years since she'd been living here. *This house will always be a large part of my memory*. She knew every nook and cranny. The bedrooms – her's and Buddy's at the southeast corner and the kids' on the northeast just off the back porch. They would not sleep in theirs ever since Buddy left. They played in it, but at bedtime, they came into her's. It had become a storage room since then. In her mind she passed Buddy's bookcase. Tears came to her eyes every time she passed it. Buddy had cherished the books there. The poor pages were ragged from all the times he'd fingered them. Her mind carried her on into her bedroom where the guitar and fiddle were still leaning up against the wall in the corner. Neither had been touched since he last played them. Should she keep them for the boys when they got older, or maybe give them to old man Richard – more decisions.

She ran her fingers along the rungs of the old wooden chair. Back then, the chair sat away from the tree trunk and faced the back porch. Buddy would go out there with his guitar or fiddle on a night when the wind, blowing in from the northwest, pushed the mosquitoes to the south side of the island. He would serenade her while she cleaned up after supper, then she would go out and sit in this very spot under the tree and listen to him play and sing for an hour or more. When it was over they would walk hand-in-hand back into the house, very much in love then.

Her reverie was broken by Junior's screams. Nobody screamed like him. It was continuous – he didn't pause even for a breath. She ran around the house in the direction of the noise and found him in the arms of Lucy. She was beating the bottom of his foot with a flat board. Lucy smiled at her when she ran up. Flo felt instant relief. He had stepped on a nail and Lucy was trying to get it to bleed to prevent him from getting lockjaw. Lucy threw the board down and squeezed the puncture until she was satisfied that enough blood had come out, then let Junior go. He stopped screaming and ran into the house.

"Thanks, Lucy. Where'd he find the nail?"

She pointed to the upturned boat in front of her house. "King and the boys were workin' on that boat and may've got careless. I just happened to be out there when he stepped on it and caught him before he got too far away. It ain't rusty. He's all right now."

"Yeah, if that's all I had to worry about."

Lucy looked at Flo with pitying eyes. "Bill comin' on Friday, aye?"

"I've got very mixed feelin's, Lucy. Still don't know it's the right thing to do." She thought about her earlier decision to make it on her own and follow her dream. She started to cry. Lucy went to her, held her close and tried to soothe her with calm words. "Lucy, I'm gonna miss you and this place. I kind of feel like I won't ever be back. Christmas just won't be the same."

"Hush, woman, you ain't goin' nowhere – not for long anyhow, lessen you want to, that is. I been watchin' you these last few months. You're all grown up now. You can handle these things all by yourself. You're gonna do just fine, mark my word," she cackled. Flo had to laugh, too.

# CHAPTER 59

It was about two in the afternoon when they came out into the Gulf and rounded the north side of Shark Point. Buddy was reminded of all the events he'd been exposed to from the last visit several days ago. He relived the terror of seeing his partner's chest blown away from his body, of the fear he felt running from the shotguns aimed at him and intent on killing him. The warmth of the buckshot as it tore through the skin on his back was as real today as it must have been then. He could taste the sweat running off his lip into his mouth. He could hear the silence of the birds watching from the trees, the lap of the waves on the shore, the shout of the men running and those out on the water. He was sweating again. He mopped it with his bandanna.

They beached the boat just north of the creek and went up to the old camp. He noticed fishing boats loosely bunched together far out in the Gulf. He reckoned they had found a good fishing hole. There were a few others farther to the south. Heck, he may be able to catch a ride right from here up to Everglades City. If he was from around these parts, one of the fishermen might even recognize him.

Toby wanted more fish and gave Buddy the task of catching them. Buddy walked past where he imagined his old bed site was and into the woods on the eastern edge of the camp. He stepped on a small tree limb – it snapped in two – the sound was like the crack of a whip. His mind immediately returned to that morning ten months ago when the same sound woke him from a light sleep. He looked around, half expecting to see men lurking in the shadows. He walked on through the trees and emerged at the creek bank where he cast his line up in the creek near the shore and in no time at all had six big speckled trout.

The strong aroma of coffee grounds boiling turned his attention back to the camp. He picked up the string of fish and moved into the woods, heading back toward the camp. Just at the edge of the clearing through the trees and underbrush, he saw several boats loaded with men at the shore. The men, many in the uniforms of police, jumped out of the boats, and with pistols and rifles drawn ran up to the campfire. The man in the lead yelled at Toby and Marty who had started to rise, "Freeze. Don't move a muscle or you're dead men. Hands behind your heads – be quick." The men rushed from three sides – from along the north beach where he'd been found by Toby, directly onto the beach on the Gulf, and from the south across the creek from which he'd just taken the fish – the boats he saw out on the water earlier were all gone. Toby and Marty jumped up, looking completely bewildered. It had all been so sudden. Nobody had heard the men coming.

"God damn it, I said hands behind heads." The man slammed a rifle butt into Toby's gut. He doubled over in pain and fell down on the sand clutching his already sore stomach. The man yanked him up and cuffed his hands behind his back. Fresh blood darkened the front of his shirt. Toby's face contorted with obvious pain. Another man cuffed Marty and sat them back away from the fire.

Buddy placed his hand on his chest. His whole upper body pulsed out of control. He breathed deep, held the breath for as long as he could, then let it out controlled and easy. He repeated the process several times until he had calmed down. He backed farther into the woods. What to do now? There must be twenty or more deputies out there. Where had they come from so quick? Were they the fishing boats he saw way out on the Gulf? Damn it. Damn it. Damn it. He was so close to getting away from these boys and back to his own life. If only he had left right after they first came back from Shark Point, he would now be free. He wondered if he could make his way back to the highway by himself. He started backing deeper into the woods.

He felt the presence of something before he heard the sounds. He wheeled about to face two big deputies. Without a thought he charged both of them at the same time and bowled them over. He was on top of the biggest one in a flash and just starting to punch him in the face when all the lights went out. He woke up later with his hands cuffed behind his back. Lying on his left side with his legs drawn up to his chest, he tried to touch his pounding head, but was unable to reach it. Right next to him were Toby and Marty both sitting with their knees up to their chests, hands cuffed behind them. All of their camping gear was piled up in the middle of the clearing. The deputies were milling around all over the place. Four men sat around the fire drinking coffee and smoking. Several were down by the boats and several were sitting or wandering around. They appeared to be waiting for someone. The sun was far out to the west and a stiff breeze was whipping up.

Buddy smelled the boiling coffee and the tobacco smoke mixed with salty seaweed. He had a strong craving for a cup of coffee and a cigarette. The birds were quiet again. One of the men stirred the fire and dropped on more wood. Ashes and sparks rose from the fire and were quickly dispersed by the wind. He was thankful for the wind.

"Toby." Toby looked at him and winked. He seemed so uncaring. He grinned. "What the hell's goin' on? What happened?"

A deputy turned from the fire and bellowed, "Knock it off. No talkin' between you. You'll get enough time to talk when the sheriff gets here." Buddy and Toby locked eyes and a silent understanding passed between them.

The stars were in full bloom when the sheriff arrived. The fire was ablaze and the aroma of cooking meat and vegetables stormed Buddy's senses. He, Toby and Marty were a good five yards from the fire and could feel only a touch of its heat. He was getting stiff from lack of movement. Buddy watched the tall lanky sheriff come up from the boat accompanied by two men in civilian clothes with badges pinned onto their light jackets. The group stopped to chat a few minutes with the men around the fire then came over and stood in front of Toby. Deakens turned to a uniformed deputy, "Jerry, ease up on these boys some. Take the cuffs off them. They're not going anywhere with those leg irons. Have they been fed?"

The deputy called for another deputy and told him to remove the cuffs. "No, sir. Food not quite ready yet. Should be about a half hour."

Deakens stared at Buddy and wrinkled his brow, then turned back to Toby. "You Toby Cypress?"

The deputy came and removed the cuffs. Toby now sat up with his back straight and seemed proud as a peacock. "I am, Sheriff."

"You want some coffee, Toby? You boys want some coffee, smokes?" Without waiting for an answer, he ordered Jerry to see to it. The birds were now chattering up a storm in the woods just a few yards away. Buddy looked to see them, but it was pitch black away from the fire and sight was restricted to just a few feet.

Deakens spoke again. "This here is Lester Johnston and this is Earl Griffin. These men are police detectives from Savannah, Georgia. They came all the way down here to ask you boys some questions." Deakens backed off. "They're all yours. Go to it." He turned and walked over to the fire.

Lester spoke, directing his voice and eyes mostly toward Toby. "We know you all robbed the jewelry store in Savannah. Know you got away with near a million dollars. Know that your boss, Robert Copolla over at Broadhouse Heavy Equipment, put you up to it, and we know that a store clerk named Echley was your contact man called 'Charlie'. You boys face the electric chair for the killing of the clerk that was not supposed to be there. The authorities just might go easy on you if you've a mind to cooperate."

Toby looked straight into the detective's eyes, "What do you want from us, Lester? You seem to know everything already."

"For one thing, I want to know where the money is? Number two, I want to know what you know about a company called Euramco."

"What money? I don't know nothing about any money. We went in there to rob some jewelry, but 'Charlie' was not there and there was no money. That man there got shot by accident. He pulled a gun and shot me first. We got scared and ran like hell. That's all there is to it, mister."

Lester stayed calm and spoke in measured terms. "Now, Toby, we have reason to believe there was a million dollars in a black bag when you all came to rob the store. After you all left, the bag was gone. Finding that money will make the judge go a lot easier on you, I can tell you that."

"I'm telling you, Lester, there was no money taken by us, and no jewels either – nothing – end of story. There was supposed to be money, but there wasn't any. We were double-crossed, and I suspect it was Copolla and the man you call Echley. Find them boys and you're likely to find your money. There was clearly a double-cross and I'm here to tell you I'm damn mad about it. Got us in a heap of trouble and damn near killed me, and all for nothing. Could I have some more coffee?"

"What about Euramco? What do you know about that group?"

"Don't know nothing about Uram . . . what'd you say that name was? Can't even say it, much less know anything about it."

A deputy brought food for the prisoners and Lester had them separated so they couldn't confer amongst themselves. He and Earl moved away. After they had eaten their fill, the detectives went back to questioning the prisoners one at a time. Toby stuck by his story, admitting to the planned robbery, but denying any knowledge of the money. Marty told the story from his perspective and also denied any knowledge of money – that the only bag he had was the one he went in with, and it was empty going in and coming out.

Buddy told them that he was a complete dupe in the whole thing and told how he happened to be there and how he got caught up in the robbery. He told them about his memory loss and what he'd been doing to try and recover it. He told them everything. They didn't seem to buy any of it because Marty had said that Buddy was a part of the plan from the beginning and Toby backed him up. They continued on into the night. It was after two in the morning before the detectives finally gave up and allowed them to sleep.

At breakfast they were allowed to sit together. Buddy glowered at both Marty and Toby. Finally, he could control himself no longer. Under his breath so the guards wouldn't hear, he said, "Toby, why the hell did you tell these people that I was part of this thing from the beginnin'? You know damn well why I was there and went along with it only because you promised to bring me back down here. I thought you were my friend."

"Damn it, Curly, keep your voice down. They told me that Marty said it and I thought it might somehow cause them to go easy on us. I figured you'd tell them your story and they'd soon come to believe it. I don't mean you no harm, Curly. Everything will be all right. Trust me."

The deputy overheard them and stood over them threateningly. "I told you guys you weren't allowed to talk among yourselves. Now knock it off."

Thunder sounded dull and ominous. Lightning flashed inside large gray clouds far out on the western horizon and lit up that part of the sky momentarily. The sun was still hiding behind the tall trees to the east of the camp, but its light was streaking through here and there and playing on the ground near the prisoners. The large campfire cast eerie shadows on the men grouped around it.

Deakens sat next to the big fire and nursed his coffee cup between long fingers. He watched as the men prepared to leave. About half he had ordered back to normal duty and they had left before first light. The one Indian with the wavy hair troubled him. There was just a hint of recognition, but it wouldn't come through. He had questioned the man after hearing his story, but got no further with it. Was it possible that this man was Jim Harrison's long-lost son? He hadn't known Buddy that well and wouldn't know him if he saw him face-to-face much less with the makeup of an Indian. He wished Jim were here. He would know if it was his son.

Deakens turned to the detectives. "Did you guys get all you want? Do you believe their story about the money?" He spat into the fire.

Lester threw the remnants of his cigarette into the fire. "They're sure solid with their story about it and I've been trying to think how it could be otherwise. You see, there were, according to our theory, two capers going on at the same time, completely isolated from each other. These boys, through Copolla, and Echley, the inside man, planned the robbery to run off with the accumulated cash. These boys were pawns. They're small-time pilferers. I suspect they went into that jewelry store to get jewelry and loose cash, none of which was taken. When we went in we found close to fifteen thousand dollars in small bills in the cash register and in the safe. Why didn't they take it? Why didn't they take jewelry which was lying all over the place? Their story just may be true. They went in there expecting somebody on the inside to hand over the goods and they ended up shot and bleeding to death. Could be they panicked and didn't get a damn thing. Jim Harrison, who was the first person on the scene, didn't recall seeing a black bag anywhere. Was it handed off before the Indian boys came upon the scene? Guess we'll never really know."

Lester poured another cup of coffee and continued. "Now this Euramco is another matter altogether. They were running a drug operation and elicit diamond importing. They were using the jewelry store to launder the drug money. The man who got shot told us there was cash there, but we have to remember that he was a regular courier for Euramco. It might just be that he was smart enough to lay the heist off on these two-bit hoodlums to protect his boss, Euramco. Makes sense, except that we suspect it was Euramco that had the boy killed. The same people were seen with Echley just before he disappeared. He hasn't been seen since. To them, the robbery was just a nuisance. They may have been killed to eliminate any trails back to Euramco, or those two boys took the money themselves, planning to lay it off on the Indians. Euramco caught them and recovered the money, then killed them. They're a world-wide organization and a couple of small timers would mean nothing to them. Interesting, isn't it?"

Deakens thought again about the Indian with the wavy hair. "Are you going after this Euramco?"

"We'll damn sure give it a try after we put these small fish away for a little while."

One of the deputies was going through the Indians' stuff and came across a large hunting knife. The handle had the image of a snake etched into it – it's oversized head at the end. He brought it to Deakens who examined it carefully. "Looks like a knife an Indian would own. The blade's been sharpened many a time." He started to hand it back to the deputy when a foghorn blew just off shore. He looked out and recognized Jim's boat. Jim was standing in the cabin waving. Deakens sent one of the deputies out to fetch him.

## CHAPTER 60

Jim Harrison, dressed all in white with his captain's hat pulled low over his brow, strode into camp and stood by the fire. Deakens offered him coffee. He still held the knife partially in the shadows, not in full view. Jim took the coffee and started to sit when the knife caught his attention. "That's a mighty big knife. Can I see it?" Deakens handed it to him. Jim recognized it immediately. "By God," he exclaimed. "This here's Robert's knife, give to him by my brother, Walter. Where'd you get it?"

Deakens jumped up. "One of these Indians had it in his bedroll. What'd you say? This knife belonged to Robert Harrison? Think these Indians could be the ones that done him in? Jim, I want you to look at . . . ."

Jim didn't answer but strode purposely toward the Indians, the knife held out in front as if shaking it at them. The sun was now over the treetops and the shadows were quickly retreating back to the wood's edge.

The sunlight bounced off the knife and into Buddy's eye. Buddy saw the knife and in an instant all the missing parts of his memory rushed over him like a flood tide. He and Robert had returned to Shark Point for that knife and the Browns had killed Robert and left him for dead. The woman in his dreams flashed across his eyes. She was there on the beach, the water running around her feet and through her toes. The little boys played in the water splashing each other. He saw her face and knew it. He said out loud, "Flo."

Jim stopped short. "What?"

Buddy looked from the knife to the carrier and instantly recognized his daddy. "Papa."

Jim looked intently at the speaker. The voice was familiar. "Buddy, is that you? My God, it is you." His legs started to give out. He reached out to Deakens who put his arm around him

411

and held him up. Jim quickly recovered and reached out for Buddy. "My God, my God. Son, I knew in my soul you were alive." He put both his large hands on Buddy's shoulder and stared into his eyes. "My son, you're alive. You're alive." He slipped his arms around Buddy's body and hugged him tightly. Tears streamed from his eyes.

Buddy hugged back just as tightly. "Papa, its been a long weary trip. I'm home. I want to see Flo and the kids." Tears streamed down his face. The camp roared. They just couldn't believe what they were seeing.

Deakens said to the deputy, "Get the irons off."

Jim led Buddy back to the fire. "You've got to tell me everything. How'd all this happen? Where've you been? What's kept you away? By God, you're Curly." They both laughed. Jim continued, "By God if I was a God-fearin' man, I'd get down on my knees right now and give thanks. Maybe I should anyhow." He dropped down on his knees and Buddy followed suit. Soon the whole camp was on their knees. Somehow, this whole thing was some kind of miracle.

Deakens stood and poured a cup of coffee. He looked out over the camp and finally had to face it. "Damn it, Jim, we can't forget we've got a big mess here. Your boy was with these Indians when they robbed that store in Savannah. The police up there've charged him with a crime and he's got to go in and answer for it. These detectives will be seeking extradition. He's told his story to the detectives, but up to now at least, they haven't believed him. Now maybe they will." He looked at the detectives.

Earl spoke up, "This scene here this morning has made a believer out of me. I don't think I've ever seen anything quite like it. When I tell it, nobody will believe me. What do you say, Lester?"

Lester intertwined his fingers, turned them inside out and cracked all of them at one time. "Well, I'm not a religious man, but this takes the cake. But . . . I guess I've got to be the bad guy here. These Indians say he was part of the whole plan and a volunteer member of the robbery. It's going to be his word against theirs, and there's two of them. We've got to take him in and let a judge decide what to do with him. I've got no choice, Jim."

Jim said, "I know, Lester. You do what you gotta do. We'll try to put together a defense for him in the meantime."

Deakens yelled at his people. "All right, men, let's get ready to shove off from here. My miss'us wants me home this Christmas. Take the prisoners to the boats."

Toby looked straight at Buddy as he was marched by. Toby's look seemed to be apologizing – Buddy's questioning. Marty went by without looking one way or the other. Midway to the boats, Toby turned and looked directly at Buddy. "Curly, I'm mighty pleased you got your memory back, boy. And I'm not forgetting either it was you that saved my life back there in Savannah." He squared his shoulders and stood taller. "So I want to say this for all the world to hear and believe. What Curly told you is true. All along he's been trying to find his memory. He came up to Savannah to get me to bring him back down here. He just got caught up in this whole mess by accident. I even forced him to drive the car because me and Marty had such a bad hangover. This is one hell of a man, and I sure don't want to see him brought down for something he had nothing to do with. I bet you that when Marty has the chance to think about it, he'll agree, too." He turned and looked at Marty.

Marty had stopped and was listening to Toby. He now spoke directly to Buddy, "I've never liked you none, Curly, not one little bit, and still don't much. If I could, I'd whip your ass right here and now. Something about you that makes my skin crawl. Don't rightly know why. Got to say this, though. I've learned to respect you. You're one brave son-of-a-buck – and honest as the day is long." Then directly to the detectives, "It's like Toby said, he had nothing at all to do with the robbery." He turned and strode towards the waiting boats.

Everybody just waited in silence. Buddy walked to Toby and hugged him. Tears welled in his eyes. In his ear he whispered,

"Toby, it ain't you what owes, it's me. I'll never forget you, friend, and I'll do whatever I can to help you. I'll look after you." He unclasped his arms and backed away. He winked where only Toby could see. Toby grasped his hand in his and looked a little confused. Buddy saw the confusion and nodded toward the south. Toby hesitated, looked to the south then back to Buddy, he winked an eye, smiled understandingly and turned away.

# CHAPTER 61

Buddy stood at the stern of the Donella and gazed at the convoy of boats following behind. He searched for a glimpse of Toby, but was unable to see him. Toby was kind of a harsh man, but underneath lay a certain kindness. Buddy certainly owed him his life. If he hadn't come along when he did, the Brown boys would certainly have finished the job and hauled both him and Robert out to sea where nobody would ever have found the bodies.

He thought back on his life since waking from the coma. The first three months after that were not good ones – too sick to even move much. Not even enough strength to help old man Andre around the place, hardly at all. It was only after he went to Liz's place that things started to pick up some. She showed a lot of understanding and really seemed to care about his recuperation. He grinned – it was probably her food that finally did the job. He owed them a lot, too, and vowed then and there that he would find a way to help them.

Buddy looked again for a sign of Toby or Marty, but couldn't see either of them. That Marty, is something else again – a rock right up to the end. Never expected him to say what he did, though. Buddy vowed to stick by them, too, and find a way to make their prison terms easier. He thought of the black bag – the money. He felt sure he knew where it was hidden.

His eye picked up a fourth boat lagging way behind the convoy of police boats. He only remembered three boats plus the Donnela. He turned and walked to the cabin where Jim, at the helm, puffed his pipe and hummed an unidentifiable tune.

Jim looked at Buddy when he came to the cabin. He had a big smile on his face. "It was sure white of the detectives to place you in my custody and allow you to spend Christmas at home. Damn, it's good to see you alive and well, Buddy. All these months I stood almost alone. Most everybody else figured you were a goner – all the evidence pointed to that, but somehow, I knew nobody could kill you. If it was at all possible, you'd survive. By God, you proved me right." The smoke billowed out of his pipe and streamed to the stern.

"What about Flo? What did she think? Did she fare all right? Must've been pure hell for a woman alone with two kids to raise all by herself."

Jim slapped the steering wheel. "By God, I completely forgot to tell you. You've got another son, three months old this month." He looked proudly at him.

"What? Another son?" The picture of the woman in his dreams flashed across his mind. There were two small boys playing in the surf and the woman was holding a baby in her arms. It was Flo. He looked at Jim almost unbelieving. "Did she believe I was dead? How'd she fare, Papa?"

"She's done all right for herself. She's done some growin' up since you left. Not completely the same woman you knew before. She worked on the farm almost right up till a month before the baby was born. I took her to Key West to be with her mama there. I understand she worked in the laundry right up to the baby's birth and some after. She came back here in November and started right back on the farm. I tried to give her light jobs at first, but here lately she's worked right along with the rest of them in the cane fields and in the syrup factory. Yes sir, she's become a finer woman than before."

Buddy shot right back. "That's not possible." They both laughed heartedly. Jim re-lit his pipe and Buddy smoked a cigarette. He thought about her long forgotten desire to be something greater than she was. It hit Buddy with a jolt. He looked anxiously at Jim. "What about men? How about men in her life? Somebody must've come callin'?"

Jim puffed on his pipe trying to stall for time, to think how to best respond. A tinge of fear forced itself into his chest. He wished he had been stronger with Flo about Bill Parkins. He wished he'd told her more strongly that he suspected that 'Curly' was Buddy. He hoped they were not too late and that Flo hadn't already gone off with Bill. "You know there's a law that says a person what's lost can't be declared dead until seven years have passed. She couldn't have got married legally for seven years."

"That may be, but a woman with three small children can't make it in this country without a man to help support 'em. She must've thought some about that. It must've crossed her mind. Besides, a woman needs a man just the same as a man needs a woman."

"You remember Bill Parkins?" Buddy nodded. "He started callin' on her within a month or two of your disappearance. She wouldn't have anything to do with him at first, but he kept at it, comin' by to see her, writin' letters and such. Accordin' to Lucy, Flo's never been alone with him. Don't think anything has gone on, but I think in the last month she's been kind of losin' hope that you'd be comin' back, and begun givin' him serious consideration of what he could do for her and the young'uns. She talked to me about it last month – I tried to encourage her to hold off for a little while longer. She's been mighty strong, waitin' and hopin' for you to come back, but I reckon she's begun to lean more in the other direction here lately."

Buddy looked straight ahead and didn't respond right away. Jim puffed his pipe. Wood Key came into view. Jim pulled on a rope at the right of the wheel and two sharp blasts from the foghorn tore into the air and drifted back to the boats following. With a turn of the wheel the boat veered to the left and headed directly towards Wood Key. When the other boats were off to the right, Jim saluted to Deakens and the two detectives. Buddy saw Toby standing in the stern of the middle boat and waved to him. Toby was smiling and waved back – gave two thumbs up. Buddy watched the boats until they disappeared around the east point of Wood Key. The fourth boat had turned to the left and also headed for Wood Key. He wondered who was in it.

Buddy turned to face Wood Key and saw all the familiar sights, the buildings, the net spreads and boats of all kinds tied to the docks and pulled up on the shore. People came out of their houses and gathered on the shore. They had heard the familiar foghorn and came to greet Papa, back from his weeklong charter. Children were romping and having a good time in the water at the edge of the shore. He couldn't make out the faces yet, but he saw his house and saw a woman come out the door and head down to the beach. His heart skipped. She carried a baby in her arms. He watched as she walked down to the shore to stand with her feet bathed in the cool water. She was dressed in a plain white, linen loose-fitting dress that went down to her ankles. She looked the same as in his dreams and the same as she had looked back in February when he went away on that awful hunting trip. Finally he saw her face – Flo. Her face was unsmiling, but had a certain glow to it. She looked older and wiser. She had endured a lot.

The other boat was coming in off to the right. He looked again at Flo. She was looking towards the other boat. His dream flashed in his eyes. He wanted to yell to get her attention. He kept his eyes glued to her. She looked toward him, then back to the person in the other boat.

As Jim docked the Donnela, the family that had gathered on the shore ran out on the dock to greet him. Flo's eyes had focused on an Indian standing amidships – her heart leapt. Was this one of the Indians Papa had been looking for, or dare she believe that it was Buddy? She looked at the man in the other boat. It was still too far to recognize him, but she knew it was Bill Parkins. He was coming to claim his prize.

She saw the Indian jump out of the boat onto the dock. The family backed away from him and opened a path as he strode along the dock towards the shore. She couldn't tell who the man was, but he was coming purposefully towards shore and she had to find out. Dare she hope? She went to the dock and started out on it. The Indian moved faster towards her. She went slowly, hardly able to breathe. She refused to let herself believe it was Buddy. The man was grinning broadly. Her heart grew as big as a melon and seemed about to burst. She recognized her Buddy.

She could hardly see for the tears overflowing in her eyes. She ran to him – they embraced. They held each other without moving for a long while. The others gathered around, not believing what their eyes were seeing.

They released each other and Buddy held her at arm's length. He looked fondly at the baby and tickled its chin with his finger. Junior and Francis came running to them, Francis hopping on one foot, yelling, "Daddy, Daddy." They both circled his legs with their arms. He tousled their hair. He looked at all the others and they yelled in unison. There wasn't a dry eye in the crowd.

Somebody yelled, "This calls for a celebration – break out the fiddle. Buddy's back home."

Buddy shook hands and spoke to all of them.

Flo glanced at the other boat as it slowly turned and went away – the pilot unidentifiable. Buddy picked Junior up with one arm and Francis with the other. They walked slowly along the dock toward their house. All the others followed, including Jim who was beaming from ear to ear.

Francis stuck his tongue at Junior and said, "See, I told you my daddy was comin' home for Santa Claus."